Rehoboth

REHOBOTH

Angela Elwell Hunt

Tyndale House Publishers, Inc.
WHEATON, ILLINOIS

Visit Tyndale's exciting Web site at www.tyndale.com

All Scripture quotations except those noted below are taken from the *Holy Bible,* King James Version.

Scripture quotations on pages 79, 131 are taken from the *New American Standard Bible,* © 1960, 1962, 1963, 1968, 1971, 1972, 1973, 1975, 1977 by The Lockman Foundation. Used by permission.

Library of Congress Cataloging-in-Publication Data

Hunt, Angela Elwell, [date]
  Rehoboth / Angela Elwell Hunt.
    p.   cm. — (Keepers of the ring ; 4)

    ISBN 0-8423-2015-6 (pbk.)
    I. Title.   II. Series: Hunt, Angela Elwell, 1957–   Keepers of the ring ; 4.

PS3558.U46747R44   1997
813′.54—dc21   97-162

Printed in the United States of America

02 01 00 99 98 97
7   6   5   4   3   2   1

It is better to light one candle than curse the darkness.
—Motto of the Christopher Society

To the weak became I as weak, that I might gain the weak:
I am made all things to all men, that I might by all
means save some.
—Paul, apostle to the Gentiles

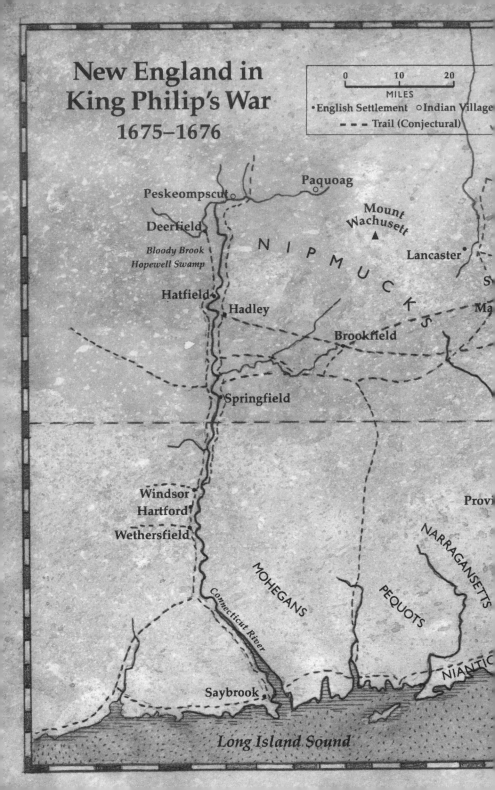

New England in King Philip's War
1675–1676

0 10 20
MILES
• English Settlement ○ Indian Village
– – – Trail (Conjectural)

Paquoag

Peskeompscut

Mount Wachusett

Deerfield

Lancaster

Bloody Brook
Hopewell Swamp

N I P M U C K S

Hatfield

Hadley

Brookfield

Springfield

Windsor

Hartford

Wethersfield

MOHEGANS

Provi

NARRAGANSETTS

PEQUOTS

Connecticut River

NIANTIC

Saybrook

Long Island Sound

AUTHOR'S NOTE

As I read and researched materials for the novel you hold in your hands, I was struck by the timeliness of certain issues faced by seventeenth-century New Englanders. Though King Philip (Metacomet), John Eliot, Benjamin Church, Mary Rowlandson, and other historical characters of this book vacated the world's stage long ago, mankind remains much the same. We resist change; we fear the unknown. Like the Puritans, we cling to familiar practices and traditions with which we are comfortable, and, like our forebears, we desperately desire to protect and shield our loved ones from the raging world outside our doors. We often attempt to isolate ourselves in our homes, schools, churches, and communities.

At this point I must surrender this opportunity to mount a soapbox and allow history to speak for itself. Aiyana, Mojag, Daniel Bailie, Forest Glazier, and Ootadabun have sprung from my imagination, but most of the other people within these pages lived and breathed and would still speak to us today.

The selections credited to Mary Rowlandson are actually from *The Captive,* originally published in 1682 as *The Soveriqnty and Goodness of God, Together with the Faithfulness of His Promises Displayed, Being a Narrative of the Captivity and Restoration of Mrs. Mary Rowlandson* (American Eagle Publications, 1990). The unusual spellings are authentic, for spelling had not been entirely standardized in the seventeenth century.

TABLE OF CONTENTS

PROLOGUE

December 1674

Fleeing westward after the departing sun, the winter wind whimpered across the blackened cornfields. The corn had been harvested and stored in buried clay pots; the women had recently burned off the remaining stubble. A party of mounted Indians, clothed in buckskin and furs, raced their horses through the cleared fields, their eyes and empty stomachs intent upon the village in the distance.

Sitting outside the sachem's wigwam at Monthaup, John Sassamon, secretary to the Pokanoket chief, tilted his head as his ear caught the sound of drumming hooves. A moment later, a series of welcoming cries broke through the usual sounds of mealtime. The messengers had returned from Boston. He made a mental note to remind his sachem that the men should be honored with a gift.

A group of children ran by, their trail of laughter reaching the chief's wigwam. Sassamon lifted an eyebrow as the messengers approached. The advancing men, five in all, moved through the village with the reluctant, careful tread of men who bring bad news. Beside him, Metacomet stiffened and lifted his chin. The women who had been bustling around their leader hurried away. Even Wootonekanuska, Metacomet's wife, retreated into the wigwam, pulling the sachem's active nine-year-old son by the hand.

"The warriors you sent to Boston have returned in good time," Sassamon remarked in a low voice, attempting to lighten Metacomet's stern countenance.

Metacomet did not answer but waited silently, his dark eyes stirring in agitation.

Sunukkuhkau, the leader of the group, came forward, met his chief's gaze, then sat on the ground, a careful and respectful distance away from the leader of the Wampanoag nation. "We are come from Boston," Sunukkuhkau said, rubbing his shaved head as his eyes skittered over the counselors who sat with Metacomet. "We asked the Yangeese about Petananuet. They said his time of forced labor was nearly finished, but someone brought the men brandy. The prisoners drank again until they had no sense. For this the English governor requires them to work another sixty days."

Metacomet's jaw clenched as he rejected the softly spoken report. "Who brought the brandy?" he asked, the muscles in his face tightening. "They are held on an island in the salt sea harbor, so who but their jailers could bring them drink?"

Sunukkuhkau shook his head. "The Yangeese say it does not matter. Petananuet will be held with the others of our tribe for another two moons."

"And then some other Yangeese will bring other bottles of brandy," Metacomet snapped. He turned to Sassamon. "Is this not true, my friend? Yet what can we do about it? Petananuet is not strong. The brandy warms his belly against the cold of winter, so he will drink. I think we will never see Petananuet again."

Sassamon rested his chin on his hand, thinking. He must choose his words carefully, for ever since he had met the minister John Eliot and professed his belief in the Lord Jesus Christ, Metacomet had looked at Sassamon with distrust in his eyes.

"Perhaps Petananuet should think of the fire in his wigwam and not the fire in his belly," Sassamon said, slowly lifting his eyes to meet his master's. "Then the Yangeese would find no reason to hold him for another two moons and Petananuet's wife would welcome her husband home."

Metacomet fingered a braided lock of his hair, signaling his irritation, then lifted his eyes to the others. "Warm yourselves around our fires," he said, nodding toward the bustle of women's activity at the center of the camp. "Eat your fill, and take your rest. Tomorrow sachems from the Nipmucks, the Pocumtucks, the Seekonks, the Pennacooks, and the Narragansetts will gather around our council fires. Together we will discuss what the Yangeese answer means."

The warriors nodded in relief, then stood and walked away while Metacomet stared into the distance, the reddened fingers of his scarred hand still toying with the long braid that hung over his shoulder. Sassamon waited, his pen in his hand, but no word fell from the sachem's lips.

"Surely this is not such a dreadful thing," Sassamon finally said, keeping his voice low. "The men held by the Yangeese are not strong. Let them spend the winter on the island. They will learn not to drink the English brandy."

"They are but one of the shadows upon my heart," Metacomet answered, unconsciously twisting his hand so that the loathsome scars were hidden from Sassamon. "Gifts from the Yangeese have hooks; they pull our people away from the pride of our fathers. Their brandy makes slaves of our warriors. Our boys learn how to shoot muskets instead of the bow and arrow. For their horses, iron plows, and copper pots the Yangeese demand our ancestral homelands. And their preachers steal the hearts of our people and turn them to Lord Jesus."

Sassamon flinched, but the sachem did not look at him. "They say we must die if we speak against their God," Metacomet continued, his eyes almost disappearing in his taut, bony cheeks. "They whip our people if we fish, hunt, or carry burdens on their Sabbath day. We should not be subject to their laws, and yet they order us as if we are children or slaves."

Metacomet lifted his face to the darkening horizon. "And they killed my brother."

Sassamon swallowed hard. Metacomet's older brother, Wamsutta, whom the English called Alexander, had assumed the leadership of the Wampanoag upon his noble father's death. As Wamsutta struggled to lead a nation of people who had grown fearful of increasing English encroachment, he abandoned his

father's easygoing attitude toward the colonists and held himself
aloof from them. Irritated and fearful of the change in Indian
attitude, the authorities at Plymouth commanded Wamsutta to
appear before them. When Wamsutta did not come, the English
sent troops to bring him by force. The sachem was forced to
march through the woods in humiliation before his wife,
Weetamoo, and eighty of his people. Sassamon had been among
those who traveled with the young leader. He had seen
Wamsutta stand proud and erect before the stern Englishmen's
interrogations and then stagger when he suddenly became ill.
Pleading on her husband's behalf, Weetamoo persuaded the
English to accept his two sons as hostages so Wamsutta could
return to his people. The delegation began the journey back to
Monthaup, but the sachem's fever worsened. He died at the
Taunton River, his head cradled in his weeping wife's lap.

Even then, Sassamon's heart had twisted at the thought of
Metacomet's reaction to Wamsutta's death. The younger brother
had been petted and spoiled by the Yangeese; he had not
expected to stand between them and the Wampanoag nation and
its many tribes. And Metacomet had adored his brother. . . .

When the powwows could not divine what evil spirit had
killed Wamsutta, Weetamoo insisted that he had been poisoned
by the Yangeese. And as Metacomet assumed his brother's place
at Monthaup and donned the ceremonial wampum belts of
chieftainship, Sassamon realized that this more severe and determined man also believed that the English had murdered
Wamsutta.

The passing of thirteen years since Wamsutta's death had
done nothing to ease Metacomet's distrust or suspicion of the
Yangeese.

With an abrupt wave of his hand, Metacomet now signaled
for Sassamon to leave. The secretary rolled up his parchment
and rose to his feet, then slipped away to find warmth in his own
wigwam.

He knew he ought to rest. On the morrow sachems from the
other Wampanoag tribes and the powerful Narragansett and

Nipmuck nations would arrive on the peninsula. Metacomet would doubtless keep his secretary busy writing letters to appease the English authorities at Boston and Plymouth. But the letters, as well as anything else Sassamon might write, would mean little.

Accustomed to memorizing and reciting oral history from generations long past, the Indians put little confidence in written documents. The substance of a man's honor was found in his words and actions. Once spoken, words were like feathers scattered to the four winds—they could not be recalled, nor could a man undo the things he had done the day before. But the Yangeese would not believe a thing unless it was written down and signed with a man's mark, even though they were quick to forget the things they themselves had written. The Indians had long ago decided that agreements made with parchment and pen were virtually worthless; but letters, treaties, and promises often bought time and favor.

On the morrow Sassamon would undoubtedly be asked to compose letters to Governor Leverett at Boston and Governor Winslow at Plymouth. Metacomet would tell him to write that all was well and that the Wampanoag wished to live in peace. And while Sassamon wrote, the sachems of the Indian nations would pass the pipe and smoke and talk of whether the time was right for war.

Trouble hovered over the country like a gray fog, but the English would not see it. Metacomet would give them no warning. He would act, and then, Sassamon knew, things would not go well for the colonies. Metacomet, whom the Yangeese called King Philip, had spent the thirty-five years of his life tallying the wrongs and injustices committed by the colonists and their governments. His patience had nearly run out. And if he succeeded in bringing the other nations to war with him . . .

Swerving from his intended path, Sassamon gripped his bearskin cloak more tightly around his shoulders and walked northward, toward Plymouth and Governor Josiah Winslow.

Aiyana

*Beat your plowshares into swords, and your
pruninghooks into spears:
let the weak say, I am strong.*

—Joel 3:10

The bright sharp morning air was wind-whipped and bitter cold. Aiyana Bailie clutched the edges of her cloak about her and ducked her head, hurrying down the main street of Chappaquiddick toward the tiny building that served as a school. Ten children would soon join her there, offspring of the praying Indians of Chappaquiddick village. Her heart sang with anticipation as she hurried to greet them. These were the children of a new generation, her father had often told her, children who would grow up in the knowledge of the Lord and the nurture of Christian parents. But for seventeen-year-old Aiyana, they were less a responsibility than a joy. Even last winter, when her mother had taken ill and died, Aiyana's heavy heart had been lightened by the sight of those dimpled, dark-eyed faces that looked to her for instruction, comfort, and a tender word.

The small clay-and-timber schoolhouse sat off the road and slightly askew, as if its placement had been an afterthought. The winter wind routinely whistled through chinks in the logs, which had been ineffectively daubed with clay, and the mud chimney often sent smoke pouring back into the schoolhouse. But the children, most of whom were only one generation removed from smoky forest wigwams, did not complain.

Aiyana's breath misted in the cold as she hurried into the darkened schoolhouse and tugged a log from the woodpile near the chimney. The coals from an earlier fire had turned to white ash; she would have to bring an armful of kindling from the bucket outside. Clicking her tongue at her own forgetfulness, she rolled the log into the fireplace, then dusted off her hands and turned toward the door.

The door swung open of its own accord, and Aiyana stepped back in surprise. A man clothed in a long traveling cape and a beaver hat stomped his feet as he entered the room. When he lifted his face and removed his hat, she ran to him, laughing.

"Father! We didn't expect you back so soon! How was your trip to Plymouth?"

"Very good, Aiyana." Her father, Daniel Bailie, caught her in a fierce embrace, then released her. "Brr, 'tis colder in here than outside. Haven't you a fire?"

"I was about to fetch some kindling when you came. I will do it now, if you'll wait—"

"No, Aiyana. There'll be no need."

She had been about to move through the doorway, but something in his voice stopped her. She turned to him, her brows lifted in a silent question.

He gave her a tentative smile. "You should send the students home today. We have much to discuss. I have come straight from the docks, and I want to take you home so we can speak with your brother. I'm afraid our lives are to be very different from this day forward, and I'd like to talk to you and Mojag at the same time."

Despite a sudden feeling of resistance, her heart pounded in anticipation. "Different? What will be different, Father?"

"We'll discuss it with Mojag." Her father's blue eyes smiled at her in reassurance. "The letter from Reverend Eliot will explain everything. So put a note on the door, dear, and don't light a fire. The children will return to their homes today, and another teacher will be found."

"Another teacher?" Aiyana's smile twisted. "Why will the children need another teacher?"

"Come." Her father opened the door, then made a sweeping gesture with his hand. "Don't worry about the children. God will provide for them even as he provides for us."

▼▲▼▲ "We are to work with the Indians?" Mojag asked, confused. He eased his long frame onto a bench at the table in the front room. "But, Father, we already work with Indians—"

"The Christian souls here are well nurtured in the faith," his father explained, smoothing the parchment letter on the table before them. "John Eliot is concerned for the natives who still live in spiritual darkness. The Indians at Chappaquiddick are secure under the ministrations of the Mayhew family, but there is no one to work with the Wampanoag."

"The Wampanoag?" Aiyana asked, her eyes meeting Mojag's for a fraction of a second. "But our Indians are Wampanoags."

"The Wampanoag are a nation composed of many tribes," her father said, crossing his long legs as he turned to her. "We must not forget the Sakonnet, the Pocasset, the Agawam, the Sokonesset, the Mattapoisett, and the Pokanoket on the mainland. All the praying villages in Massachusetts are located near Boston, and Reverend Eliot fears that the southern Indians have not been sufficiently exposed to the light of the gospel." He folded his arms. "Our job is to help him bring the gospel to those people."

Mojag rested his elbow on the table and thoughtfully rubbed the slight growth of hair on his upper lip. *A journey into the wilderness!* The idea at once excited him.

"I don't understand," Aiyana was saying, waving her hands in a fluttering gesture. "Why should we leave Martha's Vineyard? We are happy here. I have my work with the children, and Mojag has always helped you with the villagers and the church—"

"Don't you see, Aiyana?" Mojag interrupted, leaning forward. "This is our chance to prove ourselves. Can we take the truth to our people? Will they accept it? Will they accept *us?*"

Aiyana sank back in her chair, frowning slightly. "I don't know what you mean. I've been teaching truth to the children for two years. And they are Christian Indians, which is what we are—"

"We are *Indians*," Mojag said, half-aware that his voice had increased in pitch and volume, "and yet we live like Englishmen here in this village. We wear English clothes; we read English books; we attend an English church."

"You are English as well as Indian." Their father's brow knitted in a frown as he looked at Mojag. "Never forget, Son, that though your mother was a Pequot, *my* father was an Englishman. Indian and English blood mingle in your veins, but your spiritual heritage is more important than your physical lineage. You know and serve the true God. You should not long to return to the savage world of the heathen tribes."

"I don't long for that, Father, truly." Mojag ran his hands through his hair, struggling to find words to express what he had been feeling for many months. He was twenty-one, old enough to step out and find his life's calling. He had received no clear direction of what he should do, but a restlessness stirred in his soul. "It is just that I feel so *stifled* in this village. Christ has commanded us to win the world, and yet I am surrounded with believing Indians like myself. Entire nations of Indians exist across the bay, and I am kin to them, but I do not know how to reach them because I do not understand their way of life—"

"Their way of life is depraved," his father said softly. He looked at Mojag with something very fragile in his eyes. "Trust me, Son. I have lived alongside the Indians and in civilization, so let my experience speak to your heart. Beauty and honor, evil and pain exist in both worlds. But we must go where God has called us." He turned his gaze to Aiyana. "And I believe God has called us to help John Eliot. He is presently working out the details of our journey and our settlement in a new place, but we are to sell what we have here, say our farewells, and prepare to leave immediately."

Across the table, Aiyana cast Mojag a worried glance, but he smiled at her, fascinated by the possibilities of a new fork in life's road.

▼▲▼▲▼ Six days later, Aiyana stood with her feet firmly planted at a ship's rail. The future looked as vague and shadowy as the mainland against the distant horizon, and she lowered her eyes as a host of perplexing emotions assailed her. She could not look toward the stern, where Martha's Vineyard slowly retreated in the distance. She and Mojag had been born on the island, and a windswept hill there bore the tombstone of their mother, Dena Bailie. It was hard to believe they were leaving the only home they had ever known.

She turned her eyes toward the north, toward her destination. The late-afternoon sun streaked the water crimson as the ship crawled into the teeth of the bitter wind that blew across Buzzards Bay. Her father and brother stood a few feet apart at the bow of the pinnace, each alone with his thoughts.

Her father would cut an impressive figure wherever he went, she realized, studying him. Tall and still slender at fifty-three, Daniel Bailie had lightly tanned skin, a full head of hair that shone like burnished silver, and eyes the color of the sky in summer. Mojag had inherited his father's tall and slender form, as well as his clear-cut profile. But his eyes were coffee-colored and his skin the coppery shade of an autumn leaf. His eyes and skin had come from their mother, but any stranger could see that the two men were father and son. In form and gestures, they were as alike as two slivers of wood split from the same piece of kindling.

Shivering, she walked forward and stood between them. Her father noticed her immediately, but Mojag kept his eyes on the foggy horizon, his thoughts a thousand miles away.

"Speak your thoughts, Brother. 'Tis not for nothing we named you He-Who-Talks-Much," she whispered, reciting one of her mother's favorite sayings.

Mojag's face split into a wide grin. "Can't a man be quiet if he wants to be?"

"Not if the man is you," Aiyana answered, stepping closer. "What on earth are you thinking about? Home?"

"No." Mojag leaned over the rail toward the blue water rippling toward the faint and distant shoreline. "About what lies ahead. 'Twill be so different; I scarcely know what to expect."

Smiling, Aiyana's father tucked her under his arm, then

turned to the sea, covering her cold hands with his. "There is nothing to fear, children. Do you remember how I told you that your mother and I left Connecticut to work with John Eliot before you were born?"

"Of course, Father." Aiyana answered.

"John Eliot was like a father to us then, and we owe him a great deal. 'Twas he who suggested that we work with Thomas Mayhew on Martha's Vineyard. And I firmly believe that his fervent prayers brought you and Mojag to us, for your mother and I spent many years praying for children until you two were born."

"The Reverend Eliot is old now," Mojag inserted, speaking in the superior tone of voice he often adopted when addressing Aiyana. "Seventy and one. God will not allow him to remain with us much longer."

"So we must leave our home when he calls us?" Aiyana asked, trying to keep the edge of frustration from her voice. "Just like that? Mother is buried on the island, and all my memories of her are there. And the children—I was the only one willing to teach the smallest ones; now they will have no one."

"Your memories will remain in your heart and mind," her father answered, squeezing her hand. "And God will send someone else to the children. Your mother, if God had willed that she live, would have encouraged us to join John Eliot. And we leave the work on Martha's Vineyard in the capable hands of the Mayhew family. We are not needed there so much as in Rehoboth."

Rehoboth. The name of the village stirred vague memories in Aiyana.

"'And he called the name of it Rehoboth; and he said, For now the Lord hath made room for us, and we shall be fruitful in the land,'" Mojag quoted, thrusting his cold hands into the warmth of his buckskin sleeves. "The English established the village several months ago."

"And this is a praying village?" Aiyana asked, shivering.

"No," her father answered, smiling as he drew her closer. "But there are Indians in the area, including the Pokanoket, whose chief sachem is a man the English call King Philip. His village,

Mount Hope, is nearby. If even a few of his people accept the goodness of the Lord's salvation, a new praying village might be established between Rehoboth and Mount Hope."

Might be established? Was her father moving them to a settlement that did not even exist?

"Father, I don't understand—"

Keeping her hands in his, he turned to face her. His eyes darkened with tenderness. "Aiyana, my dear daughter, this is one of the most difficult things I have ever had to tell you. Mojag and I will be living in a rough hut in the woods, rougher even than the wigwams of the Indians. Such a place is neither safe nor suitable for a woman, especially one of your youth. John Eliot has suggested that you work in an English home as a hired servant."

Aiyana took a quick breath, stunned by the news.

"Even the best and wealthiest families put their children into service," her father went on, "for Reverend Eliot assures me that unmarried persons are not allowed to live alone in a Puritan settlement. In this way, children learn to honor and respect their elders as they learn a useful trade."

"A servant?" Aiyana repeated, frowning. "I'm not to be a teacher?"

"You might teach," her father said, squeezing her hands. "Your master might allow you to do any number of things. And you will not be indentured or contracted in any way. If at any time you wish to leave, you may." He chuckled. "You may even find a godly young man and wish to marry. You are certainly of age. We will only have to secure the proper permissions and arrange your dowry. . . ."

Aiyana stared at the wavelets that flecked the surface of the bay as her father's words drifted away. She was a daughter, a woman, someone to be married off and disposed of. Mojag would follow in Father's footsteps and continue his work; she would marry a fine Christian man and bear him many children.

She should have known this day would come. Her mother's illness and death had prevented her from receiving suitors while upon Martha's Vineyard, but Aiyana's time of mourning had ended. Was her father truly so anxious to be rid of her?

"How can you send me away?" she asked, cutting a quick look to her father's face. "You and Mojag need someone to keep your house. Who will cook for you?"

He slipped her hand through the crook of his arm and squeezed her to him. "We will be traveling among the praying villages and journeying often to Roxbury to meet with Reverend Eliot," her father answered, patting her hand. "We will be gone for days at a time and cannot leave you alone and unprotected. God has called me to John Eliot's right hand, Aiyana, I have no doubts. Please understand—I must do his will."

"Is it God's will that I be a servant?" she asked, her voice breaking.

"Of certain it is," he answered, turning to the rail again. "We are all called to be servants of Christ, and we honor him by serving others. Trust God, Aiyana, and trust me to do what is best for you. And remember—" his mouth curved into gentleness as he looked back at her—"'For my thoughts are not your thoughts, neither are your ways my ways, saith the Lord.' God will grant you a calling, too, if you listen for his voice. And he will make your heart willing and happy to do his pleasure."

As her father leaned over the ship's rail, Aiyana looked down at her hands. They were small but capable, strengthened by her care of her father, brother, and the schoolchildren. Soon they would tend an English family's hearth.

Aiyana knew she should be like Mojag, thrilled at the likelihood of new challenges and adventures, but the prospect of working in an English village left her as cold as the icy January wind that bit through her cloak.

▼▲▼▲ "Daniel Bailie, my friend! It is good to see you!" The rich timbre of John Eliot's voice cut through the crowd at the dock. Tall and clean-shaven, he approached with a distinctive lumbering gait, rocking on his hips as if they were stiff.

Aiyana noticed that her father embraced the aged minister gently, as if he clasped a priceless treasure.

"John, it is good to see you. We have missed your visits to the island."

"Ah, there is no need for me to visit Martha's Vineyard. John Mayhew has the missionary Mayhew heart." Stepping back, John ran an appraising glance over Aiyana and Mojag. His dark eyes, set into deep wrinkles, sparkled with delight as he exclaimed, "Surely these two fine people are not your children!"

"Yes." Her father's face colored with pride as he held out a hand toward them. "Aiyana is seventeen; Mojag is now twenty-one. They are eager to begin their work here in the Massachusetts colony."

John Eliot shook Mojag's hand, then clasped Aiyana in a delicate embrace.

"A fine pair, Daniel, and a testimony to the influence of you and your sainted wife," John said, subduing Aiyana's anxiety with the warmth of his smile. "I welcome you both. Mojag, I am eager to show you the fields white unto harvest. And I have found a place for you, lovely lady. You will not be far from your father's heart nor his home. But I tarry needlessly. There are horses waiting for us if you are ready to begin the journey."

"We are ready." Daniel gestured for Mojag to see about their trunk; then he offered his arm to the elderly minister. "And we are eager to hear about the praying villages. How many are there now, fourteen? I cannot believe that the work has spread so far."

"Ah, the work is not without its frustrations, but the harvest is good," Eliot answered, leaning heavily upon his cane as he took Daniel's arm and walked down the dock. "And I have been praying for harvesters like you to help me in the work. The time is right, Daniel; I can feel it. The lump is thoroughly leavened. Over eleven hundred praying Indians live in our fourteen towns. The Mayhews have conquered the islands for Christ. John Cotton is a mighty evangelist for the Lord at Plymouth. James Fitch and Abraham Pierson are working in Connecticut, the Bourne family labors at Mashpee—all are striving to reach the

Indians with the gospel. Within the next year, if our efforts do
not falter, I believe we shall see a mighty movement among the
tribes. Their thirsty souls will turn to the source of living water."

"I have every confidence that you are right," Daniel
answered, turning for a moment to glance over his shoulder.

Aiyana met his eyes and smiled, following him, even though
her heart rebelled at the thought of living among the English in a
strange community. Her father believed that God had called him
to this place. She had already lost one parent, and she would not
lose her father and brother by refusing to follow.

▼▲▼▲▼ They had landed at Dartmouth, a tidy settlement sandwiched between the bay and the looming forest.
Aiyana eyed the monstrous, never-ending sea of wilderness and
shivered, a sense of foreboding descending over her. Tall evergreens and bony oaks stood like armed warriors safeguarding
the interior against intruders, and suddenly she yearned for the
quiet, cleared village she had known on Martha's Vineyard.

No roads led into the woods, only a narrow pathway. John
Eliot had procured four horses, one of which pulled a parfleche
to carry their trunk. "A series of Indian trails runs throughout
the country," Eliot explained, stiffly mounting his horse. Though
his face contracted in pain as he pulled himself up, he did not
make a sound of protest or complaint. "The trails are one of the
best gifts the Indians have given us. We will follow this one to
Middleborough, then turn westward on another trail, which will
lead us first to Taunton, then to Rehoboth." He gave Aiyana a
compassionate smile. "They say the Indian runners can travel
sixty miles a day on these trails, but even on horseback I have
never been able to equal their record. The woods are thick, and
travel will be slow with the parfleche, but we will have a chance
to talk. I am sure there are many things you want to know about
the work ahead."

"Of certain, yes," Mojag answered, flinging himself across the
broad back of a handsome stallion. The beast tossed its great

head and bounced in agitation as Mojag turned him to face Reverend Eliot. "I have many questions about the tribes in this area. I thought the southeast had been evangelized."

"Some of the tribes," Eliot answered as Aiyana mounted the steady mare her father selected for her. The minister paused, waiting for Daniel to mount the horse that pulled the parfleche. When they were all ready, Eliot pulled his horse alongside Mojag's and pointed toward the woods beyond. "There are many tribes among the Wampanoag," he said, kicking his horse as he led the way forward, "and many of them are hostile to the gospel of our Lord. But I have been praying, and God has inspired me to believe that a village of converts near Rehoboth might calm the frenzied spirit of King Philip—"

"Philip?" Daniel called from behind Aiyana. "The son of Massasoit?"

"The same," Eliot answered over his shoulder. "Philip is now the sachem of the Pokanoket tribe. They call him the Fox, for he is clever and very intelligent. I have prayed for his salvation ever since his secretary, John Sassamon, became a Christian. Sassamon has proven to be our friend and keeps us informed of this sachem's intentions. For years Philip has protested and led savage parades of armed warriors past our villages, but he has done no harm. It is my prayer that he will find salvation before his heart leads him to commit mischief."

"Have none of the nearby village ministers tried to meet with him?" Daniel called, his voice a ghostly echo among the gray-green shadows of the forest. "Surely one of them would have more influence than I, for they know him well "

"The ministers of Taunton, Rehoboth, and Swansea," Eliot answered, not turning around, "care only for the souls in their churches." His saddle creaked in the stillness as he shifted slightly, composing his thoughts. "When we Puritans came to this land many years ago, we sought to make our communities a light to the world. We built our towns, based our laws upon God's, committed our families and our hearts to the Lord, but in our zeal for holiness we have closed ourselves off. Our ministers,

I fear, believe that the untamed wilderness will somehow uncivil-
ize them. They now seek to make our churches and towns a refuge *from* the world. Christ's command to 'love thy neighbor' has
become 'love thy family and lead thy children to repentance.'"

"Surely there is nothing wrong with that?" Aiyana asked, daring to speak her thoughts. "Children are so receptive when their
hearts are young—"

"Of course we want to reach our children." The great minister
slowed his horse to a walk and turned in the saddle to look at
her. "We ought to lead our families to Christ, but we should not
close our eyes to the lost souls around us. So many of our
brethren came to this New England to leave lusty old England
behind, but sin in all its forms has followed—indeed, it waited
here for us. Once a chorus of opinion held that we should move
our villages farther into the wilderness, but those voices have
stilled in the past few years. Prosperity and wealth have convinced us to be content in the world, and so we close our eyes,
ignoring the world's need as well as its evil."

The old man grew silent for a moment, then wiped his mouth
with the back of his hand. His voice, when he spoke again, was
tinged with sorrow. "In the guise of making ourselves belong to
God, I fear we have made him so much our own that the Indians
cannot understand him. We speak a Christian language that is
foreign to them. We expect them to obey our religious precepts
without comprehending the conviction that supports them. We
scrupulously punish every breach of God's laws in order to
demonstrate that God does not condone sin, but sinners' lives do
not change after punishment and public humiliation. Sin grows
more subtle and more sly, and the Indians wonder what kind of
power a religion has if it does not change a man's life."

"You said that the Indians do not speak our language," Mojag
said. "But you have translated the Bible into their tongue. You
have offered the gospel in a way they can understand—"

"And I hear in the winds of rumor that the Algonquin Bible
will not be reprinted," Eliot said, turning back to face the woods.
He clucked softly, and his horse picked up the pace. "They say I

should make the Indians learn to read English," he called over his shoulder.

They rode silently for some time, and Aiyana lifted her thoughts from the minister's troubling words to the mushrooming canopy of trees overhead. On Martha's Vineyard the sea's quiet shushing was a constant undercurrent of sound. The woods around her now seemed strangely silent. Her horse stepped nimbly over thick, snaking roots from hemlock, pine, red cedar, and mountain laurels that either towered over her head or stood as broad as houses. Off to the side, a deer trail pointed a curving finger through the bare-boned trees. Silently, she prayed that John Eliot knew where he was going. She would not like to be lost in these dense woods after dark.

The treetops stirred with the whisper of a chilly breeze, and Mojag urged his horse forward until the stallion walked alongside the minister's mount. "Tell me again exactly what my father and I will be doing in Rehoboth," Mojag said, his voice brimming with energy and enthusiasm. "I am eager to begin the ministry."

"I am glad of it," Eliot answered, turning to smile at Aiyana. "Are you as impatient to begin your work, my dear?"

She painted on as warm a smile as she could manage. "I am ready to work wherever I am needed," she answered. "I have always taught children. I would love to find a little house and open a school—"

"But Rehoboth is no place for an unattached lady," Eliot said, looking to her father. "'Tis against the law, in truth. For reasons of safety and civility, all unmarried persons must join families. Unless you'd like us to find you a husband—"

"Hold a moment, John," her father interrupted, grinning. "I'll not be losing my only daughter the week we come to Rehoboth."

Reverend Eliot grinned mischievously. "I wouldn't marry her off without her opinion and liking for a husband," the minister replied, his voice calm and soothing. "And since Rehoboth has no place for unmarried women, I have arranged that she should be employed as a servant in one of the town's leading families. Never fear, Miss Aiyana. We will watch over you, and your father and brother will not be far away. With God's blessing, they will have converts ready to establish a new praying village by the time spring warms the earth again."

Aiyana returned his smile, reluctantly trusting the love and concern she saw in his eyes.

For two days they traveled northward through the woods. Aiyana marveled at the ease with which the aged minister rode the trail, but he confided that he had always been at home in the wilderness. Though the Indians might not always accept his message, most tribes welcomed him and bestowed their usual hospitality. "Of course, the natives are not as populous as they once were," he said, a shadow falling across his face. "Once I could encounter twenty different villages in the space of twenty miles. Sickness has devastated many of the tribes, and the remaining groups have pulled together. But there are at least twenty thousand Algonquin-speaking natives in these woods, and for their sake I love to travel here."

Finally they came upon the wider, more deeply etched trail that ran east and west. Even the horses seemed to relax upon the ancient Indian path, and Aiyana felt her spirits lift as they rode through thinner forest toward the setting sun. In a few hours, Reverend Eliot promised them, they would be at Taunton where Matthew Glazier, a selectman from Rehoboth, would meet them. "Glazier is a fine man, a credit to God and to his community," Eliot said, riding beside Aiyana as Mojag led the way along the trail. "He came to Massachusetts as a young man and is one of the founders of Rehoboth. He claims he will be a ten-thousand-pound man before he is fifty."

"How old is he now?" Daniel asked.

"Forty and nine, I think," Eliot answered, winking at Aiyana. "And he is not married."

Glancing backward, Aiyana saw her father frown at this bit of information. "How can a Christian man care so much for worldly wealth?" he asked, leaning forward in the saddle. "If you have any doubts about whether or not I should entrust my daughter to him, I would hear them now, John."

Aiyana gripped the reins in her hand as her heart skipped a beat. An image of Matthew Glazier rose in her imagination: a ponderously wealthy old man with beady eyes and thin lips. His talonlike hands would reach for her. . . .

"Glazier, like most of us, believes that God blesses hard work," Eliot answered. "And wealth is but one of Matthew Glazier's blessings. He has also been gifted with health, godly children, and a spotless reputation. Never fear, Daniel. Glazier has a daughter, Constance; a son, Forest; and a housekeeper to keep the house in order." The minister smiled carefully at Aiyana. "I am certain you will be safe and happy there, my dear. If you are not, you have but to ask, and I will see that another place of service is found for you."

Aiyana nodded, not entirely relieved. She felt as if she were drowning in circumstances over which she had absolutely no control. Even if Matthew Glazier was a pillar of the community, he still sounded like an older man in search of a wife and mother for his two children. In their eagerness to do God's work, her father and brother had thought nothing of consigning her to life as a common servant, and hints of marriage had been on their tongues since their departure. This wealthy and ambitious Matthew Glazier, whoever he was, would look at her either as a potential wife or as a penniless maid fit for nothing but cleaning his house and emptying his fireplace. Neither prospect brought Aiyana joy.

Her father's heavy voice interrupted her thoughts. "Master Glazier's wife is deceased?"

"She died birthing her daughter, many years ago," Reverend Eliot answered. "His housekeeper runs the house and prepares their meals. The son, Forest, has been apprenticed to a merchant in Rehoboth and will doubtless set out on his own soon. He is a bright lad. I hear he may be a ten-thousand-pound man at the ripe old age of thirty."

Her father laughed then, his mind obviously at ease, and
Aiyana envied his ability to toss anxiety to the wind. So the son
was not a child! He was an apprentice, most likely around
Mojag's age, which meant that he probably lived at his master's house. She would share the house with the daughter, the
housekeeper, and the master. . . .

"The Taunton River," Reverend Eliot said, pointing to a silvery stream at the end of the path ahead. "The village lies just
beyond. We will rest tonight, friends, and then I must say my
farewells. I am to meet emissaries from Philip's camp before I
return to Roxbury."

▼▲▼▲▼ Taunton was much like Dartmouth, Aiyana
thought as she glanced around the next morning. The heart of
the village lay along a single frozen road that broadened at its
midpoint to make room for a cleared field surrounding the meetinghouse and an adjacent cemetery. A dozen cattle grazed upon
handfuls of hay scattered across the clearing. At the northern
and southern points of the main road, two long, boxlike houses
had been enclosed with tall, timbered walls. But despite the forbidding aspect of the garrison houses, the settlement wore a
casual, calm look as villagers moved past the orderly row of
homes and shops lining the street.

"We are to meet Master Glazier at the church," Reverend Eliot
said, doffing his hat to several men who had stepped out of their
courtyards to inspect the newcomers. "Mojag, why don't you
take your sister for a walk? I believe your father would like to
interview Master Glazier in private."

"I'd like that," Aiyana inserted, eager to be away from the
curious eyes examining her from every direction. The sky had
been dark when they had arrived last night; only the innkeeper
and the man at the livery had seen them. But apparently the
word had been broadcast: John Eliot had come to town, bringing
three supposedly *civilized* Indians with him. She moved into
Mojag's shadow, remembering one of the few times she had trav-

eled with her father to the English settlements on Martha's Vineyard. "Look, a squaw in a pretty dress!" one little girl had shouted, tugging on her mother's hand. "Do you think she stole it from someone?"

Aiyana flushed at the memory and settled her hand into the crook of Mojag's arm. He groaned, obviously not thrilled with the idea of escorting her, but jerked his head toward the street and hurried away, with Aiyana lengthening her steps to keep up.

The sun caressed her with living warmth, and a delicious tingling spread through Aiyana's limbs as she stretched to match Mojag's stride. Beyond the end of the street, the silver waters of the river beckoned, and she walked toward them.

"Let's stop at the water," she said, pulling away from her brother after they had passed the garrison house. "I feel dusty and dirty. I want to splash my hands and face."

"Don't fall in," Mojag called from behind her, but Aiyana hurried away from him and his overbearing concern. Mojag had been her nursemaid for as long as she could remember; he could not seem to realize that she did not need a protector. While he had labored in a stuffy schoolroom studying *Masusse Wunneetupanatamwe Up-Biblum God,* the Algonquin translation of the Bible, she had run with the children over the island beaches as free as a cloud.

Leaving Mojag behind, she hurried to the riverbank, longing for privacy. A border of ice-covered stones lined the bank, and she scampered easily over them. Mojag would be hard-pressed to follow her. She felt as sure and swift as an arrow; he was a clumsy, powerful bear that should be hibernating the winter away.

Kneeling on a rock, she plunged her hands into the water, which was so cold it stole her breath.

"Aiyana, come back!" Mojag called in the distance, pinwheeling as he teetered on the rocks. "You will hurt yourself!"

"Oh, no I won't," she murmured, splashing her face. She gasped at the invigorating tingle of the water, then slipped away from the river into a stand of evergreens. Compared to the bleak, tidy arrangement of the village, the woods now seemed a comforting, almost holy place. She entered quietly, her hands reaching out to caress oaks, hickories, birches, and towering maples. The trees grew so much bigger here than on the island! She spied dogwoods that would burst into flower in springtime, and oaks that would cover the floor of the woods in dense shade.

A shuffling sound caught her attention, and she ducked, crouching behind a stout oak tree. A white-tailed deer, heavy with an unborn baby, moved slowly among the blue-black shadows, snuffing the hard ground for a bit of greenery or moss.

The sharp crack of voices broke the stillness, and the doe fled in a burst of movement, her long legs barely making a sound as she sprinted away. Aiyana tensed. The voices came from downstream, but Mojag still lumbered toward her from the opposite direction. Who else was in the woods? Instinctively, she pressed her back against the tree, feeling the bite of its winter-hardened bark through the soft folds of her cloak.

"The devil take you, Forest!" A girl's voice, high and shrill, echoed along the riverbank, and Aiyana closed her eyes in relief. These were not hostile Dutchmen or French traders. The girl spoke English, and youthfulness rang in her voice.

"What's wrong with gathering kindling in the woods?" *A man's voice!* "If I don't do it today, Master Hammond will send me out to do it tomorrow."

"But it's the Sabbath! Father will scold you if he learns that you've broken the law."

"Father won't know. And it doesn't matter, Constance. 'Tis a waste of God's good energy to walk here and not pick up the branches that lie at my feet."

"I don't know why Witty and I put up with you. You're such a rogue."

"But a lovable one, in truth."

Aiyana crouched forward, ducking behind an evergreen shrub near the river's edge. A couple walked there, a man about Mojag's age and a young girl, probably no more than thirteen. The girl was pretty in a fresh-faced, pink-cheeked sort of way, but Aiyana's eyes froze on the young man's form. Tall and beardless, he was built like a sturdy oak tree, with dark hair, fair skin, and a quick smile. Mischief danced in his eyes, and though he professed to be diligently storing kindling away for the morrow, Aiyana noticed that he carried only two twigs in his right hand. As she watched, he stooped to pick up another branch but flung it into the river and grinned at the resulting splash.

Aiyana put her hand to her mouth and smothered a smile. When Mojag appeared a moment later, huffing in exasperation, she lifted her finger to her lips and gestured for him to come closer and be still. For once in his life, he did as she asked, but only for a moment.

"Let's be away," Mojag said, obviously uninterested in the approaching pair. He tugged on her kirtle. "Come, we don't know who these people are."

"They are amusing," she whispered, swatting his hand away. "Be quiet! I want to listen!"

"We need to go back to town. Father will not want to wait for us, and we've been gone for some time—"

"Go without me!"

"Aiyana," Mojag's voice deepened into a threatening growl, and she turned to him in annoyance. If he did not keep quiet, the couple on the riverbank would spy out her hiding place.

"Go away!"

"No! I cannot leave you unprotected in the woods."

Footsteps pounded the earth behind her, and Aiyana stood up, knowing they had been discovered. Embarrassment pinked her cheeks as she struggled to slip away, but Mojag's heavy foot was on her kirtle, holding her down.

"Who are you, and what is your business here?"

Aiyana closed her eyes and exhaled slowly. Turning, she lifted her gaze to answer the stern question.

▼▲▼▲▼ Forest Glazier had not known what he would find in the shrubbery, but he had never imagined that he would come face-to-face with beauty so rarefied, so pure that it took his breath away. An Indian couple stood before him, but unlike the Indians in the area who occasionally donned a shirt and jacket of English origin, these two were dressed fully in the manner of the English. The young man was his own age, a remote, majestic figure with an intimidating glare. Every fiber of Forest's body tensed, warning him not to tread too closely.

But the girl! She wasn't tall, but she held herself like a queen. The blasphemous notion that she might be one of the heathens' spirits of the forest whipped through his mind, but her flesh was real and pink, her breath quick and warm in the frosty air. Hair the color of midnight framed her face and elongated her slender neck, emphasizing her flawless complexion. Large pools of deep, rich blue lifted to meet his gaze, and for a moment he forgot his determination to intimidate whoever had been lurking in the brush. Those blue eyes were so unearthly, so unexpected, that his stomach knotted.

Constance came puffing up the bank behind him. "I cry you mercy, why did you run away? And why—" She looked up, suddenly aware that they were not alone. "Forest, who are these people?"

"I just asked that question," he said, never taking his eyes from the girl's face. He gentled his voice. "You are not from Taunton. Are you from Swansea?"

"No," the young man answered, deliberately stepping forward so that he blocked Forest's view of the girl. "We are traveling with John Eliot, who has stopped to meet a man in Taunton."

Forest grinned in pleasant surprise. "My father has come here to meet Reverend Eliot," he said, unwillingly transferring his attention to the other man. Reflexively, Forest lifted his hands from his belt to show that he had drawn no weapon. "I am sorry if I startled you. I was surprised to hear voices in the brush. The Indians have been . . . restless lately."

Like the searching light of a lantern, the blue eyes peered out from behind the fierce man's shoulder. "I am Aiyana Bailie, and this is my brother, Mojag," the girl said, smiling timidly. She spoke in a wonderful low voice, soft and clear. "We are here to meet a Master Glazier so we may journey with him to Rehoboth."

Forest felt a warm glow of relief flow through him. This man was not a suitor, but family! "Then the Lord has directed your path directly to us. I am Forest Glazier, and this—" he jerked his thumb toward his sister—"is Constance." He forced himself to take a deep breath. "It would appear that God has brought us together even as our fathers meet in the village."

"It would appear so," she answered, her voice like a warm embrace in the chilly air. Entranced, Forest fought the urge to knock her brother aside in order to see her more clearly.

"Forest—" Constance's whine cut through his thoughts— "Father will be expecting us. You know he doesn't want us to wander far on the Sabbath."

"Yes," Mojag answered, his eyes as hard and bright as glass. "We should return to the village."

Forest gestured toward the path along the riverbank. "After you, sir." Forest had hoped that the disapproving brother would march off and leave the bewitching girl free to walk with him, but Mojag Bailie took a step forward, then savagely gripped his sister's hand and pulled her through the trees toward the riverbank.

Grinning despite his frustration, Forest reached for Constance's arm and followed the Indian couple through the woods and into town. On the small porch outside the meeting-house, his father, Matthew Glazier, stood beside the elderly Reverend Eliot and a distinguished-looking gentleman who wore the buckskins of a trapper. The unfamiliar man wore his silver hair long like an Indian, tied with a leather cord at one shoulder. As his clear blue eyes raked Forest's face, the young man felt as if the older fellow had read the contents of his heart—and somehow disapproved of what he saw there.

But the gentleman offered a serene smile, which quickly concealed his inner thoughts. "May I assume, Master Glazier, that these are your children?"

"Indeed they are," Forest's father replied, thrusting his chest

forward. "My son, Forest, is apprenticed to a merchant in Rehoboth. My daughter, Constance, is but thirteen."

The blue-eyed man nodded slowly, then thrust his hand
toward Forest. When Forest took it, the handshake was firm.
"I am Daniel Bailie, father to these two with you," he said,
keeping a steady grip on Forest's hand. "I am pleased to meet
you, and even more pleased to hear that you have found your
calling. I wish you every success as you finish your term of
apprenticeship."

Though the gentleman was too well-mannered to speak
frankly, Forest suspected from the protective gleam in the man's
eye that he meant to say, *I am pleased to know that you will not be
living in the same house with my daughter.*

"Well, then, gentlemen, our business here is nearly settled,"
Reverend Eliot said, rubbing his hands together. "Aiyana Bailie
will accompany the Glaziers to Rehoboth and serve as Constance's maid until such time as the arrangement is no longer
mutually agreeable. Her wages will be two shillings a week,
room and board provided. She will be under the complete
authority of Master Glazier. On the Sabbath, after church, she
will be free to do as she pleases for the remainder of the day.
Are these terms agreeable to all?"

Forest held his breath until his father nodded and Master
Bailie nodded as well.

"I'll have a contract drawn up according to those terms," his
father said, patting his coat in an absent, searching gesture.
"Where shall I reach you, Master Bailie?"

"Mojag and I will set up a camp near the Indian village at
Mount Hope," Daniel Bailie answered. "You will be able to find
us there."

"And a year from now, if God wills, that camp will be the site
of another praying village," John Eliot said, placing a confident
hand on Daniel Bailie's shoulder.

Snow blew across the Indian camp at Monthaup, moving snake-like in long, thin lines, piling up against the wigwams. Women and children hurried from the cook fires to their shelters, taking refuge as quickly as possible. Men crawled into their furs and sat outside by the central fire, determined to wait until the council had adjourned.

Inside Metacomet's wigwam, the presence of a dozen unwashed bodies warmed the space around his fire. The sachems from several tribes and nations had come to talk, and each would have his turn to speak.

"Listen to the words my father spoke to his people when he had lived one hundred years," Wannalancet said, lifting his hand. Every eye in the circle turned in the Pennacook sachem's direction. His father, Passaconaway, had been highly esteemed. These words would be heeded and respected.

Wannalancet paused, indicating that he was about to recite the words of another. Finally he spoke in a mesmeric voice: "Hearken to the last words of your father and friend. The white men are sons of the morning. The Great Spirit is their Father. His sun shines brightly upon them. Sure as you light the fires, the breath of heaven will turn the fires upon you. Listen to my advice. It is the last I shall ever give you. Remember it and live."

The others stirred, lifting their pipes to smoke in agreement, but Metacomet ignored their sympathetic reaction. The old ones had spoken against war for years; they were old and tired. Even Metacomet's father, the great Massasoit, had chosen to befriend the English instead of warring against them. But the Yangeese had not been so bold and cruel while he had lived.

"I hear your words, my brother," Metacomet said, raising his voice to be heard above the rumblings in the circle. "And yet I fear your heart has been twisted. You have listened to the Yangeese, who speak of Lord Jesus. They have taught you to leave the spirit songs and sing praise to Jesus."

The rumbling intensified, and every face turned toward Wannalancet, who flushed at this unexpected attention. "It is true that I listened to John Eliot," he said, his hands gripping each other since he carried no pipe or tomahawk. "For four years that English man applied himself particularly to me and my people, to press and persuade us to pray to God. I used to pass by him in an old canoe, but he exhorted me to leave my old boat to embark in a new canoe. I was unwilling but have since yielded myself to his advice and have entered into a new canoe, and engage to pray to God."

"You see!" Metacomet shouted, thrusting his unscarred hand into the air. "The spirit of the Pennacook people is lost. The People of the Foothills are now the people of Lord Jesus."

"Not all of us!" One warrior stabbed the earth with his blade. "Our sachem does not speak for every man in his tribe."

"Nor does the son of our dead sachem." One of the elders from Metacomet's own tribe lifted his head to speak. His eyes, keen as a hawk's, moved over the circle, lighting on every face save Metacomet's. It was proper, for the elder spoke of Metacomet's father.

"The Fox's father was a man among men. You will not see his like again. From anger he was soon reclaimed; he was easily reconciled to those who had offended him. His reason was such that he could receive advice from mean men. He governed his people better with few blows than others did with many. Truly loving where he loved, often he restrained the malice of our people against the Yangeese. He was the most faithful friend the English had. When he died in the fortieth winter of the coming of the strangers, we grieved."

A heavy silence fell upon the group as each man contemplated Massasoit's legacy. In another moment, Metacomet knew, they would mentally compare his leadership with his father's, and the son would undoubtedly be found lacking.

"We grieve for him still," Metacomet said, in an effort to divert their speculation. "And as winter follows summer, a season of peace has become a season of war. The time has come for us to show the strength of the Wampanoag nation. We are the daybreak people, the people of the rising sun, yet the sun no longer rises first over our land. We have been pushed away from the sea. The Yangeese have taken our weapons, our rivers, our hunting grounds. They build fences in the rivers so the fish cannot enter our fishing places. They make our warriors drunk with brandy and keep them in chains to build English forts."

The younger men howled and stabbed the earth with their blades; the elders sat impassive, their eyes as untroubled as a cloudless sky. Metacomet knew their minds. Many thought he was an upstart, too proud of his fragile friendship with the Yangeese and the ridiculous title, King Philip, by which he was known among the English. Others thought he tried to unite the tribes only to broaden his power. Many, including his own sister-in-law Weetamoo, thought him mad with the desire to avenge his brother's death. But despite their misgivings, the sachems of the Narragansett, with four thousand warriors, and the Nipmuck, with three thousand, had indicated that they might join his effort to repel the Yangeese. But hundreds more would be needed to recapture the land stolen by the English.

"We will think on these things," Metacomet said finally. The elders nodded and stood to join the dancing warriors outside or those who gambled within the wigwams. As the crowd dispersed, Metacomet gestured to three of his most loyal and trusted men.

"John Sassamon has reported our plans to Josiah Winslow in Plymouth," he whispered when they were alone. He pulled his dagger from the sheath at his belt. As the trio watched, he pushed back the sleeve of the shirt he wore, then dragged the tip of the blade over the inside of his forearm. As the wound opened and bled, he lifted his gaze to study the three men before him. "I grieve because John Sassamon has betrayed his people. For this he must die."

The three warriors nodded as one.

"These things I command you, that ye love one another."

Constance spat the words out against her will, hoping that her bitter voice would be swallowed by her father's baritone rumble. Witty Greene, the housekeeper, kept her eyes closed during the recital of morning prayers, and Aiyana kept her eyes on her prayer book as if she did not quite know the words by heart. After a lifetime of daily prayers and weekly catechisms, Constance knew every phrase in the black book her father held reverently between his thick hands. Never in her life had she despised the words that rolled off her tongue—until today.

"If the world hate you, ye know that it hated me before it hated you. If ye were of the world, the world would love his own: but because ye are not of the world, but I have chosen you out of the world, therefore the world hateth you. . . ."

Constance hated Aiyana Bailie. Completely. She had despised the Indian girl ever since that morning in the woods when Forest had gaped at her like a gigged fish. It wasn't fair! She had been the center of Forest's world for a lifetime, spoiled and petted, the sworn apple of her big brother's eye. But he had taken one look at the half-breed girl and lost his reason. His single-minded determination, a strength Constance had always admired, had suddenly blazed into fascination with the Indian girl who slept upstairs in the servants' loft.

The journey from Taunton to Rehoboth had been unendurable. Ignoring harsh glances from Mojag Bailie, Forest had pressed his horse to keep pace with Aiyana's, making a fool of himself in front of the entire company. Constance had seen a sly, bemused expression upon Daniel Bailie's face and knew that she wasn't alone in understanding that her brother was completely besotted with the dark-haired girl. Such things were not done and could not be borne! No matter that her eyes were blue, her English flawless, and her Christianity genuine—Aiyana Bailie had no place in their home and no right to Forest's heart.

It would have been easier to bear Forest's infatuation if Aiyana had been properly modest, retiring, and shy. But like a moth to a flame, she returned his searching glances, obviously drawn to his laughter and easy charm. No doubt Aiyana would have pestered Constance with queries about Forest's personality and past if Constance had not made it clear that she was completely uninterested in any conversation with her maid. "Attend to my dresses, and air my shoes," she had commanded Aiyana as soon as they returned home to Rehoboth. "Help Witty when your service for me is done. And understand this—I am perfectly capable of taking care of myself. You were not employed to be my friend, my companion, or my nurse. I am nearly fourteen, old enough to be married, and I'll not waste my time in idle conversation with an Indian . . . a half-breed . . . or whatever you are."

Fury had lurked beneath Aiyana's smile as she curtsied stiffly. And then, like a fleeting shadow, some other emotion had flickered in her deep blue eyes, but Constance had turned and left the room.

And so Constance avoided Aiyana. But even in her determination to ignore the older girl, Constance burned with curiosity about her. She often placed herself outside the house near the shuttered windows to eavesdrop on conversations between Aiyana and Witty. On these occasions, she had learned that Aiyana was seventeen, that her mother had died during the previous winter, and that she missed her home on Martha's Vineyard.

"Do you never long for your husband?" Witty asked one afternoon. Listening outside, Constance dropped her jaw. A *husband*? Had she missed something?

Aiyana's gentle laugh rippled through the window. "I'm not married. Why would you think I was?"

"Oh, dearie, I'm sorry. But you're seventeen and more than an age to be wed, and you wear a ring upon your right hand. I supposed you to be a widow."

"No." The girl's voice was so low that Constance had to rise to her knees and place her ear against the crack in the shutters. The women inside were kneading bread, and the rhythmic thumps of their hands against the table nearly drowned out Aiyana's next words: "I've never wanted to be married. My life on the island was happy and full. I taught the little children and loved it."

"But—the wedding band?"

"'Twas my mother's." Aiyana's voice took on a wistful tone. "And my grandmother's, I think. 'Tis inscribed with our family credo—a charge my father has often repeated to my brother and me."

"What credo?" Witty asked. Constance gritted her teeth, frustrated because she couldn't see what was happening. She imagined Aiyana holding up her hand, pointing to an inscription on the gold ring she always wore.

"*Fortiter, fideliter, feliciter.*" The rhythmic thumping stopped, and Aiyana's voice cut cleanly through the stillness of the afternoon. "'Tis Latin for boldly, faithfully, successfully. We are to go boldly into the world, faithfully share the gospel of Christ, and remember that success is to be found in meditating on and obeying the Word of God."

Constance again heard the slapping sounds of Witty working the dough. "Well, there is no fault to be found in such a credo," she said, her plump fists pounding the table. "'Tis truly a Christian charge, that one."

"And difficult to uphold," Aiyana murmured. "My father has told me stories about my ancestors that thrill my very blood. They lived for God in the most dire circumstances imaginable. My father's mother lived with Pocahontas for a time and survived Opechancanough's uprising against Jamestown."

"I'll not be longing for that kind of thrill," Witty answered, laughing. "I thank God that the savages in this place have been at peace for the past fifty years. I wouldn't have come to New

England if I'd thought I'd have to fear every red-painted Indian I
met in the woods."

"We only fear what we do not understand," Aiyana answered.
"There was a time when I was afraid of the sea itself, but one day
my father took me walking along the shore. . . ."

Her voice faded away, and Constance clenched her fists,
annoyed that the women had left the table and turned to the
oven. She'd be hearing no more from Aiyana today unless she
spoke directly to the girl, and that she would never, ever do.

▼▲▼▲▼ Matthew Glazier's thoughts were heavy as he
escorted his household home after Sunday morning services.
Witty and Constance walked ahead of the others, the older woman's arm tucked affectionately around his daughter's waist. Forest
and Aiyana followed them, and though Aiyana kept her eyes modestly downcast, Matthew could not help but notice the shy smile
that curved her lips whenever Forest looked in her direction. She
had joined the church that morning upon a profession of faith in
Jesus Christ and as a member of his household, and the congregation had been pleased to receive her. The fact that she was of
Indian blood and not purely English made no difference, for Mistress Frances Bromfield and her two Negro slaves had been taken
into the church the week before.

But the obvious attraction between this girl and his son could
not be encouraged or even tolerated. During the week Matthew
scarcely thought about it, for his son lived with the merchant
William Hammond, and during the first few weeks of her service
Aiyana had spent the Sabbath with her father and brother. But
this week Daniel Bailie had gone to Roxbury to meet with Reverend Eliot, and Aiyana had been forced to worship with her master's family. She had not been forward or unchaste in either her
words or manner, but the mutual attraction between the two
young people was unmistakable. And because his seven years of
apprenticeship were rapidly drawing to a close, Forest would
soon be setting up his own business and household. He would

need a wife, but a penniless half-breed Indian woman was an improper and unsuitable choice, no matter what Forest's addled heart might tell him.

Frowning, Matthew folded his hands behind his back and searched for an answer. His son *would* need a wife. Forest had always been dutiful and obedient; he would honor his father's wishes. The task, then, would be to find another girl, someone convenient, someone from a family prosperous enough to provide her with a dowry generous enough to balance the handsome sum he planned to bestow upon Forest.

He grappled with the question for a moment, then remembered William Hammond. The merchant had a daughter of about fourteen or fifteen, a plain, sweet-natured child. Undoubtedly she saw Forest every day, and unless she possessed an unusually peevish and tetchy nature, she had to be attracted to Forest's charming personality. Perhaps she was already fond of him. In any case, if a marriage were arranged, affection could easily grow between them as Forest finished his time of service.

Satisfied that he had found the answer to his predicament, Matthew moved confidently toward his house. He was not a man who accepted second best in anything—he would not have a half-breed for a daughter-in-law.

▼▲▼▲▼ "But what is wrong with celebrating Christmastide?"

Breathless from their furtive escape into the woods, Aiyana turned to Forest. They had quietly slipped out of the house after Sabbath dinner, and now they walked slowly to catch their breath.

"Nothing especially," Forest answered, continuing his slow stroll. He kept his eyes on the ground, watching his shoes crunch into the powdery snow. "My father says the old pagan customs included stage shows, caroling, gaming, and other heathen merrymaking. So we ought to work on Christmas Day. The General

Court of Massachusetts has imposed a five-shilling fine on anyone caught observing the holiday."

"Five shillings!" Aiyana gasped, stunned by the amount.
"Why, I never heard of such a thing! We taught the Indians to celebrate Christmas!" She lowered her voice to a conspiratorial
whisper. "Your father would not like to hear this, I know, but we
even taught the Indians a carol written by a Catholic priest."

"I'd like to hear it," Forest answered.

Genuine interest radiated from the depths of his eyes, and a
trembling thrill raced through her. Dreaming of Forest through
the week was wonderful, but being with him was so much more
exhilarating. . . .

"Will you sing it?"

"The carol?" She blinked, distracted by his eyes.

"Yes." He stopped and leaned back against a tree, folding his
hands. His broad smile was unlike anything she'd ever seen
before. "Sing, madam, for me, please."

She stepped back, considering, then tilted her head. "You
promise you won't fine me five shillings?" she whispered, teasing. "I am a poor girl, sir, and could not afford to pay."

"If your singing is poor," he answered, raking her with a suddenly possessive look, "I may fine you ten shillings. And if you
have no money, you will forever be in my debt."

"Oh?" She lifted an eyebrow. "Then I had better sing, and
well, for I do not know if I could bear being with you forever,
debtor or free."

His eyes snapped, and she lowered her gaze, embarrassed.
You are playing with fire. She folded her hands and began to sing:

> *"Within a lodge of broken bark, the tender Babe was found;*
> *A ragged robe of rabbit skin enwrapped His beauty round—"*

"Enough of that foolishness," Forest whispered, coming
toward her. Suddenly his fingers touched her lips, his eyes bor-
ing down into hers, his breath warm upon her face.

She said nothing, scarcely daring to move. *If this is love, what is to be done about it? If 'tis not love, better to do nothing at all. . . .*

There was a protracted silence as they stared at each other. Then, by tacit consent, they stepped away.

The late afternoon air was burnished with sunlight, but she shivered, feeling cold for the first time. "No matter what Massachusetts says—" she said, folding her arms but not looking at him. She cleared her throat to steady her trembling voice. "I still think it folly to ignore the birth of Christ. The day is special; it should be commemorated and not treated like any other."

"Do not say so to my father," he answered, gesturing toward the path they had taken. One corner of his mouth rose in a slight smile. "He is a Puritan within and without. He would be horrified that you think such a thing."

"Are you?" she asked, daring to look up as they began the walk back. "Horrified by me?"

"No, Aiyana," he murmured, falling into step beside her, "you amaze me."

The sky was pure blue from north to south, with no more than a little violet duskiness lingering in the west. It was a cool, crisp day, perfect for ice fishing. John Sassamon dropped his gun and hat by the side of Assawompsett Pond and stretched. He had left his wife in their wigwam not far from the lake, and he looked forward to a morning of quiet and calm. He needed time to think, to consider his options should Metacomet choose to make war upon the English.

Relishing the warming tingle that spread through his arms, he pulled his hatchet from his pack and bent to chop a hole in the ice. The forest stood absolutely quiet around him, as if it watched to see what he might catch. Settling back upon a grass mat, Sassamon lowered his string and hook through the opening in the ice, then crossed his legs and waited for a fish to strike.

The sun, a dazzling white blur, stood fixed in the blue sky, a certain promise of spring to come. A warming zephyr rushed down the hill behind him, blowing the scents of earth, animals, and bear grease over his shoulder.

Bear grease—Sassamon had not greased his skin that morning! Though he did not move, the fine hairs on his upper arm lifted. Warriors waited in the brush behind him. Through treachery or some sort of black magic, Metacomet must have learned that Sassamon had spoken with Josiah Winslow. Unless God intervened with a miracle, the day had come for him to die.

"You may come out and face me," he called, not turning to see who might come forth. "You cannot fool me. You are silent and sure, but my God keeps watch."

An angry, rebellious war whoop shattered the silence, startling John from his determination to remain still. A cudgel met his jawbone, snapping it. As a rock smashed across his kneecap, colors exploded in his brain.

No tomahawks, he thought, slipping to the ground. This was not an execution but a deliberate and deceptive murder.

He was an old man; he could not fight them. *Father, forgive them. They know no better.* He curled into a ball, trying to protect his head and ribs from the punishing blows that fell like rain, but a pair of hands reached for his head, lifted it, and with a single wrench sent his soul winging toward heaven.

▼▲▼▲▼ Lounging on the skin-covered platform inside his wigwam, Metacomet tucked his talkative son into the crook of his arm and looked up. The brightly painted leggings outside could only belong to Sunconewhew, his younger brother. After a moment, Sunconewhew stooped to enter, then sat down and drew the back of his hand across his brow.

Metacomet rested his hand on his son's head, silencing Mukki's chatter. "What news?" he asked, studying his brother. Sunconewhew's durably boyish face concealed a quick mind and dynamic intellect. He had been educated at the Indian college at Harvard and thoroughly understood the Yangeese. Metacomet trusted his reports more than anyone else's.

Sunconewhew's eyes were dark and wild like storm clouds. "In the past months, John Eliot and Daniel Gookin have spread their teachings among the Nipmuck. The people have built seven new praying villages with wooden houses like the Yangeese. They have put aside their guns to plant crops."

The news lit a hot, clenched ball of anger at Metacomet's center, but he was careful not to show his temper. He was not one who punished the bearers of bad news.

"How many?"

"Probably eighty families." Sunconewhew's mouth twisted into a cynical smile. "But at Wabquissit, a Mohegan messenger told John Eliot that Uncas was not well-pleased that the English should call his people to pray to God."

Metacomet silently digested this news. Perhaps Uncas's displeasure could work to his advantage, but the powerful Mohegan sachem had given no sign that he would be willing to fight the Yangeese. Uncas and his people had grown rich through trading with them; they had gained power by assisting the English in the slaughter of the Pequot. And after the Pequot War, in which one of the land's fiercest tribes was nearly exterminated, Uncas had captured and executed Miantonomo, a sachem of the Narragansett who had called for unity among the Algonquin tribes.

Metacomet doubted if Uncas would support him now. The Mohegan did not want tribal unity. He wanted to sleep with the Yangeese, to lick their feet and grow fat off their foods.

"Tell me, Son," he said, nudging Mukki's slender shoulder, "do you remember the words of Miantonomo who spoke so many moons ago?"

"Yes." The boy nodded solemnly. "Would you like me to tell you?"

"Your uncle wishes to hear them," Metacomet answered, lifting the boy from his lap. He stood Mukki near the center of the wigwam, then folded his arms. "Prove to your uncle that you have learned your lessons well."

Stiffening in dignity, Mukki opened his arms to deliver the oral history. "Miantonomo, sachem of the Narragansett, said, 'You know our fathers had plenty of deer and skins, our plains were full of fish and fowl. But these English having gotten our land, they with scythes cut down the grass and with axes felled the trees. Their cows and horses eat the grass, their hogs spoil our clam banks; and we shall all be starved. We must make a common cause before all is . . . all is . . .'"

Mukki's serious expression broke into confusion, and he scratched his head. Sunconewhew smiled at him. "'Before all is ruined,'" he finished. "You have learned your lessons well."

The boy beamed in appreciation, and Metacomet leaned forward to playfully swat him on his rear. "You should be helping your mother, little frog. But you have done well."

Mukki looked up quickly, his winning smile crinkling the corners of his dark eyes, then bounded through the door. Metacomet thought the light faded in the wigwam when the boy had gone. With a sense of foreboding, he turned to his brother. "Have you been to Rehoboth?"

"Yes. Jack the trader let me buy brandy and rum. Watered down, as usual."

"And did you drink?"

"I pretended to. And I smiled and let him talk until I learned that the English still think you are preparing for war. They are afraid you will ally yourself with the French."

"The black robes? Bah! They preach Jesus as much as John Eliot. And they will take our land just as the Yangeese do."

"Jack the trader agreed that we are right to be aggrieved when the Yangeese animals trample our crops. The magistrate of Rehoboth has agreed to fine anyone we find trespassing on Pokanoket lands. And remember, Brother—they did build fences to keep their animals off our land."

Metacomet bit back the first words that sprang to his lips. The English were quick to make promises and enact halfhearted measures! But the fences were regularly breached and rarely repaired. And the Yangeese, bent on keeping him in his place, frequently demanded that he meet with them and sign away his lands. They wanted him to bow and scrape, to lie down before them.

Four years before, he and seventy of his warriors had been stripped of their muskets as they met with the English. Without considering how they would feed their families or defend themselves, the Yangeese had demanded every musket in their village. When Metacomet refused to deliver the rest of the weapons, the English leaders demanded that he proclaim himself a subject of Plymouth. For his so-called insubordination he was sentenced to pay an annual tribute of five wolves' heads and a heavy fine of one hundred pounds sterling.

Biding his time, he sold more Pokanoket land to pay the fine.

And over the years he killed the required number of wolves and took their bloody heads to Plymouth, gambling upon the future. His father, the great friend to the English, would have cut himself in mourning if he had lived to see his people in such a pitiable and humiliating condition. He would not have wanted to fight, but he would have lifted the war club against such injustices. As sachem, as leader, the calling would have fallen upon him.

But Massasoit was dead and so was Wamsutta. Now Metacomet heard the call of war and knew he must answer it. If he and his warriors were successful, the Wampanoag would regain all they had lost. And though his people now grumbled and spoke openly of Metacomet as a "white-livered cur," he bore their complaints and criticism, understanding what they could not. Sometimes a nation had to placate an enemy until its strength had fully ripened. And that time had not yet come.

"So, my brother," Metacomet said, tossing Sunconewhew a brittle smile. "The men of Rehoboth told you they would build fences and fine trespassers. Are you taking their part? Do you think we are wrong to fight the same Yangeese who taught you in their school?"

"I am Wampanoag and your brother," Sunconewhew answered. "I will stand with you. But I urge you to wait. Passaconaway despised the Yangeese at their first coming and tried all possible ways to destroy them or prevent them from settling here, but he could not stop them. He advised us never to contend with the English, nor to make war with them."

"That sachem is dead," Metacomet answered, annoyed that his brother would dare to use the great chief's name. Often Sunconewhew was too much like the Englishmen who spoke the great ones' names without reverence or regard for their eternal souls. No well-behaved Indian ever addressed another by name, nor would he disturb the spirits by calling a dead man's name aloud.

A great shouting and whooping rose from outside the wigwam, and Metacomet's eyes flitted toward the sound.

"Will you go outside?" Sunconewhew asked, bending his knee.

"I do not have to," Metacomet answered, leaning back upon his elbow. "Trouble always finds its way to my wigwam."

Within minutes, a group of warriors entered with three captives, two pale English boys and an Indian man whose tribe Metacomet could not discern. The man's face was unpainted, his arms empty of tattoos, and he wore the buckskin leggings and shirt of an English woodsman. Metacomet suspected the man was a praying Indian, but he chose to ignore him and deal first with the two children.

He gave his attention to Sunukkuhkau, the warrior holding the tallest child. "These two we found hunting near the pig fence," the warrior said, his hand momentarily dropping the noose he held around the oldest boy's neck. "They were trespassing on Pokanoket land."

Metacomet lowered his eyes to the boy's face. The child was probably twelve or thirteen, not yet old enough to carry a musket and fight should war come. Sandy-haired and freckled, the boy reminded Metacomet of an English lad he had played with many years before.

"Do you know who I am?" he asked the boy in English.

The boy's lower lip trembled; fear flashed in his eyes. "Yea. You are King Philip."

Metacomet smiled. "Yes. And because you and this other one—"

"My brother," the boy blurted out.

Typical of the English, always interrupting. Metacomet forced a smile to his lips, forgiving the insult. "You were found on our land. If we hunt on English land, our warriors are fined ten shillings or five days' labor."

The boy's face paled, but he did not answer. Good.

"Because you are young, and because I wish to show my English neighbors that I mean them no harm, I will send you and your brother back to your village. But do not cross the fence again."

"Yes, sir. Thank you, sir."

Metacomet's warriors untied the boys' hands and removed

the trusses from their necks. After bowing awkwardly, both boys turned and fled from the wigwam. Metacomet jerked his head toward Sunukkuhkau. "Take them out, and see that no harm befalls them before they reach their village."

Sunukkuhkau nodded, then left to follow the children.

Metacomet looked next at the stranger who stood between two other warriors. "What shall I do with you?" he asked in English, his generosity evaporating. "You are not of the Pokanoket nor of the Nipmuck."

"I am Mojag, from Noepe, which the English call Martha's Vineyard," the man answered fluently in Algonquin. "And I must commend you, great Sachem, for the kind manner with which you released the English boys. Their mother and father will have cause to bless your name in their evening prayers."

Metacomet frowned. His assumption had been correct. "So you are a praying Indian."

"Yes."

Sniffing with satisfaction at the young man's honesty, Metacomet studied him more carefully. He was strong and well-favored, as tall as Metacomet himself. His clear brown eyes were as gentle as a she-dog's. His name meant "He-Who-Talks-Much," and Metacomet knew he would have remembered if he had met this man before. "I am sachem over all the Pokanoket Indians, including those on Noepe, and yet I have never seen or heard of you," he said, speaking slowly and deliberately. "How can this be?"

"I never lived in a Pokanoket village," the young man answered, meeting Metacomet's eyes with an unflinching gaze. "I have followed Jesus Christ since my childhood. My mother was Pequot, my father the son of an Englishman and a woman of the Powhatan tribe."

Metacomet lifted an eyebrow. "And you have lived in a praying village all your life?"

"Yes."

"You are like the chameleon—you change your colors."

"I am an Indian." The young man's chin rose in a flash of defensive spirit.

"Then live as one." Metacomet impulsively threw out the challenge, half-hoping the young man would take it, though he had never seen a Christian Indian with boldness enough to remain as part of the tribe. "I have seen the praying villages. I have seen strong men gelded by the tears of the preachers. Those men put aside their muskets and bows and arrows. They plow like women and sing like the Yangeese. Their courage fails in the face of the English God. They beat their breasts and weep for wrongs committed by one called Adam and his woman."

"Perhaps you do not understand."

Metacomet frowned with cold fury, astonished by the blunt answer. "You are the one who does not understand!" The rage in him lifted its head to roar, but Metacomet clenched his fists, determined to overrule his anger. This was not the time to vent his feelings. This young man was not the enemy; the time was not right.

This praying Indian from Noepe knew nothing of life in the tribe. And yet he stood before Metacomet with his head high; his spirit had not yet been cowed by the English God. Perhaps if he could be convinced to stay with the Pokanoket, his heart could be stolen away, one small victory for the nation that had lost so many to Lord Jesus.

The sachem regarded his visitor with renewed interest. "Why were you in the woods?"

The question caught Mojag off guard. He tilted his head for a moment, then the barest of smiles played briefly upon his lips. "I wanted to meet you, great Sachem. My father and I would like to be friends of your people. If any of your tribe would like to follow our God, we plan to build a new village nearby where they can worship and grow their own crops in peace and safety."

Metacomet rested his chin in his hand and lifted an eyebrow. So, John Eliot was now sending his men directly onto Pokanoket land to steal hearts for Lord Jesus. And this youth had the courage to walk into Metacomet's own wigwam and announce his intentions!

No. Courage would know better. Foolishness had brought this young man to Monthaup.

Metacomet's mind curled lovingly around the thought of revenge. If this one could be stolen from Lord Jesus, his youth and strength would serve the Wampanoag well in the days to come.

After a long moment, Metacomet drew a breath and stared at the interloper with deadly concentration. "If you would befriend our people, you must understand us. It is obvious from your manner that you do not."

"But, great Sachem, I am an Indian—"

Metacomet scowled, and Mojag fell silent. When he was certain the young man would not speak again, Metacomet continued, "When one of our sons reaches fifteen winters, we blindfold him and lead him into unfamiliar woods with only a bow and arrows, a hatchet, and a knife. There he must remain for a month, supporting himself only with what the earth will furnish in the dead of winter. As the snow melts we fetch him out and feed him poisonous and bitter herbs, which he must drink until he can retain them without complaint. During this time of testing, the spirits give each of our sons the name by which he will be known as a man."

Metacomet narrowed his eyes. "You say you were born on Noepe, and so you are one of my tribe. Will you pass the winter in this way so you may prove yourself worthy of this friendship you seek?"

Doubt and despair wrestled for a moment upon the young man's face; then he nodded. "I want to prove myself to you, great Sachem," he said, his voice quiet, tranquil, and stubborn in the silence of the wigwam. "If I must winter in the woods in order to do this, I will. Only let me tell my father what I am doing—"

"A grown man does not need to consult his father about a matter so important," Metacomet snapped. "A man acts when he has opportunity. You trespassed on Pokanoket land, and I have the right to kill you. But because you are one of my people, I will let you live if you prove yourself worthy of life. We do not need praying Indians, He-Who-Talks-Much, we need men of courage."

"I agree with your words," Mojag answered, lifting his head. "To confirm my loyalty to your people, I will do as you suggest."

Metacomet felt the corner of his mouth lift in a smile. "Go then." He shifted his gaze to the guards who waited patiently in the doorway. "Give him a full meal, then take him to a wintering place and give him the weapons he will require. When the snows melt, we will see if his heart is still with us."

▾▲▾▲▾ As he followed a pair of warriors from the sachem's house, Mojag shook his head, shocked by the unexpected turn of events. When he had awakened in his little hut this morning, he had never imagined that he'd be spending the next month alone in the woods.

John Eliot had assured Daniel and Mojag that any sort of evangelistic work in this part of the country would be impossible without the support or tolerance of the Pokanoket sachem, so for weeks they had been praying that God would grant them an opportunity to meet and talk with King Philip. Daniel had urged Mojag to be patient, to pray and study and seek God's leading, but Mojag had chafed at his father's plodding plans. And after Daniel had left for Roxbury, a sudden inspiration had seized Mojag—why not visit the Pokanoket camp and introduce himself to the sachem? What harm could it do? After all, they were both Indians, and the blood of distant Powhatan sachems flowed in Mojag's own veins. . . .

He hadn't gone more than a mile into Pokanoket territory before he had been apprehended. Then, without his even having to ask, he had been hauled before the sachem and practically commanded to join the tribe! Never had Mojag dared to dream that God would work so quickly, so drastically, or so . . . fearfully.

One of the warriors who had found him in the woods now gestured toward the central campfire, where several black iron kettles sat upon glowing coals. Men, women, and children served themselves by scooping their hands into the cauldrons. Though Mojag's sensibilities rebelled against the notion of sharing a common pot and eating with his hands like an animal, he followed the example of the others and walked toward their fire. Inside the nearest kettle he found a stew made of some sort of stringy meat, acorn nuts, dried corn, and various roots.

He hesitated, a bit bewildered. A strangely musical voice interrupted his thoughts. "For you," a girl murmured, offering him what appeared to be a bark plate. In an instant, all thoughts of Philip, his father, and the wintering ordeal fled from his mind.

Fingers as gentle as an evening breeze brushed his hand as the young woman gave him the plate. Mojag stood motionless, his heart thudding erratically as he looked down into a face as luminous as a full moon. A sense of tingling delight flowed through him as he studied her, and her warm dark eyes examined him in return. "Thank you," he finally managed to stammer as she moved away. Though everything in him wanted to call her back, he sensed that such an action would not be proper. He had only just seen her, and there were surely proprieties to be addressed, a father to be reassured, a mother to be charmed. Not even in the praying villages could a man approach a young woman without first pleasing her parents.

Swallowing his frustration, he scooped out a handful of the pottage, placed it on his plate, then sat cross-legged by the fire with others who were eating. Thoughts of the girl were foolish, for he would soon be leaving for the woods. He had much to consider and would need to pray for strength and cunning he had never needed before. But first—

"Excuse me, friend," he said, nudging the man who ate next to him, "but that girl over there—the one with white feathers in her hair. What is her name, and who is her father?"

The man's face cracked into a sly smile. "That one is daughter to Dyami. She is called Ootadabun."

Ootadabun—"daystar." Mojag smiled his thanks and lowered his head, pretending to concentrate on the food before him. But the meal was bland and tasteless, especially now that his brain hummed with thoughts of survival and the girl who would make his life complete.

A fierce, freezing wind shrilled through Rehoboth, and Aiyana pulled her cloak more tightly about her neck. Despite the miserable weather, she was thrilled to dress and go outside. It was Sunday, time to go to church . . . and see Forest.

Constance, Witty, and the master joined her outside in the courtyard for the walk to the meetinghouse, and she hoped that the approaching figure was Forest coming to spend the Sabbath with his family. But her spirits sank when she recognized her father's lean form.

"Good morrow," her father said, tipping his hat respectfully to Master Glazier. "I wonder if I might take the pleasure of my daughter's company from you today?"

"Well met, Daniel Bailie," Matthew Glazier answered, thrusting his hand forward in a stiffly polite handshake. After the greeting, Master Glazier herded Constance and Witty toward the gate. "We'll be on our way and allow you a private word with your daughter."

"Thank you kindly," her father answered, stepping aside so the family could pass through the courtyard gate. When they had gone, her father sat on a garden bench and patted the empty space at his side. A momentary look of discomfort crossed his face. "Sit down, Aiyana. There is something I must tell you."

Something in his tone made her heart beat faster. She obeyed, automatically sinking to the place next to him.

"I came to ask—I had rather hoped—that you have heard from Mojag."

The hard fist of fear clenched in her stomach. "Has something happened to him? I haven't seen Mojag since the last time you both visited."

"'Tis probably nothing," her father answered, leaning forward with his elbows on his knees. Absently, he twirled his hat in his hand. "But when I returned from Roxbury, Mojag was not in our hut."

"If he is missing, we should organize a party of men and search for him," Aiyana said, placing her hand on her father's arm. "I could borrow a horse from the Glaziers. Forest would help us search, and there are others here—"

"No. Mojag is a man, and he must make his own way in the world," her father answered, patting her hand despite the anxiety that hovered behind his eyes. "I know he was trying to find a way to reach the Pokanoket, and perhaps he set out with a hunting party. I searched for him myself yesterday but found no traces of him. If evil had befallen him, I am sure we would have heard something by now. From the appearance of our hut, I would say he has been gone at least a week."

Aiyana's mind reeled with the dark possibilities of danger in the woods. Mojag could have been mauled by a bear, attacked by a mountain lion, or murdered by robbers, renegade Indians, evil seamen intent on terrorizing solitary wayfarers—

"Father, we must do something! Why would he go off alone? If he wants to help the Pokanoket, why didn't he go with you to Roxbury?"

"Mojag has been struggling over the last few weeks, Aiyana. My ways are not his ways."

"But you are his *father*. Why must he always be difficult? You know how to build a praying village. All Mojag has to do is follow you and do what the Reverend Eliot suggests."

"We must trust Mojag into God's care."

"But the woods here are full of Indians—"

"You forget yourself. Your brother is an Indian, as are you." Her father stood, then held out his hand. "Come, my dear. We'll go to church and pray for Mojag there."

Choking back a frustrated sob, Aiyana took her father's arm

and walked to church in silence. When they reached the door, where men and women parted to sit on their respective sides of the building, her father bent and whispered in her ear, "Pray for him, Aiyana. Pray for his safety and that Mojag would find his calling."

Through the entire service she prayed, her head bowed, her hands in her lap. Once she felt eyes upon her and looked up to see one of the selectmen glaring at her from across the aisle. *He probably thinks I'm sleeping!* she realized, horrified. If so, she'd have to pay a fine or face some other punishment. Aiyana gave the man a penitent look, hoping that a properly repentant attitude might dissuade him from reporting her. When the man looked away, she promptly returned to her prayer for Mojag's safety.

She couldn't bear losing her brother now. When her mother died, they had each mourned in their own way. Her father had spent hours alone in his chamber; Mojag had preferred to walk endlessly on the beach, alone with his memories and his thoughts. Both father and son had adored Dena, but Aiyana had considered her mother a friend and soul mate unlike any she would ever know. Even now she missed her mother terribly.

She had once made the mistake of mentioning her loss during the Glazier's family prayer time.

"You are wrong to mourn, Aiyana, and you should confess that sin so that God may cleanse your heart," Master Glazier had rebuked her, staring sternly over his Bible. "'Tis a sin to grieve immoderately, for grief is but a result of not keeping your love within proper bounds."

"I was wrong to love my mother?" Aiyana had asked, disbelieving.

The master had shaken his head and lifted a wagging finger. "We must give all our love and complete devotion to God and not value our fellow creatures too highly. Death parts all of us— husbands from wives, children from parents. God would not have you so torn apart by grief that you are unfit for his service. Remember that our Lord said, 'He that loveth father or mother more than me is not worthy of me.' Love discreetly, dear girl, love carefully, but delight yourself only in the Lord."

Now, remembering his words, Aiyana blinked back tears. Master Glazier would probably say she was sinful to worry about Mojag, but she loved him so. And Jesus knew what love was, for he wept when his friend Lazarus died. Master Glazier and the other Puritans might keep emotions in neat, orderly packages, but she could not love tidily. She had grown up under two parents who showered her and Mojag with love and affection, and she could not see that she had been harmed by their "immoderate" adoration.

When at last the church service was dismissed, she caught up to her father and linked her arm through his. Not caring what anyone might think, she pressed her head to his shoulder and released the tears that had been building behind her eyes all morning. Despite buzzing whispers and reproachful glances, her father stopped in the center of the street and drew her into his comforting embrace.

▼▲▼▲▼ Aiyana's father assured her that all would be well, but the next morning she rose with a heaviness upon her heart and soul. She moved slowly through the house as she worked, and more than once Constance complained about Aiyana's distracted attitude. "I've heard that Indians are indolent and lazy," the younger girl snapped, lifting her kirtle to march across a mound of dust Aiyana had just swept into a pile. "And now I see that the tales are true."

Angry words rose to Aiyana's tongue, but she held them in check, closing her eyes against the rebellion in her soul. If Constance had been more of a friend, or even a tiny bit sympathetic, she might have confided the source of her anxiety and mental distress. But Constance would not care that Mojag had vanished into the heart of the wilderness, where Philip's warriors roamed. She would only make a glib remark about untrustworthy, lying Indians, and Aiyana would be tempted to slap sense into the girl.

She pressed her lips together and returned her broom to the scattered dust. *Dear God, give me patience. Bring Mojag home safely. And forgive me for thinking harsh things about Forest's sister.*

A blast of arctic air ripped through the house as Witty stumbled through the doorway.

"Witty, I am glad you are here," Constance called as the housekeeper slammed the door. "Father has invited Master Hammond to visit after supper. Make sure the house is particularly presentable."

"Is there news regarding Master Forest's apprenticeship?" Witty asked, a smile lighting her reddened face as she untied her hat and cloak. "Will Master Hammond set Forest up in business? Mayhap—" her eyes twinkled at Aiyana—"he's willing to make our Forest a partner!"

"'Tis better news than that," Constance said, plopping down on the high-backed settle before the fire. "The visit is to discuss Forest's marriage to Serenity Hammond."

A curious, tingling shock jolted Aiyana; the broom fell from her hands. Embarrassed, she bent to retrieve it even as her heart pounded in denial. *No! Forest cannot be engaged to another! He loves me, and I've endured weeks of suffering in his father's house to be closer to him, to understand him better. . . .*

Witty's gaze met Aiyana's in a moment of understanding. "Surely this thing is not yet settled," Witty said, tearing her eyes away from Aiyana's. She moved toward Constance. "Why, Forest has known Serenity for years, and he's never spoken a tender word about her. Methinks he considers her a sister, more like a cousin than a wife."

"You heard Father's sermon the other night at prayers," Constance said, smiling impishly beneath her cap. "A man and woman marry not for love but to render each other's life easy, quiet, and comfortable. Forest will be a good husband for Serenity, and she will provide him with many children." She shrugged. "Who could argue against the match?"

Dropping the broom onto the floor, Aiyana grabbed her cloak and ran out the door.

▼▲▼▲▼ Witty found Aiyana in the barn. "Come here, my dear," she called, climbing through the straw to wrap her arms around Aiyana's trembling shoulders. "Do not weep. 'Tis not the end of the world, you know. Anything can happen on the morrow."

"No," Aiyana whimpered, hiccuping. "Every day brings me more sorrow! Mojag is missing, Witty. He has disappeared, and no one knows where to find him. I can't lose him, Witty, no matter what the preacher or Master Glazier says. And I have come to love Forest, and I thought he loved me. But all will come to naught if he is wed to Serenity—"

"Serenity is but a child, and Forest can think for himself," Witty said, turning Aiyana so that they faced each other. "Wipe your tears, child, and trust me. I have known that boy since before he could walk, and I know his heart. Love for you shines on his face every time he looks at you. Have you not seen it?"

"I don't know," Aiyana whispered, clumsily palming tears from her cheeks. "My mother told me that I would know love when I had found it. I think I love Forest, but Master Glazier says my will must command my affections, so perhaps the feeling is not love. I know I cannot command this unruly feeling. If I must command my will *not* to love Forest, then I am a soul most miserable. I do not believe I can ever stop loving him—"

"Hush, my girl," Witty whispered, drawing Aiyana close. "If you love Forest, trust him to do what is right. He is a godly young man. If he loves you, he will not fail you."

Aiyana sniffed. "Do you think he would speak to my father about me?"

"I have no doubt of it," Witty answered, brushing straw from Aiyana's hair. "This talk of Serenity Hammond is not of Forest's doing. I know that as sure as I know the sun will rise on the morrow."

Gulping in relief, Aiyana threw her arms around the older woman and hugged her fiercely.

▼▲▼▲ Matthew Glazier finished his prayer time with his household and sent the women off to bed. When he was certain that Constance was safely tucked away and that the servants would remain in the attic, he lit a lantern in the window and waited for William Hammond's arrival. The two men had agreed that these discussions should not be mentioned to the prospective bride and groom until the details were settled and the arrangements made.

At length the awaited knock sounded upon the door. Matthew rose eagerly and greeted his friend, offering him a chair by the fire.

"Ah, and 'tis good of you to think of me," William said, bending his long frame to fit the chair. "And good of you to think of my daughter with regard to your son. You know, Matthew, I often think of Forest with fatherly affection. For these past seven years he has served me honorably and with respect. He is a credit to you and to our Lord."

"Thank you," Matthew answered, trying to smooth the pride from his features. "It gives me great pleasure to hear you say so. But as you know, within the year Forest will finish his contract of service and must think about his own future."

"I'm glad you mentioned business," Hammond said, leaning forward. He lifted a hand and pointed a finger at Matthew. "He's such a hard worker, I've been half afraid he would prepare to compete against me. Competition would drive prices downward and impoverish both our families."

"Why should there be competition?" Matthew asked, shrugging. "Why not a partnership between equals? With our children wed to each other, what is good for Forest's business will be good for your own. A marriage of our children would yoke equals in birth, education, and religion. And if my son's character has pleased you as you say it has—"

"Indubitably, it has," Hammond asserted. "And my daughter is very fond of Forest. I daresay she already thinks of him as a brother, so 'tis but a small step to consider him a husband."

"Well, then." Matthew slapped his legs in approval. "If we are agreed, let us settle the terms of the espousal before we approach the children. I know of too many marriages that were unhappily stalled while the parents tried to work out the terms of the endowment and dowry."

"Amen, I agree," Hammond answered, crossing his legs. He ran a finger over his thin, carefully clipped mustache. "It is customary, I believe, for the bride's father to give half as much as the groom's."

Matthew blew out his cheeks. "Customary and, I daresay, a good idea. We have only to determine what that amount will be."

"Well, Matthew, knowing your generosity, I know I shall not need to worry about my Serenity. Life is uncertain at best in this wilderness, and in case Forest should die before her, she may be left with many small children. She will need some small fortune to trust for her provision."

"Likewise, if Serenity predeceases my Forest, he will need to hire a servant to care for those many small children." Matthew paused for a moment, studying the friend who had now become an opponent. As the groom's father, he ought to propose a figure first, but if he suggested too small an amount, he would appear unloving toward his son and future daughter-in-law. On the other hand, why part with good gold if he did not have to?

"I propose," Matthew said, drumming his fingers on his knees, "that I shall give Forest twenty pounds and the portion of land behind my house. Since the land is worth at least eighty pounds, my contribution will total one hundred pounds. If you provide Serenity with fifty, it will be an equitable arrangement."

"Twenty pounds?" Hammond's face reddened. "And a plot of worthless land? Matthew, my friend, you forget yourself! How can they set up a household with naught but twenty pounds?"

"The amount would be seventy pounds, with your fifty," Matthew pointed out.

"My fifty is to be put away for safekeeping, in case my Serenity becomes a widow," Hammond interjected. "Twenty pounds? I'm amazed, man, simply amazed. I thought you would offer at least one hundred fifty pounds in gold—"

"One hundred fifty pounds?" Matthew forgot to lower his voice until a board creaked overhead. He had disturbed the servants, and he knew they must be awake and wide-eyed, staring at the floor. "One hundred fifty pounds?" he whispered, grinding the words out between his teeth. "Do you think I'm made of gold? I love my son, William, but I'll not be paying a fortune to dress your daughter in silks and feathers and lace and ruffles and whatever other fripperies she may have in mind—"

"My daughter is not set on frippery!" William roared, standing to his feet. "She is a God-fearing and righteous girl, as happy in homespun as she is in silk. With her to manage his home and affairs, your son will prosper far more than he ever would without her—"

"So now my son is not a good manager, eh?" Matthew stood to meet his companion's eye. "So why did I hear that 'tis he and he alone who has kept your shop in business while you visit the public houses of Swansea and Taunton? 'Tis not all business you conduct in those towns, I've heard."

The line of Hammond's mouth tightened. "So now you are calling me a drunkard?"

"Those words are yours, but by the words of a man's tongue shall he be convicted."

"I—I—" Hammond closed his eyes and opened his mouth, his signal that Glazier had transgressed the bounds of human endurance. As words failed him, Hammond gathered his hat from the mantel and stormed out of the house, refusing even to bid his host a good night.

When the merchant had disappeared into the darkness, Matthew sank onto the settle. Sighing heavily, he folded his hands across his stomach and brooded. All in all, compared to reports he had heard about other prenuptial meetings, this first one had gone fairly well.

"If you would befriend our people, you must understand us. It is obvious from your manner that you do not."

"But, great Sachem, I am an Indian —"

Mojag's mouth curved into a mirthless smile when he recalled his boasting to the great Wampanoag sachem. *I am an Indian,* he had thought. *I am just like you!* Then Metacomet's men had left him alone in the Squannakonk swamps, and within a few hours Mojag had begun to understand the depths of his foolish pride.

He knew nothing about being an Indian. The children in Metacomet's camp had scampered through the cold wearing little but buckskin shirts and leggings, but though Mojag wore buckskins, fur-lined moccasins, and a beaver hat, the cold came at him like a mortal enemy and wearied him with its bite. It entered through his mouth and nostrils as he shivered in the sun. It sucked moisture from his body, drying his skin and cracking his lips until they burst open. The wind pressed through his leggings like an icy hand intent upon forcing him farther into the darkness of the swamps, far away from civilization. His father had once told him that the Indians considered the swamp a sacred place where family members could be sheltered in times of war. But Mojag agreed with the English: The swamps were the hiding place of the devil, unreclaimable and useless land where wolves and other dangers lurked and waited for the unwary.

The brief winter days were at their shortest; the nights, cold, black, and interminable. During the first few days of his isolation, Mojag rose from his sleeping place with the pallid yellow sun and prowled like a wolf himself, his empty stomach driving him to find food. Glistening with frost, the bare trees and shrubs mocked him with their emptiness. He fumbled through barren owls' nests and abandoned beaver lodges; once he came upon deer prints in the mud and desperately tracked the animal for hours before losing the trail and giving up the chase.

Though blood from the Pequot and Powhatan tribes flowed in his veins, he could not master the land his ancestors had subdued and dominated. He had given his life to books and the study of theology; he had imagined himself above the need for knowledge of the wilderness. To indulge Aiyana, he had occasionally joined her on the beach to fish and dig for clams, but that bit of experience would do him no good in the swamps. His father was an expert hunter and scout, but Mojag had never coveted his father's skills.

As he retreated from the claws of the wind and huddled against a frozen tree, Mojag realized how little he knew. His body trembled with weakness, cold, and hunger, but his senses had never been sharper. Odd wind-borne sounds came to him: animal cries, the snap and crackle of ice in shallow pools, the groanings of the trees. The forest wrapped around him like water around a rock, at once overwhelming him with its vastness and intimidating him with its might. His senses reached out into the night as he heard, smelled, and touched the fullness of God's created earth.

Metacomet had said that spirits talked to boys as they passed the solitary winter of their manhood, and Mojag understood how a lonely soul could imagine himself a captive of the spirit forces. Not a single human voice save his own disturbed the haunting, low moans of the wind, and after many days he fancied himself able to understand even the cries of a hawk that circled overhead. *I see you, weakling!* the hawk cried, its sharp eye tuned to the spot where Mojag cowered before the wind. *And I will pick your bones if you fail!* Choirs of wolves gathered at night and lifted their mournful dirge, waiting for him to die.

After a week without finding food, Mojag crawled into a hollow spot in the earth. Pulling his head to his knees, he fought against despair. Why had he ever thought himself capable of surviving this ordeal? He looked like an Indian, but the Englishman John Eliot was more Indian than Mojag would ever be. The old preacher knew enough to survive in the woods!

Mojag had no idea which of the tubers in the ground would feed him and which would make him ill. Any fifteen-year-old boy had a better chance of surviving the winter ordeal than Mojag did. He would never win Metacomet's respect; he had made a fatal mistake. Pride, not God, had led him to the Pokanoket camp. Like the villainous King Herod who brought forth the head of John the Baptist on a platter, he had hoped to present his father with King Philip's soul. He had yearned for the praise of men, but instead the low moans of the wind and the chattering of eagles filled his ears.

A cold fog covered the swamp; the ghostly blanket thickened and congealed around him. Mojag pressed his hand over his face. "Father God, if I have offended you, forgive me. Show mercy, dearest Lord, and have pity upon me."

Two sleepless nights bore down on him with an irresistible weight, and he closed his eyes, withdrawing into a vague half-sleep. Sometime later the pressure of a hand upon his shoulder woke him.

"What?" Mojag murmured, unwilling to quit his sleep. There, at least, hunger did not gnaw at his insides.

"Rise and eat," an iron voice commanded.

The words jolted Mojag like a bolt of lightning. He forced his eyes to open and nearly stopped breathing when he saw the man who stood before him.

Of average height and weight, the man wore buckskins like the English and French trappers, but his resemblance to an earthly creature ended with his clothing. Lustrous white hair covered his head and flowed in a rich tide down to his waist. His skin was pale, practically translucent, his eyebrows as white as his hair. His bright eyes glowed like light, piercing to the core of Mojag's soul.

"Are you not hungry?" the man spoke again. The grooves

beside his lips deepened into a sure smile. Wind-scented breath rushed from his mouth as he gestured to a clearing beyond.

Mojag sat in a stunned huddle, unable to answer.

"The Lord has heard your cry," the man answered, extending his hand. For an instant, wistfulness stole into his expression. "Come, you must eat if you are to remain strong."

Mojag clenched his hand, trembling as if the devil himself had offered a handshake. "Who are you?" he asked, afraid to look into those eyes of light.

"In the Indian tongue, my name would be Hania," the man answered, withdrawing his hand. He stepped back and stared at Mojag with eyes as indecipherable as water. "I am a servant of the most high God, Mojag Bailie. You need not fear me."

"Spirit warrior," Mojag whispered, interpreting the name. He felt a tiny tremor of fear but rose to his hands and knees and looked up at the stranger again. "You are an angel?"

Hania nodded. "Yes. And if you are hungry, you should eat. Don't grovel before me like a dog. I am not the Almighty."

"Of course not." Mojag swallowed against the unfamiliar constriction in his throat and forced a lighthearted note into his voice. "I hope you can cook, Hania. I am starving."

"Come and see."

Mojag stood to his feet, absently patting his body to make certain he was not dreaming. The rising sun had burned off the fog, and the scent of roasting meat set his mouth to watering. He brushed the dirt off his breeches and walked toward the clearing, anxious to discover more about his unearthly visitor.

Hania had prepared a venison stew, a dead doe lay gutted on an earthen bank nearby. The stew bubbled in a kettle Hania had fashioned from a hollowed-out tree trunk. Mojag frowned. There was no sign of a miracle. No shiny copper pots, muskets, or gleaming swords had appeared from thin air.

"Do you expect me to do everything for you?" Hania asked, his eyes gleaming as he looked at Mojag. The angel sat on a fallen log and gestured toward the kettle. "This is how the Indians lived before the English brought them iron pots. This is how you must learn to live if you are to remain with the Wampanoag."

"I won't be remaining with them," Mojag said, his senses reeling as he breathed in the heady scent of the food. Reaching into the pot, Indian-style, he brought forth a handful of the steaming stew. The warmth invigorated his cold fingers, and he nibbled at a piece of venison, then brought his hand to his face and greedily devoured the delicious portion.

"Why wouldn't you remain with the tribe?" Hania asked, his bright eyes searching the horizon beyond. "Metacomet needs to hear the voice of one who will bear witness of the truth. John Sassamon has departed this earth."

"I don't know him," Mojag said, dipping his hand into the pot again. "But I can't live as an Indian. You see how I have failed. Metacomet will have no respect for me. I'm grateful God sent you to spare my life, but—"

"You will always fail when you attempt to do God's work in your own power," Hania answered, resting his chin on his powerful fist. "But if you are obedient, God will tax the resources of the highest star to assist you in your calling."

"I've not been obedient," Mojag argued, scooping up another handful of the delicious pottage. "So please thank God for saving my life—"

"Do you think I have come only to spare your life?" The angel's eyes fastened on Mojag, glittering with an inner fire brighter than the sun. "If you are not willing to be used, then what does it matter if you live on earth or in heaven? God wants to use you among the Wampanoag. I am here to teach you."

"Teach me?" Mojag snorted in disbelief. "I have studied the Bible all my life. I know the law and the prophets. I can recite any catechism you choose."

Hania's mouth twitched with amusement. "I am not here to prepare you for the church, Mojag. I am here to teach you how to live in the *world* to which God has called you. You have asked God to reveal your calling; he has sent me to prepare you for what you must do."

Suddenly ashamed of his physical appetite, Mojag lowered his greasy hand to his side. An angel had come from heaven to reveal God's plan, and all Mojag could think about was filling his belly!

"I thought my calling was to help my father and Reverend Eliot," he said, heat stealing into his face.

"They are one part of the body of Christ; you are another. Yours is a different calling, Mojag Bailie." Resting his hands upon his knees, Hania closed his eyes and let his head fall back so that his silver hair swept the ground behind him. The bone-numbing cold that had held Mojag in its grasp suddenly faded, and when Hania spoke again, his voice rushed like a wind through Mojag's soul. "You are God's chosen one, called to give light to a darkened people, to bring understanding where there is folly. The Almighty sends you to a people whose hands are defiled with blood, their fingers with iniquity. With their lips they speak falsehoods; their tongues mutter wickedness. 'Their feet run to evil, and they make haste to shed innocent blood: their thoughts are thoughts of iniquity; wasting and destruction are in their paths. The way of peace they know not; and there is no judgment in their goings: they have made them crooked paths: whosoever goeth therein shall not know peace.'"

Too startled by the authority in the angel's voice to offer any objection, Mojag fell to his knees on the moist earth, clasping his hands as he bowed his head. "My Lord and God," he prayed, awestruck at the significance of Hania's words, "truly, I thank you for sending this messenger to me. But how can I do this alone? I cannot even survive in the woods without your help."

The sun seemed to rise from behind his closed eyes; a bright light filled his soul. A new and unexpected warmth surged through him as the voice of God spoke directly to his heart: *"Look at the swamp around you, my son Mojag. My people are like this desolate swamp—they reek from the stench of their own stagnation. In their quest for purity they have isolated themselves from my heart. They venerate acts of men and familiar traditions, but they ignore the fresh, moving river of my Spirit."*

"What shall I do?" Mojag whispered, covering his face with his hands.

"I have called you to the Wampanoag, and to their sachem, Metacomet. Be as wise as a serpent, my son, but as gentle as a dove among the people to whom I have called you. And my Spirit, which is upon you, and my words, which I have put in your mouth, shall not depart from your tongue. Boldly, faithfully, successfully arise and go forth, for I am with you always."

Suddenly, in a breathless instant of release, Mojag understood. No wonder he had always felt uncomfortable and stifled in the praying villages! God had been working on his heart for years, molding him, preparing him for this responsibility. While his father and John Eliot had been content to reach the Indians who would come forth from their heathen villages, Mojag had yearned to go further. He had often wondered if his concern for the Indians sprang from a peculiar desire to know the Indian part of himself better, but now he understood. God had made him, had shaped his deepest yearnings, for this task. In fulfilling God's call, he would realize his dreams and fill the empty places of his heart.

A cry of relief broke from his lips. He swayed upon his knees, caught up in the most profound joy he had ever known, then crumpled to the ground. When his heart finally stopped racing, he lifted his eyes to meet Hania's.

The angel sat on the log, waiting. "There is one other thing," he said, giving Mojag a wistful smile. "The Wampanoag will expect you to have a new name when you return. You shall be known to them as Askuwheteau, He-Who-Waits. Watch and wait, Askuwheteau, and see the glory of the Lord revealed in this land. But do not expect to find God in one people or the other. He is everywhere, in the hearts of all who turn to him."

Overcome by emotion, Mojag struggled to find his voice. "Will you help me?" he finally stammered.

The angel gave him a boyishly affectionate smile. "I will teach you to hunt, to cook, to walk as soundlessly as a thought, to find food in the earth. The rest you must learn yourself."

Ootadabun paused inside her wigwam when she heard the returning warriors' cries of celebration. Stooping to look out the doorway, she searched the crowd, anxious to see whether they celebrated the stranger's death or his victory. There! He walked among them, his face wreathed in a triumphant smile, his arm lifted as he proudly displayed his bow. The newcomer had endured! She felt a smile cross her face and hastily corrected her expression. Rumor had it that this one prayed to Lord Jesus; the tribe had yet to see whether or not Metacomet would allow a praying Indian to join his people.

Outside his wigwam, the sachem watched with his wife and son but made no sign of pleasure or anger as the whooping warriors entered. The newcomer stopped to salute the sachem, and Metacomet remained silent as Sunconewhew praised the stranger's prowess and twined a pair of white eagle feathers, the mark of manhood, into the stranger's hair. "He not only survived but he has killed a deer for our feast!" the sachem's brother proclaimed, pointing toward a huge buck two other warriors carried upon a pole. Ootadabun hurried from her house to join the women who would cut and cook the meat. A buck that size would keep them feasting throughout the night.

Another party returned not long afterward with a pitifully thin boy at its center, but the young man lifted his arms in victory and saluted his chief as well. More than thirty boys had grown to maturity and proved themselves this winter, and on their return Ootadabun was always grateful that women did not have to endure a winter alone. Between caring for a family and continual planting, reaping, and cooking, a woman's work was ordeal enough.

But for this new man, this one called Mojag, Ootadabun would endure women's work and more should he ask her. She had been struck by the honest emotion in his eyes when first she saw him, and today she felt herself blush as his eyes sought hers again. Had the spirits whispered her name in his time of travail? And would his successful wintering prove to Metacomet that this man would be a valuable addition to the tribe?

Jabbering in frustration and hurry, one of the women pointed Ootadabun toward a kettle that needed stirring. She picked up a wooden paddle and lowered her gaze to the pottage, feeling the intensity of the young man's eyes upon her. When the time was right, he would speak to her father, she knew. And when her father asked if she could love this newcomer, she would reply that she would give herself to no other.

▼▲▼▲▼ Instantly alarmed by the sound of movement in the brush, Daniel Bailie lifted his head from his book. A moment later Mojag walked into the clearing, an impenitent grin upon his face.

"Mojag!" Dropping his book, Daniel rushed to embrace his son, a wellspring of love rising in his heart. For weeks he had prayed for this moment. A hundred times he had imagined how he would rebuke his son for wandering into the wilderness without so much as a "by your leave," but now he wanted only to hold his son and never let go.

"It is good to see you, Father," Mojag said, his voice unnaturally loud as he strained to push his embarrassment aside. Was he as relieved as Daniel?

"And you," Daniel answered. "Let me look at you!" Keeping his hands upon his son's shoulders, he stepped back. Despite the cold, Mojag wore no shirt, only a breechcloth and leathern leggings. A belt of wampum hung loosely around his waist, and a blanket draped his shoulders. Painted designs adorned his chest and face, and his formerly close-cropped hair had begun to grow into the longer tufted style preferred by the Pokanoket. Two white feathers had been woven into a braid that hung over his ear.

But the real changes in Mojag went far deeper. He had been gone but a few weeks, and yet he seemed five years older. The last traces of awkwardness, uncertainty, and boyishness had evaporated from his face and body; he had become a man. An *Indian.* An aloof strength emanated from his features; he stood tall and impressive. *My son.*

Pride and alarm stirred in Daniel's heart. "Mojag, I am glad you have come home. You must have many stories to tell me."

"I do, Father."

Daniel hesitated, suddenly aware that they spoke as awkwardly as casual acquaintances. Mojag made no move to sit down, and Daniel realized that his son waited for an invitation. "Good, good, let us sit," he said quickly, hurrying over the formalities. He sank to his mat and gestured for Mojag to sit beside him. "When we have talked, I will write Reverend Eliot and tell him of the progress you have made. And when we visit the Indians together . . ."

He paused. Mojag had averted his eyes.

"Son?" he asked, leaning closer. "Is something wrong?"

"What I have to tell you is not easy," Mojag said, lifting his gaze to meet Daniel's. "When you left for Roxbury, I decided to visit Monthaup alone. Mayhap I went in pride or curiosity, I don't know. But Metacomet received me warmly and asked that I spend a month alone in the woods in order to prove myself. I think he wanted to see if we Christians were truly made of stern stuff. Frankly, Father, I would not have survived but for the grace and provision of God." A shy smile crept over his face. "But while I suffered in the woods, God revealed my true calling. I am not to work with you and Reverend Eliot, though we shall be working toward the same end. God has called me to live among the Wampanoag, to serve Metacomet as best I can, to be like the lone voice crying in the wilderness."

"Mojag!" Daniel hesitated, torn by conflicting emotions. He

shook his head in dismay. "You can't live among the heathen. Reverend Eliot has instructed me to wait before progressing further. It appears that even now Philip is planning to make war upon the English. What will you do when he does?"

"I would not fight," Mojag answered softly, looking at the ground again.

Exasperated, Daniel tossed his hand into the air. "You are so naive! You cannot close your eyes to the threat of war and pretend it does not exist! Mojag, I have taught you better than this. The natives are best reached through our work in the praying villages. And I am depending upon your calling to follow me into the ministry."

"Father, you have lived among the English too long. You sound just like a Puritan! Do you forget your days among the Pequot? You ate with them, played with them, hunted with them; my mother was one of them. I am following your example. How can you fault me for that?"

"The Pequot are nothing like the Wampanoag! Nixkamich's people were a Christian clan, who knew the Lord and his salvation. They lived much as their ancestors did, but they did not worship the spirits or behave as barbarians." Daniel closed his eyes as he reflected on the people he and his family had lived near for so many years. "While with Nixkamich—your grandfather—and his people, we had nothing to fear from them. We were welcomed as brothers in the Holy Spirit. My father would never have left us alone in a pagan tribe."

"But, Father, who converted that clan in the first place? They were not always Christian." Mojag's eyes filled with a curious deep longing. "Grandmother and Grandfather taught them of Christ—that was their calling. I feel called to the same task. I respect and honor what God has done, but I cannot resist what he is presently doing."

"What he is doing?" Daniel shook his head, dumbfounded. "Son, God is working through John Eliot. Hundreds of Indians are coming to Christ and settling in the praying villages. How shall I explain to the Reverend Eliot that *my son* believes God wants to work in a different way? He will not understand how a Christian could choose to live among the heathen barbarians."

"Why wouldn't he understand?" Mojag's handsome face darkened. "Jesus lived among the heathens! I have studied, Father, and in the biblical record of Jesus' ministry, two-thirds of his personal encounters were with those who did not follow him. Our Savior won the hearts of men and women by telling stories that farmers, mothers, fathers, fishermen, slaves, and soldiers could understand. All people, *especially* the Indians, appreciate honorable qualities. God has prepared their hearts to receive the gospel, but we must live it among them; we must respect them—"

"Respect them?" Daniel's mood veered sharply to anger. "Mojag, you have not spent much time among them. I have. They are noble people, but they are in spiritual darkness. The powwows call upon demons and evil spirits. You may think their way is honorable, but Satan is an angel of light, eager to deceive even you. I know you are eager to serve God and make your own way in the world, but in this you are wrong."

"Father, I cannot explain how God works. But can you forget the example of William Tyndale? He was called to be different. One hundred years ago he was tied to a stake and strangled because he dared to print an English Bible people could actually read and understand! And John Wycliffe was condemned and excommunicated for translating the Bible into the common man's language! God called those men to move in a new direction, and the church did not understand! I do not want to be safe and sure. God has called me to risk everything—"

"John Eliot has translated the Bible into Algonquin, and I would not call that *safe*," Daniel snapped. "But he has kept himself pure, in the church, and in a civilized society. He does not walk around half-dressed, painted like a savage, with feathers in his hair!"

Daniel's anger resonated faintly in the clearing while Mojag stared at him with burning, reproachful eyes. "John Eliot has seen the problem, but he is not an Indian," Mojag said finally, his words clipped. "He cannot do what I am doing. Don't you remember, Father? When Reverend Eliot rode with us to Taunton, he said that the Puritans had made God so much their own that the Indians could not understand him. But Jesus spoke in the language and pictures of ordinary people. The Indians will never understand the English. You cannot remain in this hut, reading your books, and possibly hope to win their souls."

Daniel flinched, stunned by the sudden declaration of war between them.

Mojag's fists were clenched, his chin trembled, his jaw flexed and set. After a moment, his eyes softened into an expression of sadness. "I am sorry, Father, that you do not understand," he said, his voice choked with sincerity. "Mayhap you will, in time." Without another word, he stood to leave.

"What will your sister think?" Daniel called after him, his heart breaking. "What shall I tell her?"

Mojag did not turn around. "Tell her that I am well and happy and following God's call," he said, his voice ringing with absolute finality. He looked briefly over his shoulder. "And give her my love."

And then, like the most skilled of the Indian warriors, he moved silently into the brush and disappeared.

The freezing winds of March softened into the gentle rains of April. Like flowers that appear under melting snow, hope bloomed anew in Aiyana's heart when her father sent word that Mojag was alive and well in King Philip's village at Monthaup. "He is striving to give feet to the prayers of John Eliot and others who pray daily for this sachem's salvation," her father wrote. Though she squirmed at the thought of Mojag living in the village of a heathen leader, she was relieved to know that he was safe and well.

Her father had relocated to Roxbury, abandoning his dream of a praying village near Rehoboth. Mojag's departure had shaken him more than he cared to admit, Aiyana realized, and her father was too sociable a man to work alone. And so he wrote to Aiyana from Roxbury, offering more than once to send an escort if she wished to leave Rehoboth and join him in John Eliot's ministry.

She refused. In letter after letter she cited her great affection for the Glazier family as her reason for remaining in Rehoboth, but the real reason she would not leave was Forest. The warm kernel of happiness that occupied the center of her being sprang from the breakdown of negotiations between Master Glazier and the merchant William Hammond. As time passed and the difficulties between the two men continued, Aiyana hoped that Master Glazier would come to see her as a possible daughter-in-law. If given enough time, she was certain she could convince him to allow her and Forest to marry.

She went about her work with a light heart, sharing confidences with Witty, enduring Constance's cold diffidence, and coming to genuinely admire Master Glazier as a man of wisdom and integrity. As one of the town's selectmen, his opinion was often solicited, and Aiyana noticed that he usually did not reply until he had considered the question in the light of prayer and Bible study.

One warm afternoon, the town magistrate and the committee of selectmen met at the Glazier house. The men sat around the board, drinking ale and sampling Witty's cooking while the two serving women attended to their needs. Aiyana's heart leapt when the magistrate mentioned the need for a new school.

"The law requires that a town with fifty families have a school for boys," the magistrate said, leaning back in his chair, "and Master Hobbit has agreed to teach the boys seven years and older in the meetinghouse. But he is greatly vexed that his pupils will be coming to school with little knowledge of the alphabet."

"We need a dame school," Master Glazier said, resting his hands on his stomach. He looked around the circle. "Does anyone know of a goodwife willing to teach the little ones?"

Surely there had never been a more heaven-sent opportunity! With a discreet servant's cough, Aiyana stepped forward.

"Aiyana?" Master Glazier looked at her, lifting a brow.

"If it please you, sir, I used to teach the little ones on Martha's Vineyard," she said, curtsying slightly to the other esteemed men at the table. "I taught them their catechism and the alphabet. I taught the boys to write and the girls to embroider their samplers."

"Mark me, there's an idea," Master Glazier said, turning to the others. "I'd be willing to hold a dame school here in my house. My Constance can assist Aiyana. 'Twould be good training for her."

"But were you capable with the children?" the magistrate asked, a glittery challenge in his eye. "Did you teach them proper table manners? To speak not, hum not, sing not, and wriggle not?"

Aiyana looked at the floor for a moment as she smiled. "Well, sir, not exactly," she said, lifting her eyes. "You see, Indian parents are not as restrained as English folk. They are more free with their children."

"Indians!" Another of the selectmen wrinkled his nose. "If your only experience is with Indians, Miss Bailie, I hardly think you will be capable of educating our children. And we cannot expect a squaw to know what our children must learn."

"A squaw?" Aiyana answered, irked out of a servant's proper demeanor. "Why shouldn't an Indian woman teach the English alphabet? Is an *A* not an *A* when I write it?"

The selectman's face reddened as he caught a breath to answer, but Master Glazier interrupted by placing his hand on the man's arm. "There is a simple solution to this problem," he said, the coaxing timbre of his voice calming the agitated men at the table. "My daughter, Constance, shall be the teacher. My servants, Miss Bailie and Miss Witty Greene, shall assist her. And with so many able hands put to the work, our children shall have the finest education we can offer."

The other men nodded, albeit grudgingly, and Aiyana flushed as she walked from the room. On Martha's Vineyard she had been able to forget about the Indian blood flowing through her veins, but here in Rehoboth she frequently felt like Cain, marked across the forehead with the sign of a curse.

▼▲▼▲▼ The dame school began one week later, and though Constance received four shillings a week as teacher, Aiyana actually taught the children. As she helped them scratch on their hornbooks and thumb through the precious pages of their primers, she told herself that the judgments and opinions of misinformed men did not matter. She was teaching again, and never had she felt more blissfully happy or fully alive. Forest had noticed the change in her, too, and once had remarked that she looked "as pink as a flower and radiant as the sun."

The world remained rosy and blue until one Sabbath dinner in June. Aiyana had worn a blush of pleasure ever since Forest appeared at the door to escort them to church, and at dinner she had listened enthralled as he regaled his family with his plans for the shop he would one day open.

"'Twill be the biggest and best emporium in Massachusetts," he predicted, helping himself to a heaping portion of butter. "When the trade routes from Boston are better established, there will be no stopping the supplies. Whatever a man wants, he'll be able to get in a month—two at the most."

"And what will your master say when your store outshines his, heh?" Master Glazier joked, elbowing his son.

"I don't know, but I'm a bit worried about Master Hammond," Forest answered, his smile fading. "He has been much bothered of late by a story he heard at the Swansea trading post."

"What story?" Witty asked.

Forest raised his eyes to his father's face in an oddly keen, swift look. "John Sassamon was King Philip's trusted secretary," he announced, passing Witty a bowl of creamed corn. "And in January he was found dead under the ice at Assawompsett Pond. Everyone assumed he had fallen under the ice and drowned, until Governor Winslow ordered that the body be exhumed." His voice fell as he leaned across the table. "The Governor, you see, had heard from this secretary that Philip was planning to make war upon the English settlements. And when they dug up Sassamon's body, they discovered that his face was purple with bruises, his neck broken, and his lungs empty of water!"

"What are you saying, Forest?" Constance asked, her pretty face clouded with anxiety. "Is there really going to be a war?"

"Not likely," Forest answered, helping himself to two of Witty's biscuits. "They found a witness who saw three of Philip's Indians murder the man. One of the murderers, Tobias, was one of Philip's closest counselors."

"I heard," Witty interjected, "that this witness owed money to Tobias. By accusing him of murder, he is absolved of his debts."

"If he is guilty of murder, he must suffer the consequences, regardless of who owes him money," Matthew Glazier answered, his voice rumbling through the room. "I'm sure there will be a fair trial to discover the truth of this matter."

"The trial's already done," Forest said, setting his glass of cider back on the table. "A jury of English and Indians heard the case."

"Philip's Indians?" Aiyana whispered, her heart in her throat. Had Mojag been involved?

"Of course the Indians weren't allowed to vote on the verdict," Forest assured her. "But the three defendants were found guilty and hanged. As they strung up the third man, the rope broke. The experience left the savage so shaken that he confessed that Philip had sent them to kill Sassamon. The judges thanked him and strung him up again. The second time, the rope held."

"Will they attack Philip?" Aiyana asked, thinking of Mojag. "Will they send an army to Monthaup?"

"They have arranged for John Easton, attorney general from Rhode Island, to meet with Philip and see how the wrongs against the Pokanoket can be righted," Forest answered. His eyes softened as he looked at her. "Easton is a Quaker, Aiyana, and he does not want war. No one does, neither Philip nor the English. We have lived in peace for fifty years, and we can live in peace forever if reasonable minds prevail."

Despite his profound doubts that talking with the Quaker from
Rhode Island would do any good, Metacomet traveled to Rhode
Island's capital with forty of his best men, including the newcomer who now called himself Askuwheteau. The young man
spoke English even more fluently than did Metacomet, and the
sachem had long ago learned that the Yangeese would not
believe an Indian's word unless it was written on paper and
signed, or spoken by a praying Indian. The new man, Askuwheteau, was literate and a professing Christian, therefore doubly
valuable.

John Easton heard Metacomet's list of complaints without
interruption; he was the first Englishman who had ever honestly
listened. The sachem spoke of the burdens of English law upon
his people, the interference of Christian ministers, the wrongs
committed by trespassing farmers.

As an hour drew to a close, Metacomet held out his hand to
the only Englishman he now trusted. "The English who came
first to this country were but a handful of people, forlorn, poor,
and distressed," he said. "My father was then sachem. He
relieved their distresses in the most kind and hospitable manner.
He gave them land to plant and build upon; they flourished and
increased. By various means they got possession of a great part
of his territory, but still he remained their friend till he died. My
elder brother became sachem. He was seized and confined and
thereby thrown into illness and died. Soon after I became sachem
they disarmed all my people, and our land was taken. Only a
small part of the dominion of my ancestors remains."

Metacomet paused, struggling for self-control. "I am determined not to live until I have no country."

With forthright friendship and respect shining in his eyes, John Easton promised to assemble a panel of mediators. He nominated Sir Edmund Andros, recently appointed royal governor of New York, to serve on the panel and asked Metacomet to choose a representative from among the country's great sachems. While the sachem mulled over his decision, Easton suggested that they return to their homes to wait until the details had been settled.

Metacomet brought his company home. On the seventeenth day of June, as the hot sun increased the flies and shortened men's tempers, his warriors brought him several horses that had strayed from their English owners. Metacomet told his men to return the horses to their owners at Rehoboth and Swansea. He was determined to do whatever he could to maintain the fragile peace.

Forest

*And the king of the South will be enraged and go
forth and fight. . . . He will enter the richest
parts of the realm, and he will accomplish what
his fathers never did, nor his ancestors; he will
distribute plunder, booty, and possessions . . .
and he will devise his schemes against
strongholds, but only for a time.*

—Daniel 11:11, 24

Heavy clouds blocked the merciless rays of the June sun, but the air was hot, humid, and heavy—the sweltering stillness before a storm. As Aiyana entered the blessed shade of the house, she set her garden basket on the floor and paused to wipe a trickle of perspiration from her forehead. If it would only rain! But at least the house was cool and quiet, for the dame school had already been dismissed and Constance had gone to visit friends.

The scent of ripening strawberries rose from her basket, and Aiyana bent to lift a board onto the trestle that stood by the fireplace. Once the board was in place, she hoisted her basket onto its broad surface and took a seat on the bench. She loved to cull strawberries, for no one cared if she ate one every now and then, and soon her fingers would be red with their delicious wet sweetness. The fruits grew wild in the fields outside Rehoboth, enough for every family to enjoy fist-sized strawberries throughout the summer.

A sudden thumping noise sounded overhead, and she lifted her eyes to the ceiling and frowned. Though the wooden houses of the English tended to creak and groan, they did not thump of their own volition. Had a thief slipped in while she and Witty worked outside? Wiping her hands on her apron, she stood and moved toward the ladder.

All was silent as she pushed the trapdoor open; then a swift movement startled her, and she ducked, dropping the door. She stiffened, momentarily embarrassed at her reaction. She'd seen a small animal, nothing dangerous, and yet she had jumped as if she'd been shot. "Aiyana," she whispered, carefully pushing the door again, "how can you be so frightened?" More confident now, she flung the trapdoor away and climbed into the loft.

The interloper, a bushy-tailed squirrel, perched on her bedroll, its tiny paws moving in agitated frustration. "Do not fear, friend squirrel," Aiyana murmured, moving slowly toward the tiny window through which it must have come. "This is no place for you. Let me show you the way home."

A trunk partially blocked the opening, and Aiyana shoved it aside. A breeze, heavy with the summer scents of grass and rain, gushed through the room, and the frightened animal turned its head toward the window.

"That is the way," Aiyana whispered, standing back. "Go home to your family, little one."

In a flash the squirrel darted toward the opening, then flew out, landing squarely on a broad branch of the oak tree just outside the house. Aiyana smiled in relief, then looked around to be sure the animal had not damaged her master's things.

The wooden sole of one of Witty's slippers was slightly chewed, but the squirrel had not had time to do any other harm. Aiyana glanced at the trunk by the window. It was a small wooden box not more than two feet wide, and unlocked. Curiosity urged her toward it. An inner voice whispered that she shouldn't pry into her master's things, . . . but she was responsible for cleaning the house, and wasn't this trunk part of the house? She had never noticed the box before, for when she and Witty climbed to this room after dark they were usually too tired to do more than unroll their beds and fall asleep.

Her decision made, Aiyana slipped to the floor, ran her hands over the smooth wood, and lifted the trunk's lid. She gasped in delight at what she saw inside. The trunk was filled with children's clothes, stacks of neatly pressed garments, little shifts and hats arranged alongside tidy little breeches and shirts. The Indians had always let their children go naked once they learned to walk, but the English dressed their young ones like little adults. These clothes must have belonged to Forest.

She lifted out a small shirt and breeches, marveling at their tiny size and the intricate stitching that bound the edges of the fabric. Someone had lovingly crafted each of these garments for Forest—of certain the careful hand had been his mother's. Her love and devoted care were evident in each tiny stitch.

Enthralled, Aiyana pressed the tiny boy's suit to her cheek, breathing in the lingering scent of life. Forest had worn these.

"Put those things down!" Constance's sharp voice cut through the attic like a knife. Startled, Aiyana let the shirt and breeches fall to her lap.

Constance stood on the ladder, her face a glowering mask of rage. "You will not steal those things. They are mine and my brother's."

"I did not intend to steal them. I was just—"

"I know what you were doing. Everyone knows that savages steal whatever is not nailed down. Why would you be up here, unless you are entertaining thoughts of thievery?"

Aiyana turned to face her. "It is my room."

"No, 'tis *our* attic. You only sleep here."

"I heard a noise, and I came up to see—"

"You heard no such thing. You took advantage of my absence to come up here. People have warned me to watch you. They say Indians are lazy, that they plot mischief and murder when their masters are away. You'd probably be working wickedness right now if I hadn't spied the open door and come up here!"

"Enough!" Aiyana cried, flashing into sudden fury. She dropped the baby clothes back into the trunk, slammed the lid, and stood to face her young mistress. "I have worked for this family with all the energy I possess since the day I first came to this house," she said, glaring down at her accuser. "As God is my witness, Constance Glazier, I would not take anything from you, nor would I hurt you." She wanted to add, *I love your brother, and I would not do anything to harm those who love him,* but caution stilled her tongue. She had not spoken openly of her feelings to anyone but Witty.

Constance twisted her mouth and looked away, suddenly dropping her attack. A blush ran like a shadow over her cheeks.

Good, Aiyana thought. She deserved to be embarrassed after such a baseless assault. Crossing her arms, Aiyana tried to regain control. The weather was hot and unbearable, and perhaps the active children had frayed Constance's nerves.

With an effort, Aiyana summoned a smile. "Why don't you come down with me?" she suggested. "I will get you a cup of cool apple cider."

"Yes," Constance agreed, her voice defeated as she moved back down the ladder. She took a deep breath. "I suppose I'm just upset about the espousal. Things will change soon, and I know I will miss my brother. He won't visit us as often when he is married."

Aiyana felt a thin, cold blade of foreboding slice into her heart. The espousal! She had heard no news of progress since the shouting match between Master Hammond and Master Glazier. She had almost managed to convince herself that the espousal would not happen.

She moved toward the open trapdoor and looked down. "Is there to be an engagement?" she murmured, struggling to mask her fear.

"Oh yes," Constance answered, not looking up as she climbed down the ladder. "My father and Master Hammond have been working out the details. If God is willing, Forest and Serenity will celebrate a December wedding."

Constance reached the first floor and moved toward the stoneware cider jugs along the wall, but Aiyana froze on the ladder, her thoughts fiercely concentrated. How could it be true? She had thought she had earned Master Glazier's respect, and she felt eager affection from Forest each time they were together. So why hadn't Master Glazier discerned the obvious? And why hadn't Forest spoken to his father about her? Didn't he know that she remained in Rehoboth and slavishly served his family only because she adored him?

One sudden, cold, lucid thought struck her. Maybe both Forest and his father thought she wouldn't be happy marrying a Puritan. Truth be told, she couldn't imagine spending the rest of her life in a stuffy English village like Rehoboth, but Forest would follow her anywhere, she knew it! She had only to tell Forest that she loved him.

By the time her foot touched the floor, she had made a decision. Rather than love Forest from a distance and pray that God would see fit to bring them together, she would take an active part in her own destiny. Her father had always told her that prayer was good, but there was a time to rise from her knees and walk on the path God had set before her. After all, the Almighty expected man to work *with* him.

She would speak to Forest. And if Constance was right about her father's negotiations with Master Hammond, Aiyana would have to speak to Forest soon. She could not wait until the Sabbath when he came to visit his family, for Master Glazier might settle the terms of the espousal in the week ahead. She would have to see him today. But where? He wouldn't be coming to the house, and she couldn't go to the store—too many listening ears lingered there.

She would have to disobey the curfew and call him out after dark.

▾▲▾▲ At sunset, after Master Glazier led his household in bedtime prayers, Aiyana told Witty to go to bed without her. "I'll be up directly," she said, moving toward the broom. "I'm not ready to sleep. I thought I would sweep out the house while the fire still casts a light."

If Witty understood what kept Aiyana awake, she did not mention it but climbed the ladder to the loft. After a few moments, Master Glazier left with the lantern to check the barn and Constance retreated to her small chamber off the keeping room. When Aiyana was certain she would not be seen, she put the broom away and pulled on her cloak, lifting the hood to cover her hair. She paused a moment before the brass mirror that hung by the door. In the dim firelight she could see little of her reflection, only the desperate dark pool of her eyes.

She drew back the bolt on the door and slipped out into the night, lingering in the shadows to avoid the town watchman, who patrolled the streets after dark. A sliver of moon scuttled behind the rooftops; an occasional lantern pushed at the gloom as she slipped down the street.

Master Hammond's house lay off Rehoboth's main street, between the cobbler's shop and the wheelwright's house. The shades were drawn over the windows of the store, but Aiyana slipped through a narrow alley that led to a side door and the part of the house where the family lived. A dim light shone through the shutters. Gathering her slippery courage, Aiyana knocked.

A little spasm of panic shot across her body as footsteps sounded from inside the house. What would she say if Master Hammond answered the door? She had spent the afternoon carefully crafting the words she would speak to Forest, but common sense now attacked her dreams. She had given no thought to the excuse she would give for being out after curfew, and the thought of facing Master Hammond left her tongue-tied.

The latch creaked; the door opened. Behind it, in a thin sliver of light, Serenity Hammond stood with a light blanket modestly gathered around her shoulders. "Aiyana!" she whispered, her pale blue eyes widening. "Is there trouble at the Glaziers' house?"

"No," Aiyana answered. She took a deep breath and adjusted her stiff smile. "Nothing is wrong, Serenity, but I need to speak to Forest."

"He's in his room," Serenity said, tilting her head toward a small alcove away from the family's living quarters. "Shall I have my father wake him?"

"No." Aiyana threw her hand up and stepped closer, then rested her fingers lightly on the girl's wrist. "Don't bother your father, Serenity. Just rap on Forest's door and tell him that his sister's maid wishes to speak to him."

Serenity stepped back, blushing, and Aiyana suddenly realized that her request was highly improper. Serenity was not the sort of girl who would rap on an unmarried man's door in the middle of the night.

"Let me in, and I will wake him," Aiyana suggested, summoning her warmest smile. "I promise you will come to no harm."

A look of doubt flickered over Serenity's face, but she swung the door open wider. Aiyana stepped into the house, cast a hasty glance around for the merchant, then moved toward the small door of the alcove.

"Forest," she whispered, rapping lightly. "It is me—Aiyana. I must speak with you."

Within a moment he appeared, his eyes wide with alarm, his hair tousled. "Is all well?" he asked, his voice crisp in the quiet.

Aiyana pressed her finger over her lips. "Yes. Forgive me for bothering you at this untoward hour, but I need you. Will you come with me for a moment?"

"Let me find my shoes."

He did not debate, but fumbled for his shoes and shirt in the darkness. When he had dressed, he followed Aiyana out of the house. As they walked past Serenity, Aiyana noticed that the girl blushed furiously and pulled the blanket more closely about her. *Despite her youth, she is well aware of Forest as a man*, she thought, stepping out into the night. *And whether or not she will admit it, her face reveals that she loves him, perhaps as much as I do.*

▼▲▼▲▼ Years of obedience to the proper standards of behavior fell away from Forest as he crossed his master's threshold. A servant did not venture out at night without his master's permission, especially with a beautiful young woman. And Serenity had watched him go! In the morning she would ask what emergency had called him away in the night, and Master Hammond would hear of it. Forest would face a severe rebuke, maybe even a fine. His face twisted in wry amusement. Oh, how his father would squirm if Forest was forced to spend a morning in the stocks!

But the pull of Aiyana's magnetic eyes was strong enough to

draw him to the very gates of hell. He had long suspected that
she held an alarming degree of power over him, and now, with
one beckoning gesture of her hand, she had confirmed his fears.
Did she know how his heart reacted to her gaze?

"Where are we going?" he whispered as she led the way
through the shadowy streets.

"Somewhere private," she whispered back. She turned so suddenly that he nearly ran into her; the warmth of her breath
struck his cheek. "Can you suggest a place?"

The impulse to reach out and touch her was almost tangible,
but he forced his mind to function. The streets were deserted, but
strong men with listening ears and alert trigger fingers lingered
inside every dark house.

"The meetinghouse," he said, reaching for her hand. A dangerous sense of exhilaration possessed him as her fingers slid into
his. All his life he had been such a good, dutiful boy, a favored
son—but now he held magic by the hand.

Two days from full, the moon lit the sloping rooftops of the
houses with a cold yellow radiance and threw black shadows on
the street below. Toward the village green they hurried, pausing
once behind a towering oak as the night watchman passed on his
horse. Finally they reached the church and paused at the steps.
"Let me check to be sure no one is inside," Forest whispered, his
heart hammering with more excitement than he had felt in his
lifetime.

With an adventurous toss of her head, Aiyana nodded. He
climbed to the porch, his tongue trying to frame the words he
might say if he found the building occupied. But when he
opened the door, the room beyond lay neat, dark, and still. He
turned and gestured to Aiyana, who flew like a dream up the
steps and into the building.

"Here," he said, indicating a pew on the men's side of the
room. He sat and pulled her down next to him, while some part
of his brain hummed with the knowledge that he might never
again sit with a woman in church. Such things were not done,
but here he was, sitting before God with the loveliest girl he had

ever known. Her admiring gaze thrilled him; his masculinity
responded to her femininity. But what madness had caused her
to call him out of his master's house?

He reached for her hood and lifted it from her head, exposing
the mass of glossy black hair that billowed from her head like a
silken cloud. "What is it?" he asked, finding his voice with difficulty. "What has brought you out in the night like this?"

Even in the darkness, her smile shimmered like sunbeams on
the surface of the river. "You bring me out," she whispered, one
of her hands stealing to touch his. "You, Forest. I have heard Constance speak of your espousal, and I had to talk to you."

"My espousal?" He shook his head, amazed by the strange,
dreamlike lunacy of the night. "I have made no espousal. I want
to wait until I have established myself in business before taking a
wife."

Her eyes lit with hope; her hand upon his tightened. "Oh, I
am so glad to hear it! But your father, Forest, has already held
meetings with Master Hammond."

"Surely they are discussing my apprenticeship. That contract
will be concluded soon."

"No, Witty and I have heard them arguing. They plan for you
and Serenity to be married so you can be a partner in Master
Hammond's shop."

"Serenity? And a partner?" He laughed and squeezed her
hand. "Serenity is a child. Why, she was but eight years old
when I came to live with my master. And I do not wish to be any
man's partner. I will make my own fortune, by my own wits.
With God's blessing, of course."

An uncertainty crept into her expression. "Serenity is fifteen
now and of an age to be married." She shot him a half-frightened
look. "And I believe she loves you."

Shaking his head, Forest listened with a vague sense of unreal-
ity. He did not want to believe Aiyana's words, but some part of
his soul suspected that she spoke the truth. Serenity's wide, wor-
shipful eyes followed him everywhere. She hung on his words;
she prepared special dishes to please him. Marriage might well

be on her mind, and on her father's. And his father, steady and careful as always, would like nothing better than to see his son tied to Rehoboth and an established business.

But Serenity was more like a sister to him than Constance. He liked her, he even held her in affection, but she was not what he wanted in a wife. This woman—Aiyana—was all he wanted.

"Serenity is a fine young woman who will make some other man a wonderful wife," he said, placing his free hand atop Aiyana's. "But I do not love her. As soon as my term of apprenticeship is completed, I plan to write to your father for his blessing so that we might be wed."

She closed her eyes, pulling her hand from his, and for a moment his heart lurched, afraid he'd misread her smiles and glances through the months. But then her arms slipped about his neck; her lips brushed against his ear. "I'm so glad to hear you say so," she whispered, trembling like a frightened child in his arms. "I was afraid you would not want me. I was afraid your father would not allow you to marry me."

"Why wouldn't he?" he asked, stroking the thick black hair that tumbled over her back. "You are the most extraordinary woman in town. You have a strength beyond the others; you think your own thoughts, and you're not afraid to say what you think."

He caressed her cheek with the knuckle of his index finger. "I want you to spend your life with me, Aiyana Bailie. I know not what God has planned for the future, but I know he would not have given me this love for you unless he meant for us to be together."

One corner of her lovely mouth lifted in a half-smile. "I will be yours, Forest Glazier," she said, her hand capturing his. She turned to press a kiss into his palm, then her eyes moved into his so that he saw nothing else. "I will love you with my life, now and forever."

▼▲▼▲▼ Aiyana never knew whether her nighttime excursion was discovered. Shortly after sunrise the next morning, a trio of men rode into Rehoboth on lathered horses, galloping for the town green as if the hounds of hell were giving chase. Almost instantly, the alarm bell began to toll, and the people of Rehoboth poured from their homes and gardens and hurried to the meetinghouse. Inside the building, Witty, Constance, and Aiyana clustered on the front pew, and Aiyana frowned in puzzled amazement when Constance gripped her hand. "Are the Indians coming?" Constance whispered, breathing in shallow, quick gasps. "Shouldn't we run to the garrison houses? Why are we wasting time here?"

"The bell tolled slowly," Witty said, straightening in a nononsense posture. "When it rings quickly, that's when we worry. Never fear, girl. God will not let us be harmed."

When everyone had assembled in the meetinghouse, the town magistrate stood and held his hands up for silence. "These three men," the magistrate said, jerking a thumb toward the exhausted riders as he stared out over the crowd, "have come from Swansea. Our scouts are reporting that armed Indians from several tribes are joining Philip at Mount Hope—"

"Monthaup," Aiyana muttered, correcting him.

The magistrate glared at her. *"Mount Hope,"* he continued, insisting upon the English pronunciation. "Philip is sending his women away in canoes. Those who know the tawny foe swear that he intends to fight."

The assembled settlers emitted a collective gasp, then broke into muffled buzzing.

"Why would he send the women away?" Witty whispered.

"To spare them," Aiyana answered, fear spurring her heart to beat unevenly. For once, the English had not misunderstood the natives' intentions. Algonquin warriors valued their women and children above all else, even sparing the women and children of an enemy whenever possible. If Philip was truly sending the women and children away, he was certainly readying for war.

She looked across the room toward Forest, who stood with

Master Hammond against the far wall. His eyes blazed with determination, and he joined the rabble of voices that met the magistrate's announcement. "Shall we ride forth to join the militia?" he asked, striding to the front of the room amid a handful of other young men.

"Forest, no!" a young voice cried out. Serenity Hammond, her face blazing like white parchment, stepped out of a pew and ran to Forest's side, her hands clutching his arm in desperate entreaty. "You can't go away! What will we do without you?"

As the entire town watched, Serenity crumpled in a dead faint and pitched forward into Forest's arms.

"Faith, what's this?"

"Scared to death, is she?"

"Welladay, I didn't expect *that*," Witty murmured.

Aiyana lifted herself from the pew to see better. Clearly embarrassed, Forest knelt by Serenity's side, attempting to fan her face with his hand. Several women and Master Hammond rushed forward to aid the fallen girl, but after a moment it was clear that they were willing to let Forest care for her.

Aiyana sat down, bewildered, then caught Constance's gaze. The younger girl's eyes blazed with satisfied triumph.

Benjamin Church possessed neither military credentials nor patience with military minds, but he had been born and bred in the wilderness of New England. His father had served in the Pequot War, and since that time Benjamin had been pleased to count the Indians as his friends and teachers. Like them, he knew the woods, and his survival instincts were sharp. He was a woodsman and hunter, his uniform the buckskins and furs of the wilderness, his weapons the knife, musket, bow, and arrow.

He and his wife had planned to settle and build a house near Sakonnet Point, but rumors of war interrupted his work. Curious about the Indians' intentions, he accepted an invitation to attend a dance conference at the village of Awashonks, an esteemed female sachem of the Sakonnet tribe. Awashonks was a cousin of King Philip and an old friend of Church. He was certain he could understand the troubles between the Indians and English if he could talk to the sachem.

He traveled to the Sakonnet town with Charles Hazelton, a boy who spoke Algonquin as fluently as he did English. As they entered the village, the pair was greeted with the usual friendly yells and generous offers of food and tobacco, but Church waved away the offers until he found Awashonks. She was with the dancers, moving around the fire. An arrogantly handsome woman of inestimable age, Awashonks danced with fervor. Her ceremonial costume gleamed in the sun; the body paint on her hands and bare arms ran with sweat. Church lingered at the fire until he was certain she had seen him; then he took a place outside her wigwam to wait for the end of the dance. As his eyes drifted over the gathering, he spied six warriors of the

Pokanoket tribe, their faces and shoulders smeared with bright red war paint, their heads shaved for battle.

Church smiled as the light of understanding dawned. Awashonks had invited him because she knew Metacomet would send his most impressive warriors to convince her to join his war. She wanted to resist the overtures of her cousin, to whom she was nominally subject, but needed her people to hear a dissenting opinion before she could reject the prospect of war.

Awashonks called an end to the dancing. As the dancers dispersed, she walked to her ceremonial mat, one hand smoothing her tangled hair. Her face was as smooth as carved alabaster, but the legs beneath the edge of her buckskin skirt were withered and blue-veined.

Church nodded to her, impressed as always by her courage and intelligent strategy. "I thank you, my friend, for the invitation to join you here," he said, remaining seated. "The dance is a good one."

"Yes." Awashonks sat upon her mat; the Pokanoket warriors moved immediately to sit at her right hand since Church sat at her left. After a respectful moment of silence, the warriors began their impassioned pleadings to persuade Awashonks to bring her three hundred Sakonnet braves to join Metacomet's cause. A handful of Sakonnet elders stood outside the circle, their eyes as hard as granite. Not a flicker of emotion crossed their faces, but their minds, Church knew, recorded every word.

After hearing the Pokanoket arguments, Awashonks turned her bronzed face to Benjamin. "The Yangeese are preparing to fight against the Wampanoag, our people," she said, a film of sweat glistening on her face. "They are assembling an army in Plymouth town."

While Charles translated, Church assured her that the English were not preparing for war and the Sakonnet, therefore, had nothing to fear. "Would I," he asked, "have begun to build my house near you if the Yangeese were planning to make war in this land?"

While the faces of the Pokanoket warriors grew hard and

resentful, Church urged the sachem to make an immediate alliance with Plymouth so she and her people would be protected. But even as he spoke, he feared he fought a losing battle. A few days before, he had met with Weetamoo of the Pocasset, another squaw sachem and Metacomet's sister-in-law. From her, Church had learned that Metacomet was having difficulty containing his hot-tempered braves. His people hungered for the warpath even as Metacomet tried to find a road for peace. But if peace could not be preserved, Metacomet would fight as fiercely as a famished wolf.

"Metacomet is a dynamic and forceful man," Awashonks was saying now, her dark eyes softening as she thought of her cousin. "He is able to persuade, charm, and inflame warriors to do his will. The Yangeese have no one like him."

And as Benjamin Church looked across the fire toward the Pokanoket warriors, he had to admit she was right.

▼▲▼▲▼ Smoking in silence, Metacomet sat outside his hut and watched his wife and son tease each other. He had not sent them to Narragansett territory with the others; time with them was too precious. If all did not go well in the days to come, he would not see them again.

A bloodcurdling war cry sounded from the edge of the camp, and his stomach knotted even as he took pains to keep his face in regular lines. "What's that?" Mukki asked, running to his father's side. His new teeth gleamed large in his small face.

"Nothing," Metacomet answered, lightly running a finger down the boy's painted cheek. "You should run and play. But stay clear of the canoe landing and the pig fence."

The boy sprinted away; the sound of the warriors' cries grew closer. "Are you hungry, my husband?" Wootonekanuska asked, hovering nearby. He understood what she really wanted to ask: Will you come inside and eat so the trouble will go away?

He turned to her, his anxiety diminishing at the sight of her delicate face. "I will eat later. I must see what this noise is about."

Wootonekanuska bit her lip, then ducked into the wigwam. Metacomet steeled his nerves, readying himself for the confrontation to come. His young and headstrong warriors dreamed of nothing but killing the Yangeese. Most of their wives were safely away; they had heard rumors of English soldiers assembling in the towns of Boston and Plymouth. Unless Metacomet stilled their eager hearts, the war could begin this afternoon.

A crowd approached, a steadily expanding group of screaming warriors with a knot of pale Yangeese at the center. The mob paused before Metacomet, and the warriors screeched their fury for a full minute before the sachem held up his hand for silence.

Tihkoosue, his eyes as hard as dried peas, spoke first. "These Yangeese trespassed on Pokanoket land. They say their horses have escaped."

"Have they?"

Tihkoosue nodded. "We found two mares and a stallion near the water's edge."

Metacomet pressed his lips together and pretended to consider his options, but he knew what his answer would be. Somewhere to the north, John Easton worked to assemble a peace-keeping council, and just south of this wigwam Mukki played in the woods. For both their sakes, the peace must last.

"Give these men back their horses and release them at the pig fence," he said, gazing at the Yangeese with chilling intentness. "And you—" he broke into English—"tell your English fathers that we have released you in peace."

The men's sweaty faces bobbed in unison; one of them looked as if his knees would buckle at any moment. Metacomet then turned to Tihkoosue, whose features had twisted into a maddening leer. The demons of war would not be restrained much longer.

Forest's mind churned with unruly thoughts as he paced in the moonlight outside one of the outermost garrison houses. His musket seemed heavy on his shoulder, and his sword slapped awkwardly against his knee. Ever since the town had heard that Philip prepared for war, tempers had shortened and fear blazed like kindling. Furthermore, in the last week Forest had discovered that many of the bedrock beliefs on which he would have staked his life were as insubstantial as mist.

He had believed that the Indians in the area of Rehoboth were calm, placid people who fished and hunted and came to town to trade for whiskey, iron kettles, and tools. He had always imagined them too cowed by English superiority to attempt a rebellion. What did they have to rebel against? He and his family had done nothing to them. And yet there was talk of insurrection, of bloody battles to come, of financial ruin. If the Indians were to attack, as the selectmen said, they'd be quickly chased away, but not before inflicting substantial damage on crops and cattle.

Thoughts of war were not all that troubled Forest. He had always believed that his father wanted life's best happiness for him. Yet when Forest had pulled his father aside on this Sunday afternoon and told him that he loved and wished to marry Aiyana Bailie, his normally reserved father had exploded in a fit of anger.

"You are a fool, Forest," his father had yelled, his face brightening to the shade of a ripe strawberry. "You have allowed the devil to reign in your thoughts. Infatuation, the love of passion, has done this to you. Passion can cause violent emotions, sickness, and even death."

"Father, I—"

"No! You think I don't understand, Forest, but I do. I was once young, and I am still a man. I know she is beautiful. But the power of what you're feeling comes from some place outside the body—heaven or hell, depending upon the object of your fantasies. But given that the object is *that girl*—"

"Father." Forest had restrained his own temper with difficulty. "I have never done anything to displease you since leaving this house for my master's. In all things I have striven to honor your kind upbringing and devoted guardianship. You taught me to love God, to not shirk from hard work, and to revere my family—"

"And I have been well pleased with you. You have a head for business, and someday your prosperity will surpass mine." His father's meaty hand had fallen upon his shoulder. "Ah, my son," he had said, sighing deeply. "Would that you were able to remember your mother better. I regret that she did not live long enough so that we might model a Christian marriage for you. There are things about men and women you do not understand."

He had motioned to the garden bench, and Forest had sat down, his emotions bobbing and spinning like a piece of flotsam caught in the river current.

"Women," his father had begun, shaking his head in disapproval as he sat beside his son, "are creatures without which there is no comfortable living for men. It is true of them what is wont to be said of governments, that bad ones are better than none. Those who despise and decry women and call them a necessary evil are a sort of blasphemer, for women are a necessary good. Even God's holy word tells us that it was not good for man to be without one of them."

"Why, then, can I not marry Aiyana?" Forest had asked. "She is a virtuous woman. She is witty and creative. She works with a will—"

"She is an Indian." His father's voice had rung with finality.

"But she doesn't *look* much like an Indian. Her eyes are dark blue."

"She is an Indian, Son. There is no denying it. The blood of a barbarous and heathen tribe runs in her veins and is evidenced even in her speech. Did you not hear her interrupt the magistrate at the meeting?"

"She corrected him. She is a teacher; such things are natural to her."

"She wanted him to speak the name of Philip's village in the *Indian* way. Her loyalties lie with them. I could not allow you to marry an Indian even before the threat of war loomed over us, and I must not allow you to think of her now." His mouth had dipped into an even deeper frown. "I have already spoken to Master Hammond. When your apprenticeship has expired, he is willing to give Serenity to be your wife."

"But I do not love Serenity!"

"Do not love her?" His father's face had flattened into a mask of amazement. "Son, can you not *learn* to love her? And if your love does not grow, what does it matter? The materials and relationships of this life are like footprints left in sand; in heaven there is not the least appearance or remembrance of them. In the Holy City the king will not recall his crown, the husband his wife, nor the father his child. He who loves too deeply risks placing a creature before the Creator himself."

Forest now cringed at the memory of his father's words; he shook his head as if he could dislodge them from his brain. How could a God who loved man beyond all reason not allow his people to love in like measure, or at least as much as they were able? For surely the all-consuming passion he felt for Aiyana was but a shadow of the limitless love that caused Christ to abandon the holy halls of heaven and venture to a war-torn earth.

A bird flapped in a nearby tree, and Forest slammed his musket to his shoulder, squinting down the barrel toward the dark horizon. A soft summer wind blew the meadow grass in the grayness of dusk, but nothing else moved in the vast and endless plain of evening. Thoroughly unnerved by the way his world had turned upside down in the last few hours, he was altogether too jumpy.

He lowered his musket and forced himself to breathe again. Aiyana would smile at his fears, for she moved as easily in the darkness as a cat. . . .

How could he give her up? The thought of her sent fire coursing through his veins, but part of her allure lay in her very uniqueness. He had promised to love her always, but had he spoken without thinking? Since her arrival, he had been fuddled by longing, spellbound by new and compelling sensations. His body ached to enfold hers, but his father would draw back in horror if one day Forest presented to him a grandchild with Indian features.

Though his father had not mentioned it, another difficulty hovered at the back of Forest's mind. Aiyana's brother lived in Philip's heathen village, and several Rehoboth men had spied him skulking in the woods. He had worn a wooden cross around his neck and claimed to be engaged in missionary work, but he had been dressed in a heathen's breechcloth with paint upon his bare chest and face. Surely John Eliot would cast him off if he ever saw the young man dressed in such a way. But Aiyana assured Forest that her brother was completely devoted to God and very concerned for Philip's eternal salvation.

He gave himself a stern mental shake. The Puritan church leaders constantly spoke of the "civil man," a man who behaved beautifully, obeyed the laws, carried out his social obligations, and would not hurt so much as his neighbor's dog, but was still hell-bound for not professing Christ in faith. Such a man walked and talked like a Christian but did not know the Lord. Was it possible, even conceivable, that an opposite kind of man existed? One who did *not* walk and talk like a civilized man but *did* know the Lord? Maybe Aiyana's brother would prove to be such a one.

Forest turned, moved his musket from one shoulder to the other, and tried to concentrate on the work at hand. He had to remain alert, for the lives of everyone in Rehoboth depended upon the sentries. His sister, his master, his father, even Aiyana counted on him.

His mind skated back toward his unsolvable dilemma. He recognized and appreciated the logic in his father's counsel, but his heart longed to hold Aiyana in his arms. He could close his eyes and imagine her hair flowing across his chest, as soft as silk around his neck—

"Well met, Forest."

Forest jumped, the blood draining from his face. Another sentry, his relief, stood beside him in the dark.

"I cry you mercy, Thomas, I didn't expect you so soon." Forest sighed, relieved that the darkness had covered his inattention and the flush that burned his neck.

"Have things been quiet?"

"Yes, thank God."

Thomas touched his fingers to the brim of his cap and turned resolutely to face the wilderness. Forest lowered his gun and turned onto the main road, suddenly more weary than he had ever been in his life.

A pretty little town centered around a Baptist church, Swansea stood like a sentinel at the entrance to Metacomet's land on the peninsula the English called Mount Hope. Smaller than Rehoboth, the settlement consisted of only a few dozen farming families whose homes were scattered throughout the woods rather than clustered for safety. A small sister community of about eighteen houses was located some distance to the south, actually within the narrow neck that led to the Pokanoket village of Monthaup. For years the Indians and residents of Swansea had been cooperative neighbors, exchanging food, services, and agricultural labor, but the relationship had not been without its flaws. The farmers' animals often escaped to spoil the Indians' fields, and the Pokanoket disliked being told what they could and could not do on the English Sabbath.

Metacomet knew that the past few days of tension had been especially difficult for the settlers at Swansea. His impatient warriors, encouraged by their increasing numbers and the throbbing and relentless drums, had looted the house of Job Winslow on the eighteenth of June. But trouble had begun in earnest on Sunday the twentieth. A company of warriors, encouraged by the injustices of the English and their own blood lust, had traveled to the farms in the southern settlement and had proceeded to loot and plunder, setting two of the houses afire. The few terrified settlers who still remained in their homes had escaped and hurried toward the main village to spread the alarm. From Swansea, a rider had sped to Governor Winslow in Plymouth.

On the twenty-first of June, after the terrified rider had spilled his news, Governor Winslow had penned a letter to Governor

Leverett in Boston, informing him of the trouble at Swansea. Since the Nipmuck of Massachusetts were believed to be allied with Philip, Winslow had requested that the Massachusetts governor take steps to prevent their participation in the uprising. But while recognizing the potential danger, Plymouth's governor had believed that he and his men could handle the problem. "If we can have fair play with our own," he had written, "we hope with the help of God we shall give a good account of it in a few days." Winslow had then sent an order for the immediate raising of seventy men from Bridgewater and Taunton. They were to leave immediately for Swansea and put an end to Philip's insolence.

▼▲▼▲ After hearing of the looting in Swansea, Metacomet reached for his wife's hand and squeezed it gently. "Find the one who now calls himself Askuwheteau, and bring him to me," he said. "Keep Mukki outside while we talk."

Wootonekanuska clutched his hand with both of hers, then left the wigwam, leaving Metacomet alone with his thoughts.

So much to bear. His warriors had begun to strike, which meant the Yangeese would soon be upon him. As a child he had admired the English, wondered at their many clothes, and trembled at the sound of their muskets, especially after one had exploded in his hand and scarred the tender flesh forever. Many of the sachems had thought the Yangeese gods until it became apparent that they died like other men. If they were not gods, the tribes had reasoned, the secret to their superiority must lie in Lord Jesus.

Many of them had blindly followed the Yangeese ministers, but Metacomet's father, Massasoit, had never become a Christian. Over the years Metacomet began to understand why. Though the Yangeese talked of love and patience, they constantly and persistently fought with one another. Their greed drove them to commit murder and steal even from the mouths of their neighbors' children. They stripped and fenced the land, depriving the animals of the woods. They had many goods but did not share them as the Indians did. Whoever entered an Algonquin camp was invited to share freely in all things, but when the Indians entered English towns, they were forced to pay in gold or labor for even a drink of water or a sorry bite of food. The Yangeese said they had come to help the Algonquin, but they were quick to accuse, eager to arrest, ever ready to disarm and take back the goods they had sold. One Yangeese man would sell a musket to an Indian for ten beaver skins; another would take the musket away and deprive the Indian of a weapon necessary to feed his family. The Yangeese were an accursed and troublesome lot; Metacomet's suspicion of them now matched theirs of him.

But his father had loved them. In the early days, when the English did not know how to plant or how to feed themselves, Massasoit had treated them like children. When they had grown strong, his ties to them gave him status among the other tribes. Metacomet's father had forgiven the English many evils and catered to their strange quirks. He had even petitioned the colonial courts to give his sons English names, but Metacomet had been secretly relieved to hear that the Yangeese suggested the names Alexander and Philip because those names once belonged to great warriors who did not worship their Lord Jesus. Neither would he, no matter how many praying Indians might want to lodge in his camp.

A soft, discreet cough interrupted his thoughts, and he looked up to see Mojag, lately called Askuwheteau, crouching in the doorway. "Come," Metacomet said, gesturing for the younger man to enter. Askuwheteau seated himself on a mat before the sachem, but, as was proper, did not speak.

Metacomet puffed on his pipe, then lowered it and slid his eyes toward his guest. "You wish to take Ootadabun as your woman?" he asked, lifting a brow.

The young man stiffened, obviously surprised that Metacomet knew what the entire camp had buzzed about for many weeks. "Yes," he answered slowly, shifting his weight on the mat. "If her father approves."

"Her father died during the winter. I will speak for him," Metacomet answered.

Askuwheteau's brows rose in obvious pleasure, and amber flames lit his eyes. "May I speak to her? I will go now."

"Wait." Metacomet lifted the pipe again, weighing his words. This experiment still interested him; it alleviated the tedious contemplation of war.

He lowered the pipe. "Would you cease praying to Jesus in order to marry Ootadabun?"

The young man's face collapsed in disappointment. "No." His voice was hoarse. "I could not."

Metacomet tilted his head. "Would you fight the Yangeese for Ootadabun and her people?"

"I would defend Ootadabun with my dying breath," Askuwheteau whispered, meeting Metacomet's eyes without flinching.

"The power of love and honor is great in you," Metacomet said, tapping the bowl of the pipe in his hand. "Then listen to this, my friend, for I will say it only once. War is coming. Because you have a sister among the Yangeese, you must go to Rehoboth and take your sister from that place. Leave here before the day has passed. If you return, I will give you Ootadabun."

"I will return." Askuwheteau leapt to his feet and had nearly reached the doorway when he whirled suddenly. "Why would you do this?" he asked, his eyes flashing. "And what will happen to Ootadabun if war comes while I am away? I will not be here to protect her."

"I do this because you have been honest with me," Metacomet answered, looking the newcomer straight in the eye. "And if your Lord Jesus is so powerful that you will not give him up, can he not protect the girl in your place?"

Askuwheteau seemed preoccupied for a moment, as if a memory had suddenly surfaced and overshadowed his awareness.

Then he turned and left the wigwam, sprinting toward the out-skirts of the village.

▼▲▼▲ On Wednesday, June twenty-third, a boy and an old man watched over the fields on the outskirts of Swansea. The afternoon passed quietly, but as darkness came on, the pair looked out upon a sight that curdled their blood: a band of Pokanokets slitting the throats of cows put out to pasture. The boy followed the instructions he'd been given; he lifted his musket and fired.

An hour later, Metacomet stared at the mortally wounded man on the ground before him and listened as his warriors told the story triumphantly. "They fired the first shot," one of the looters cried, thumping his chest. "The powwows have said that we will win if the English draw first blood. Victory will be ours!"

Metacomet turned away without answering. The Yangeese thought him a king, able to control and mold his people with a single word, but the English had never understood the Wampanoag. A sachem was but a counselor who led by strength of wisdom alone, and the fragile peace Metacomet had tried to maintain was now broken. The demon of war had been released; the fighting would not stop until one people or the other lay too bruised to rise again.

He looked around for Askuwheteau, but the young man had not returned to the village. Perhaps now he would never return. Ignoring Sunconewhew's steely gaze, Metacomet looked to his powwows, who were preparing to strike the war pole and dance with the feverish warriors.

"It is begun," Metacomet said, moving toward the bowls of clay and pollen with which he would paint his body for war.

▼▲▼▲ Plymouth decreed that the twenty-fourth day of June would be observed as a day of fasting and humiliation in order to beseech God to aid his people in this time of crisis.

Together with seventy soldiers who had arrived from Taunton and Bridgewater, the citizens of Swansea huddled in three garrison houses.

Finally free of all restraints, the Wampanoag hid themselves along the roads and paths of Swansea. As patient as spiders mending a web, the Indians waited for opportunities to strike. At one house they fell upon a small group retrieving corn from a deserted farm; six English were killed, including the boy who had inadvertently begun the war by firing his musket. Toward the end of the day a war party ambushed a group of citizens returning from church. One man was killed, several others wounded. Two Swansea men slipped away toward Rehoboth to fetch a doctor, but the next day mediators from Massachusetts discovered their mutilated bodies. Before nightfall of the first day of the war, nine Englishmen died.

At Monthaup, the Wampanoag celebrated.

"Who goes there?"

The voice, high and reedy with fear, was hardly one to inspire fear, but Mojag froze at the click of a musket and slowly lifted his hands above his head.

"My name is Mojag Bailie," he said, careful to speak precise and clear English. He turned slowly. "My sister, Aiyana, is a servant in the household of Master Matthew Glazier."

The sentry, a gangly youth with a blotchy face, trembled as he lowered his musket, but his eyes narrowed as he studied Mojag. "Why are you dressed like a savage?"

Mojag dropped his hands and gave the boy a lopsided grin. "I am living with one of the tribes near here. But I need to see my sister in Rehoboth. Please, I am a Christian. Do you see the cross I wear? I am unarmed and mean you no harm."

The boy studied Mojag for a moment more, then jerked his head toward the road. "Go on," he said, deliberately deepening his voice. He kept the barrel of his gun aimed in Mojag's direction. "But I'll have to escort you to the Glazier's house."

Mojag nodded his agreement. As he walked through the town with the boy at his back, passersby froze or recoiled at his approach. He should have taken time to don an English coat, but he'd been so frantic to reach Aiyana that he had not considered his appearance.

"Here." The sentry waved the muzzle of his musket toward a large, impressive-looking house. Children spilled through the doorway. "This is Master Glazier's home. His daughter runs the dame school."

Mojag made the mistake of approaching the gate. The children looked at him, screamed, and scattered in frantic flight. A plump, pink-cheeked servant came to the door and yelled for help.

"Please," Mojag called, lifting his hands again. "I mean you no harm, but I must speak to my sister, Aiyana."

"Mojag?" Aiyana's voice danced ahead of her, and he turned toward the sound. She came from the garden, a pretty picture in her frilly English dress and slippers. Like the women he had passed on the street, she wore her hair curled on each side with long ringlets spilling over her neck. Beribboned and blushing, she was scarcely recognizable.

Running to him, she gave him a quick embrace, then stepped back and playfully tilted her head. "In faith, Mojag, must you dress like that when you visit me? 'Tis bad enough that you insist upon living with the Indians, but when you come to Rehoboth you should at least don a shirt and proper breeches."

"I haven't time to listen to a scolding," he said, glancing around. He took her arm and stepped inside the courtyard. "We must talk. Is there some private place?"

She fell silent before the seriousness in his eyes, then motioned toward a small orchard at the side of the house. "Come," she said, taking his hand. She looked back at the young sentry, who had not yet lowered his musket. "You have done well," she said, dismissing the teenager with a spirited toss of her ringleted head. "This is my brother, and I can assure you he is no threat. I beat him up quite regularly when we were children. Go back to your post lest some truly dangerous savage attempts to slip by."

The young man colored before her attention, and Mojag smothered a smile. Did she torment every admiring man this way?

"You should not be so hard on him," he said, chiding her as they walked away. "He thought I was a dangerous barbarian, and then you teased him. I fear both of us have deeply embarrassed the boy."

"Well, Mojag, the attitude of this town is really rather extreme, don't you think? They are so frightened! They speak of the damage Philip's Indians will do to their property and their crops. They ramble on and on about a war that never comes. The Indians I know would never do the horrible things they describe—"

"War is coming." They had reached the orchard; Mojag squatted on the ground and pulled Aiyana down to his level. "You must leave and come with me right now. There is no time to waste."

Her face emptied of expression as a sudden icy silence surrounded her.

"No," she said, lifting her chin in the stubborn gesture he knew all too well. "I can't leave. And I won't."

"You must! War is coming."

"They've been saying that for months."

"This time they speak the truth. I may already be too late."

"Then you should stay here with me instead of playing in the woods. The English have guns and horses, Mojag. Their prayers have called forth God's protection—"

"I can't stay here. Metacomet—Philip—needs me."

She snorted softly. "*He* needs you? I can't believe that he would even listen to you. More than that, I can't believe that you would speak to him."

"He doesn't listen to me—not really."

"Then why, in faith, do you stay there? I've heard such terrible things about him. They say he paints himself and rides before the towns, daring anyone to look out and rebuke him. He is a heathen. He prays to the spirits of the earth and the wind. He rejects Christ, and they even say he has caused many a good Christian's death. So how, Mojag, can you think that God wants you to minister to *him?*"

A dim ripple ran across Mojag's mind. He had argued with God using the same reasons Aiyana had just mentioned, and he knew his father felt as she did. But God had given him a simple and profound answer to silence the questions.

"Philip matters to God," he said softly. "Who are we to say he does not? And God has called me to minister to him."

"I cry you mercy, Mojag." Frustrated, Aiyana turned and sat

on the ground, hugging her knees. A shadow of annoyance crossed her pretty face. "Tell me the true reason why you insist upon living with the Indians. Have you fallen in love?"

Mojag felt himself flush; Aiyana lifted a brow and laughed. "You have! Tell me, is she pretty? So pretty that you will not leave her in the face of war?"

"Aiyana!" He wanted to shake her, to pound sense into her head. "Listen to me! God has told me that I am to stay with Metacomet. He is not ready to profess Christ, but if war comes and his losses are severe, mayhap he will relent and surrender his eternal soul. No one else could do this thing, Aiyana. He would not allow an Englishman into his camp. But he tolerates me because I have wintered . . . and because I have promised to marry a Pokanoket woman."

Aiyana arched her delicate brows into triangles. "I can tell when you're lying, Mojag."

"I'm not lying. Every word I have spoken is true."

All traces of humor fled from her face as a blue flame of defiance lit her eyes. "You are truly in love? Then do not disguise your feelings with a cloak of spiritual concern for Philip. If you love this girl, stay with her. I would not leave the one I loved if a hundred wars broke upon the land."

He tilted his head back, studying her. She spoke with a maturity and sense of self-possession he had not known in her before. "What has happened to you?" he whispered. "What has changed you, little sister?"

Her eyes clouded with hazy sadness. "I, too, have found love," she murmured, her voice suddenly husky, golden, and warm. "Forest Glazier. We have pledged our love to each other, but I have not spoken to him since the riders came to tell us that Philip prepares for war. I'm afraid, Mojag, that this war will make things . . . difficult. Forest will of certain join the militia; what will I do if he is killed? Or what if the war turns his heart against Indians? He will hate *me*, Mojag, and that I could not bear. . . ."

Her voice broke, and tears rose in her eyes like a slow fountain. Reaching out, Mojag drew her to him, realizing for the first time that their separate paths might keep them apart forever.

"I have promised to stay with Metacomet," he said, his own voice thick with the sound of tears as she nestled against his chest. "The Wampanoag have many just grievances, Aiyana, and the English drew first blood. But I have promised God that I will not venture forth to kill; I will only stand to defend my wife and Metacomet."

"Why can't you leave him? He is a savage, Mojag. I have heard stories—"

"They are all lies," he answered, clasping her hands. "Metacomet is a devoted sachem, husband, and father. The English have pushed him into a corner from which he cannot escape without fighting." His eyes drifted to the edge of the orchard. "And he has personally changed my life. Until I wintered, until he forced me to spend time alone in the woods, I knew nothing about being an Indian. And then God sent Hania—"

"One of Metacomet's warriors?" she murmured.

"One of God's," he answered. "An angel."

"A what?" The heavy lashes that shadowed her cheeks flew up at him. "You saw an angel?"

"Yes," Mojag said, knowing full well that she would think him crazy. "And Hania taught me how to survive in the woods. When I take Ootadabun as my wife, I will be bound to the Pokanoket tribe forever."

She lifted her head and looked at him; her hand traveled to his cheek, where she wiped a tear away. "My poor brother," she whispered, her smile fading. "What shall I tell our father when I write him again? I dare not tell him that you are thinking of marriage, or that you are seeing angels—"

"Where is he? I should tell him myself."

"No." She gently shook her head. "I would advise you not to speak of it. Father has gone to Boston. At present, he is helping John Eliot debate with the Massachusetts authorities, none of whom, I'd wager, has ever seen an angel."

"Tell Father that I will strive to be bold, faithful, and successful in the things of God," Mojag answered, smiling in the calm strength of peace. "And that I will seek to do him honor."

▼▲▼▲▼ From his window near the orchard, Matthew Glazier lingered near the closed shutters and held his breath. In the hush of the afternoon, he had heard every word of the conversation between his servant and her heathen brother, and prickles of cold dread now crawled along his back.

Philip was coming. Soon!

Breathless, he sank down upon his bed and gripped his walking stick, forcing himself to think. The thought of Philip sent his blood racing. Almost equally unsettling was the knowledge that the girl had been offered a chance to flee the battle to come, and yet she had chosen to remain in Rehoboth to bedevil his son. He had not worked a lifetime to accumulate a fortune so an Indian could inherit it when he died.

He had hoped that his frank discussion with Forest would put an end to the boy's infatuation with the girl, but such a determined woman would not surrender easily. Maybe she had bewitched him by the power of heathen demons, or perhaps the potency of her exquisite beauty held him in thrall. But the problem with Forest would not disappear if she would not leave. When the trouble with the Indians was settled, something would have to be done about her. But at the moment, Philip was the more dangerous threat.

Struggling to gain his breath, Matthew rose to his feet and hurried out the door.

▼▲▼▲▼ As the alarm bell began to toll, Forest dropped the feather quill he had just dipped into the inkwell and stepped out from behind the merchant's ledger book.

"What is it?" Serenity asked, hurrying out of the storeroom.

"I don't know," Forest answered, holding out his hand to lead her to the meetinghouse.

A few moments later, Forest's whole body tightened when he looked up to see his father mount the platform. Matthew Glazier's brows were drawn together in an agonized expression, his mouth tight and grim. When a sizable gathering had filled the hall, the magistrate pounded his gavel, then stepped aside to allow Matthew to address the crowd.

"King Philip is coming," Matthew bellowed. His furious voice, lifted in a shout, stopped every movement dead. A dense silence fell upon the room.

"This afternoon I heard my Indian servant speaking with her brother, who now lives in Philip's camp," Matthew went on, slamming his hand on the pulpit in front of him. "Philip is coming, there is no doubt. He may even be on the trail now, so we must prepare! Bring in your cattle; guard your possessions; ready the muskets! There is no time to linger in idle talk!"

A strange and tangible whispering moved through the air, then absolute furor erupted. A woman screamed, children whimpered, men shouted and stood atop the pews, ready to leap over them and return to their homes. But the magistrate, walking to the platform with long, purposeful strides, slammed his hand on the lectern and commanded the villagers to be of good cheer.

"Quiet, my friends. Do not let yourselves be dismayed," he said, casting a quick glance of reproach toward Matthew Glazier. "Why should Philip come to Rehoboth? We have done nothing to offend him. And Swansea stands between us and Philip—if there is trouble, we will hear of it in time aplenty."

A rush of relief echoed through the room. "That's right," called another voice. "And the militia from Plymouth would come in time to crush Philip. What's he got, three hundred savages? Our militia can handle that many with no trouble."

"You're right. Philip could never get this far," the magistrate answered, smiling as he leaned one elbow on the lectern. "So trust in God, friends, and do not panic. Go home, bring in your cattle if you like, and prepare your muskets. But do not behave rashly. There is a way we can ensure that Philip will not attack us."

What? The question glimmered in the eyes of every man and woman present.

The magistrate lightly flicked a speck of dirt from his jacket. "Our leaders in Plymouth have kept the peace for years by venturing into the countryside and gathering the Indians' children. We have no Indian children, but we do have Indians." He looked pointedly at Matthew Glazier. "Your servant is an Indian, is she not? And her brother, Philip's man, is with her now? Fetch them here. We will hold *them* as hostages. And should Philip approach our town, we will send out a runner to tell him whom we hold. If he values this man and woman at all, he will not attack. God has brought this good fortune to pass, and we have nothing to fear."

Every eye turned expectantly toward Matthew Glazier. Forest felt his heart pound against his rib cage as his father's mouth thinned with displeasure. "You'll not be holding them in my house. What if Philip attempts to free them?"

"We will hold them in the jail," the magistrate answered, smiling. "'Tis a safer place, by far."

Matthew Glazier drew his lips in thoughtfully, then tapped the fingers of one hand against his chin. "We must hurry," he said. "You will find them in my house."

The mob inside the church broke and ran for the street.

▼▲▼▲ Ignoring the alarm bell, Aiyana packed Mojag a light supper of bread and cheese, then paused by his side as he gripped her hand and bowed his head. "Heavenly Father, our God," he prayed in an awestruck voice she scarcely recognized, "you know the paths you have planned for us. You created our hearts and minds. Your will is sufficient for each of us, whether we walk to death or to life. Guide my sister, Lord Jesus, and protect my Ootadabun. Give our father wisdom, and bless John Eliot for his work."

"Hide your holy words in the Indians' hearts," Aiyana joined in, clasping her brother's hands. "Cause them to see your hand in war as they would not see it in peace. And bring this conflict to a swift, merciful end."

"Amen," they said together.

Despite Mojag's grim news of war, Aiyana felt a bottomless peace and contentment. "I still think you would be better off working with Father than in the Indian camp," she whispered, running her finger along one of the wampum belts he wore over his chest. "But I will be happy if you are happy, Mojag. And I'm glad you were able to come here. I do not know when we will see each other again."

A look of tired sadness passed over his features as he turned to face her. "While I wintered in the woods," Mojag said, taking her hands, "the Lord spoke to my heart and brought words from the prophet Isaiah to my mind. He said he would bring me to a dark people whose hands were defiled with blood, their fingers stained with iniquity. These people speak lies with their lips; their ears do not hear. 'Their feet run to evil, and they make haste to shed innocent blood . . . The way of peace they know not; and there is no judgment in their goings.'"

"The Wampanoag," Aiyana murmured.

"Mayhap he spoke of the English," he answered.

"Mayhap," Aiyana whispered, resting her hand on his shoulder, "God spoke of both." She paused, relishing his company, wishing he did not have to go.

Suddenly the door flew open, and two men burst into the house, their muskets squarely leveled at Aiyana and Mojag. Assuming that the men had come for her brother, Aiyana stepped forward to defend him, but then Master Glazier entered the room. A slight hesitation flickered in his eyes. "Take them both," he said, a faint thread of hysteria in his voice, "to the jail."

▼▲▼▲▼ His breath ragged with impotent anger, Mojag followed the pompous Yangeese to the jail. An animal-like instinct from deep within urged him to run, but reason stayed his feet and kept him by Aiyana's side. He could not outrun the muskets at his back, and if he fled he could not protect his sister. But even if she had not been at his side, he would have remained under the English guns. A dead man could not escape to rejoin Ootadabun.

The jailer, an obese, balding, sloppy man of middle age, gaped in astonishment as the assembled mob pushed Mojag and Aiyana toward his small jail. "What's they done?" he yelped, recoiling from Mojag as if he were Lucifer himself.

"Nothing, as yet," the magistrate said, his brows set in a straight line. "But we're holding them as hostages in case Philip shows his face here. And we're being certain," he tipped his head back and stared at Mojag, "that these two aren't spying for Philip. No matter what, we're holding them."

▼▲▼▲▼ Because New England Puritans believed that public humiliation served as a far more effective punishment than incarceration, the jail at Rehoboth was a small, rarely used building. Behind the front room where the jailer kept his watch were two small cells separated by a solid wall. The magistrate led Mojag and Aiyana to these two rooms, then warned the jailer to keep a sharp watch lest they try to communicate with one another and escape to warn Philip of Rehoboth's preparation.

Aiyana had hoped that the mass hysteria would vanish in the calm light of a new day, but by sunset on the second day of their captivity word of the bloodshed at Swansea had reached Rehoboth. Genuine terror lit the jailer's eyes as he paced in the outer room and regarded his two prisoners.

"Swansea," he said, swaying unsteadily on his feet as he paused in the center of the room, "is destroyed. Scouts say that over one hundred men died there."

"Impossible," Mojag answered. From the small window in her door Aiyana couldn't see him, but she took comfort from the strength in his voice. "There weren't one hundred people *in* Swansea a week ago. Most of them had fled to other towns."

"I'll not be believing you!" the jailer roared, flinging a hand in Mojag's direction. "You're one of *them*, as savage as any lying barbarian that ever walked the earth!" The man's face purpled as he shook his fist at Mojag. "There's a meeting at the church now. The selectmen are telling the people to make ready for war. When Philip comes, I'd be more pleased to take *your* head off than let him harm one soul of this town!"

The man started toward Mojag's cell as if he meant to execute him immediately, and Aiyana screamed, afraid of what might happen next. But a sudden pounding at the front door broke the jailer's concentration, and he turned as Forest came into the jail-house.

"Quick, man," Forest said, not even glancing in the direction of the cells. "Get your musket. They are coming."

"Philip?" the jailer asked, the color draining from his face.

"No." Forest shook his head and moved to a shuttered window. "Our own people. The reports of Swansea have stirred them to anger, and there is talk of killing these two in retribution."

Sheer black fright swept through Aiyana, and she sprang to clutch the bars in the window of her prison door. Forest's eyes turned to meet hers. "Quick, man, give me your musket," he told the quaking jailer, not taking his gaze from her. "I will help you defend this place."

Aiyana heard the noise then—a steady roar that grew louder with every second, a cacophony of voices, shouts, and running feet, the uncontrolled sounds of mayhem. The entire village of Rehoboth, it seemed, would be breaking through the door at any moment.

"Hand 'em over to us!" One nasal voice cut through the din; then others joined in. Icy fear twisted around Aiyana's heart; even women were calling out for her death. "String them up outside the gate so Philip will know we will do the same to him!"

"Let us have them!" "Hanging's too good; I'd like to draw and quarter the heathens."

Gasping weakly, Aiyana slunk away from the door and coiled into the shadows, her hand covering her mouth. She heard Forest speak to the jailer, his voice rough with anxiety.

"Lock the door behind me, and open it for no one. If anyone comes through the door while the rabble is present, shoot first and ask questions later."

"I'll not be shooting my own neighbors to save the hides of two Indians," the jailer protested.

"You will uphold your sworn duty," Forest answered, a bitter edge to his voice. "Protect your prisoners, for these two have done nothing wrong."

Aiyana heard the door open and slam shut, and she knew that Forest stood alone to face the unruly mob. She clenched her eyes shut and began to babble a prayer: *Dear God, protect him; protect us. O Lord, why is this happening, and what can we do about it? We are here only to serve you. We have been about your business since we were small. Will you require our lives and the life of the man I love in order to work your will today?*

The noise outside crescendoed as Forest confronted the throng; then waves of silence seemed to begin at the front of the jail and spread outward. There was a long and brittle hesitation; then Aiyana peeked through her fingers as a different voice addressed the crowd. Matthew Glazier had stood to finish what his son had begun.

"I have heard reports from the survivors at Swansea," Master Glazier said, his voice rumbling like thunder through the windows of the jail. "And from the reports I have learned that the screeching rabble acted to avenge the death of one of their warriors. On Wednesday, the twenty-third, one of Philip's men was shot and killed; yesterday Philip's warriors took their revenge. I have lived in these parts many years, my friends, and know that the Indians have no stomach for prolonged war. They will strike, kill, and consider the matter settled. 'Tis not their nature to engage in a bloody and protracted war."

No one answered. Aiyana could not hear even the whisper of a sound.

"Now let us depart this place in peace," Master Glazier went on. "Philip has no reason to attack Rehoboth, so let us not give him one by harming the two innocent people inside this jail. We will keep them as hostages to ensure our safety. Philip knows the young man Mojag, and the girl is the daughter of a man who works with John Eliot. Both are valuable prizes. Should Philip wish to redeem them, he will pay dearly."

Voices murmured; then Forest spoke again. "My father is right," he said, his voice gentle and eminently reasonable. "We do not want to spill blood lest we invite Philip's wrath upon our own heads. Let each family return home and pray that God will protect us in this troubled time."

The silence remained; the crowd must be dispersing. Aiyana ran to the door of her cell. "Mojag?" she whispered, clinging to the iron bars in the window.

"Aiyana?"

"Are you all right?"

"Yes, thank God. And you?"

She managed a crooked smile. "If your angel friend is still around, this might be a good time to call him."

Through the embracing folds of sleep Metacomet heard the wind whisper his name. Knowing that he dreamed, he stirred from his bed and crossed the thin river to the island where he had buried his father's flesh and bones.

Massasoit's ghost, a pale, ghastly image that would have frightened anyone other than Metacomet, separated from the swirling greasy fog like oil from water. The eyes, veiled and liquid, seemed to stare through him as the voice spoke: "Son of the Fox, the fire is lit of your own will. Watch carefully, lest the flames turn upon you as they did the Pequot tribe. Feed the flames, but do not forget the burned flesh upon your left hand. Thus will your nation be scarred if you fail."

Struggling against the pull of the recurring dream, Metacomet clasped his head in his hands and sat up in an effort to throw off the lingering wisps of sleep. He did not want to believe in ghosts, but he did believe in dreams. And the spirits had spoken to him again, personally, without revealing their will through his powwows. The fire of war was lit and would not be quenched until he had won or he was no more. He would fight until the dreams stopped . . . or until he slept forever.

The gleaming coals in the hearth fire at the center of his wigwam threw a reddish light over the sleeping figures of his wife and son. Would Mukki grow to be a strong sachem? Or would the fire of his father's war devour him?

He reached out and rested his hand upon the boy's slender shoulder. Mukki stirred, smacked his lips, murmured some unintelligible word, then settled back to sleep. "I fight so you will not have to, my son," Metacomet whispered as the bitter gall of sorrow burned the back of his throat. "Those at war with others are seldom at peace with themselves. I wish you peace, little frog, and rest."

Listening to the steady sounds of his son's deep breaths, Metacomet settled back on his mat and allowed his eyes to drift to the circle of night sky visible through the vent in the roof. He would not have chosen to be a warrior. He would have postponed this war for many more months, if possible, but the Yangeese had given him no choice. His war was a measure of last resort.

The narrow cobblestone streets of Boston were encumbered with horses and tight with pedestrians. In the midst of the bustling activity, Daniel Bailie stood motionless, completely stunned. He had just left the governor's office, where he had heard frightening reports from the frontier, rumors of murder and full-scale assault on nearly defenseless colonists.

The three Puritan colonies—Massachusetts Bay, Plymouth, and Connecticut—however, were confident that the army of their New England Confederation could handle the "red king's rebellion." In a voice of remote dignity, Governor Leverett had assured Daniel that the Massachusetts militia would soon capture and execute the troublesome King Philip.

But Daniel held private doubts. The governor had spoken like a brash Englishman who did not understand Indians. John Leverett did not realize the very great danger New England would face if the Indians decided to organize and unite their efforts.

And the governor could afford to be confident. He did not have a daughter working in a frontier town and a son living in Philip's own village.

▼▲▼▲▼ Anxious to rid the land of this upstart Indian king, Boston authorities appealed to its veterans: aged soldiers of the Pequot War and other wars. One hundred ten volunteers, most of whom were now more suited to the tranquillity of home and hearth than to the battlefield, kissed their wives good-bye and buckled on their rusted swords. Among the fattened soldiers of the past marched apprentices, seamen, servants, and recently freed convicted pirates who looked for yet another chance to cheat death. Captain Samuel Mosely, a fierce buccaneer from the West Indies, led this rabble, accompanied by a pack of hunting dogs and three Christian Indians he had persuaded to act as guides.

The Massachusetts army moved southwestward toward Swansea and paused at sundown in the vicinity of Dedham. As the men munched their food in the moonlight, the earth's shadow began to obliterate the face of the moon. Though most of the men were devout and God-fearing, they possessed fierce imaginations, and someone pointed out that an eerie shape on the surface of the darkened moon resembled a scalp lock. For more than an hour fear gnawed away at their bold confidence as the men of the militia pondered this decidedly evil omen. When the lunar eclipse finally passed, the sober men resumed their midnight march.

Plymouth's contribution to the war effort, a contingent of ill-trained and terrified Pilgrims, proved to be a sorrier lot than the Boston rabble. Major Matthew Bradford and seventy-year-old Major James Cudworth commanded Benjamin Church to lead the Pilgrim contingent to the Swansea battlefront as an advance guard for the Boston troops. Cudworth had reason to believe that Weetamoo of the Pocasset was ready to help Philip's people escape from the Mount Hope peninsula.

Church did not hesitate but set forth into the brush, challenging his men to keep up with him as best they could. A few followed his lead and kept his pace, but the others, accustomed to walking in straight, regimented lines, fell so far behind that Church had time to hunt, kill, flay, roast, and eat a deer before the officers and the rest of the Pilgrim company caught up to him.

"Aiyana."

The softly spoken summons woke her, and Aiyana lifted her head from the floor, conscious of a dimly lit face in the window of the cell door. "Who is it? Mojag?"

"No, Forest."

Awareness hit her like a punch in the stomach, and she sat up, brushing dirt from her face and shoulders. "What has happened?" she asked, fearing an attack.

"Nothing. I just wanted to be sure you were well. I am sorry. The hour is early, but Master Hammond would not want me to neglect the shop—"

"I am fine, thank you."

She stood slowly to her feet, aware that they spoke as formally as people separated by vast age or social status. She crossed to the door and smiled at him, hoping he would see that she did not hold him responsible for her situation. "I want to thank you for what you did yesterday. You and your father probably saved my life and Mojag's."

Forest shrugged. "'Twas only what had to be done. Sometimes fear makes people do things they ought not to do."

"I know." She looked down at her hands, debating whether or not to suggest an idea that had germinated in her brain. "Forest, will you do something for me?"

"Anything in my power."

"This is in your power—I hope." She lowered her voice. "Is my brother listening?"

Forest left the window for a moment, then returned. "He is asleep."

"Good." She stepped closer to the door and lifted her eyes to his. "He must be released from this jail, and very soon. If Philip comes, or if he strikes another town, you and your father will not be able to stop the mob. They will come again, even more furious than before, and they will take Mojag out and kill him."

"They will not!" His denial was automatic, but both of them knew he lied.

"Yes, they will." She pressed her hands to the door. "You must help Mojag escape this jail. He must leave Rehoboth."

"What about you?" His eyes gripped her. "Do you think an angry crowd will spare you?"

She shrugged. "I am a woman; they will not harm me. I have been among the people here, and they know me. I do not fear the people of Rehoboth. But Mojag has been with Philip, and he frightens them because they do not understand."

Thinking, Forest stepped back and combed his strong dark hair with his fingers. "Aiyana," he finally said, his eyes studying her thoughtfully, "I want your brother to survive, but I can't release him to fight with Philip. You are asking me to betray my own people!"

"Mojag will not fight for Philip. He is trying to win Philip to Christ before the war escalates further. He can't do anything if he is trapped here."

A cold, congested expression flitted across Forest's face. "Philip is an unregenerate. He has heard the gospel and rejected it. There is no more hope for him."

"There is always hope for a soul for whom Christ died. Mojag will not give up, and I will not stop praying. Mojag has promised that he will not fight except to defend his or Philip's life—"

"And you believe him?"

"Yes. Just as I would believe you if you gave me the same promise."

"I don't know, Aiyana." Forest paced slowly outside the jail door. "You have the most unorthodox ideas, but what your brother is doing is near heresy. One does not become a sinner in order to save some—it's inconceivable!"

"Mojag hasn't become a sinner. He's only living with them, the same way Jesus lived with and talked to the sinners of his day."

Doubt flickered in Forest's blue eyes. "My father would disown me if he knew that I would even consider such an idea."

"Forget your father, Forest. There isn't time to consult him. Mojag will not harm you or any of the people in this place. But if he stays here, he will die. You know that I speak the truth."

Forest lifted both hands in entreaty. "You would release him to pray for the savages. Can he not do that here?"

"I would release him to live! Yesterday the eyes of the people in Rehoboth were no less savage than Philip's. Please, Forest, if you love me, if you love God, you must do this."

"I don't know," he murmured, walking toward the jail's main door. "I love you, Aiyana, but this is bigger than the two of us. I must think about this—and pray."

With a sudden slam of the door, he was gone.

▼▲▼▲▼ Forest left the main street and turned for the fields, anxious to avoid his fellow townspeople as he considered his choices. His steps were long and quick, spurred by the maddening inability to break free of Aiyana's suggestion. She was right. He ought to release Mojag, but what a traitor he would be in their eyes if the people of Rehoboth ever found out! The thought of being discovered made his stomach knot; the idea of standing guilty before his father's implacable gaze made his blood run cold.

Why couldn't he have gone with his master and the others who rode out to join the Plymouth militia? Master Hammond would have understood if Forest had chosen to fight. His father thought Forest remained behind to manage Master Hammond's store and protect Serenity and Constance, but his real reason was far more selfish. He had not gone because Aiyana remained in Rehoboth.

The undeniable logic of her reasoning struck him again.

Rumors of unimaginable atrocities had already begun to sweep through the village. In every rumble of thunder the townspeople imagined the sounds of Philip approaching with a screaming army of mounted riders. If Philip did attack, if even one citizen were killed in a skirmish, the angry, frightened mob would tear Mojag limb from limb.

Unless he were gone. Then they'd turn on Aiyana.

But because Forest loved her, he'd protect her. And because he loved her, he'd release her brother.

▼▲▼▲▼ "Hello, Master Johnson." Forest gave the jailer an easygoing, confident smile. "Our servant, Witty Greene, has sent over a basket of fried pies for you and the prisoners. Of course, you'll want to take yours with you to the meeting."

"What meeting?" the man asked, lifting the cloth that covered the basket. The movement released the aroma of Witty's cooking, and the jailer eyed a sugar-dusted apple pie with covetous delight. "I didn't hear aught about a meeting today," he said, lifting a pie in his pudgy fingers.

"'Tis an emergency gathering of the selectmen, for something has come up. My father sent me to relieve you here at the jail while you attend. He said you'd only be needed for an hour or so."

"Um," the jailer answered, biting into the pie. "Faith, this is delicious! Will you give my thanks to Miss Witty?"

"I will," Forest answered, carefully moving aside so the man could slip by him. "Take another to fill your stomach in the meeting. I'll mind the jail until you return."

"Um," the man answered, taking another pie. Smacking contentedly, he slammed out the door.

Forest moved immediately toward Aiyana's cell. "I've come back," he said, his voice flat in his own ears. "I'm ready to help, but we'll have to hurry. There is no meeting, and Master Johnson will be back before long."

"Thank you, Forest," Aiyana answered, understanding. Her mouth curved with tenderness. "Mojag will thank you, too."

"I'm not going without you, Aiyana," Mojag shouted from the next room. "I am thankful for what you intend to do, Forest, but I will not go without my sister."

"I can't go," Aiyana whispered. Her eyes caught and held Forest's. "Mojag, believe me, I won't go."

"I will protect her," Forest answered. With an effort, he pulled himself from Aiyana's gaze and lifted the key ring from the outer wall. "Nothing shall happen to her as long as I live."

"Can you protect her in war?" Mojag asked.

"Can you?" Forest asked as he unlocked the door and swung it open.

Mojag did not answer but stepped out of the cell, dirty and disheveled. The tensing of his jaw betrayed his deep frustration, and Forest knew he would not find it easy to leave Aiyana behind.

"Mojag," Aiyana called, her voice breaking with the sound of tears. "Don't go yet. I have something for you."

"I'm here." Mojag said, turning with a quick snap of his broad shoulders. Bringing his face close to the window, he pressed his hands against the door of Aiyana's cell, his body slumping in the silent language of sorrow. Forest felt his neck burn as he observed the intimate scene.

"You must take this," Aiyana said, frantically pulling a gold ring from her finger. "Wear it always, and do not forget what is inscribed inside. If you insist upon going back to the Indians, you must go boldly, faithfully, and successfully."

"Would that I could," Mojag answered, straightening. He slipped the ring on his smallest finger; then his hand closed over Aiyana's. "May God keep you until we meet again."

"We shall, soon," she answered, her eyes darkening as she gave him a small, tentative smile. "And I shall pray that God will bring you safely back to us."

Mojag turned to face Forest. "I do beg you, take care of her."

"I will protect her with my life," Forest answered, moving toward the empty cell. He stopped when he and Mojag stood eye to eye. "And as much as I despise deception, I fear I must resort to it now. What should my story be?"

Mojag glanced around. "You came to offer me something to eat," he said, pointing slowly to the basket, "and opened the door to give me food. But instead of taking a pie, I grabbed the keys and hit you so hard that you lost consciousness."

Forest tossed the basket on the ground, scattering the pies. "I suppose," he said, rubbing his cheek with a rueful smile, "that I shall need a bruise to prove the tale."

A melancholy frown flitted across Mojag's features. "You will take care of her?" he asked again, an edge of desperation in his voice.

"Yes," Forest answered. "And you, do not give up on Philip."

"I will not." Mojag paused, then clenched his fist. His mouth curved into an unconscious smile. "I would not have you lie for me, Forest Glazier. If you need a bruise, you shall have one."

As Aiyana screamed in protest, Mojag's fist connected with Forest's jaw.

Mojag

My soul, my soul! I am in anguish! Oh, my heart! My heart is pounding in me; I cannot be silent, because you have heard, O my soul, the sound of the trumpet, the alarm of war.

—Jeremiah 4:19

Constance Glazier's smile wilted as she looked around Master Hammond's shop and saw no sign of Forest. "Where is he?" she muttered aloud, afraid she could easily guess the answer. His fascination with Aiyana had undoubtedly drawn him to the jail again. If he wasn't careful, the entire town would realize that prosperous Matthew Glazier's son—*her brother*—fancied himself in love with an Indian girl. Forest's good sense would be questioned, his reputation tattered. And if he actually went as far as to suggest an espousal to Aiyana, no decent suitor would ever approach the family to negotiate for Constance's marriage. . . .

That thought stood in front of the morning, killing all joy.

"Are you looking for Forest?" Serenity asked, bobbing up from where she'd been kneeling behind the counter. "He left a while ago and asked me to keep an eye on things."

"Did he say where he was going?"

Serenity shook her head. "No."

Constance pressed her lips together, then flashed a bright smile to cover her annoyance. No sense in worrying Serenity about her brother's foolishness. "Well, naught can be done about him, I suppose. I'll wait with you until he comes back." She moved to a tall stool and perched upon it. "I was hoping to talk to Forest about our father's notion of joining the militia. A man his age has no business tramping through the woods where that devil Philip waits for scalps."

"My father couldn't be dissuaded from it," Serenity said, her gray eyes clouding as she leaned over the counter. "Forest was upset when he learned that my father intended to go. He insisted that only young men should fight, but Father insisted that the younger men were needed to remain here in case the savages attacked." She closed her eyes and shivered slightly. "Will they, do you think? I could hardly sleep last night for imagining it."

"I wouldn't worry," Constance whispered, slipping from her stool. She moved to the older girl's side and patted her shoulder in sympathy. "My father says Philip attacked Swansea only for revenge. He wouldn't dare attack another English settlement."

Serenity sniffed and dabbed at her eyes with a lace handkerchief. "Your family is such a comfort to me, Constance. I cannot begin to express my gratitude to your father for sending Witty to stay with me while Father is away. I have no closer friend than my father."

"You have me," Constance said, resting her hands on the girl's shoulders. She gave Serenity an affectionate squeeze. "And mayhap I shouldn't be saying anything as yet, but my father and your father have begun to negotiate."

"Negotiate?" Honest confusion shone in the girl's eyes. "Is your father aiming to buy something?"

"Would that he were," Constance said, regarding her friend with a lurking smile. "Can you honestly tell me you don't know?"

"I don't know *what?*"

Constance turned Serenity to face her. "That we're really and truly to be sisters! Forest wants to marry you!"

For a moment Serenity stared at Constance in a paralysis of astonishment; then a sudden weight of sadness fell upon her round face. "Oooh," she whispered, pressing her hand to her heart. "He thinks my father will be killed. 'Tis but pity that turns his heart toward me."

"No, no, that's not the way it is! Our fathers began to treat together long before the trouble with the Indians. Forest is fond of you, Serenity. Haven't you noticed?"

The sadness evaporated, and a smile trembled over the young girl's lips as twin stains of scarlet appeared on her cheeks. "I had not dared to hope," she said simply, lifting her eyes to Constance's face. "You are not playing a game, are you?"

"No, I swear it," Constance said, lifting one hand as if she were taking an oath.

"Oh, dear me, mind your manners!" Serenity said, giggling in the face of Constance's irreverence.

"I would not lie," Constance said, dropping her hand. She leaned on the counter and gave Serenity a confident smile. "There is only one stumbling block that might stand in the way of your happy betrothal and marriage. But that thing is of no great import—"

"What?" Serenity asked, a pensive shimmer in the shadow of her eyes.

"My servant, Aiyana Bailie." Constance idly traced her finger over the wood grain of the counter.

"The Indian girl?"

"The same. I have good reason to suspect that she believes herself in love with Forest. She is a terribly passionate person, as undisciplined as a woman can be. Of course, naught could come of this, but I've heard that Indian powwows can cast spells of love and death. Though Aiyana claims to be a God-fearing Christian, if she knows these spells, I'm afraid Forest might be swayed from his rightful intention."

"Surely no Christian could be influenced by a spell of the devil!"

"I don't know," Constance said, hardening her voice. "I don't know what power the savages have. But if you want Forest as a husband, Serenity, you must keep him away from Aiyana, whether she remains in the jail or is released to my house. We must not let her hold sway over his feelings. And you should pray for Forest, Serenity, as if he were your husband already."

"I will." Serenity remained motionless behind the counter, blank, amazed, and very shaken.

Constance sniffed in satisfaction as she moved toward the door. She knew her brother better than he knew himself. Forest might fancy himself in love with Aiyana Bailie, but he was too kind and gentle to hurt his master's daughter. And if Serenity pressed her case even a tiny bit, Aiyana would never have her way.

The Massachusetts troops had scarcely arrived at the Miles garrison house and taken note of their surroundings before some of them began to wonder where the hostile redskins were. About a dozen of Captain Prentice's men, guided more by enthusiasm than by sense, wanted to demonstrate their military prowess without further delay, and gained permission from their superiors to make a foray into enemy territory. . . . Benjamin Church . . . readily agreed to accompany them. The whole army watched with interest as the little party of hot-bloods on horseback trotted out of the camp. . . . Apparently they intended to go some distance into the peninsula, for they took with them as a guide a Rehoboth man, William Hammond.

—Douglas Edward Leach, *Flintlock and Tomahawk*

Lying low in the brush beyond the bridge that led into his territory, Metacomet and his men waited as quietly as a held breath as the cocky Yangeese approached. Erect and proud on their horses, the soldiers' bulging bodies made fine, wide targets for his warriors.

As they came into view, Metacomet set the lock of his musket to half-cock. At the heavy thud of a hoof upon the bridge he calmly rammed the musket ball and its patch down the barrel. More hooves thundered as Metacomet poured powder from the flask at his belt into the priming pan. Stones clattered over the path. The lead man's horse trotted safely away from the bridge, nearly into range. Metacomet closed the pan cover and set the musket lock to full-cock position. Finally, when the last hoofbeat had echoed across the bridge, Metacomet squinted down the length of the musket's barrel, aimed it squarely at the first man's chest, and fired.

The brush erupted with warbling war cries as a volley of bullets flew. The first rider clutched his middle and slumped in the saddle. Another man was hit in the leg while his horse crumpled under him. A cloud of gun smoke rose from the grasses as bullets whizzed among the English. Within a moment, the proud Yangeese turned and galloped back across the bridge like a pack of scalded dogs.

But not all of them ran. The wounded guide slipped to the ground, and another man in buckskins leapt from his saddle. Using his horse as a shield, he pressed forward, trying to reach the injured man.

Metacomet lowered his musket and motioned for his warriors to hold their fire. The Yangeese were a pack of cowardly dogs, except for this one. The sachem studied the Englishman more closely. He wore his long, dark hair tied behind him like a warrior, and the woods did not seem to frighten him. While the others had come across the bridge like conquering heroes, the eyes of this man alone shone with the alertness of an owl.

Crawling low on his elbows, Sunconewhew appeared at Metacomet's side. "That one is Benjamin Church," he whispered, nodding toward the man who lingered. "Awashonks knows him. She trusts him."

"And yet he comes against us," Metacomet said, his eyes narrowing as he watched the scene before him. No longer interested in killing, he lowered his musket and lifted his head above the grass.

One other Englishman, a man in a brightly decorated coat, had returned to help Church lift the wounded man. They heaved the guide over the saddle of the second man's horse, then hurried across the bridge. As Benjamin Church left, he raised his fist into the air and screamed insults at his comrades.

Metacomet felt his face crack in an unwilling smile.

▼▲▼▲▼ Returning to camp, Metacomet ordered his people to gather their belongings. Stored foods had to be taken in the canoes. The wigwams were to be left where they stood and not disassembled. "Take only what you need," he told the remaining women, his eyes meeting his wife's for the first time that day. "Prepare the children. They must not be afraid."

Though the sun had climbed only halfway across the sky, the morning's skirmish had drained him of energy. He slipped away from the circle of wigwams and retreated into the woods, finally sinking to the ground at the base of a stout oak tree. The rattle of cicadas laced the hot air; everything else seemed to sleep under a clouded fog-colored sky.

Against his will, Metacomet slid into a thin sleep, where the ghost of his father met him. Massasoit's reddened eyes fastened upon the musket lying near Metacomet's scarred hand. "Did you kill today?" he asked, his voice a quiet rebuke that set his son's teeth on edge.

"The English rode over our bridge to kill us," Metacomet answered, tightening his fist. "We fired shots and sent them running. Two men were hit."

He turned his face away from the pale image, but the spirit asked another question. "Will the men die?"

"Only if their god is not powerful enough to save them," he muttered, impatiently ripping out the words.

Massasoit lifted his pale hand as if he would argue, but Metacomet hardened his heart to the sight. His father's ghostly visits no longer unnerved him.

"We are leaving this place, great father," he said, staring boldly into the lifeless black eyes. "If you haunt me further, you must look for me elsewhere. Tomorrow your friends the Yangeese will come to Monthaup, but we will not be here."

A sudden sound disturbed the fabric of the dream, and when Metacomet blinked, the ghost vanished. The space it had occupied vibrated softly, as if a residue of Massasoit's presence remained in the air, a noticeable afterimage that faded only when a young woman walked through the vague form and shyly peered down at her sachem.

Metacomet shivered, then recognized the woman. She was Ootadabun, the one Askuwheteau loved. When the praying man came again to this place, *if* he came again, he would find it empty.

"Your wife sent me to find you," she said, modestly ducking her head. "I will tell her you are resting."

"Wait," Metacomet said, holding out his hand to her. She lifted her face; her large, timid eyes were tinged with sorrow. "Do not let your heart mourn for the praying man. When we are settled in a new place, I will give you another husband."

"I will wait for Askuwheteau," Ootadabun said, lowering her dark eyes to the ground. Her slender shoulders slumped. "He promised he would return."

"We will see," Metacomet said, waving her away. "We will see if he can find us."

▼▲▼▲▼ Two days later, on June thirtieth, Benjamin Church rode with a larger force across the bridge leading to the Mount Hope peninsula. The bridge had remained under heavy guard throughout the previous day, and unless Philip had rowed his entire nation across the water, he would be trapped like a rabbit in its burrow.

Once across the bridge, the men of the militia spread out in a broad line and proceeded through the woods and fields like a giant comb, their eyes and ears attuned to any sight or sound of the Wampanoag. They had conducted a brief search of the area yesterday but had succeeded only in mistaking each other for the enemy and shooting one of the officers' sons.

As the company swept across the peninsula, they passed the blackened ruins of the Swansea houses that had bordered Pokanoket country. Two or three miles farther south, they reached Kickamuit, the narrowest part of the neck. Here they found a grisly reminder of battle: upright poles decorated with the severed heads and hands of several Swansea men. After burying the grim remains, the troops continued southward until they came upon Philip's abandoned village.

The wigwams stood empty; the cornfields had been plucked clean. While the vexed and angry officers shouted that the savages had to be *somewhere* on the peninsula, Benjamin Church trotted down to the water's edge. Not a canoe remained.

A riotous celebration had broken out by the time he returned to the empty village. Several men were proclaiming victory, others had begun to sketch diagrams for parceling out the land joyously hailed as "the best in New England."

"We've got 'em on the run!" one soldier crowed, but Church silenced him with a harsh look.

"'Tis true they have fled from this place," he said, spitting in contempt as he eyed the arrogant soldier who had probably never seen a battle, "but look around. There are no signs of haste or panic. Philip's people left *before* we pursued them. They've gone to gain a more advantageous post and to strengthen themselves."

As if to counter the noise of their celebration, the winds picked up, howling across the fields and tossing empty baskets from wigwam to wigwam. As night drew on, rain hit with a sudden dense rush of thick drops. Withdrawing into one of the wigwams with the other officers, Church sat silently and tried to keep his temper under control. A circle of commanders debated their next action around a smoking fire, and Church could not help but grit his teeth in agitation. One captain declared that a secret stone fort existed on the peninsula and the army should not leave until the fortress had been found and destroyed. Another officer stated that they could not leave this hard-won land without claiming it for Massachusetts, so a fort should be built near the mouth of the Kickamuit River to prevent the Indians' return.

"Beshrew this nonsense!" Church finally roared, forgetting for the moment that he was not of very great rank in this expedition. "Not a one of you could pour water out of a boot if there was a hole in the toe and directions inscribed on the heel! Mark my words—Philip is in the Pocasset swamps. His sister-in-law Weetamoo has obviously lent him canoes and help for his journey. If we depart at once, we can catch him before further harm is done."

"Further harm?" A starched captain from Massachusetts drizzled gray disapproval as he looked at Church. "You forget yourself, sirrah. You backwoods greenhorns think this Philip is some fierce warrior, but he is a hare running before the hunters, and what harm can a frightened rabbit do? We have of certain chased him into the woods—"

"While you sit here planning your fort and eating the clams from *his* seashore," Church answered, venom in his voice, "Philip is courting his sister's people. On the morrow you will not only fight the Pokanoket but the Pocasset as well. The Sakonnet live in that area, too, and they may be persuaded to join him. He is far more dangerous now than when he was penned up in this narrow place—"

"Relax, Church; you fret too much," Captain Matthew Fuller said, tossing a stick onto the fire. "Philip is not going anywhere. We are the combined strength of three colonies; we can take him whenever we want to."

Church only closed his eyes in answer.

The next day, perhaps in an effort to silence his protests, the commanders assigned Benjamin Church to a company of three dozen men under Captain Fuller. Their mission was to journey to the Pocasset shore and confirm Awashonks and her Sakonnets as friends of the English. Contemptuous of the English plan to build a fort on Pokanoket territory, Church was glad to leave the others.

After crossing the bay, Captain Fuller's party divided into two groups. Fuller commanded his men to bivouac in the darkness without campfires in the hope that at least one of the enemy would inadvertently stumble into their camp. Such a man, if captured, might be convinced to lead the English to Philip.

Church quickly denounced Fuller's idea as ludicrous. "Too many of your men are troubled with the epidemic of tobacco lust," he told the captain. "They need to strike fire to smoke their pipes, and the sight and scent will reveal their presence to any Indian within a mile of this place."

Though Church disagreed with Fuller's order, he obeyed it; and he was not surprised when no Indians showed themselves during the night. Upon rising the next morning, he discovered that the soldier in charge of provisions had left their entire food supply at Mount Hope. With a few small cakes in his pocket, Church fed the entire company a morsel so they would have something in their bellies; then he led the group under his command toward Awashonks's village.

"When are we going to see these Indians of yours?" one of the more noisome soldiers chided. Church glanced behind him. The man who had spoken was Richard Smith. Smoke oozed from the corner of his mouth as the man puffed on his pipe. "You keep talking about Indians, and yet I've not seen one of the horrid savages since we came to this place."

"You'll see them soon enough, I'll wager," Church answered, picking up the pace. "Now fall into line and keep quiet. And toss away that pipe before I ram it down your throat."

Relying on tracking skills developed from a lifetime in the wilderness, Church soon found a trail through the swamps. He hadn't led his group more than ten feet upon it when one man spied a rattlesnake. The soldier screamed, fired his musket, and sent the reptile hissing into the bushes. The rest of the men beat a hasty retreat to higher ground, refusing to venture into the swamps.

Certain now that he led a pack of misfits and cowards, Church retreated from the swamp trail and continued along the beach. At Punkatees Neck he spotted a pair of Indians and hailed them in his broken Algonquin, but the Indians ran into the brush.

"They always run," Smith remarked dryly. "I still haven't had a good look at an Indian, Captain Church."

"In time," Church answered, gripping his musket more tightly. He knew the Indians hadn't run in fear as his men imagined. Even now they were spreading word of the English approach. Church wiped a trickle of perspiration from his forehead, then pocketed his handkerchief and motioned his men forward. Within a few hours he would know whether Awashonks had decided to join Philip or not.

A few miles southward, Church and his men found themselves in a broad field filled with blooming rows of spring-planted peas. Prompted by their growling bellies, they stopped to pluck off a few handfuls of early ripening pods, but the sharp crackle of musket fire from the nearby woods interrupted their peaceful grazing. Whirling around, Church lifted his gaze to a wooded hillside that seemed to move before his eyes. Like diamonds in grass, the landscape glittered with the bright guns of Indians as the enemy converged upon the Englishmen.

"Run for your life!" Dropping his hat and cutlass as he dashed for cover, Church led his men to a group of stone outcroppings along the beach. A short distance across the bay, the shores of Rhode Island glistened, as welcome as land to sailors long at sea. "Strip off your coats!" Church ordered his men. "The men from Rhode Island will see our white shirts and know that we are Englishmen. If God smiles upon us, they will come to our aid."

"And if they don't come?" Richard Smith jeered. "Those cursed Quakers are not likely to come to the aid of Puritans such as us."

"Mayhap 'tis time to rethink your position on the Quakers," Church retorted, slamming a musket ball down the barrel of his gun. "Load your muskets and fire at will!"

"Captain, we don't have much powder!" another voice yelled. "We weren't expecting this!"

Church smiled, discovering a perverse pleasure in the challenge. It was true—each man had only one powder flask at his belt, and in the terror of the moment, more than a few had spilled their powder as they ran willy-nilly through the peas.

"Listen to me," Church shouted, holding every man's attention with the power of his voice. "When your powder is low, you must make every shot count. Don't fire into the bushes and pray that your musket ball will find a mark. Wait until you see the enemy, line him up with the barrel of your musket, then fire and pray that your aim be true."

Sensing the urgency in his voice, the men obeyed, but the afternoon wore on without respite. The enemy in the woods, at first estimated to be sixty strong but now reckoned to be nearly three hundred, did not ease its attack. As soon as a man put his head around the edge of a rock, musket balls peppered the boulder. Church had nearly decided that he had lived his last day when one of his men spied a sail upon the water. "Look, Cap'n," the man cried, pointing at the small white canvas in the distance. "I trow that's an English ship!"

"Hail her," Church replied, keeping his eye toward the field of peas and the woods beyond. If the Indians came closer, they would surely be lost.

Church's man stood and waved his arms, then hit the dirt as a round of fire from the woods answered him. The ship's commander, hearing the noise of battle on shore, turned his vessel and retreated. The sight of the withdrawing ship encouraged the screaming Indians, whose bullets continued to ping and whiz off the sheltering rocks.

"Awashonks," Church muttered to no one in particular, "if you had wanted me to dance like Metacomet's men, you had only to ask."

"Captain! Another ship approaches!"

A second ship, commanded by a braver man, came near.

"Thanks be to God, there is at least one fire-eater in Rhode Island," Church said, peering over his shoulder at the vessel. He grinned at the soldier who had mocked the Rhode Islanders. "And he's probably a Quaker."

The sloop anchored within range of the enemies' guns, her bold crew hiding themselves behind barrels and masts. One brave soul exposed himself long enough to push the sloop's canoe toward shore, where Church and his men waited.

"What do we do now, Cap'n?" one young voice asked. Distracted from his thoughts, Church looked down at the freckle-faced lad beside him. The boy couldn't be more than sixteen. Why on earth had he chosen to join up with this motley crew?

"We pray, son," Church answered, his eyes roving over the shoreline. "And we take that canoe, two by two or one by one, if necessary, until we are all safely aboard that sloop."

"I'll fetch it in, sir," the lad replied. He pulled himself up to his full height, a full foot shorter than Church.

"Aye, son, and so you will," Church said. "You're the smallest man here, and therefore a smaller target. Go there among the reeds in the water, and hide yourself until the reeds thin completely. Then swim as if the devil himself were giving chase, and pull the canoe in toward us."

"Aye, Cap'n," the boy answered, flashing a good-natured grin.

As the boy crawled on his belly toward the water, sudden tears stung Church's eyes. If all his men were as able and willing as that youngster, the war would be won in a day. But war had a way of killing the young, able, and willing first.

"Aaargh!" A sudden shout from down the line caught his attention, and he looked up to see one of his men clutch his arm. A red spot bled through the cloth of his uniform, and the man grew pale, then crumpled into a heap. Church snorted softly. The fellow was obviously the sort who loved his wounds. He wouldn't last long.

"Take him to the water, and see that he's the first to go," Church commanded the man's comrade. "We'll have no time to deal with the wounded here."

"Captain Church! Look who comes yonder!"

Church turned and dropped his jaw as the canoe nudged the sand. The boy crouched inside, an oar in his hand and a wide smile upon his face.

"Name of a name, I hadn't expected you to do it so well," he said, laughing. "Smith, take the wounded man and go first. Take the canoe to the sloop and send it back for the next pair."

"How are we all going to cross in one canoe?" Smith challenged, his eyes measuring Church with a cool, appraising look.

"Two at a time," Church answered, refusing to be daunted. "With bullets and arrows whistling about us, no doubt." He lifted his voice. "Listen, men! We're going to the sloop, so those who remain must keep the Indians in the woods until we are all safely across."

"In truth?" Smith said, his mouth pulling into a sour grin. "But I suppose you're waiting here until the crossing is safe."

"The crossing will never be safe," Church answered, turning back to face the woods. He cocked his musket and tapped another load of powder into the pan. "They have us and will not give up until our heads are on poles. So cross or not, Mr. Smith, but do not waste time debating the matter."

Smith crossed. And two by two, as bullets tore holes in the water around them, Church's men rowed out to the sloop, then pushed the canoe back toward shore, where the boy hauled the boat in. Finally only the boy and Benjamin Church remained.

The Indians, realizing that their quarry was escaping, streamed from the woods as the number of defenders lessened. Now, as darkness came on, Church could see their forms skulking among the rows of peas. Another few moments on this beach would prove fatal.

"Come out of that canoe and cover me," he called, thrusting his musket toward the boy. "I'm going back out there."

"Wh-what?" the lad stammered, splashing toward the shore. Fear had gnawed away at the boy's confidence. "Come, Captain Church, there is no time to waste. The sun is nearly set—"

"I left a perfectly good hat and cutlass in that field, and I'll be drawn and quartered before I'll let any of Philip's men have them," he said, tossing his musket to the boy. "Just aim over my head, and reload as quickly as you can. I'll run fast, boy, and never you mind about us getting away. We'll be home in time for supper."

"Captain Church, I don't know about this," the boy said, his hands trembling as he lifted the musket.

"Don't fret," Church said, crouching beside a huge boulder as he prepared to run. "And I beg you, don't hit me."

Breaking from the rocks, he ran doubled over as musket fire snapped around him. Amid the crackle of weapons fire, the Indians shrieked in frustrated fury and his comrades yelled from the deck of the sloop, probably figuring he had lost his wits from the pressure of battle. If they only knew—he never felt more alive than when gripped by the mad happiness of a man about to do something utterly insane.

He saw his hat, dived, and tapped it on his head. The cutlass— where was it? There, gleaming like gold among the peas. He scrambled on his hands and knees like a determined terrier, then reached for the hilt of the curving sword.

An unexpected frisson of terror gripped him when a warrior stepped into his return path and pointed a musket directly at

Church's head. The Indian's stone face rearranged itself into a grin.

Church's heart stopped. *One risk too many.*

The Indian's finger pulled the trigger.

The gun clicked. The musket did not fire.

"Sorry to disappoint you, my man," Church whispered, his voice breaking. Grinning in relief, he scrambled to his feet and ran forward, butting the man with his shoulder and knocking the startled savage out of the way.

"Now, boy, to the canoe!" he yelled, galloping over the ground. He flew past the sheltering boulders, splashed into the canoe behind the boy, and hurriedly dusted his musket pan with the precious little powder he had left. A wave of warriors, still firing, appeared over the rim of the rocks, and Church aimed at the fiercest of them and pulled the trigger. He had intended to leave them with one last shot, but the pitiful remnant of powder in his gun sent the musket ball plopping uselessly into the water only a few feet away.

Church tossed his musket to the floor of the canoe, picked up an oar, and rowed with the frantic energy of adrenaline. He grinned. Once again death had crooked a bony finger at him, and he had refused to follow.

▼▲▼▲▼ Hidden by the covering veil of darkness, Mojag spied the light of campfires on the shore of Metacomet's land. Something was amiss, for the Pokanoket did not usually camp near the water but farther inland.

He pulled the oars into his canoe and rode the waves in the darkness, thinking. These had to be English fires, not Indian. And if the English had ventured this far south, they had totally traversed the village. Either Metacomet had escaped or he was dead.

Doubt and despair flooded his mind in a rush of emotion. Had he failed? Could he have lost both Ootadabun and Metacomet in the space of a few days?

He stared past the shoreline into his own thoughts. No. God had provided him with the opportunity to warn Aiyana. The Almighty would not have called Mojag to the Wampanoag and suddenly yanked them away.

He struggled to remember what his father had told him about the local Indian tribes. The Narragansett villages lay to the west, but they had not yet allied themselves with Metacomet's cause. If Metacomet were to flee, he'd go east toward the Pocasset, where his sister-in-law Weetamoo waited. If the Pokanoket yet lived, they would be found in the east, with other tribes of the Wampanoag nation, the daybreak people.

He dipped his oars into the water and turned the canoe toward Weetamoo and her people.

For the third day since Mojag's escape, Aiyana sat in a straight-backed chair and wearily faced her jailers. No, she repeated, she did not know where Mojag was. Yes, she was certain he meant the settlers of Rehoboth no harm. No, she was not a spy for Philip or his people. She had never even met the sachem.

From a stool in the corner of the room, Forest sat and watched silently, the bruise on his face now an off-green color. When they first came to question her, Aiyana was certain they would ask if Forest had somehow arranged Mojag's escape, but apparently these men did not believe it possible for an Englishman to take pity on an Indian. Day after day they grilled her, asking details of her past, present, and future, hoping to find in her words some clue to Mojag's whereabouts, some certainty that would dispel their fears. For from Mount Hope had come the news that Philip had fled into the wilderness, and for all the people of Rehoboth knew, the wolf could be outside their own doors.

"I know only that my brother is concerned for King Philip," she replied again, resting her head on her hand as she leaned upon a desk. "Mojag is a godly man, as godly as you, and he intends to do his part to staunch any further bloodshed. My brother is a man of peace."

"Then why is Forest Glazier's face bruised?" the magistrate cried out, pointing a trembling finger at Forest. "You are lying! Tell us again, young lady, where your brother has gone!"

"I speak the truth, I know not where he is! He might be with Philip, but if that sachem has fled his lands—"

"Your brother runs to consort with the very devil himself!"

"He went out to win this one you call the devil! You forget, sirs, that Philip matters to God!" She gulped, realizing that she defended Mojag with his own words, words she herself had refused. She shook her head, desperately wishing her tormentors away. "Does not the Bible say that we should venture into the world and carry the gospel to every creature?"

"You are right to call him a creature, for such as Philip are not men. They are incapable of being redeemed." The dour-faced selectman who had spoken pressed his thin lips together.

"No man is beyond the grace of God," Aiyana breathed, lowering her eyes so she would not have to look at her inquisitors for one minute more. "We are all the vilest of sinners: Philip, his warriors, me, and you."

The group before her uttered a collective gasp, amazed that she would have the temerity to include them in such a bold statement.

"Let her go." Forest's voice, weary but strong, echoed from the shadowed corner. "You've hounded her for three days. She knows nothing. Her brother followed his own mind, and she does not know where he is."

"Forest, be quiet!" Matthew Glazier snapped.

"She is too profane to be released!" the magistrate shouted, thumping the table in his earnestness. "You have heard her, Forest. She would include even the screeching savages among the elect of God—"

"She is as godly as we are, gentlemen, and you may trust my word," Forest answered. He stood with an easy grace, and Aiyana thought him more regal than any of the esteemed men who sat before her. "She is a servant in my father's house and is under his authority. I beseech you, sirs, let me return her to that house that she may keep her place. I can assure you that she will not do any mischief in this town. I know her heart, and I know it is bent toward God and his people."

"I do not know her," the magistrate huffed, rising to his feet. "And she will remain where she is."

Forest lifted his chin and met the magistrate's icy gaze

straight on. "She is guilty of no crime. And Philip has no affilia-
tion with her, so she is of no use as a hostage."

"She is not one of us," Master Glazier answered, moving
toward the door. "She is the spawn of the people who are making war upon us. Let her remain here, so we may sleep in our
beds without fear."

"You fear her? Your own servant?" Forest's voice cracked in
weary astonishment, but his father left the jail without answering. One by one, the others followed Matthew Glazier out the
door until only the jailer and Forest remained. Shaking his head,
the jailer moved to Aiyana's side and roughly gripped her elbow.

"Let her be," Forest snapped, authority ringing in his voice.
"I'll see her safely put away."

Surprised into obedience, the man dropped her arm. Aiyana
stood, trying to recapture some semblance of dignity. The days
of questioning and fear had left her an empty shell, and she
clenched her jaw to kill the sob that wanted to escape from her
throat. She would not cry before this jailer, nor any of them. Not
even Forest.

Forest led her back to her cell. Glancing behind him, he made
certain that the jailer had not followed. He stood in the doorway
and rested his hands upon her shoulders.

"I can't stand to see you in this horrible place," he said, his
face clouding with uneasiness. "The danger Mojag faced now
waits for you, Aiyana. If Philip comes, the people will want to
take their revenge upon an Indian. And now you are the most
Indian of any among us."

"I will not fear them as long as you are near," she whispered,
letting her head fall to the rough fabric of his shirt. For months
she had dreamed of being crushed within his embrace, and yet
the actual feel of his arms brought more comfort than passion.
Despite the misery of the jail, her weary heart stirred with contentment as she listened to the steady pounding of his heart.

"But therein lies the problem, Aiyana. If you are here in the
jail, I can't protect you. If trouble comes, there is no guarantee I
can reach you in time."

"It is of no import," she murmured sleepily, her voice as hollow-sounding as she felt. "If they come for me, I'll meet you in heaven."

"*You* are important," he insisted, his hand falling upon her head. "When you pray for your brother tonight, bring my name before God, too," he said, lightly fingering the strands of hair that now flowed down her back. "I have a plan, but I will need courage to put it into effect."

She tilted her head to look at him, and her pulse skittered alarmingly when she saw the seriousness in his eyes. A flicker of apprehension coursed through her. What plan would make him speak with such quiet but desperate firmness?

"Forest, what are you thinking of?"

His fingers fell across her lips, and she stilled beneath the warmth of his touch. Without saying a word, he bent forward and claimed her mouth in a slow, thoughtful kiss. The gentle caress sent the pit of her stomach into a wild swirl, and for a moment her mind emptied of all thoughts of Mojag, Philip, and the jail. The kiss seemed to lift her to a separate world, a delightful place where no one and nothing else mattered but the indescribable sensation of Forest's nearness, his lips upon hers.

He pulled away suddenly, leaving her knees atremble. "Forest!" she cried, reaching out for him, but he would not look at her as he locked the door and left her alone.

The land spoke from all around. Insects whirred from tall grasses as a silken breeze whispered through the woods. Mojag listened intently for the sounds of men. He had found traces of recent canoe landings in the muck of the shore and had followed a subtle trail deep into foreign territory. He knew Metacomet and his warriors would hide deep in the swamp, but in this, his first foray into thrilldom, he felt competent and sure. *If Hania is watching in that great cloud of heavenly witnesses,* he thought, kneeling to examine a footprint in the earth, *surely he is pleased that I have done so well.*

Pressing his finger to the muddy footprint, Mojag felt his stomach drop like a hanged man as a shadow crossed his. A dark and vigilant guardian presence suddenly materialized before him in the quivering heat. With an indolent, tomcat grace, a greased and painted warrior moved toward him. The man carried neither musket nor spear, but a cold lump grew in Mojag's stomach as he looked up at his powerfully built foe.

Chilly tendrils of apprehension spread through his body. "I—I am a friend," he stammered in Algonquin, struggling to find his tongue. "I am Askuwheteau, a friend to Metacomet."

The warrior did not answer but regarded Mojag with a taut and derisive expression. Mojag closed his eyes with rueful acceptance. What a fool he was! He had imagined himself as clever as Metacomet's warriors, finally an Indian, but he hadn't heard this man coming. And now he knelt helplessly, without a weapon or an escape plan.

The brush behind him rustled, and a blade bit at his throat as a hand yanked his hair, jerking his head back. The warrior before him was not alone.

"I wish to see Metacomet, sachem of the Pokanoket," Mojag said, straining away from the pressure at his throat. He lifted his hands slowly to signal that he meant no harm. "Tell the sachem that Askuwheteau is returned and seeks his counsel."

Two other warriors, their bodies painted in the red designs of the Pocasset, stepped out of the brush and eyed Mojag critically. The knife at his neck lowered a fraction, and Mojag slowly swallowed. One man remained behind him, the odds were four to one. Truly he had blundered this time.

"You are very foolish to walk so openly in daylight," the warrior before him said, placing his hands on his hips. There was something familiar about the way he held his head, something in the man's stentorian, rumbling voice. . . .

The fierce warrior threw back his head and released a great silvery peal of laughter that ricocheted off the trees and filled the woods. Before Mojag's startled eyes the man's savage visage melted into Hania's classic features. Gleaming white hair tumbled from the formerly bald head; the copper skin took on a translucent glow.

The other warriors, too, were similarly transformed, chuckling to themselves as they shed their primitive disguises and took on the aspects of holy warriors. Alabaster robes replaced the buckskin breechcloths. The eyes that had been veiled in Indian black now shone toward him in holy humor.

Mojag stood, surprise siphoning the blood from his face. When he could finally speak, he sputtered in helpless fury. "This," he said, pointing to the earth where he had been kneeling, "this was a cruel trick, Hania! I did not think that one of God's own would resort to threatening violence!"

Hania's laughter stopped as though he'd suddenly turned a valve in his throat. "Cruel?" he said, lifting a silver brow. "I thought it a most effective tool against pride. You grow too self-assured, my friend, and the Pocasset are not likely to ask questions before they shoot strangers. The English have been trying to find Metacomet, and the Pocasset are on the alert. You would be a dead man now, had you not been walking in the wrong direction."

As Mojag's raw fury turned to embarrassment and humiliation, Hania looked to his companions and seemed to speak, though his lips did not move. The other men's faces spread into affectionate, delighted smiles, and then, while Mojag watched, the trio of angelic helpers disappeared.

Coloring fiercely, Mojag crossed his arms and turned back to Hania. "I would have found Metacomet sooner or later."

"By following English footprints?" Hania asked, laughing. He came forward and slapped a heavy hand on Mojag's shoulder. "Let me show you the way, He-Who-Waits, so you may return to the work to which God has called you. Metacomet's heart is heavy with fear, but he cannot speak of his feelings because his people look to him for courage. He needs a counselor. Right now he is listening to Weetamoo, whose heart is filled with bitterness."

"I don't know Weetamoo," Mojag said, following Hania.

"You will," the angel answered, slinking as easily as a shadow through the woods.

▾▲▾▲▾ Because he had expected to find Weetamoo in a cleared, fortified village like Monthaup, Mojag was surprised when Hania led him over a serpentine, confusing path through low-lying swampland. Water seeped into his moccasins, shriveling the skin of his feet, and more than once he nearly tripped over treacherous submerged roots. Finally they came upon a spot of higher ground. There, hidden among the trees, Mojag saw the thatched roofs of hastily built dwellings.

"Go there and find Metacomet," Hania said, pointing with his massive arm.

"You're not going with me?" Mojag asked, his courage suddenly failing.

"No," Hania answered. His good-natured smile suddenly flattened, and he leaned forward in the vaguest of movements, a mere shifting of shadows. "You must be more careful in the woods. These are but the beginnings of sorrows, my friend."

"But you'll come if I need you. I'll have courage, Hania, if I know—"

"I am a messenger, not your arm of salvation," the angel answered, his voice softening in reverence. "Understand this, Askuwheteau. You needed help, and I was sent to give it. But your help comes from the Lord who made heaven and earth. Look to him and him alone."

With these words the angel disappeared as utterly as a shadow at noonday. Mojag hesitated, staring upward as if Hania would leave a passing trace of his presence, but nothing remained save the echo of his voice in the stillness.

Finally Mojag moved toward the camp. A guard at the entrance of the palisade questioned him roughly, then grabbed his arm and escorted him to a central wigwam. Mojag stooped to enter. Inside, sitting upon a red ceremonial mat, Metacomet held conference with his counselors. The tense set of the sachem's jaw betrayed his deep frustration, but his lips parted in honest surprise when Mojag entered the hut. Next to him sat a woman, her face bronzed by wind and sun. She looked at Mojag and touched her gleaming black hair in an absent gesture as her lips twisted into a cynical smile. Weetamoo.

Metacomet nodded absently in Mojag's direction, then turned to continue his conversation with his counselors. "Brothers," he said, spreading his hands, "you see this vast country before us, which the Great Spirit gave to our fathers and us; you see the deer that now are our support. Brothers, you see these little ones, our wives and children, who are looking to us for food and clothing; and you now see the foe before you. They have grown insolent and bold. All our ancient customs are disregarded; the treaties made by our fathers and us are broken, and all of us insulted. Our council fires are put out, our brothers murdered before our eyes. Their spirits cry to us for revenge. Brothers, these people from the unknown world will cut down our groves and spoil our hunting and planting grounds. They will drive us and our children from the graves of our fathers, and our women and children will be enslaved."

The men in the circle murmured in agreement; Mojag's own heart stirred to hear the sachem's impassioned plea. The Indians *had* been injured, and grievously so. How could he blame them for resisting English tyranny?

Metacomet turned from the circle toward Mojag. "I did not think we would see you again," the sachem said, looking toward him with easy familiarity. "You went to the Yangeese. Within a day and a night, the Yangeese came to Monthaup."

"I did not send the Yangeese," Mojag inserted, afraid the sachem's words contained an oblique accusation. "If I loved the Yangeese more than you, I would bring them with me even now."

Metacomet inclined his dark head. "I do not blame you. The Yangeese have been waiting to take our land for years. They drew first blood, and now they intend to strike until the last Wampanoag has left the land."

"No, they want peace, as do you," Mojag answered, trying to lace his voice with the proper measure of humility. Weetamoo, he noticed, had not spoken but studied him with eyes brimming with dislike.

"You should kill this one," she said suddenly. Leaning forward, she clasped her hands together like an eager child. "Send his head to the Yangeese at Rehoboth. He wears the cross of Lord Jesus, so let us be rid of him."

The reassuring sound of Metacomet's laughter silenced Mojag's quick fear. "The Yangeese will not know what to do with this man's head," the sachem said, resting his hands upon his knees. He cast a quick glance at the squaw sachem. "He is welcome among us."

Weetamoo's brow furrowed. "But you know nothing of him, and the praying Indians are cowardly. They do nothing but cry to Lord Jesus."

"He is not afraid, for he dared to come back even though he knows I think little of praying men."

"Bah!" Weetamoo spat on the ground. "I would still like to kill him. Let his God save him if he can."

"Not this one," Metacomet answered, lifting his hand. He looked to Mojag. "The woman I promised you is outside with the others. Go to her, my friend, and take your place among us."

"I cannot fight," Mojag reminded him, afraid the sachem had misinterpreted his motives for returning.

"Again you remind me why I dislike the praying men," Metacomet answered, his smile fading. "And yet you said you would defend me if the Yangeese come against us. For this reason, I welcome you. Take your bride with my blessing."

Scarcely able to believe his good fortune, Mojag stood, bowed his head in respect to the sachem, and hurried out of the hut.

With heavy steps, Forest turned toward his own home. He knew he'd find his father waiting by the fire, disappointment and frustration evident in the hard frown and glint of temper on his face. Back at the jail, Forest had committed the nearly unpardonable sin of disagreeing with his father before the magistrate and the other selectmen. If his plan were to work, he would now have to submit to paternal authority and make amends for his misconduct. Aiyana's life depended upon his willingness to swallow his pride.

He rapped on the door and heard his father's throaty command: "Enter."

Forest's jaw tightened as he stepped into the dimly lit house. Though the sun was at least an hour from setting, darkness had already come to this room, and black fury rode his father's brow. His eyes, when they rose to meet Forest's, glimmered with anger.

"Well? Why aren't you at the jail shirking your duties?"

"Forgive me, Father." Forest slipped his hat from his head and inclined his head in what he hoped was a properly contrite gesture. "I know I have neglected Serenity, but she is in no danger, and she knows how to manage the store—"

"I have told Witty to bring Serenity to this house. We will take care of her."

"No, Father, 'tis my place. Master Hammond asked me—"

"The merchant," his father said, deepening his voice, "is your master no more. We have just received word that William Hammond was killed while making the first attack in the enemy's lands. As his friend, I will take responsibility for his woefully orphaned child."

Forest took a quick breath of utter astonishment. "Master Hammond? Dead?"

His father lifted his granite jaw. "He rests in Abraham's bosom, a far safer place than Rehoboth. And since you have shown no concern for his daughter—"

"Please, Father, hear what I have come to say before you rebuke me." Forest moved to a stool near the empty fireplace and sat down. Twisting his hat in his hands, he searched for the words he had rehearsed on the walk from the jail. "You are a man of some esteem in this town. The others respect you, and they will listen to your advice."

His father folded his arms across his chest. "And flattery is the devil's tool."

"I don't mean to flatter you. I speak the truth," Forest pressed on. "I apologize for neglecting Serenity these past few days, but concern for Aiyana overwhelmed me." He lifted his eyes to meet his father's bright gaze. "She is also under the care of this family. Because she is our servant, we are responsible to God and the colony for her welfare."

"You do not have to remind me of my responsibilities," Forest's father answered, his voice flat.

"Of course not," Forest said, lowering his eyes again. The words he had prepared tumbled forth in a rush. "But it appears I need to be reminded of mine. Now that Serenity is orphaned and will need a home, I beg you to let me provide one. If you will implore the magistrate to release Aiyana from the jail so that you may protect her in this house, I will ask Serenity to be my wife."

For a moment his father blinked, surprise blossoming on his face. "You will freely marry Serenity?"

"If you will relieve me from my worries about Aiyana, I would be happy to become Serenity's husband," Forest answered, dropping his hat onto the floor. His father pinned him with a long, silent scrutiny, and Forest knew the older man was sorting through a maze of considerations. *He knows I love Aiyana, and he knows this is the very devil's bargain. However, he is nothing but practical, and he will have all that he has ever wanted and more—a*

prosperous son, a dutiful daughter-in-law, and even the satisfaction of
knowing that Master Hammond's wealth has been transferred to the
Glazier family.

"My son." For a moment a wellspring of emotion broke
through the man's glacial dignity; pride, delight, and doubt
struggled on his countenance. "Can you promise me that you
will learn to love the girl? The great God commands you to love
her in action. If you cannot be kind, loving, and tender in your
words and carriage to her—"

"I have been kind, gentle, and tender in my words and actions
toward Serenity since I have known her," Forest answered, his
mind blocking the protests of his heart. "What else does love
require? I promise you, Father, that she shall not be harmed or in
any way injured in marriage to me."

His father's eyes narrowed in a calculating expression. "There
remains the other matter. I will see to Miss Bailie's release if
Serenity accepts your proposal. But what, exactly, do you propose I should do with the Indian woman?"

"Aiyana shall abide with you for as long as she wishes," Forest
answered, the words sticking in his throat. "I expect that I will not
have many occasions to see her, and thus shall not think of her."

These last words were a bald lie, for he could do nothing *but*
think of her, but perhaps time and absence would erase her image
from his heart. For as soon as Serenity was willing and New
England peaceful again, he intended to sell Master Hammond's
business and move to Swansea or Taunton, mayhap even to Boston. Aiyana would forget him and return to her father or marry
one of the Indian men from one of John Eliot's praying villages.
His father would say this was what God willed for them all.

His father stood and came forward to place his broad hand
upon Forest's head. "Go in peace and in the name of our
almighty God," he said, his voice trembling with unexpected
emotion. "Out of conscience to God, study and strive to render
Serenity's life easy, quiet, and comfortable. Please, gratify and
oblige her as far as you lawfully can. Look upon her as a tool
that you may be better fitted for God's service, and so she may

bring you nearer to God. But do not take too much pleasure in her or any creature, for such great affection will benumb and dim the light of the Spirit that is within you."

"Do not worry, Father," Forest answered, a heavy, sodden dullness settling in his heart. *It is done. Peace is made. And Aiyana is saved.* "I will love Serenity as best I can. And you will see to Aiyana's release—"

"She shall be freed on the morrow," his father answered, his hand falling from Forest's head. "My word in this shall be as binding as yours."

Forest stooped to pick up his hat, then stood before his father. His height nearly matched the older man's, and yet he had always felt as though he gazed up at his father from a great distance below. Tonight, for the first time, he looked at his father as an equal.

"I suppose I should speak to Serenity," he said, the hat swirling in his hands again.

"You have but to sit and wait, for Witty is bringing her here," his father answered, indicating the settle. "I will go to bed, and you must speak to the girl when she arrives. We'll publish the banns in the morning and confer with the magistrate about the wedding. The law requires eight days to declare your intention to enter into a contract of espousal and another eight days until the wedding."

He clapped Forest on the shoulder. "In sixteen days, Son, we'll see you a married man." Inexplicably, his eyes misted. "My son, Forest—a husband. Faith, I had ill-imagined such joy until now. Thank you, Son. God bless you."

He turned toward his bedchamber, chuckling to himself, and Forest sank back down onto his stool, his heart too full for words.

▼▲▼▲▼ "What's this you're asking me?" Serenity's weepy eyes went wide with wonder, her mouth gaping in surprise.

"I'm asking you to join your hands with mine," Forest

answered, dropping one knee to the floor. He lowered his eyes, praying she wouldn't see the pity, frustration, and desperation that raged in his soul. "Since your father has been killed, Serenity, and because you cannot live alone—"

"Father," she whimpered, caught up in a new wave of grief. She sank onto the settle and stared miserably into the fireplace. Someone from the militia had broken the news an hour before, but her grief was raw, angry, and very new. For a stunned moment she did not move, but then tears streamed down her round cheeks. "He shouldn't have gone," she whispered, sobbing into her hands. "With my mother and father in heaven, now I have no one—"

"You have me." Forest rose to sit next to her. Carefully, protectively, he slipped one arm around her shoulder while the other one reached for her trembling fingers. "Take my hand, Serenity, and become my wife. We shall be married, you and I, and work the store as we have always done. Please say you'll marry me. Nothing will change. You will not have to move or disrupt your life—"

She lifted her head, gazing at him through red-rimmed eyes, and pressed a hand to her mouth. "Marry you?" she whispered, hiccuping. "Forest, my father is dead! I don't know what to do!"

"Say yes to me," he whispered, pulling the sobbing girl to his shoulder. She turned to him, her arms heavy about his neck. He placed his hand on her cap and murmured words of consolation until she finally lifted her face to look at him.

"I will do whatever you think best, Forest," she whispered, sniffling.

Carefully, awkwardly, he thumbed tears from her cheeks. "Thank you," he said, sighing in relief as a faint smile trembled over her lips. "Thank you very much."

Securely concealed in the Pocasset swamps, Metacomet sat with Weetamoo and listened to reports of the fiery war that had sprung from the musket in his hand. In the past few days the Wampanoag and Nipmuck had attacked Taunton, Dartmouth, and Middleborough, though his Pokanoket warriors had only been directly responsible for the attack at Taunton. His dream of a united offensive had finally become reality, for throughout the land, the Nipmuck, Wampanoag, and other nations were rising to strike the Yangeese who had forced them to abandon their territory and their way of life.

The name King Philip had become a curse. Metacomet heard that the English blamed him even for atrocities at Dartmouth, but he and his warriors had not been near the place.

From other Indians he heard the truth: The Indians of a small village called Indian Town had peacefully lived near the Yangeese at Dartmouth for years, even plowing English fields and working in Yangeese homes. But terrified by reports of the attack on Swansea and suspicious of the Wampanoag tribes nearby, the English residents of Dartmouth had withdrawn into their garrison houses.

Not long after the trouble at Swansea, one brash young warrior from that village stood by the river and made a rude gesture in defiance of his English masters. In answer, a shot rang out from a garrison, and the warrior fell dead.

Inflamed by the man's murder, the neighboring tribes struck the war post and set fire to the outlying farms, then concentrated on one of Dartmouth's garrison houses. The building was strongly fortified, however, and by the time the colonial militia arrived, many of the Indians had retreated and over one hundred had been taken captive.

"Benjamin Church found the captives under guard," Weetamoo told Metacomet and his counselors. "They had surrendered under the promise that they would be restored to their lands. But without regard to those promises, the Yangeese militia carried them away to Plymouth to be sold and transported out of the country. My scout told me that this action was so hateful to Benjamin Church that he has renounced friendship with many of his English brothers."

Metacomet listened to the news in bitter silence. These captives, forever wrenched from the land of their fathers, would not have been so cruelly treated if not for his actions. *Philip, Philip, Philip. The English curse that name. In that name warriors are separated from their women and children and sold as slaves.*

But the English were themselves a curse. If they had not been, he would not have gone to war.

Aiyana stared, tongue-tied, when the magistrate entered the jail and ordered her release. "She is to return to Master Glazier's house and resume her duties. The council has this morning determined that she is worthless as a hostage and no threat to the village."

The heavy wooden door of her cell swung open, and Aiyana stepped forward, still stunned. Why had the council experienced this sudden change of heart?

"I am free to go now?" she asked. "And free to do whatever I like?"

"Whatever the law of God allows," the magistrate said, turning to leave.

"Wait," Aiyana called, catching his sleeve. "Did Forest—did Forest Glazier have aught to do with this?"

"Forest Glazier?" An eyebrow lifted in amused contempt. "Why would you think such a thing? I suspect he has been too busy planning his marriage to Serenity Hammond to give thought to his father's servants. The banns were published this morning."

His marriage! Her breath caught in her lungs. *Forest can't be planning a wedding. Only last night he held me in his arms and kissed me. He asked me to pray for the plan he would put into effect—*

Another shock wave slapped her. Was *this* part of his plan? Had he planned not to claim her love but to kill it by marrying another? It was an insane notion, a foolish idea. He couldn't destroy her feelings; he couldn't wipe her heart clean of the passions that stirred there.

Aware that the jailer and the magistrate watched her carefully, she swallowed hard, lifted her chin, and boldly met the magistrate's piercing gaze. "I expect there will be much work ahead if there's to be a wedding," she said, her voice sounding artificial and false in her own ears. "I'd best get to the house and ask Forest what's to be done."

"Forest is at Miss Serenity's house," the magistrate said, a thoughtful smile curving his mouth. "But Miss Constance and Master Glazier will have plenty for you to do, I daresay."

"Good." With a confidence she did not feel, Aiyana squared her shoulders and walked past the two men out of the jail.

▾▲▾▲▾ She automatically set out toward the Glazier house, but the thought of Constance's gloating face spurred her feet to turn and run in the opposite direction. She had to talk to Forest. The wedding had not yet taken place—the engagement could be broken. Of course, Forest would have to sacrifice his honor, and Serenity's heart would be broken. . . .

She pushed those thoughts aside. If she could convince Forest that he did not need to marry Serenity, they could run from Rehoboth and the disgrace of a broken betrothal. There were other villages and towns; surely they could find a place where the past could be forgotten.

Without thinking, she burst through the door of Master Hammond's shop. Serenity stood behind the counter, a vision in black, strange attire for a bride-to-be. Before her stood two women, who turned and glared at Aiyana as if she were the devil incarnate.

"Of course we saw the notice this morning," one of the women said, staring at Aiyana with a prim and forbidding expression. She then turned back to Serenity. "And though this is all rather sudden, 'tis surely what your dear father would have wanted for you."

Her use of the past tense startled Aiyana, but she had no time to ponder the twists and turns of village gossip.

"Serenity," Aiyana said, stepping forward, "where is Forest?"

All three women froze. Serenity's troubled smile faded a bit as she looked at Aiyana.

"I need to speak to Forest," Aiyana repeated, acknowledging the other women with a polite smile. "Can you tell me where he is?"

"Don't tell her anything," the older woman hissed, leaning over the counter. "She's not to be trusted. Think of your father, dear."

"I . . . ," Serenity began.

"Do not think that because she serves Forest's family she means you no harm," the second woman whispered hoarsely. "The tawny foe are faithful to none but their own kind."

"Please, Serenity," Aiyana begged, reining in her temper with an effort. "I mean you no harm. Tell me where Forest is."

"Sentry duty," Serenity whispered, her expression tight with strain. "Near the river."

"Thank you." Aiyana gave the girl a smile of genuine sympathy before she turned and left the store. Her conscience smote her. Serenity was obviously upset about something having to do with her father, and yet Aiyana was on her way to break the girl's heart.

▼▲▼▲▼ She found Forest in a stand of trees near the water's edge. Behind him the western vista of silver water shimmered against the skyline of an endless cobalt sky. Nothing else moved in the stillness.

Creeping slowly forward, she crouched behind a screen of shrubs, watching him. The sight of his strong body made her heart beat more rapidly; the strength in his clean-cut profile left her spellbound. Was there another man in the world as noble? He had sacrificed his happiness and their love in order to win her freedom, but his concessions were unnecessary. They did not have to live in this thoroughly Puritan town. She'd go anywhere if he were by her side. Though she loved his generous nature, he had acted rashly.

He stirred, changing direction, and shifted his musket from

one shoulder to the other. He seemed straight and alert, but from her hiding place she could see that a vacant expression occupied his eyes. His thoughts were far away.

A curious crow hopped along the ground toward Aiyana, and she shooed him away. The bird cawed and flapped through the brush, but Forest did not flinch or even look toward the sound. He was blind to everything but his own inner reflections.

"A sentry must have better eyes and ears," she called, standing. She smiled when he jumped at the sound of her voice. "Philip and his men could creep up on you with more ease than I."

"Aiyana." A genuine smile lit his face, but he backed up a hasty half step as if to ward her off. "I suppose you know . . . everything."

"I know I was surprised to find myself a free woman this morning," she said, coming closer, "and astonished to find that you are to be married soon."

"It was the best way to win your freedom," he said, retreating until an oak tree blocked his path. "I knew my father would agree to the arrangement. Serenity needs a guardian now that her father is dead. And now you are free of Rehoboth. You can return to your father or go to one of the praying villages—"

"You could cast me out of your life so easily?" she asked, her mind spinning. All thoughts of his noble nature vanished as quickly as a burst bubble. "You want me to leave? Do you think you can make decisions for me as simply as you make them for yourself?"

"It is for the best, Aiyana. You will forget me in time, and you will be happier away from Rehoboth."

Her temper flared. "I am sure I will be, but I had thought to leave with you!"

"I can't leave Serenity. I have responsibilities. All that was my master's is now mine. The store, the business—"

She gasped as her mind blew open. Therein lay the real reason he would not leave with her! He could not leave his wealth, his work. "Are you," she whispered, the thought resonating within her, "so determined to become a ten-thousand-pound man that you would sacrifice my happiness . . . our love?"

"No," he whispered, shaking his head.

"Yes!" She stepped back, appalled to discover that a realization could hurt so much. Maybe he did love her, but he loved his ambition more. His heart belonged to Rehoboth, to the Puritan principles of hard work and industry, to the sterling reputation he had begun to build as Matthew Glazier's esteemed son. He could deny reality forever, but he could not hide from her. She knew him too well.

"I am sorry," he said, his voice choked with weariness. "I made my decision according to what was best for all."

Like a giant awakening within her, anger reared its head. "Who gave you the right, Forest Glazier," she blazed up at him, "to come into my life, to make me love you, to chart my course?" Her hands clenched into fists. "Who are you to decide what I will do?"

His expression twisted; his jaw clenched. "I am, by heaven, the man who loves you!" In one sweeping movement he reached for his hat and flung it to the ground, casting formality and pretense aside in the gesture. Defiance poured hotly from his blue eyes as he stared at her, and Aiyana trembled before him, anger and love warring in her soul. Finally, at long last, she had uncovered his fierce heart. Why hadn't he been able to stand up to his father with this kind of passion?

"I love you," he said, his face flushing as he spat out the words. "I can't sleep at night for thinking about you, worrying about you. You'll never know what I've suffered on your account. When the townspeople turned against you in the jail, I kept closing my eyes and seeing you on the gallows. I would have sold my soul to save your life. And when Mojag held your hand and told you good-bye, *my* heart broke, because I knew we must part, too. Rehoboth is not like the village where you grew up, Aiyana. Indians and Puritans do not live together peacefully in the real world!"

"'All things are possible to him that believeth,'" she said, moving to him. "If you love me, Forest, do not throw our happiness away by binding yourself to a woman you do not love! Come away with me, and let us find my father. We can live in Boston, near John Eliot or his people. If you want a business, you can set up your own shop. You can still become a ten-thousand-pound man. . . ."

He shook his head, a glazed look of despair spreading over his face. "No, Aiyana. Don't you understand? A gentleman's word is his bond, and last night I gave my word that I would marry Serenity. Would you have me hurt her? She is an innocent, an orphan child, the daughter of the master I have served for seven years. I would be ungrateful, the worst sort of scoundrel, if I walked away from my promise to her."

"What of your promise to me?" Aiyana whispered, knowing her words had the power to wound. "Or do I count for nothing because I am a servant, because I am an *Indian?*"

"Aiyana," he murmured in a choked voice, "don't."

"I don't understand, Forest," she said, floundering in an agonizing maelstrom of emotion. She turned her eyes away, unable to look at the pain on his face. "I can understand why you thought you had to sacrifice yourself. You wanted to be sure I was safe, and so you spoke to your father. You thought you would do the right thing, the noble thing. But, Forest, I am no longer one person—I belong to you. Can you not see that in sacrificing yourself you are also sacrificing me? I am incomplete without you. I will never be all that God has called me to be if I am torn from you—"

"No!" He shook his head abruptly. "You are speaking blasphemy. 'Tis sinful to love someone so much. God did not make you for me; he made you to serve himself."

She released a choked, desperate laugh. "Did not God say that two are better than one? Why, then, could he not make one for another, so that their labors may be halved and their joys doubled? The people of Rehoboth say that God formed this land in order that they could build cities and towns where he is God and Lord. If God can make a land for a people, can he not make a woman for a man? God has called me to your side, Forest. I know this to be true."

"Aiyana . . ." A muscle quivered at his jaw.

"Please, Forest," she said, trembling slightly as if a chill wind had blown over her, "Why should you resist what God has already revealed to both of us? We are of the same mind, heart, and sinew. Have you not felt it?"

His lids slipped down over his eyes, but he did not deny it.

"Yes." She reached out, daring to touch this man who was promised to another. Her hand fell upon his arm, and she felt the muscles tense under his sleeve. "You were made for me. Did we not realize it the day we met by the river? Your name was on my tongue; I had only to learn the sound of it. My name is carved within your heart; you have only to recognize it—"

"Aiyana—" For a brief moment his face seemed to open so that she could look inside his soul and watch her words slowly take hold. She saw resistance there, a quick flicker of fear, then passion more potent and powerful than anything she had ever imagined. "I do love you!" he growled, dropping his musket to the ground. His hands gripped her arms with the strength of desperation as his eyes raked over her, drinking her in as if he could never fill his heart.

Breathless, Aiyana tried to control the dizzying current racing through her. "Forest, say what you will—"

"Don't talk." His hand took her face and held it for a moment, then he pulled her to him. Her heart hammered foolishly; the pit of her stomach churned as she felt the heady sensation of his lips against her neck. Sensing surrender, hope, and victory in his kiss, she raked her fingers through his hair and wrapped her arms about his neck. Finally he pressed her lips to his, caressing her mouth more than kissing it, and she knew that she had won.

A sudden cracking sound split the stillness of the forest, and a chunk of bark flew from a tree not six inches away from Aiyana's head. Forest jerked her to the ground, his breath coming faster. Terror stole her voice; she could not speak.

"Shh!" Forest whispered, pressing his hand to her mouth. He

motioned for her to remain on the ground, then he crawled away and lifted his head above the stand of shrubs near the trees. Silence, thick as wool, wrapped around them again; then Aiyana heard the sound of canoes hissing up the gravel of the riverbank.

"Go!" Forest turned to her with the bright light of urgency in his eyes. "Run to the village. Philip is coming!"

A thunderbolt jagged through her. "But, Forest, what about you?"

"Go! Don't look back!" In one powerful movement he jerked her to her feet and pushed her forward so roughly that she nearly fell. Without thinking, she began to run, her feet pounding the earth, her ears filled with the sound of her pounding heart.

Dear God, dear God, dear God, she prayed as her feet flew over the path. *Help us; help Forest; help me help the others. And let Mojag not be among those who are coming.*

Aiyana tried to maintain her fragile control as she raced through Rehoboth. The enemy seemed to be everywhere and nowhere at once. Sounds of gunfire echoed in the distance, and her hoarse screams instantly summoned men and women from their houses and shops as though they had been waiting, tensed and ready, for this moment. The air filled with strange sounds—the terrified wail of children, the sharp and brittle crack of distant musket fire, the agitated clanging of the alarm bell—as families poured from their homes and raced toward the garrison houses.

Momentarily confused, Aiyana swirled in the center of the street. Where should *she* go? She had no real home, and for a moment her panic-stricken brain could not remember in which direction the nearest garrison house lay.

Before her eyes, the door to Master Hammond's shop opened. Serenity stepped out, her eyes glittering with stark and vivid fear. "What should I do?" she asked, her fingers twisting her apron. "Father took the musket, and Forest is gone to sentry duty. . . ."

Her voice trailed away, lost, and Aiyana stepped forward and took the girl's arm. "Come with me," she said, willing her heart to beat steadily for the younger girl's sake. Serenity must not see how frightened she was. "We'll find a garrison, and Witty will be there to take care of you. You like Witty, don't you?" Serenity nodded dully. "I thought so. Now come with me, and we'll find her."

Serenity took two steps, then hung back and pulled away. "I mustn't leave the store," she said, waving her hand toward the building behind her. "Father said I should never leave the shop unattended—"

"I'll tend it for you when everyone is safe," Aiyana promised, trying to still the panic that rioted within her. She held out her hand. "Come, Serenity, we must hurry."

The girl pressed her lips together, then took Aiyana's hand and followed her to the garrison house at the farthest corner of the street, which Aiyana had seen several families running toward. The scent of burning wood blew past them, and Aiyana realized that the enemy had begun to fire the town. Did this smoke come from one of the outlying houses or the center of Rehoboth itself?

A series of deafening explosions rent the air; flaming arrows whizzed across the sky and fell in a whistling cloud upon the villagers' houses. In a moment of madness, Aiyana turned to look behind her. And froze.

An Indian warrior, his face and shoulders painted in brilliant stripes of red and black, crouched in the center of the road not twenty paces back, a musket at his shoulder. One of his eyes squinted as he trained the barrel of the musket squarely on her.

Dear God in heaven, help me now.

Serenity turned. "Why are we stopping?"

The musket shifted slightly. A finger caressed the trigger.

Dear God, no!

Moving in a dreamlike blur, Aiyana yanked on Serenity's arm, pulling her toward the ground, but not in time to escape the bullet that struck the young girl in the chest. The Indian warrior pitched forward as a bullet struck him; his musket flew sideways and rattled on the hard-packed earth of Rehoboth's main street.

Serenity collapsed at Aiyana's feet. "Oh, dear God, no," Aiyana whispered, kneeling. She wrapped her arms around the girl. "Serenity," Aiyana said, cradling the girl's head in her lap. She lifted Serenity's hand, entwining the fingers with her own. "Serenity, dear, open your eyes. Look at me. You must open your eyes."

The girl's breathing came in ragged, shallow gasps. Her eyelids flickered, and her eyes opened for a moment. "Mama," she whispered, staring through Aiyana toward some distant place. The beginnings of a smile tipped the corners of her mouth.

"Serenity, you must listen to me," Aiyana urged, clinging to the girl's hand while she bent low to protect her from the madness surrounding them. The dark circle on Serenity's bodice bloomed relentlessly, growing ever larger.

"Mama," Serenity whispered again, arching her back. She curled upward for a moment, then wilted like a rose thrust into the cold. Aiyana closed her eyes against the avalanche of guilt that threatened to bury her. Less than an hour ago she had urged Forest to abandon this sweet girl, and now . . .

"Get up there, girl!" A male voice jolted her; rough hands jerked her to her feet. "Hurry to the garrison before they close the doors."

"I can't leave her," Aiyana said, reaching toward Serenity's lifeless body. "Please, we can't leave her here for the—"

"She's better off," the man answered gruffly. "Now get up!"

"I won't leave her!" Aiyana screamed, stamping her foot in desperation.

"Have it your way," the man answered, stooping. Before she realized his intention, he bent and heaved her across his shoulder.

"No!"

Breathing heavily, Aiyana's rescuer carried her through whizzing bullets and swirling smoke to the fortified building. Once they were safely inside, he lowered her to the ground.

Aiyana stepped back, stunned beyond belief when she recognized her deliverer as Matthew Glazier.

▼▲▼▲▼ The village's defenders repelled the savage attack, and by nightfall quiet had returned to Rehoboth. Most families remained in the garrison houses, afraid to return to their looted homes and charred farms. Only the settlements on the outlying areas had been totally devastated, for apparently this particular band of Indians had pillage, not destruction, uppermost on their minds.

Forest thanked God because the entire Glazier household had survived unscathed. Constance and Witty had hidden in the basement as the screeching rabble looted the house. After stealing whatever pleased them, the Indians set fire to the bedding. The two women would have burned alive if Witty had not climbed up to smother the flames with a wet blanket.

Aiyana sat beside Constance now in the garrison house, the flush on her cheek like the blush of sunrise, and Forest noticed that the attack had brought an uneasy truce to the warfare between the two. The entire town had heard of Aiyana's valiant attempt to save Serenity, and no one now doubted her loyalty. She had been in as much danger as any of them, and she had behaved nobly, risking her life to save another's. In light of the vicious attack, gossip linking Forest and Aiyana suddenly became as trivial and insubstantial as morning mist.

Though his heart was heavy with honest grief for Serenity's tragic death, Forest had never loved Aiyana more. She knew him too well. He *had* been loathe to leave his prosperity behind, but in the face of war his ambitions of wealth and prosperity seemed as senseless as a lamp without a wick. Fear and anger knotted inside him when he thought of how close they had come to losing each other.

He longed to find a private moment to talk to her, but conditions in the fortified garrison were not conducive to privacy. Fifty-five men, women, and children had crowded with their dearest possessions into a house designed for a dozen at most. They shared the precious space with bags of grain and barrels of water, stored in case the Indians attempted a siege. In daylight hours a few of the men ventured out to gather food and walk sentry duty, but the women and children remained safely inside. At night they divided the house into two sections, one for men and one for women, and slept on straw or blankets strewn over the floor. Sleep was usually interrupted by the crying of small children and the regular changing of the guards positioned at shuttered windows and barred doors. The fear of attack wrecked their sleep and terrorized their dreams; the unexpected barking of a dog in the night urged them to the brink of unreasoning horror.

But encouraging reports from other villages filtered in as the week passed: In order to prevent the Pokanoket from returning to their own lands, the colonial militia had destroyed over one thousand acres of Indian cornfields as well as the remaining hogs and cattle found at Monthaup. In an effort to preserve the delicate friendship between the English and the mighty Narragansett nation, a delegation from Boston had visited one of their sachems, Canonchet, and presented him with an ornate silver-trimmed coat. The English asked, among other things, for Canonchet's help in snaring Philip and his renegade sister-in-law Weetamoo. And, the people at Rehoboth learned, though Major Thomas Savage had been ambushed by the enemy in a shadowy valley, three Pokanokets had died in the skirmish, including Philip's brother, Sunconewhew.

The garrisoned settlers were cheered by the news that Uncas, the steadfast Mohegan, had sent fifty of his warriors to aid in the English cause. "Even now his son Oneko is approaching Rehoboth with a large force," one messenger told the garrison. "'Tis common knowledge that Philip and Weetamoo are fleeing with animals, women, and children, so a determined army should be able to overtake and defeat them."

Armed with hope and confidence in God, the settlers of Rehoboth left their garrisons on Sunday and met in the scarred meetinghouse. Looking across the assembled gathering, Forest noticed several empty places. Among the dead were Serenity Hammond; Master Burford, the cooper; Master Brantley and his wife; and the entire Holcomb family, the master, mistress, and six children. The Holcombs had lived farther out than the others, and from examining the remains of the burned house, the selectmen of Rehoboth had determined that the Indians killed every last Holcomb as they slept.

Several of the men in the congregation wore bandages or limped on makeshift crutches, and more than one was flushed with fever and perspiration. One woman, Goodwife Kyrk, wore a bandage around her head, the result of an Indian's attempt to remove her scalp. Fortunately, the savage was felled by her husband's bullet before he could complete the devilish deed.

The service began with the heart-felt singing of a psalm:

> I will say of the Lord,
>   He is my refuge and my fortress:
>   my God; in him will I trust.
>   Surely he shall deliver thee from the snare of the fowler,
>   and from the noisome pestilence.
>   He shall cover thee with his feathers,
>   and under his wings shalt thou trust:
>   his truth shall be thy shield and buckler.
>
> Thou shalt not be afraid for the terror by night;
>   nor for the arrow that flieth by day;
>   Nor for the pestilence that walketh in darkness;
>   nor for the destruction that wasteth at noonday.
>
> A thousand shall fall at thy side,
>   and ten thousand at thy right hand;
>   but it shall not come nigh thee.
>   Only with thine eyes shalt thou behold
>   and see the reward of the wicked.

When the congregation had been seated, Deacon Philip Walker stood to read a poem he had written:

> Let's search the Court, the Country town, and City
>   The tribe, the house, the person, find 'tis pity
>   To miss the knowledge of the thing or things
>   For which God's angry and his Judgment brings.

During his sermon, the minister exhorted his people to search their souls for whatever sins might be found there. "Contentiousness, drunkenness, profanity, Sabbath breaking, the love of the

world and its treasures, disrespect for parents, formality in worship, and personal vanity are all a stench in the nostrils of God,"
he said, pounding the pulpit as his steely gray eyes probed the
souls of his congregation. "Vanity is the worst and most obvious
vice. A proud fashion no sooner comes into the country but the
haughty daughters of Zion in this place are taking it up and
infecting the whole land. What shall we say when men are seen
in the streets with monstrous and horrid periwigs, and women
are wearing borders and false locks? Such are whorish fashions
and have kindled the anger of the Lord against this people!"

A murmur of voices, a palpable unease, washed through the
room as guilty consciences quaked.

"Rehoboth," the minister said, closing his eyes as if he could
not bear to look upon his people's sin, "I understand, with you
God is offended. And therefore he will humble you, until your
ways are mended. Repent, therefore, and do no more advance
yourselves so high. But humbled be, and you shall see these Indians soon die."

As the minister spoke, Forest chewed on his lower lip and
stole a quick look across the room at Aiyana. She had cast her
eyes downward and trembled slightly at the minister's harsh pre-
diction. *'Tis not so,* his heart whispered, hoping she would look
up and meet his eyes. *God will not destroy the Indians. He is only
disciplining us. When we have learned, the war will cease.*

But she did not look up as the congregation stood to sing the
closing hymn.

▼▲▼▲ Riders to Rehoboth brought steady news
about the progress of the war. The Mohegans, eager to prove
themselves to their English friends, joined with the militia to
chase Philip and Weetamoo through the swamps. Typically,
Philip led his warriors out to engage the pursuing enemy while
the women and children gathered what they could and fled
deeper into the swamps. The English were too afraid of snakes to
venture in after them, but the Mohegans were more interested in

plundering the goods left behind than in pursuing Philip's people. When the Mohegans could not find Philip, the English sent them back to Connecticut.

Realizing that he traveled with too many people to move swiftly, Philip divided his forces, sending Weetamoo and her Pocassets, together with the aged and infirm Pokanokets, to seek safety among the Narragansett. He and his people fled northward toward Nipmuck territory.

The Nipmuck had already taken to the warpath. In mid-July a group of them attacked the Massachusetts town of Mendon, killing several of the settlers. In early August, when Philip and his warriors arrived, the fighting accelerated. In rapid succession the Indians attacked Northfield, Deerfield, and Hadley, forcing the total evacuation of the first two towns. As the settlers fled for their lives, Indians caught the English between towns in bloody wilderness ambushes. On September eighteenth, they trapped a provision train and killed sixty-eight colonists.

Amid panic and fear, New Englanders began to resent all Indians. The colonial settlements buzzed with news of an early-August attack made by a tribe of supposedly neutral Nipmucks near Brookfield. And a few weeks later public faith in praying Indians was sorely jolted when a group of Christian Indians living outside Springfield joined in a devastating attack against that city.

"When I was last in Plymouth," the minister whispered to Forest one afternoon in what remained of Master Hammond's shop, "I heard that a praying Indian near Boston has a conscience so tender he will not eat horse meat, but he thinks nothing of killing Christians. And another who travels with Philip even now is so cruel that he wears a string of Christians' fingers about his neck."

Forest felt a shiver pass down his spine. Aiyana's brother was a praying Indian, and as far as anyone knew, he still traveled with Philip. Could Mojag have fallen to such a barbaric level?

"Surely these are not true Christians," Forest said, stiffening. "For many men profess beliefs that have nothing to do with the true state of their hearts before God."

"But in a skulking war such as this," the minister pointed out, lowering his voice as if one of Philip's warriors might lurk nearby, "who can say whether the Indian behind a tree is friend or foe? The General Court in Plymouth seeks to protect the loyal Indians, but what can they do? Mark my word, Forest—something will come of this concern. Then your family will have to reconsider the Indian girl you keep as a servant."

"We need the praying Indians," Forest interjected, ignoring the reference to Aiyana. "How are we to fight like the natives unless we can move as they can? Our soldiers are lost in the swamps, and yet I heard the Mohegan nearly caught Philip."

"If the greedy devils hadn't stopped to plunder the goods Philip left behind, they would have caught him," the minister grumbled, rubbing his beard. "And so, once again, war is prolonged because of the savages' base natures."

"I can't believe that all Indians are barbarians," Forest answered, lifting his chin. "Have you not heard how Aiyana Bailie risked her life to save Serenity Hammond? And 'twas she who shouted the alarm that forewarned the town."

"But she didn't save Serenity, now, did she?" the minister asked, pointedly lifting his brow. "And we could hear the savages' muskets by the time she warned us. There are too many dead, Forest, to think we were properly forewarned."

"*You* are alive," Forest snapped.

"Ah, Forest," the minister said. He wagged his finger like a scolding teacher and smiled. "We have a great enough enemy outside the camp; let us not make war on each other. If I have offended you, I am truly sorry. But until this war is done, I will support our right to feel free and secure in our homes. Something must be done about the praying Indians. And something will be done, soon."

Miles away in Roxbury, Daniel Bailie paced the floor of John Eliot's small office. The aged minister sat at his desk, his gray brow furrowed and his eyes troubled. The war had taken a tremendous toll on the man, and Daniel feared for his mentor's health and safety.

"The current order is too harsh," Daniel said, thinking aloud. "How can our people feed their families without their guns? And how can they travel to market their goods when they are not allowed to go more than a mile from their wigwams unless escorted by an Englishman?"

"The Council declares that we are wholly innocent, that their blood be upon their own heads if they are killed or injured," Eliot murmured, quoting from the court's order. "Like Pontius Pilate, they are washing their hands; they will not accept responsibility for this inhuman and irrational act. And yet I do not know what we can do about it, Daniel. We are but a few voices speaking on behalf of the praying Indians."

"They are starving," Daniel said, leaning on Eliot's desk. "With no guns, they have no food. Did we lead them to Christ only to lead them to death? And considering what happened last night—"

Daniel shuddered as the memory came crowding back. Captain Samuel Mosely, an arrogant hater of even loyal Indians, had traveled to Concord and taken a group of fifteen Christian Indians into custody without cause or authority. After roping them together like criminals, Mosely had marched the terrified natives from Concord to Eliot's house in Roxbury. Immediately after the Indians' arrival, thirty Roxbury residents went to the home of

Captain Oliver and demanded that he release the Indians so they might be killed "for the safety of the city." In true Christian courage, Oliver refused their demand. But accusations against the praying Indians too often were believed without proof or rebuttal. Now, deprived of their weapons, their fields, and the freedom to travel, the praying Indians faced slow and sure starvation.

"What will you do with the fifteen at your house?" Daniel asked, looking up.

Eliot's lined face cracked into a weary smile. "Hannah will feed them," he said, referring to his wife. "And we will give whatever we have to supply their lack. Even now Daniel Gookin searches for a safe place for them."

Daniel waved his hand in exasperation. "Then someone else will bring another group to you. And this harassment will continue until the light of the gospel is snuffed out—"

"The light will never be quenched," Eliot interrupted. Reaching forward, he lightly pressed his hand over Daniel's. "You are speaking as a man, Daniel, not as a servant of the most high God. It is our duty to wait, to speak for truth, and to see what God will do. We have carried the gospel into the dark world. God will do what he must to sustain his holy light."

October 13, 1675:

It is ordered that all the Natick Indians be forthwith sent for, and disposed of to Deer Island, as the place appointed for their present abode. . . . None of the Indians shall presume to go off the said island voluntarily, upon pain of death, and it shall be lawful for the English to destroy those that they shall find straggling off from the said places of their confinement, unless taken off by order of authority, or under an English guard. . . . It is ordered that the county Treasurer take care for the provision of those Indians that are sent to Deer Island, so as to prevent them from perishing by any extremity . . . for

want of absolute necessaries . . . and for that end he is to
appoint meet persons to visit them from time to time.

A black veil moved painfully at the back of Daniel's mind as
he watched John Eliot read the order a second time. The minister's age-stained fingers trembled as they held the parchment;
his lips thinned as the full impact of the words sank into his
consciousness. When he had finished reading, Eliot lowered
the page to his desk and covered his face with his hands. After
a long moment, he wiped his eyes. "The profane Indians have
proved a sharp rod to the English," he said, folding his arms
upon his desk, "and the English have proved a very sharp rod
to the praying Indians." He looked away as if distracted, then
turned to Daniel, his expression darkening with an unreadable
emotion.

"What are we to do?" he asked, moving his fingers so that
they brushed the surface of the parchment before him. "They
will not stop with the Indians at Natick. All fourteen of our praying villages will be emptied, for the English will now assume
that a free Indian is an enemy. We must bring all of our converts
here for transport to Deer Island, and we dare not wait."

Daniel felt the wings of tragedy brush lightly past him. Indian
blood flowed strongly in his veins and his features, even as it did
in his children's. "I must send word to Aiyana and Mojag," he
said, gripping the arms of his chair. "They must come to Boston.
I'll find them—"

"There is no time." Eliot shook his head. "By the time you
travel to Rehoboth and escort Aiyana here, the English settlements will be frenzied with desire to destroy the Indians. And as
for your son—" The crescents of flesh below his eyes drew up
into half-moons as he managed a tremulous smile. "You might
never find him. Does he still travel with Philip?"

Daniel looked away as tears stung his eyes. He had not heard
from his prodigal son since their angry meeting outside Rehoboth. "I don't know. I pray he does not, but I have not heard
from him."

"God will hold him," Eliot answered, his voice soft and reassuring. "Send a letter to your daughter and instruct her to find a safe passage to Roxbury. We must make arrangements for the transporting of our other people. I know these soldiers—they will not be patient. They have their orders. They will move our Indians or shoot them."

Aiyana received her father's letter at the end of October, and from the terse tone of his words she knew she would have to depart immediately. The thought of leaving tore at her heart in an unexpectedly savage way. She had thought she loved Forest and heartily disliked Rehoboth, but at the prospect of leaving she realized that she felt great affection for Witty, Constance, and her master, too. The Indian attack had melded their hearts in a way everyday life could not.

When the Glaziers gathered for Sabbath dinner she announced that her father had summoned her to Boston.

"What?" Witty said, forgetting that servants should defer to their masters. "You can't leave us!"

"I must," Aiyana murmured, the heaviness in her chest like a millstone.

"How are you to get to Boston?" Constance asked. "The woods are alive with murderous savages."

"Write and tell your father that you cannot leave," Master Glazier said, his voice rumbling over the table. "I will not release you into the wilderness. You are safer here with us."

"My father is quite insistent," Aiyana said, touching the folded parchment on the table. "He says the General Court has issued an order. Effective immediately, any Indian found in the land without an English escort will be killed without question." She paused, swallowing the despair in her throat. They would not understand. How could they? The General Court had just declared that any colonist could, in good conscience, shoot her dead at any time, in any place. In his letter her father had hinted that soon the English might even offer rewards for Indian scalps, and who could say whether a dead Indian's scalp had come from friend or foe?

"I will be your escort," Forest said quietly. Every eye at the table turned toward him. He put down his spoon and folded his arms on the table. "Why are you surprised? Aiyana should obey her father and go to Boston. Rehoboth is not safe, especially for her. And she is fortunate enough to have another place to go."

"But, Son—"

"Father." Forest's eyes shone with a steadfast and peaceful determination. "I am going to do this with or without your blessing, though I pray you will give it. Since God has seen fit to call Serenity home, I have decided to ask Aiyana to become my wife. It is only right that I meet her father and ask his blessing on our marriage."

Aiyana sat back, stung by the unexpected turn of events. She had seen little of Forest in the past few weeks, and they had not spoken privately since that awful day of the attack. In light of the situation, she had feared that he had come to loathe the Indian part of her. Yet he had just declared his intention to marry her regardless of what his father might say.

Cautiously, Aiyana studied her master's face. William Glazier's mouth had gone slack at his son's announcement, but now his lips clamped firmly together, his brows knotted over eyes that glittered with uncertainty. But the harshness, the unyielding granite stubbornness of days past, had vanished from his countenance. Swiftly, his eyes moved to meet hers. The heavy power in his gaze laid hold of her entire being.

"Aiyana," he said, his voice like iron, "do you love the Lord our God with all your heart, soul, and strength?"

"Yes, Master Glazier," she said, not wavering. "You know I do."

He nodded slowly, almost imperceptibly. "And will you love my son? Will you live with him in an English village and strive to find peace among your people and ours? Will you bring my grandchildren up in the nurture and admonition of the Lord?"

"Master Glazier," she whispered, her heart softening toward

the older man. "I promise that I will follow your son wherever God calls him. Any children born to us will be taught to revere God, to love their father, and to adore their grandfather."

His stony face cracked at her words. "Then *if your father approves,* I will consent for you to be married," he said, his hand tightening into a fist. He gave his son a warning glance. "But only if Master Daniel Bailie knows and gives his permission. You'll not be stealing a daughter from her father. I've a daughter, and I know I would never forgive such a thing."

"Do not fear, Father," Forest said, relief heavy in his voice. "And thank you." He looked around the board, smiling fondly at Constance and Witty. "I suppose I should take my leave of you. We will leave on the morrow for Boston."

"Go with God, my son," the master answered, his hand coming to rest upon Forest's head.

As he bowed his head and offered a heartfelt benediction for their peace, happiness, and safety, Aiyana noticed that his voice trembled.

▼▲▼▲▼ Aiyana and Forest slipped out of town with no fanfare or great leave-taking. People left Rehoboth regularly these days—families too discouraged to rebuild their burned-out homes and others who could not bear the pain of empty places at their dinner tables. Master Glazier promised Forest that he would take over the running and repair of Master Hammond's shop, and Constance gave both Forest and Aiyana parting embraces. Weeping loudly, Witty wiped a profusion of tears from her eyes and smacked kisses on both Forest's and Aiyana's foreheads, making them promise to return safely and to remember Rehoboth in their prayers. "For," she said, dabbing at her eyes with the edge of her work apron, "God knows that we are in as much danger as you. I never thought I'd live to see the day when I worried about parting from my scalp."

As they rode out along the trail leading to Swansea and civilization, Forest spoke little. His eyes darted from bush to tree to shrub, ever alert. He kept one hand on the horse's reins and the other upon a pistol in his belt.

Aiyana rode behind him, silently studying the proud lift of his head and the muscular build of his strong shoulders. For the hundredth time since his proposal, she wondered why he had volunteered to go with her. He could easily have stepped aside and allowed her to find another escort to Boston. It would have been just as easy for him to tell her to ignore her father's letter and remain at Rehoboth. He could have pretended that she meant nothing to him—and his life would be ever so much simpler.

If not for her, he'd be safely at home with his family.

If not for the war and Serenity Hammond's death, Forest would be quietly married to the merchant's daughter. He'd be a prosperous, wealthy businessman in the thriving village of Rehoboth. That was all he had ever wanted to be.

But the war had come, their lives had altered irretrievably, and the whirlwind had not yet stilled.

Metacomet

The words of his mouth were smoother than butter, but war was in his heart: his words were softer than oil, yet were they drawn swords.

—Psalm 55:21

Aiyana and Forest journeyed northward from Rehoboth through mostly uninhabited woods. The trail, heavily trampled by the movements of the colonial militia in weeks past, curved beneath shedding trees hung with straggling yellow and brown leaves. Though a drowsy contentment filled Aiyana's heart because she was leaving Rehoboth and was finally free to love Forest, the dismal sounds and sights of the dying earth touched a secret pool of sorrow within her. Somewhere in this war-scarred country Mojag lived with a ruthless savage, and she could never be completely happy until she knew that he was safe and that he approved of her upcoming marriage. If she could only arrange to have Forest, Mojag, and her father together, she was certain all misgivings would be erased, all doubts forgotten. Forest would come to understand her family, and Mojag and her father would learn to appreciate Forest.

A strongly fortified building rose out of the dusk. "Can we stop there for the night?" Aiyana asked, leaning forward. "A soft bed would be comforting after a full day in this hard saddle."

Forest shook his head. "That is Woodcock's garrison house," he said. "Of all places, we would be least welcome there. The militia quarters at that house when they are not on maneuvers, and if they get one look at you—"

He didn't finish, but Aiyana understood. Despite her beribboned hair and elegant dress, in the current state of heightened panic an English settler was likely to see her dark complexion and pull the trigger without asking questions. Unnerved, she kicked her horse, urging him to walk abreast of Forest's mount.

She did not want to be left in the rear as they passed the garrison house.

Before nearing Woodcock's garrison they left the main trail and drove their horses into the forest. Slender fingers of golden light probed a colorful carpet of fallen leaves as their mounts crashed through the woods. They continued until the time of half light between day and dark; then Forest pulled his horse to a halt and cocked his head, listening. Aiyana's mare whickered uneasily. The bit jangled in her mouth, a strangely metallic sound in the chilly stillness, and Aiyana murmured gently and leaned forward to pat the animal's neck.

"We can stop here for the night," Forest said, his tone brusque and businesslike as he dismounted.

"The horses will need to drink," Aiyana added, slipping from her saddle.

"I can hear running water, so there's probably a stream down that bank." Forest jerked his head toward the darkness beyond. "We'll water them in the morning."

Taking her cue from Forest, Aiyana pulled the heavy saddle from the mare's back, hobbled the animal's legs with a length of rope, then yanked the saddle blanket from the horse. The blanket was heavier than she had supposed, and she nearly dropped it, but Forest's hand caught the edge. "You should have waited," he said, his smile bright in the advancing moon's light. "I would have tended to your horse."

"I can help," she said, suddenly self-conscious. He had not stood so close to her in days, and they were alone and in the woods . . . again. But this time there was no village to which they must return, no spying eyes from a farmer's window. She stepped back and lifted the blanket to her chest like a shield. The urgency of her father's letter and her surprise at Forest's proposal had completely occupied her mind; she had not given any thought to this inevitable moment. She loved him, and he her. And she had longed for his touch ever since they were torn apart on the day of the attack. But surely this was too much freedom for a couple not yet married. . . .

Forest moved closer, extending his hand, and she reflexively took a half step backward.

"What's wrong?" he asked, still smiling as he took the saddle blanket. She thought he would toss it aside and reach for *her*, but he stepped away and shook the blanket until it snapped in the night. "You won't want to wake with horsehair all over you," he said, moving back toward her with killing casualness. As his hands expertly fitted the blanket around her shoulders, she lowered her gaze in confusion. What did he intend? And did it matter? They would be wed, of that she was certain, so would what she contemplated truly be a sin?

Forest tossed his own saddle blanket over his arm, then reached for her hand. Uncertain of what would come next but loving him desperately, she slid her palm into his and let him lead her to the base of a sprawling oak.

"I'm sorry, Aiyana, that I have nothing more than dry ground to offer you," he whispered, a measured degree of warmth and concern in his voice. "But the blanket is warm. If you keep it about you, you should sleep well."

She found his tone vaguely disturbing. Why, he spoke to her like Mojag did, like a protective older brother! Where was the passion she had tasted the last time they were alone together? Why were his eyes not crackling with desire? Why didn't he reach out to hold her?

"This is fine," she answered, her voice cool. Abruptly, she sank to the ground at his feet and gripped the blanket more tightly about her. Turning her back to him, she lay down and settled her head on a huge gnarled root. After a moment, Forest stretched out, his body angled away toward the horses, but his head only inches from hers.

A warning voice whispered in her head. Maybe his passion had disappeared. Maybe she had guessed correctly when she thought he had grown ashamed of her after the Indian attack. Oh, he would still offer to marry her, of course, because he was a man of unyielding honor. The same integrity that had driven him to propose to Serenity, a girl he did not love, had propelled him to propose to her, a girl he no longer loved. He would see her to Roxbury, if she did not meet with an eager settler's bullet on the journey, and he would ask her father for permission to marry his only daughter. And if Forest was cold, as distant and uninvolved as he had been throughout the past day, her intuitive father would sense that something was amiss, and he would not grant Forest's request. And so Aiyana would remain in Roxbury with her father while Forest returned to Rehoboth to settle down with a sweet Puritan girl who would mind his successful business and bear him many fair-haired children. . . .

Congested with sudden doubts and fears, she bit her lip and lifted her eyes to the velvet black sky. Oh, why had Mojag left her? She needed to talk to him; he would know what she should do. But somewhere tonight, beneath these same stars, Mojag slept with the devil—or at least the devil's emissary. Perhaps he and Philip were running for their lives at this moment. Or he might be praying, mingling his prayer with hers.

Oh, God, if you would send an angel to Mojag, why won't you send me a sign? My love burns as bright as ever, but Forest has grown so cold! Has this war driven a wedge between us?

No answer came in the night, the only sounds in her ear the occasional shuddering of the horses and a whisper of wind in the trees. She had not really expected to hear a voice. The God she knew spoke through his preachers and his holy Word in neat, predictable commandments and laws. He did not send angels or blow the answers to one's problems in the breath of the wind.

But Mojag would not lie. Had he truly experienced a calling from God? Or perhaps he had endured a bout of temporary madness, for surely in the Indian camp he had seen sights not fit for civilized eyes. . . .

She'd give every hard-earned shilling in her purse for Mojag's counsel. But since he was absent and God was silent, only she could plumb the depths of Forest's heart. If Forest truly bore ill will toward the Indians—*toward her*—his heart would be revealed in his words.

She turned her head toward him. "Forest," she asked, as casually as she could manage, "do the English truly hate the Indians? This order from the General Court is severe, and I am worried about Mojag. Though I don't agree with his mission, his intentions are unselfish and honorable."

"If he knew of the court's order," Forest answered, cool assurance in his voice, "do you think he would turn himself in to the authorities?" He paused for a moment. "I do not. Your brother is stubborn. He will do what he wants to do."

"So you think Mojag is wrong? He believes he is obeying a holy call to the Indians."

"I have considered that question many times." Forest shifted and rested his head on his elbow, tilting his face toward her in the darkness. "I am sure my father suspects that I helped Mojag escape from the jail. But he has not asked me about it."

"Why not?"

"Because if I confessed, his conscience would force him to disown me." A flash of humor crossed his face, then vanished. "Many times since the attack on Rehoboth I have wondered if I did the right thing. I allowed Mojag to leave, knowing he would offer help and comfort to the enemy, and now Serenity and Master Hammond are dead."

"But Mojag didn't kill them," she whispered, clutching her blanket to her. "And what if he is right? Your people built Rehoboth to create a Christian society in the wilderness, but Jesus told us to go into the *world*, not to cloister ourselves in the meetinghouse. And yet how many Indians has your father invited to worship?"

He groaned in disapproval. "We should not talk about my father."

"Then let's talk about you and me." She sat up, folding her arms inside her blanket. If they couldn't get beyond this, maybe they didn't have a future. "I don't know what you're thinking, Forest, but in the light of Mojag's actions I have examined myself. What calling did I fulfill in Rehoboth? I reached no one. I was not even allowed to teach the children. I grew comfortable in the daily work, and there were times that I forgot that my mother was a Pequot and my father descended from the Powhatan. I nearly became a part of Rehoboth. I did not even protest when the townspeople criticized Mojag and my father for attempting to take the gospel to a people considered barbaric and uncivilized."

"You have to admit," Forest drawled, "the Indians *are* heathens. They worship the creation rather than the creator—"

"Why should we be upset because heathens act like heathens? The English expect them to be saints, which they are not, and consecrated, which they cannot be until someone leads them to salvation. When my father asked the selectmen of Rehoboth if they would financially support a nearby praying village, they refused. They said the Indians were too lazy to build a proper town."

"The natives do sit around and gamble for hours," Forest murmured. "I work hard, at least ten hours a day, and an Indian plays that long. They get up only to eat—"

"So why does their behavior offend you?" Aiyana asked, leaning toward him. "You have been a Christian since you were old enough to understand faith; you are not a weaker brother. So why are you so bothered by what the Indians do? Their gambling does not tempt you or make you stumble. But instead of offering a hand of help to the Indians, the people of Rehoboth look away in offended dignity. The stronger people spurn the weaker, and Rehoboth grows suffocatingly stagnant. If Philip and his warriors do not completely destroy the town, Rehoboth will wither and die on its own."

"Do you hate the place so much? Were you not happy there?" he asked, gentle reproach in his voice.

"Happy? Yes. Comfortable?" She paused. "No. Rehoboth accepted me, but only when I wore a proper English dress, curled my hair in the English fashion, spoke English, went to the English church, and sat quietly on the women's side of the meetinghouse. I was happy as long as I conformed, but when I embraced my brother or spoke of overreaching my place, I was rebuffed." She lowered her voice and looked down at her hands. "I was happy there, Forest, but I shouldn't have been."

Stunned by the intensity of her own words, she pressed her

hand to her cheeks, glad that the darkness hid the flush there. She had not intended to speak her mind so freely, but she had to share the things that were on her heart. And since Forest seemed too preoccupied to talk to her—

"So do you believe," Forest said, his brilliant blue eyes glinting toward her, "that this war is God's way of punishing the English for the way we have treated the Indians?"

"Mayhap." She paused, hesitating. A torrent of honest words might drive him away forever, for Puritan men were unaccustomed to forceful speech from their wives. "A woman is to guide the house and children, but not the husband," Witty had often instructed Constance. But if Forest could not abide her true thoughts, maybe he was right to doubt the wisdom of their marriage.

"God can use whatever he chooses," she said, meeting his eyes in a steady gaze. "But isn't the sin of hate more serious than that of wearing a periwig? Don't you think God is more displeased with his children who ignore their spiritually ignorant neighbors than with those who wear silk and fine laces?"

"I don't know," Forest answered indulgently, dropping his head back upon the ground. He chuckled softly. "Since my clothes were burned in the attack, I haven't had an occasion to wear silk and lace."

He thought her amusing! She swallowed hard, trying not to reveal how deeply his laugh had raked her. She had opened her heart and he had . . . snickered. Well, he might as well know the full extent of her feelings.

"I fear God's hand is upon the Yangeese because they have failed to see that God is a God of diversity," she whispered. "Each man, each tribe, each village is different from another. We are not intended to be the same, and yet the Puritan fathers would have us be one of a kind. Even John Eliot—" her voice wavered—"has urged his praying Indians to put aside their buckskins, their wampum belts, their wigwams. He would like to put them into the mold of New England, and I fear many of them will not fit it."

Forest was silent; maybe he already slept. Or maybe he wished for time to pass quickly so he could rid himself of the talkative, troublesome woman who would not let him sleep.

A cold wind blew past her with soft moans, and Aiyana shivered and crawled back into the warmth of her blanket. "My father spoke often of this problem," she said, talking more to herself than to Forest. The thought of her father made her throat ache with loneliness. "He often told Mojag and me about the Pequot tribe his parents led to salvation in Christ when he was a child. They worshiped in their own way, but they worshiped truly until the English—"

She bit her lip. Forest was English, and she would not make him feel guilty for a war that had occurred nearly forty years before.

"We ought to get some sleep," he murmured, startling her. "The day ahead will be long. And we should stop to find food, for the bread and cheese Witty packed are nearly gone."

"Do not worry about me," Aiyana answered, lying back on the cold ground. Closing her eyes against the despair in her heart, she prayed that the journey would pass quickly.

▼▲▼▲▼ Forest waited until her breathing slowed and quieted. Then he shook off his blanket and stood in the darkness, gazing down at her. Why had he thought he could do this? He was a young man in the company of the woman he loved, and yet he had to treat her like any other woman, as chastely as if she were his sister.

It was torture to look at the living richness of her full red mouth and not claim it! Impossible to behold her slim, wild beauty and not hear his heart hammering in his ears!

He strode blindly through the darkness, searching for the rushing water he'd heard earlier. A frigid splash upon his face might shock thoughts of her from his mind and ease the burning of his blood. With every step of the horses on the trail he had been aware of her shapely shadow on the ground behind him.

When he had slipped the blanket around her shoulders, an unwelcome surge of excitement had seized his mind—and his body. How could he pass the night alone with her? Her nearness, her dark beauty made his senses spin, and she had no idea how sensuous her voice sounded in the dark as she opened his mind to new ideas and troubling thoughts.

Smothering a groan, Forest stumbled through the woods, not caring who or what might hear him. The sound of water grew louder, and he pressed forward, then tumbled down an embankment.

He grabbed for a low-hanging branch, stopping himself just before he would have fallen into the creek below. Some remaining rational part of his brain reminded him that he'd catch a fever if he spent the night in freezing, wet clothes. And how would he ever explain his bedraggled condition to Aiyana?

"God have mercy," he cried, embracing the stout limb as if it were the only reality in a mad, shifting world. Words from Scripture whirled in his mind: *It is good for a man not to touch a woman. . . .* "Give me strength, God," he prayed, dropping to his knees on the carpet of the forest floor. "If you want me to deliver Aiyana to her father in honor, you must help me put her out of my mind. My love is driving me to distraction."

▼▲▼▲▼ For three more days they continued through the wilderness, and Aiyana found that the countryside matched her increasingly bleak mood. They came upon charred English towns as well as desolate Indian villages with burned wigwams and ravaged cornfields. After skirting the English village of Dedham, which had not been attacked but whose inhabitants were certainly uneasy, Aiyana breathed a sigh of relief when Forest spied a signpost for Roxbury, John Eliot's home. Only two miles from Boston, Roxbury was secure in English hands. The Indians had not made a single attack in this area.

From the east came a frosty wind with the scent of the sea in its breath, and Aiyana breathed it in and stretched her frozen fingers as their horses slowly walked into town. She would be grateful to slip off this horse and sit by a roaring fire; she must look as weather-beaten as one of the Indian squaws. Forest had asked a passing traveler for directions to Reverend Eliot's home, and at length they stopped in front of a prosperous-looking farmhouse. As distant as ever, Forest dismounted and went to the house without a word to her. A few moments later he came out to tell her that Mistress Eliot waited inside to greet them.

Hannah Eliot was a short, rosy-cheeked, white-haired woman of at least sixty-five years, Aiyana guessed, and her hands were gentle and competent as she pressed Aiyana's frozen palms between her own. "Oh, my pretty child, you are chilled to the bone," she said, her delicate features twisting into a frown. "Come inside and let me take care of you. I'm so sorry that John is not here, nor your father, but Daniel has been detained with the others on Deer Island."

"My father is *detained?*" Aiyana gasped, unable to think clearly. "For what reason?"

"Oh, my." The woman's rosebud mouth took on an unpleasant twist. "You don't know about Deer Island?"

"My father wrote that I must come to him immediately on account of the court's order," Aiyana answered, puzzled and more than a little nervous. "He said it would be dangerous for me to remain on the frontier in Rehoboth."

"'Tis dangerous everywhere, my dear, and so the court has ordered all friendly natives to Deer Island." Suddenly Mistress Eliot's face went grim. "Though I don't know how anyone is supposed to survive the winter in that harsh place. I suppose God will preserve our people as he always has."

A soft gasp escaped Aiyana. She had never imagined that her father, so valuable an assistant to the esteemed Reverend Eliot, would be counted as an Indian. Why, his father had been an Englishman!

Mistress Eliot read the surprise in her face. "Yes, my dear, I'm afraid the authorities are quite unyielding in their commands. Anyone who looks, talks, or even thinks like an Indian is sus-

pect. Your father was quite willing to follow the others to Deer
Island, God bless him, because he said he could better look after
their needs if he lived among them. And my John, who used to
spend all his weekdays on the forest trails, now spends much of
his time on the island, trying to gather supplies for the nearly
four hundred who are held there—"

"This island," Forest asked, stepping closer. "It is habitable?"

"It's not like Martha's Vineyard or Nantucket, if that's what
you're thinking," Hannah answered, pulling a stool near to the
fire. She gestured for Aiyana to sit down. "Deer Island is a tiny
spot and almost totally barren of trees or wildlife. The Indians
have no guns, nor knives, no bows or arrows—nothing with
which they can provide their own food, if there is any to be
found. John says they are existing only on the clams and shellfish
they can find in the mud at low tide."

"Is my father in any danger?" Aiyana sank to the stool and
frowned into the fire. "If people are frightened enough to send
even my father away—"

"The people here are terrified, for they hear the most brutal
stories," Hannah answered. Her hand fell upon Aiyana's shoulder and gave it a gentle squeeze. "But do not worry, my dear.
Men like John Eliot and Daniel Bailie give higher priority to
God's orders than those from the civil authorities. Even so, both
John and Daniel Gookin, another of my husband's assistants,
have been receiving death threats since summertime."

"Death threats?" Forest's brows drew downward in a frown.
"Who would threaten a minister?"

"The forces of evil have always aligned themselves against the
goodness of God and those who exemplify it," Mistress Eliot
said, moving toward the large Bible that sat on a bench near the
fireplace. She lifted the cover and withdrew a slip of parchment.
"These notices are being planted throughout Boston," she said,
handing the slip to Forest. "Read it and judge for yourself
whether or not God's work is a dangerous enterprise."

Holding the paper aloft, Forest read: "Reader, thou art desired
not to suppress this paper, but to promote its design, which is to

certify (those traitors to their King and Country) Gookin and
Eliot, that some generous spirits have vowed their destructions.
As Christians we warn them to prepare for death, for though
they will deservedly die, yet we wish the health of their souls. By
the New Society, A.B.C.D."

"What is the new society?" Aiyana whispered, turning to look
at Mistress Eliot. "And why would they call for the death of
these good men?"

"We don't know who the cowards are, but they despise my
John and Daniel Gookin because they have persisted to visit the
Indians on Deer Island and help them to survive this miserable
winter," Hannah said, her body slumping slightly. "We have
even heard rumors that men from the vicinity of Lynn are planning to invade the island and slaughter the Indians there."

Aiyana felt a whisper of terror run through her. "They would
murder defenseless people?"

"'Tis what the warring tribes have done," she said. Her hand
came to rest upon Aiyana's. "The unredeemed natives have murdered innocent and defenseless women and children in the frontier villages, and some folk feel that the praying Indians deserve
killing as well. But though my countrymen call themselves Christians, they forget that our Savior stands against war and pillage."
Her eyes softened as she looked into the fire. "I fear that men
will carry guns until they learn to carry the cross."

Aiyana's thoughts filtered back to the day her father had announced that they would move to Massachusetts. Had he since
regretted hearing God's call? Had he heard a call at all? Surely
not, for how could God take him from a thriving ministry and
insert him into the middle of a harsh captivity—

"Please, Mistress Eliot, I must go to my father at once," Aiyana
said, taking the woman's hand. "I would bring him what comfort
I can, and there is something important I—well, Forest and I—
must ask him."

The woman returned her gaze to Aiyana, then looked up at
Forest with an understanding smile. "I can see that you are in a
hurry," she said, turning from the warmth of the fireplace. "So be

it. I shall draw you a map and write a letter explaining your presence in case you are detained in Boston. If you avoid the main roads and ride directly to the docks, you should not meet with trouble. And you should wear a wider hat, my pretty girl, to cover that dark hair. But first you must eat a good dinner, something warm and filling."

"Please, Mistress Eliot, we do not wish to trouble you," Forest said, clasping his hands behind him.

"Nonsense." She lifted a chin of iron determination. "John always says that we must not sit still and look for miracles; we must up and be doing, and the Lord will be with us. Prayer and pains, through faith in Christ Jesus, will accomplish anything. If you want to join Master Bailie, you shall, but not until you've a decent dinner inside you."

After eating as much as they could hold, Forest and Aiyana returned to their horses and rode eastward toward Boston Harbor. Mistress Eliot had given them explicit instructions to avoid the bustling center of town, for that area would be full of angry men and women who lusted for the sight of Indian heads upon poles. They then followed a southern road that skirted the town itself and then wound northward until it reached the docks.

Soon the harbor came into view. The sky was clear from rim to rim over the crushed-diamond water. Massive black rocks roared up from the water's edge, and in the distance a ship left the pack and lanced her way out of the harbor, her sails full and round.

Overcome by a sudden nostalgia, Aiyana reined in her horse and paused. Aware of her movement, Forest did the same, and for a moment they said nothing and listened to the mingled sounds of wind and sea.

"Is this much like Martha's Vineyard?" he asked, a flicker of compassion lighting his eyes.

Aiyana tilted her head and gave him a wistful smile. "A little," she admitted, peering out at him from underneath the wide brim of Mistress Eliot's hat, "though the ships that came to our island were not as grand as these." Her eyes misted as she searched the enormous sheet of water that shaded off into a blurred horizon. "I had not realized how much I missed the sea."

"Come," Forest said, gently nudging his horse forward. "You will not feel so homesick after we have found your father."

After making arrangements for the care of their horses at a stable, Forest consulted the note in his jacket pocket. "Mistress

Eliot was not very explicit in her directions," he said, studying the parchment in his hand. "She has written that the captain of the *Howard Edward,* a pinnace, will carry us to Deer Island, but she does not mention where we are to find that ship."

Aiyana looked around. Shops, wagons, and merchants crowded the port of Boston while seamen and ships clogged the docks that jutted out to sea like the spokes of a rimless wheel. Under the docks the sea was scummy with waterlogged scraps of parchment, bottles, dead fish, and greenish brown seaweed. Rust bloomed like a skin rash in great orange blotches on a huge anchor that lay abandoned in the shallows. A group of bleary-eyed, bearded seamen lingered on shore around a fire in the sand, waiting for darkness and whatever the night would bring.

"Perhaps we should set out upon the docks and ask for the ship," Aiyana suggested, narrowing her eyes as she glanced toward the western horizon. Already the sun had dipped low; darkness would be upon them in an hour, and she had no idea where they would spend the night if they did not reach Deer Island. The sights and sounds of the docks made her uneasy. This place was far more frightening than the woods.

"You're right," Forest said. Stiffly, awkwardly, he tucked her arm through his. "Stay close to me and keep your head down. I'm certain we'll find the right dock shortly. Mistress Eliot would not have sent us this way if the dock were not somewhere in this vicinity."

Aiyana moved closer to him, aware that several seamen on the docks had not taken their eyes from her since she and Forest stepped out of the livery stable. A steady stream of curses and catcalls echoed from the docks, and Aiyana understood why there were no other women near the wharf. No wonder Mistress Eliot had worried when she heard that Aiyana would have to journey to the dockyard! Still, if she was to reach her father, this part of the voyage could not be helped.

Lowering her head, she walked with Forest toward the first long pier reaching out to the sea. A mighty ship lay at anchor there, and Forest shook his head and moved past it. "We are looking for a pinnace," he said, hurrying her on. "Nothing so big as that."

They made inquiries at several berths, but none housed the *Howard Edward*. The sun had set as they neared an empty berth, and in the fire-tinted darkness of the docks Aiyana saw two rough-looking seamen squatting around a low, open kettle in which a fire burned.

"I cry you mercy," Forest called, pausing just beyond the rim of the light. "We are looking for the captain of the *Howard Edward*. We seek passage to Deer Island as soon as possible."

One of the men stood, and in the orange light of the fire Aiyana could see that he had a harsh, grayish yellow face and deep violet rings under his eyes. He did not look capable of any pleasant emotion.

"The cap'n is not here, and neither is 'is ship," he said, spitting over the side of the dock. A stream of spittle clung to his lower lip, and Aiyana stared at it in horrified fascination until he wiped it with the back of his hand.

"But this is that ship's dock?" Forest asked, the muscles of his arm tensing beneath Aiyana's hand. "If we wait here, will we find the captain presently?"

"Very soon, I'd 'spect," the man answered. Tearing his eyes from Forest's, he regarded his companion with a smirk. "Any minute, wouldn't you say, Wills?"

"Aye," the second man answered. He stood, too—a hulking man with an enormous stomach protruding like a tumor over his belt. His air proclaimed his unutterable boredom, but neither the darkness nor his ragged clothes could conceal the muscle in his thighs or the strength of his arms. His eyes were as gray and wild as storm scud, and they fastened directly on Aiyana. Her nerves tensed immediately, and she clung more tightly to Forest's arm.

"What's your business with the cap'n of the *Howard Edward?*" the first man called, a gold tooth winking in the firelight. "Can that be a squaw you've got there? If 'tis, we'll keep her for you. We've got a right and a license to hold her."

"Miss Bailie is not a *squaw*," Forest answered in easy defiance. "She is my—"

He halted when the man called Wills pulled a pistol from his belt. "Come closer," Wills said, waving the pistol slightly as he squinted at them. "Y'are too much in the dark. These are dangerous times, you know, and a man's liable to shoot what he can't see, 'specially if he fears there are Indians about."

"Forest," Aiyana whispered, holding him back. Panic like she'd never known welled in her throat.

"'Tis all right," Forest answered. His voice, without rising at all, had taken on a subtle urgency. "This must be the right dock. We have only to wait for the ship to return. It is natural that these men should want to examine us."

"But Forest—"

He stepped closer to the fire, pulling Aiyana's unwilling feet forward. The men gave Forest a cursory glance, then both turned to study Aiyana, their eyes probing her face and form in a way that made her blush.

"I hope you're satisfied, sirs, that we mean you no harm," Forest went on calmly, his voice like a steel blade wrapped in silk. "We have business with Reverend Eliot, who is probably on board the *Howard Edward* at this very moment."

"She's a mighty pretty one, but I seen her black hair. I'm thinking that's a squaw." Wills pointed the pistol directly toward Aiyana's chest. "And any Indian found off Deer Island without a military escort is to be shot."

Aiyana stifled a scream as Forest stepped in front of her, shielding her with his body. "No, sir, Miss Bailie is the daughter of an assistant to Reverend Eliot. If you don't stop harassing her, I'll be forced to press charges against you."

The sailor threw his head back and released a drunken cry that split the night. Aiyana's heart contracted in sudden shock.

"Charges for capturing an Indian? They'll give me a medal if I bring her in, dead or alive. That's a squaw behind you—I saw her black eyes!"

"Miss Bailie's eyes, I assure you, are blue."

"Lemme see her close up."

Heavy footsteps pounded toward her, and Aiyana closed her eyes and pressed her forehead to Forest's back. *Please, God, don't let them come any closer.*

"You'll not bother Miss Bailie. She is not a doll for you to ogle. Now tell us, sirs, where we may wait for the ship in peace and quiet."

"I don't think I like your tone," Wills sneered. "And I know I don't like you."

The incoming tide made slapping, sucking sounds beneath the dock, but all else was quiet as the men stood on the dock. Peering over Forest's shoulder, Aiyana saw that both sailors seemed to swell, sizing Forest up as if in some primal territorial dispute. The man with the pistol caught her eye and grinned, then tucked the gun securely in the belt at his waist.

"Though I'll warrant she's prettier than most I've seen, I still say that's a squaw behind you," he said, resting his hands on his belt. "Now you be cooperative and let us have her, or we'll shoot you for dressing her up like an Englishwoman."

"I'll not give her to you," Forest answered, spreading his feet in a wider stance. "And you'll not kill me, for Reverend Eliot is expecting our arrival. He'll have you hung if you dare lay a hand on either of us."

"No one listens to that Indian-loving preacher," the first man growled, stepping closer. He put up his fists, glaring at Forest over the top of his grimy knuckles. "You're bluffing. You probably mean to collect the bounty for her scalp yourself."

Bounty? For Indian scalps? Aiyana felt her skin prickle into gooseflesh. When had the colonial government descended to such lows?

"'Tisn't her scalp that interests me," the second man said, eying Forest steadily. He spoke in a dark, liquid voice that signaled the end of his games. "Step aside, my lad, and leave the woman with us. You've done your duty. We'll see that she's taken to the island when we're done with her."

"I won't leave her."

"Then get ready to die."

Aiyana let out a tiny whine of mounting dread as Wills pulled the pistol from his belt. Without hesitating, Forest lunged forward, leaving her suddenly alone on the dock, and she covered her mouth with her hand as the two men grappled for the gun and rolled over the dock. The first seaman, cheering his comrade, pulled a dagger from his sleeve. The shining blade, alive and dancing in the moonlight, sliced through the air as the first man jumped into the fray and managed to score a few well-aimed kicks to Forest's back.

Fear like the quick, hot touch of the devil shot through Aiyana; every nerve leaped and shuddered. What should she do? What could she do? If she had more time, she could think of a diplomatic solution, but she was helpless in the face of this kind of male madness.

A shot rang out, the blast ripping through the darkness like an early thunder of war. Forest and the sailor, still locked in a death grip, suddenly parted. Both their hands gripped the gun, but a widening circle of blood spread over the seaman's shirt.

Regaining his feet, Forest stood with his hands on his knees while the other sailor gaped at his companion, who fell motionless to the dock. "You've killed Wills!" he screamed, turning to Forest with a look of complete stupefaction. For a moment he stood as if paralyzed; then he lunged at Forest, the dagger gleaming in his hand.

Aiyana screamed. The blade barely missed Forest's neck, and Forest drew his hand back and struck the sailor's wrist with a blow that sent the dagger spinning over the dock. Scrambling forward, Aiyana sprang for the knife, but her hand caught hold of the blade, not the handle. Grimacing in pain, she flung the dagger into the water, where it winked through the shallows and disappeared into the murky depths below.

For a few moments the figures on the dock struggled against each other. In a dance of death they pirouetted over the wooden dock, tripping over the dead man's body, slapping flesh, tearing garments. Finally a shoulder throw sent the sailor crashing onto the dock, and then Forest's boot slammed into his stomach, forcing out the man's breath.

As the sailor struggled, gasping and kicking viciously at nothing, Aiyana pulled on Forest's arm. "Quickly, we must be away," she cried, pointing to lights that suddenly gleamed from a ship anchored nearby. "Forest, this place is not safe! If the authorities come, they will take me even as these men tried to!"

"Not like these men," Forest said, wiping a trail of blood from his nose. Looking at her through a puffed and bruised eye, he managed to nod. "But we'll leave."

They hurried from the dock, grateful for the darkness, and Aiyana left Forest in the shadows while she retrieved their horses from the stable. After paying the livery master, she helped Forest mount, and they rode back to Mistress Eliot's house.

A servant had heard the approaching hoofbeats and met them at the gate. "Who are you, and what is your business?" he called harshly, holding a lantern aloft. The man pursed his lips suspiciously when he saw Forest's battered face.

"If you please, we must speak to Mistress Eliot," Aiyana said, leaning forward in the saddle. "I am Aiyana Bailie, and this is Forest Glazier. We were at the dock to meet Reverend Eliot, but two seamen there waylaid us and would have done us harm. And Reverend Eliot did not come—"

"Reverend Eliot nearly died tonight," the servant said. "His ship was rammed by another, and only the gracious hand of God saved Master John and his companions. He's inside now with the missus and his doctor."

"Oh no!" Aiyana whispered, her hand at her throat.

"Is he well?" Forest asked, gathering his reins. "We will not trouble him if he is in no condition—"

"Master John would not turn Daniel Bailie's daughter away even if he lay at death's door," the servant answered, opening the gate. "Come in, and I'll see that you each find a bed and something to eat. You can speak to the master and mistress in the morning."

Aiyana bowed her head in relief and dropped her reins, suddenly bleary-eyed and unspeakably weary.

▾▴▾▴▾ The next morning, John Eliot heard their story while propped up in his bed, a downy white quilt spread over his lanky frame. As Hannah tenderly fussed over him, the aged minister listened without interruption while a bruised Forest told the story of the seamen who had threatened them the night before.

"You did right, my boy," Eliot answered when Forest had finished. His clear, observant eyes blazed despite his exhaustion. "You acted in self-defense and in defense of our young lady here. And, of course, you had no way of knowing that the *Howard Edward* was lying under a mile or so of water. In truth, I would have been on that dock to greet you if the devil's own accomplice hadn't destroyed our ship on its errand of mercy."

"My father," Aiyana whispered, hesitant to break into the conversation. "Is he well?"

"Forgive me, Aiyana, dear," the minister said, his eyes gentling. "How like us to ramble on about our misadventures when 'twas your father that brought you here in the first place. Yes, my dear, he is well. But a bit low in spirit, I'm afraid, since you and Mojag are both away from him. Thoughts of Mojag have particularly distressed him."

"Is there news about Mojag?" Aiyana asked, her heart jumping in her chest.

Eliot paused to blow his nose, then shook his head. "No news at all, I'm afraid," he said, smiling despite his reddened eyes and nose, evidence of a cold caught during last night's plunge into the freezing bay. "And with every day that passes, your father grows more concerned. He is a devout man, our Daniel, and a most unconventional one."

"I know," Aiyana whispered. She smiled brightly, though tears stung her eyes. "I would like to see him."

"Then you shall," Eliot answered, pounding the quilt with his fist. He looked to his wife. "My dearest Hannah," he asked, his tone suddenly humble and penitent, "since you will not allow me out of this bed, will you make arrangements with Master Gookin so these two young people can join Master Bailie today? And there's a shipment of blankets to be sent over, as well as a barrel or two of peas and some other provisions."

Hannah turned to Forest. "This one doesn't look as though he should be out of bed, either," she said, frowning. "Why, the sight of that black eye alone would cause any God-fearing soul to turn and run in the other direction—"

"I assure you, ma'am, that I am not the brute I appear to be," Forest answered, placing his hand upon his chest in a humble gesture. "And I am so beholden to your hospitality that anything I can do to make your life easier will be tantamount to a command. You have only to tell me what you need done, and I will do it."

The lady lifted a brow; then her mouth tipped in a faint smile. "I am beginning to understand what this young lady sees in you," she said, her wise little eyes bright and bemused. "Come, Master Glazier, and let me show you what has to be transported. Master Gookin will arrange everything, if he's yet out of his own bed. If all goes well, you should be under sail before midday."

Forest flashed Aiyana a grin and followed Mistress Eliot out of the room. Before Aiyana departed, she leaned forward and squeezed the minister's hand. "God bless you, sir, for all you have done."

"He already has, my child," the minister answered, amusement lurking in his deep-set eyes. "He already has."

▼▲▼▲ Aiyana thought Deer Island the most desolate place she had ever seen. Obeying the wind, the captain of the pinnace circled the island in the brief space of ten minutes, and Aiyana shifted closer to Forest's side as she stared at the place that was to be her prison and sanctuary for the indefinite future. A chilly, pearl-colored mist hung over the bare and bleak island, blown occasionally by a wild wind that hooted and slid over the rocks. A handful of leafless trees stood at its crest, and one abandoned gray field bore deep black wounds in neat, evenly spaced rows, the recent work of grave diggers.

On the opposite side of the island, far from the graves, clusters of people moved around a series of fires. Aiyana noticed that there were few wigwams and no materials from which they could readily be made. Over four hundred Indians, mostly citizens of the fourteen praying villages, had abandoned their homes and comforts to crowd into this dismal place and try to avoid certain death.

The air is lifeless here, Aiyana thought as she stepped onto the island. *If the English had tried to find the most melancholy spot in the world, they could not have found a more dreary spot than this one.*

But her father, thank God, was alive, his embrace warm and comforting. "Aiyana, it is good to see you," he murmured as he held her close. "I am so glad you have come."

"Father," she cried, choking back the words of protest that sprang to her lips. It wasn't right that he—that she—that *any* of them should be confined to this place. But he was powerless to change things, and she wouldn't spoil their reunion by complaining of events that couldn't be helped.

"So you have come to join me here on Deer Island?" he asked, his bright blue eyes twinkling as she pulled out of his embrace. "I'm sorry it's not the paradise you probably expected."

"I didn't expect paradise," she answered truthfully, noticing that his face seemed more lined than when they had parted a few months before. "But I didn't expect this, either. It's very . . . *depressing,* Father. How can you stand it?"

"Ah, Aiyana, I have come to thank God for it." He linked her arm through his and glanced back toward the dock. "Did you come alone? I thought mayhap Reverend Eliot might accompany you."

"Forest Glazier came with me," she said, lowering her eyes as she felt an unwelcome blush creep into her cheeks. This was not the time to talk of Forest. "But he is belowdecks helping Master

Gookin unload supplies. I think mayhap he wanted to give us time alone together."

"Very considerate of him." Her father smiled and gestured toward a lean-to that had been erected high on a hill behind a stand of scrubby trees. "Come, let me escort you to my cottage, where we can have a cup of tea."

His *cottage!* Shock caused words of protest to wedge in her throat as she examined the rough shelter to which her father led her. No walls, no floor, not even a decent roof. He had not a book, a chair, nor even a mat to lie upon. Only a fire, gleaming with a few reddened coals, and a charred stump of wood that someone had carved to serve as a pot.

A terrible sense of bitterness assailed her as she looked at the pitiable condition to which her father had been reduced. How could he accept this unfair treatment so graciously? He had always been a fighter, ready to battle for the values and ideals he believed in, but the English had given him no recourse but to surrender. With only his wits and the tools God had furnished, he had been able to richly provide for himself in the wilderness, but the English had forced him from the woods. And here he had to care not only for himself but also for four hundred mouths begging to be fed, four hundred souls who could not understand why God would punish them when they were trying their best to be civilized.

A dozen Indians sat under the shelter around a pitifully small fire, but they moved without complaint as Daniel and Aiyana approached. None of them had stools, mats, or furs beneath them, so Aiyana sank onto the damp sand and gave them a polite smile.

"We thank God for this exile," her father said, sitting beside her. "We rejoice in it. What our enemies intended for evil, God meant for our good. Through the years, Reverend Eliot and I have heard complaints that our Indians were not genuinely converted. 'How can the Indians be true Christians?' the Puritan leaders have asked us. They were convinced that the Indians sought our God because the natives were so deeply impressed by their English tools and knowledge." He raised his eyes to the sky. "My Puritan brothers do not realize that these natives have always recognized the Creator's hand. They only needed to know his name and learn of his Son's provision for salvation."

He lifted a hand and swept it over the group. "These are truly my brothers and sisters in Christ. The seed so easily planted in the wilderness and cultivated in the praying villages has taken strong root in the fertile ground of suffering. When we leave this place, all will see that the gospel has flourished in these hearts. It will bear fruit in happier, more productive years."

Tears slowly found their way down Aiyana's cheeks as she looked into the eyes of the people before her. Deer Island had etched pain and suffering onto their faces and pitifully thin bodies, but peace shone from their eyes. Even the children, clinging to their mothers' necks, smiled shyly as she looked at them, though of certain those little bellies were empty and those coppery arms chapped from the bite of the wind.

A sudden realization struck her. She had been looking at them with the eyes of an outsider. But she was an Indian and had been exiled to this barren, forsaken island until the war should cease. This pathetic lean-to was now her home, too.

"Aiyana, 'tis time to pray," her father said, pointing to the white sun overhead. "In the praying villages, we paused at midday to offer thanks for the food before us." He spread his empty hands. "Now we pray because our hearts hunger to know God better. Listen, Aiyana, and translate the prayers for me. Let me see if your ear is still quick after so many months with the English."

She tented her frozen fingers. A man in the circle lifted his dignified countenance to heaven and began to pray in Algonquin. "*Amanaomen Jehovah tahassen metogh.*"

"Take away, Lord, my stony heart," Aiyana whispered.

"*Chechesom Jehovah kekeowhogkow,*" he continued.

"Wash, Lord, my soul."

The words caught in her throat, their simple beauty overwhelming her. In the howling loneliness and scarcity of this place, this man thought first and foremost about the unworthiness of his heart. In the last few weeks she had thought of little but her own loves and concerns—her worries about Forest, Mojag, and her father, her own safety and comfort—while hundreds of men, women, and children here grew strong in the Lord and cleansed their hearts in the fire of testing.

Back in another compartment of her head, she heard Master Glazier's voice at evening prayers: *"We glory in tribulations also: knowing that tribulation worketh patience; and patience, experience; and experience, hope: And hope maketh not ashamed; because the love of God is shed abroad in our hearts by the Holy Ghost which is given unto us."*

Under a few scornful glances and belittling words, she had thought she suffered in Rehoboth, but now she shuddered in humiliation as the Spirit of God spoke to her heart. Her experiences paled in comparison to what these people had endured.

Her heart cried out in regret and repentance; then the comforting warmth of her father's hand slipped around her own.

▼▲▼▲▼ "Forest," Aiyana called, walking down to the dock, where he stood helping Reverend Eliot's men unload barrels and baskets of donated goods, "may I have a word with you?"

"Of certain," he said, straightening. He pressed a hand to his back as if he were exhausted, but his quick smile assured her that he was only teasing. Did his broad shoulders ever tire of the burdens he carried? He had escorted her through dangerous woods without complaint, he had endured a beating and nearly lost his life, and he had spent the morning hauling cast-off clothing and faded blankets for no reward other than a heartfelt thanks. He was noble, her Forest, too kind to speak his true thoughts, too well-mannered to abandon her.

"Forest," she said again when she had reached his side. She dropped her eyes before his steady gaze and spoke with quiet firmness. "According to the court order, I must remain here with my father and his people."

"I know, Aiyana," he said. She looked up; his expression had stilled and grown serious. "But this situation cannot last for long. And I have decided to ask Reverend Eliot if I might stay with you. I will write to my father, and he will understand why I am remaining."

"I want you to go." Her voice was heavy, dull, like a weight of iron falling to the ground with a resounding thud.

The impact of her words made him stiffen in surprise. "I beg your pardon?"

"I want you to go, Forest. You were kind to bring me to my father, but I don't want to be reminded of you while I am confined here." She bit her lip until it throbbed like her pulse, her anguish nearly overcoming her control. Freedom was her parting gift to him. *Please, God, let him understand and walk away without making a scene. Then my memories of him will always be sweet. . . .*

He stared at her without speaking, and then his blue eyes flashed with outrage. A wave of fear overwhelmed her—she had expected protestations, hurt, and refusal, but not anger.

"Aiyana, what makes you think that I could just go? You once accused me of making decisions without consulting you, but now you expect me to walk away as if you mean nothing—"

"Forest, you must understand," she interrupted, averting her eyes. "I can't ask you to remain here on this pitiful island."

"Then I will wait for you in Boston. Reverend Eliot will help me find work in the city."

"No, I don't want you to wait. Your father and sister need you in Rehoboth."

"They will be fine without me."

"Then what about—" she could not keep the edge from her voice—"your *business?*"

He said nothing, but stood motionless in astonished silence. Even while looking at the ground, she could feel his eyes upon her.

"If that's what you think, then so be it." His voice was crisp.

"I'll return to Rehoboth until the war is over, but I must speak to your father first. When the fighting is done, I'll come back here for you."

"No." A sensation of desolation swept over her. "I don't expect you to marry me, Forest. I know this has all been . . . too much."

"Too much?" His fist clenched. "For whom, Aiyana?"

"For me." She tore herself away with a choking cry and sprinted toward her father's lean-to on the hill.

Mojag was home on Martha's Vineyard. Gentle clouds sudsed the blue
sky as his village shimmered in the slanted sunlight of early morning.
Scents of spring wafted through the air, mingling with the aroma of
roasting venison. As the day opened peacefully before him, Ootadabun
slept next to him, rosy-cheeked and tempting.

Something nudged his foot, and Mojag's mind gripped at the
dream, held onto it with terrible longing.

"You must wake, my husband." The whisper slashed his sleep
like a knife, rousing him to wakefulness. He opened one eye and
smiled. His wife sat beside him on her knees, her eyes wide with
entreaty. She threw a quick glance over her shoulder to be certain
no one else in the wigwam would hear. "Come outside and tell
me what happened to the one called Abram."

Though he wanted to pull her to him and linger in the sweet
embrace of sleep, he grunted and sat up, tossing his blanket from
his shoulders. A thrill shivered through his senses when he
looked at the girl who had become his wife, but he disguised his
joy and gave her a discreet nod. Standing, he walked outside the
crowded wigwam, listening for her gentle footfalls behind him.

They had taken refuge deep within the Narragansett territory
north of Worden's Pond with the other Pokanokets who remained
with Metacomet. The sachem felt secure here, knowing that the
English were too clumsy to maneuver in the mucky terrain. On a
small rise, Metacomet's people had helped build a village protected by tall stakes set upright in the ground and surrounded by
thick masses of tree limbs and brush several yards thick. Within
the wall, the village consisted of many crowded huts in which

lived more than a thousand Narragansett, Nipmuck, and Wampanoag Indians united to make war against the English.

Wandering through crowds of men, women, and children, Mojag led his wife toward the edge of the encampment, to the very wall itself. When he was certain no one had followed, he sat upon the hard ground and pulled Ootadabun down to sit in front of him. "Where did I end the story yesterday?" he asked, gripping her cold hands.

"Abram heard God's call and left his people," she answered, her dark eyes glowing with excitement and curiosity. "Your God called him from the place called Ur."

"I remember," Mojag answered, feeling his heart turn over the way it always did when she looked at him. She was so open, so eager to learn, and so receptive to the gospel! If only Metacomet would listen with half the interest Ootadabun did!

"God called Abram to leave his parents and his people," Mojag said, entwining his fingers with hers. "But God never calls a man without a reason. When God told Abram to go, he promised to make from him a great nation. God said that Abram's name would be revered and that all the nations of the world would one day thank God for him. So Abram departed from his people and his place, taking his wife and his nephew, and they journeyed into an unknown country, a land of fierce kings who did not know Abram's God."

His wife's soft, watchful eyes missed nothing. She sat silently, waiting for him to continue, her face like gold in the early morning light. Mojag had to restrain himself from gathering her into his arms. Her innocence and willingness to learn were the precious fuel that kept him dedicated to his task of proclaiming God's truth to Metacomet.

"What happened next?" Ootadabun whispered, squeezing his hand. "Did this Abram become a mighty man?"

Mojag nodded. "Yes. He obeyed God, subdued kings, and from his lineage came the Redeemer, Jesus Christ, who has power to cleanse sin from the stained heart of any willing believer. In him all the nations of the earth have been blessed, including the Wampanoag. Many of your tribe have followed Jesus and renounced the old gods."

"Like me," she whispered, her face lighting up like sunshine bursting out of the clouds.

"Yes," Mojag answered, keeping his voice low. He leaned forward and brushed a strand of dark hair out of her face. "And like Abram, I have left my people to come among the warriors of a fierce king. As you work today, my wife, whisper a prayer to the true God and ask him to soften Metacomet's heart. Ask him to protect us until the time—"

A shadow fell across them, and Mojag looked up to see one of the sachem's counselors standing nearby. "He calls for you," the man said simply, staring down at them. The counselor's smile was strained, his eyes hard and wary.

Mojag squeezed his wife's shoulder, then stood to his feet. "Remember what I have told you," he said, then he lifted his chin and followed the warrior to Metacomet's hut.

▼▲▼▲▼ As the leaves fell and the gray bones of the trees began to show, Metacomet's thoughts turned from war to winter. Though his warriors still rode out on occasional sorties to harass and perplex the enemy, the Indian sachem's primary concern was feeding, housing, and caring for the thousand men, women, and children who traveled with him. He had asked many tribes to join his cause, and since they had, he could not abandon them to winter's merciless winds and hunger.

The huts in the great swamp fortress held many clay pots of dried corn, enough to feed the company through the winter, but his warriors needed meat if they were to remain strong for battle. Even Mukki, Metacomet noticed, had grown lean from the hungry days of forced marching through the woods. He wanted his son to enjoy the fullness of health and strength that he and his brothers had known in the prosperous years of Massasoit's leadership. So for a time, his warriors must become hunters.

Last night, as he had looked out over the camp to select men who might prove adept at finding meat without encountering trouble with the English, his eyes had fallen upon Askuwheteau, the praying man. Though the man still insisted he would not fight against the English, he had on several occasions ventured out to hunt. But hunting was hardly a test of loyalty, and Metacomet had been much troubled of late. His scouts had brought back reports of disloyal Indians who, lured by promises of bounty and riches, had turned to cooperate with the English. Though Ootadabun bound Askuwheteau to the tribe, a woman was not worth a man's life. Under duress this praying Indian might be convinced to betray those he called his brothers.

A sudden thought whipped into Metacomet's mind. He had allowed the praying man to remain in the village to see if his heart could be swayed, so why not test him in a more direct way? He knew the praying man often spoke of his God. Some said that Ootadabun had already begun to pray to Lord Jesus. But if Askuwheteau and his God were put to the test, they would surely fail. In the face of defeat Askuwheteau might consider returning to the English, but Metacomet would have him hunted down and killed before he could betray his people.

But perhaps the praying man would not leave. Metacomet smiled and tipped his face to the sun. Love burned bright in Askuwheteau's eyes. He might return to his woman no matter how shameful his disgrace. Then Metacomet could feed him and his false heart to the flames, the proper place for all traitors. If the woman protested, she would burn, too. And the people would see and know that He-Who-Waits spoke falsely, that no man could speak of peace and live with war.

The quiet clicking of wampum beads brought Metacomet's eyes from the sky. He looked down to see Annawon, an esteemed sachem of Squannock, approach with Askuwheteau. Without ceremony, the pair sat down on mats beside Metacomet's smoldering fire.

"Go play with the other boys," Metacomet called to Mukki, giving his son a playful smile.

"Will you paint my back later?" the boy asked, turning.

"Later," Metacomet promised, nodding. "Now go."

Mukki scampered away, and Metacomet turned toward the men who waited for his attention. Three other elders had also come to sit by his fire. Corbitant, the sachem of the Mattapoisett and Pocasset people; Matoonas, a sachem of Pakachoog who had once been a constable of a praying-Indian community; and Naonanto, a sachem of the Narragansett. Of such esteemed men Metacomet was the least, but because he had been the first to see the inevitability of war, his voice was respected. Matoonas was especially considerate of Metacomet, for the Pakachoog sachem had come to distrust the English and their God ever since the Yangeese executed his son for a murder of which he was clearly innocent.

"Brothers," Metacomet said, nodding first to Naonanto as a sign of respect, "you know that the Yangeese ministers often called our people to pray to Lord Jesus."

The sachems nodded. Matoonas put down his pipe and leaned forward in interest.

"Though they no longer move among us, another does. This one—" Metacomet looked to Askuwheteau—"from the island of Noepe, has wintered among us, taken a wife, and teaches her to pray to the Yangeese God." He lifted his brows and spoke directly to Askuwheteau. "Do you deny my words?"

Determination lay in the jut of the young man's chin. "No, Sachem, I do not."

Metacomet pressed his lips together. "Then you can understand why I am concerned that your heart is not with us. I have decided to propose a contest so the truth will be known. My powwows will pray to our gods, and you will beseech yours for the meat this village needs to find strength for the winter. You will join our hunters to search for a well-fed elk. And we will see which gods have the power to meet our needs."

"An elk?" Annawon lowered his pipe. The old man's weather-beaten face was beginning to erode like a granite cliff, but his dignity had never been more powerful. "The elk left this part of the world many seasons ago. They have moved past the river the Yangeese call Connecticut—"

"Then let the gods call the elk back to us," Metacomet said, frowning. "They are gods."

Annawon shrugged and puffed on his pipe again.

"When do we leave?" Askuwheteau asked, a flash of defensive spirit shining through his eyes.

Metacomet closed his eyes and pretended to consider the question, though he had already decided and assembled a team of expert hunters. "Today, at midday," he said, opening his eyes again. "You must return by sunset tomorrow."

"I beg you to consider one thing, Sachem," Askuwheteau said, lifting his hand. "Your warriors have muskets. I have no gun, only a bow and arrows that I have made."

A smile tugged at Metacomet's lips. "If your God is all-powerful," he said, his eyes moving over the faces of his companions, "then surely a bow and arrow—even a stone—would be enough."

Askuwheteau closed his eyes and nodded slowly in answer.

▼▲▼▲▼ Crouching in the brush, Mojag lowered his belly to the moist black earth. The slippery, wet leaves beneath his clothing chilled him. Discouraged, he thrust his bow aside and cradled his head in his hands. How foolish he had been, thrashing through the woods like a madman in the bold light of day! In his panic he had probably set every animal within ten miles to flight or even alerted passing English scouts to his presence. If he wasn't killed, lost, or frozen during the night, it would be a miracle of God.

In the hours between Metacomet's announcement and the beginning of the hunt, Mojag had time only to urge Ootadabun to pray for his success, to eat a quick meal of bread, corn, and stew, and to check his bow and arrows. As he prepared, his thoughts whirred in a confused pattern. What had possessed Metacomet to issue such a challenge, and why had he thought such a test necessary? In a surge of memory, Mojag recalled the Bible story of the prophets of Baal who begged their gods to send fire from heaven. Why hadn't Mojag suggested the sachem try *that* test? Mojag thought it more likely to summon fire from the sky than to find an elk in the woods. In his year with the Indians, he had never seen such a creature. And even if God was merciful and sent an elk, how could he kill an animal of that tremendous size? One arrow would only wound it, and he suspected an elk could run for miles at great speed before stopping.

A cynical inner voice cut through his thoughts. He had been raised among *civilized* Indians in a proper praying village; he knew more about planting corn than stalking mighty game. As always, he was in the wrong place at the wrong time. *God in heaven, what have you done to me now?*

He knew, with pulse-pounding certainty, that this was not a test of skill but of loyalty. He had wintered at Metacomet's request. He had taken a wife from the Pokanoket. He had obeyed every law of the tribe and endured hardship without complaint. And yet distrust still filled the sachem's eyes when he looked at Mojag. *Perhaps fear drives him to test me. Perhaps he fears the God I serve because God is the God of the English who make war upon him.*

"Holy God," Mojag murmured, lowering his face to the cold, black ground, "the price for failure will be high. If I run from this contest and do not return, Metacomet will mock you before the people and Ootadabun will doubt all that I have said. But if I return without an elk, Metacomet will say that my words are false and cannot be trusted. He may even brand me a traitor and demand my death."

The flash of gold on his right hand caught his eye, and his mouth twisted into a smile of amused resentment. The inscription on the family ring urged him to live boldly, faithfully, and successfully, but all he had done thus far was make his father angry, his sister miserable, and his wife confused. He had imagined himself to be a fisher of men, but while everyone else fished from the safety of shore, he had insisted on sailing out upon troubled waters where sharks roved with black eyes and razor-sharp

smiles. How could he have imagined himself called of God? It
was more likely that Aiyana was right—Ootadabun's sweet
beauty had blinded his reason and hypnotized his spirit. Perhaps
he had fantasized his own calling and Hania was but a figment
in a dream.

If Hania had truly appeared to him, where was the angel
now? Mojag's life depended upon this test—the spiritual destiny
of an Indian nation might be settled by the simple provision of
an elk. So why didn't Hania appear and solve Mojag's problem?

"I am a messenger, not your arm of salvation."

The voice rang in the halls of Mojag's memory, setting his teeth
on edge. He couldn't have invented Hania. The angel had
appeared in the past, but he wouldn't come this time. With crystal
clarity, Mojag recognized the truth. He was to look not to Hania
for help and salvation but to God. Hania had relayed a calling
and a warning; now Mojag had to depend on God for an answer.
In desperation, Mojag called out to the Almighty. And waited.

His thoughts were like gliding clouds, fading in and out of the
heavens, and suddenly Mojag realized that he was dreaming. A
bright light, more intense than the sun on a summer's day, suddenly surrounded him. Hundreds of animals swarmed in the
light: squirrels, birds, foxes, wolves, raccoons, deer, beavers,
horses, muskrat, otters, and, moving resolutely toward him, a
majestic elk with antlers as wide as a wigwam.

"'Tis but a dream," Mojag whispered, his voice echoing, ghost-
like, in his own ears. "Metacomet asks too much, God. He
requires the impossible, for though I see an elk in this dream,
there are none in this part of the woods."

A stentorian voice rumbled like thunder through the woods:
*"Nothing is too much, my child. If I cannot provide a mere creature,
how can I grant eternal life to the lost soul who seeks it? Metacomet
must see that I am able to do all things."*

His fingers trembling, Mojag picked up his bow, then reached
over his shoulder for an arrow from his quiver. As he strung the
arrow, the elk turned wide, expressive eyes upon him, then
shifted its stance as if to expose the portion of his breast where

the arrow should lodge for a quick, painless kill. Without understanding how such a thing could be possible, Mojag pulled back the bowstring, centered the arrow, then closed his eyes and let the missile fly.

He heard the whizzing of the arrow through the air, then the soft sound of impact. When he opened his eyes, the assembly of animals had disappeared, but a mammoth elk lay upon the ground before him.

Mojag scrambled forward, his hands burying themselves in the tangled, rough, *real* hair of the elk's hide. Impossible to believe, but he held proof of God's provision! The creature beneath him smelled of the woods; red blood trickled from the small wound in the beast's willing heart.

Mojag felt his eyes fill with hot tears as he fell upon the creature, spreading his arms as he thanked God for this deliverance. He would sleep here tonight to protect his kill from marauding wolves, and on the morrow he'd build a sledge to drag the heavy carcass back to the village. For whether God had summoned an elk from beyond the Connecticut or created one from thin air, nothing mattered but that his glory and power would be proclaimed among the heathen of Metacomet's camp.

▾▲▾▲ He could hear shouts of jubilation even as he approached through the swamp. The muscles in his back and arms burned from dragging the heavy carcass, and Mojag paused at the narrow entrance to the fort, dropping the dried vines with which he pulled the bark sledge. The scents of frying meat and smoke hung heavy in the air—had the other hunters found an elk, too? It was very like Satan to counterfeit God's miracles; maybe Mojag's victory would not be apparent after all.

The lookout saw him and fired his musket; the sound echoed through the camp and brought an abrupt halt to the merrymaking within the enclosure. "The praying man comes!" the guard shouted, and Mojag knew the others were lining up inside the palisade, anxious to see whether or not his God could provide.

Well, they could wait. His body ached from the bounty of God's provision.

Suddenly, unexpected strength flowed through his arms and legs as he pulled the sledge forward, his pace increasing until he could see men and children tossing aside bundles of brush as they cleared an opening for him. Excited whoops rang out as the entire village recognized the elk's huge head like a towering trophy behind Mojag's perspiring back. On and on, he pulled his burden through the exuberant crowd, until he stood before Metacomet's hut. There he dropped the ropes in his blistered hands and slowly straightened before the incredulous eyes of the sachem's little son.

"An elk?" Mukki asked, astonishment on his young face.

Mojag nodded.

Metacomet came out of his hut, then gave the elk a quick, denying glance. Lifting his chin, he turned to Mojag. "You are the last hunter to return," he said simply.

"My God has provided our needs," Mojag answered, gesturing to the elk behind him. "He not only led me to the elk for which I prayed, but he has given me the strength to kill the animal and haul it to this camp in order that our people may eat."

A vein in Metacomet's forehead swelled like a thick, black snake. "Our gods provided the other hunters with foxes, deer, raccoons, and beavers," he said, spreading his arms toward the simmering pots on the women's fires. "Our gods have answered our prayers for meat, too. Our gods will feed us as well as your God."

"But my God has provided exactly what you asked for," Mojag answered quietly. "You wanted an elk, great Sachem, and that is what he brought to me, his servant." Lifting his voice, he dared to broadcast the words that lay on his heart. "You say you want peace in the land. If you do, my God can provide it. But first you must seek him with a repentant heart and turn from the false gods who cannot satisfy."

"The Yangeese God?" Metacomet cried, venom in his voice.

Mukki stepped back, startled. "And what is his name, that I may seek him?"

"His name is Jehovah, and his Son's name is Jesus the Christ," Mojag answered. "He has promised to answer any and all who call upon him, no matter if they be Indian or English, French or Spanish. Hear me, great Sachem, and heed my words."

"Bah!" Metacomet lifted his hand to brush away the words, but Mojag knew he faced a toothless lion. The sachem would not harm him now—his honor would not allow it. Mojag had met the conditions of the test.

"Your God answered to provide for our needs, so you may remain with the people," Metacomet said, eying Mojag as if he were a bad smell. "But our gods have spoken, too, and you will not deny them." He lifted his hands toward the crowd. "We have meat, so let us eat and rejoice in this time of plenty. The Yangeese sleep in their houses, afraid of snakes and owls, so let us rejoice that the gods, even their God, provide for us."

Shoulder-high snowdrifts covered the knobby hill of Deer Island during the harsh winter of 1675–1676. The provisions for the Indians that had been ordered by the General Court were slow in coming. Indeed, supply ships came less often than did Indians, many of whom had been rounded up, bound, and herded like cattle to Boston, where leaky boats then transported them to the island. John Eliot and Daniel Gookin continued to visit as often as they could, and Aiyana and her father worked in the camp to administer medicines, blankets, food, and comfort.

Throughout the winter, Aiyana saw and heard nothing of Forest Glazier, and she could not bring herself to ask about him. Her father must have sensed that something was amiss, for his eyes often rested upon her in troubled speculation, but he respected her privacy and did not pry into her thoughts.

John Eliot visited as often as his health would allow, often bringing terrible tales of injustices committed against the Indians. One blustery afternoon in January, Aiyana huddled against the wall of their small shelter while Eliot sat by the fire and told the story of Captain Tom, a praying Indian of Natick, who had been misidentified as a participant in an attack against Sudbury. Eliot attended the trial, heard Captain Tom's denial of the charge, and visited him in prison after his conviction. "I dealt faithfully with him," Eliot told Aiyana and her father, "to confess if the charge were true, and I believe he told the truth. I accompanied him to his death on the day of execution, and on the ladder of the scaffold he raised his eyes to heaven and said, 'I never did lift up a hand against the English, nor was I at Sudbury.' This he said; then he was hanged."

"That's terrible!" Aiyana gasped, shivering in her blanket.

"There are worse things than death," Eliot went on. "While the praying Indians are sent here to Deer Island, presumably for their own safety, captives taken in the war are either summarily executed or sold to slave merchants for captivity in the West Indies."

"Slavery?" Daniel's head jerked sharply upward. "I have told you, John, that I detest slavery. One has only to spend a night aboard a slave ship to know God did not intend for men to treat one another so cruelly."

"Selling souls for money has always seemed to me a dangerous enterprise," Eliot answered, sipping a cup of birch-bark tea. "After begging the governor and the Council to pardon my boldness, I urged them to weigh the reason and religion that labors in this great case of conscience. I am afraid that the Indians' adversaries think only how to exterminate them. They do not realize that freedom is the cornerstone of Indian life. No one, not even a sachem, commands another native. They are best wooed by affectionate counsel, not force. I fear slavery will bring an end to them all."

Aiyana shivered through fleeting nausea as John Eliot then told the story of Squando, a sachem of the northern Saco tribe. The Saco, who were not affiliated with the Wampanoag, had not been involved in the war during its first few months. But shortly after the war's outbreak, Squando's wife was traveling by canoe with her baby boy when she met a boatload of English sailors. "The seamen," Eliot explained, pain flickering in his eyes, "drunken, rude, and doubtless behaving under the prevalent notion that all Indians are better off dead, had heard that Indian babies possess an instinctive ability to swim. So when they spied the child with Squando's wife, they charged the canoe, upset it, and captured the woman and her baby. While one seaman held the child's frantic mother, another dropped the baby into the water, waiting to see if it could swim."

"Did it?" Aiyana gasped, her heart in her throat.

"The child sank like any other," Eliot said, shaking his head in disgust. "And the anguished mother tore herself free and dived in after him. She finally emerged with the babe in her arms, but the boy died. And Squando, who had accepted our Lord and Christianity, has led his tribe and the entire Abnaki nation to war against the English."

Aiyana felt ice spreading through her stomach. In Rehoboth she had heard nothing but tales of Indian atrocities; now she heard stories of English cruelty. "It is all so terrible," she whispered, her voice breaking. "How could they have been so heartless?"

Eliot's gray brows flickered a little. "Many have excused the sailors' actions by saying the child would surely have died eventually." Lowering his voice, he continued, "But my heart breaks when I hear how God's people have forgotten mercy and reacted to savagery with equal brutality. 'Tis said that Captain Mosely ordered one Indian woman to be torn to pieces by his dogs. And in Marblehead, Massachusetts, a group of women emerging from church set upon two Indian prisoners and literally tore them apart with their bare hands."

Closing her eyes, Aiyana covered her mouth with her hand. Such inhumanity was unthinkable. And yet Mojag was in the midst of the Indians, and Forest undoubtedly fought with the English.

"Has Forest Glazier—," she asked, daring to speak his name for the first time since their separation. Her eyes moved into those of the white-haired minister. "Has there been word of his safe return to Rehoboth?"

The reverend's lips parted in surprise. "I'm sorry, my dear, I thought you knew."

"Knew what?"

"That he had decided to remain in Roxbury. Mistress Eliot wouldn't allow him to return alone through the wilderness, and I daresay she enjoys having a young man around the house. Our children are grown and gone, you know, and there is much work to be done. My legs are quite unable to carry me everywhere they used to, and young Forest seems tireless." He smiled at the sudden relief in her eyes.

"Thank you," Aiyana whispered, suspecting that he understood something of her feelings.

John Eliot looked over at her father. "You'll like this young man, Daniel," he said, pushing himself to a standing position. "And as I understand it, when the war is over he intends to marry your daughter. If you approve, of course."

"I have always liked Forest," Daniel answered, his eyes searching Aiyana's face as if he could read her thoughts. "But my daughter's happiness matters first and foremost. We shall see what God wills, John, when the time comes."

"Amen," Eliot answered. "And I hope and pray that peace will come soon. I have finally convinced the Council that our praying Indians could help the colonies end this struggle. Major Thomas Savage has testified that our natives have proved themselves courageous and faithful soldiers. And no one can deny that they are much more at home in the swamps than the English."

"The English army is recruiting Indians?" Aiyana asked, her heart skipping a beat. She had believed Mojag safe as long as the regimented English stumbled around in the swamps. But if Indians came against him. . . .

"Yes," her father answered. "Our people are expert trackers, and they can march rapidly along the forest trails without making a sound. They can live off the land when necessary, and unlike the English, they are at home in the wilderness. They can also act as spies, mingling with enemy Indians to gain information about hidden forts. In fact—" he paused for a moment and rested his hands on his knees—"I have volunteered to go with them. I speak both languages and can survive in the woods as well as anyone."

"No!" Aiyana cried, caught off guard by his announcement. She clutched at his arm. "Can you have forgotten about Mojag? Would you lead the English to him?"

Embarrassed, Reverend Eliot looked away while her father

patted her hand. "I have not forgotten my son," Daniel said, clearing his throat as if a host of emotions had clotted there. "But he is his own man, Aiyana. He follows what he believes is God's plan for his life, and I must follow God's will for mine. Mayhap our paths will meet."

"If God is merciful," Aiyana interrupted, her voice trembling, "they will not."

"Aiyana." Reverend Eliot, who had been squinting out at the camp, suddenly turned and gestured outside. "There is someone here who would like to see you, I think."

Stooping beneath the framework of saplings and blankets, Forest came into the shelter. At the sight of him, Aiyana felt her surroundings swirl madly around her. She had not seen him in nearly three months, and for a moment the reality of his presence took her breath away.

"Aiyana," he whispered. His voice was thick and unsteady, as if the reunion had left him off balance, too.

"John, I believe I should walk you to the dock," her father said, lifting an eyebrow in her direction as he stood and slipped his arm under the minister's hand. Aiyana waited until the two men had left; then she lifted her eyes to Forest's dear face. He seemed older somehow, and more self-assured. The shadow of a beard upon his cheek gave him an even more masculine aura, and his profile seemed more rugged and somber than when she had last seen him.

"Forest, I was so afraid for you," she whispered, scarcely trusting herself to speak. "I thought you had returned to Rehoboth—"

"I would not leave you. You may tell me to leave a thousand times, but I will not. My heart is with you, Aiyana, and will be until my dying day."

She stood and swallowed a sob as hot tears slipped down her cheeks. "I thought—you were so silent on the journey here, I thought the war had killed your love. I was sure you promised to marry me only because you are honorable and kind."

"Aiyana!" Surprise, disbelief, and blinding joy mingled on his face as he came toward her and wound his hand through her hair. "If you only knew," he whispered, gathering her into his arms. "If I was silent, 'twas because I worried about how to cope with being alone with you. If I seemed distant, 'twas only because I was afraid that I might offend in word or deed or thought. . . . I wanted to hold you. I wanted to stop and cradle you in my arms until the world went away, and yet I could not!"

"Truly?" she whispered, lifting her head to look into his eyes. "I thought my prattling about the people at Rehoboth had offended you."

"Aiyana, you are the light God has used to illuminate my path," Forest answered, his breath softly fanning her face. "I may not always understand the things you speak of, but I am willing to listen."

His eyes drifted to her lips, and Aiyana offered them freely, giving herself to the passion of his kiss. When he finally pulled away, he traced his fingers across her forehead. "I am glad you are not still angry with me. I was reluctant to come, but Hannah insisted that I speak with you."

"I wasn't angry, Forest. I was . . . confused." Her arms squeezed him gently. "I thought you no longer cared."

"A man is not like a woman," he whispered in a ragged voice. "There are . . . *strong desires* that should not be encouraged until after a man's marriage. At least, not without certain safeguards."

"Safeguards?" she asked with a teasing smile. "Like the host of people outside? Are they the reason you can kiss me now, and you couldn't in the woods?"

"In part," he answered, grinning down at her. His smile suddenly straightened. "I had to see you today because I am going away for a while. Even if you still did not wish to see me, I had to be sure you were well."

"You're leaving? Why?"

"I am joining the militia."

Her heart leapt in her chest like a startled bird. "Not you, too! Shall I lose you and my father at once?"

"Do not worry, Aiyana." His eyes held hers tenderly. "When I heard that your father had volunteered for the militia, I decided to join him. I can keep him company, and mayhap impress him of my suitability as a son-in-law." He gave her a crooked smile. "The sooner this conflict is ended, dearest, the sooner I can free you from this miserable place. I have suffered knowing the hardships you face, and if joining the army can help end the struggle—"

"You don't have to do this just to impress my father. Reverend Eliot has already assured him that you are a worthy man."

"I must do this. I know your heart cannot rest until your father and brother are safe. If you are not at rest, Aiyana, neither am I."

His announcement left her with an inexplicable feeling of emptiness. She moved into his embrace and rested her cheek against the cloth of his coat. "Is there nothing I can say to make you change your mind?"

"My happiness lies in your eyes, Aiyana," he said, his hand falling upon her head. "As my love resides safely in your heart. Pray for us and for an end to this brutal war. And may God have mercy upon us all."

▼▲▼▲▼ Forest flung the blanket from his bed as someone slammed open the door of his room. "Rise, Forest Glazier!" Even through the fog of sleep he recognized the strong, commanding voice of Magistrate Daniel Gookin, one of John Eliot's assistants. Forest opened his heavy eyes. Gookin stood in the doorway, wearing a simple cloak over a nightshirt, breeches, and boots. Only something urgent could have pulled him from his bed in the dead of a winter night.

"What is amiss?" Forest mumbled, fumbling to find his breeches in the dim light of a candlestick.

"Last month we sent two Christian Indians to spy among the enemy. Tonight they have come to my house with word that Lancaster will be attacked tomorrow."

"Lancaster?" Forest frowned, reaching for his boots. The town lay about thirty-five miles to the northwest of Boston, but it was a sizable settlement and farther north than any thus far attacked by the Indians.

"Yes." Gookin held his candlestick aloft and eyed Forest critically. "You are to take the shallop to Deer Island tonight and round up the Indians who are willing to enlist in our cause. We must advance toward Lancaster without delay."

"Aye," Forest answered, buttoning his shirt. "What exactly did these spies tell you?"

Gookin drew his lips into a tight smile. "Job Kattenanit reports that four hundred of the enemy are on their way to Lancaster even as we speak. I've already dispatched messengers to Concord, Marlborough, and Lancaster, but I do not dare hope they will reach those towns in time to do any good. But Captain Wadsworth's small force is already garrisoned at Marlborough. If word reaches him by daybreak, mayhap he can ride for Lancaster and turn the enemy into the woods before too much damage is done."

Forest slipped into his coat and threw his scarf around his neck. "I'll ride as swiftly as I can," he promised, striding past the elderly magistrate. "Is the shallop at the docks?"

"I have a man stationed there. You will have to rouse him from sleep, though," Gookin answered, following him down the hall. "He sleeps in the cabin of the *Wayfarer*, a ship docked at a northern berth."

"God will help me find it," Forest answered. He paused to give the worried man a smile of reassurance. "Pray for us, Master Gookin."

"I will, my son," the older man answered. His expression was compassionate, troubled, and still. "And if I were twenty years younger—"

"We need men like you and Reverend Eliot to command us," Forest answered. He paused and glanced toward the door leading to Master Eliot's bedchamber.

"Go," Gookin said, guessing his concern. "I'll wake John and Hannah after you've gone. I don't want to upset them unduly in the dark of night—'tisn't healthy for a man of his age, you know."

Forest nodded. He drew his scarf closer about his neck against the freezing wind as Magistrate Gookin wished him Godspeed.

Sitting in the doorway of his wigwam, Mojag's troubled eyes rested upon the smoldering fire in the center of the makeshift camp. The war's relentless fury had risen again; a war party had departed hours ago, set upon the pretty little village of Lancaster, a quiet town of about fifty homes, brimming barns, and only six garrison houses. Following Lancaster, Metacomet had announced, the exposed towns of Groton, Marlborough, and Medfield would fall. Each town would be vacated, the sachem predicted, until the English were forced to return to Acawmenoakit, the island of the strangers, the land on the other side. England.

No longer did the Wampanoag fight alone. The Norwottock, a peaceful tribe that had opposed war, had joined in the fight when the Yangeese militia demanded that the warriors of the tribe surrender their weapons. The Agawam, who had lived peacefully beside the English at Springfield, were angered to war when the people of Springfield decided they should take the Agawams' weapons and hold some of their children as hostages against the peace. And when the notorious Indian-hater Samuel Mosely burned two peaceful native villages in New Hampshire for no reason, tribes that had formerly been content to live in peace blazed in righteous anger. The Pocumtuck, the Narragansett, the Nipmuck, the Abnaki—virtually all tribes and nations in the region—had struck the war post against the Yangeese.

No longer was neutrality or peace possible. Mojag's blood still ran thick with despair when he remembered what had happened in the great swamp fortress shortly after Metacomet's people had pulled out and moved northward. A great force of English, drawn by promises of land as well as their wages as soldiers, had assembled in December. Aided by a captured Narragansett called Indian Peter, the English army slogged through the swamps and found the concealed entrance of the nearly impregnable fortress. Forgetting—or ignoring, Mojag reasoned—the ancient and honorable Algonquin tradition of warning before an attack, the traitorous Peter stood back and watched as the English sprang out of the woods in a surprise assault. They could not enter the well-defended fortress, so they fired the walls and wigwams. More than six hundred Narragansetts—most of them women, children, and the aged—had burned alive in the massacre. Three hundred warriors were taken prisoner. Of the wounded, English and Indian, forty died during the long march back through the wilderness to Wickford.

When the story of the great swamp fight spread, tribes that had been reluctant to declare war streamed forward like aroused and angry bees to attack the Yangeese who had violated their land, their treaties, and their ancient Algonquin war codes. And though the Indians knew that the English cursed King Philip as the devil incarnate, Metacomet no longer controlled the war. Canonchet, leader of a thousand Narragansetts, and Muttawmp, a sachem of the Nipmuck, wielded far more power in the war council than did the leader of the Wampanoag.

Canonchet and Muttawmp had marked Lancaster for eradication. Since Monoco, a sachem of the Nashaway known to the Yangeese as One-eyed John, had attacked Lancaster early in the war, they sent Monoco and his warriors to finish the destruction of that town.

As the united tribes struck harsh blows again and again, Mojag found himself wondering if Metacomet might not realize his dream. Out of ninety white settlements in the area, fifty-two had been attacked and twelve had been completely destroyed and abandoned. In weeks past, he had heard that Rehoboth had been attacked again and nearly leveled. Metacomet now bragged that he would invade Plymouth itself.

But though victory had never seemed so close, hunger and

want hovered over the Indian villages. The gardens and fishing places near their old homes were now denied to them, and they had not found new ones. Their winter stores were depleted, and the woods teemed with enemy scouts. Women and children grew thin and long-faced in the camps; the elders grew weak and died from illness. In private, unguarded moments, many warriors wore the faces of worried, frightened family men. Every night one or two more were missing from the circles around the fires. The absent ones had gathered their women and children and struck out to find a place to fish, hunt, and plant, and Mojag knew as well as Metacomet that the English would never allow these hungry ones to live in the land. Those who did not travel with an armed party would be killed; perhaps all of them would die. Only God knew the future.

"War is better at abolishing nations than nations are at abolishing war," Mojag whispered, staring mindlessly at the bustling camp before him. He had said as much yesterday as he sat at Metacomet's fire, but the sachem had only laughed at him.

This morning, after nearly four hundred warriors had departed for Lancaster, Metacomet and a party of his trusted counselors had ridden northward, still in search of allies from the northern tribes. Mojag's heart was heavy with despair as he watched the sachem go. Back at the swamp fort, when he had seen God's clear hand of provision, he had been certain that Metacomet would open his heart to the truth. But the sachem remained as bent on destruction as ever.

Were Mojag's prayers not working? Did some secret sin block his effectiveness? Was it possible that his love for Ootadabun stood in the way of the sachem's salvation?

Mojag could not find the answers, and he grew weary with the struggle. Hania had called him Askuwheteau, He-Who-Waits, and he was waiting still. No matter that Canonchet was now the chief sachem, Mojag's heart was still burdened for Metacomet. Something in the man's tender care of his wife and son bespoke a sensitivity to righteousness. He was not far, Mojag believed, from accepting God's truth, but his pride and the expectations of his people seemed to keep him from what he truly sought.

But in time of war, truth was the first casualty. Metacomet had heard the gospel. He had seen God's providing hand. He had escaped a hundred traps because God was merciful and sustained his life. And yet he preferred to believe the lies of his powwows . . . and his pride.

▼▲▼▲▼ Miles away, on the beach near Boston, Daniel and a host of other natives from Deer Island stripped off their English shirts and breeches and painted their bodies with cold mud from the water's edge. *The English asked us to become civilized,* Daniel thought, warming the mud between his hands, *and now they ask us to become savages again. War makes savages of us all.*

Reaching for the shiny new musket that a soldier handed him, Daniel immediately rubbed the metal pan cover with mud. He caught sight of Forest Glazier's upraised eyebrow. "Mud dulls the shine," he said casually. "The sun will not reflect off our guns if the barrels are muddied."

Forest dipped his musket to the earth, scooped up a handful of dirt, and copied Daniel's movements exactly. Daniel smiled in silent approval. His daughter might have been thinking with her heart instead of her head when she fell in love with this Puritan, but at least the young man was no fool.

On the tenth of February, 1676, came the Indians with
great numbers upon Lancaster. Their first coming was
about sun-rising. Hearing the noise of some guns, we
looked out: Several houses were burning, and the smoke
ascending to heaven. . . .

At length they came and beset our own house, and
quickly it was the dolefullest day that ever mine eyes
saw. . . . Now is that dreadfull hour come that I have
often heard of (in time of war, as it was in the case of
others) but now mine eyes see it. Some in our house
were fighting for their lives, others wallowing in their
blood, the house on fire over our heads, and the bloody
heathen ready to knock us on the head if we stirred out.
Now might we hear mothers & children crying out for
themselves, and one another, "Lord, what shall we do?"

I took my children (and one of my sisters, hers) to go
forth and leave the house, but as soon as we came to the
door and appeared, the Indians shot so thick that the bullets rattled against the house, as if one had taken a hand-
full of stones and thrown them. . . . We had six stout
dogs belonging to our garrison, but none of them would
stir, though another time, if any Indian had come to the
door, they were ready to fly upon him and tear him
down. The Lord hereby would make us the more to acknowledge His hand, and to see that our help is alwayes
in Him. But out we must go, the fire increasing, and coming along behind us, roaring, and the Indians gaping

before us with their guns, spears, and hatchets, to
devour us.

. . . The bullets flying thick, one went through my
side, and the same through the bowels and hand of my
dear child in my arms. One of my elder sister's children,
named William, had his leg broken, which the Indians
perceiving, they knockt him on [the] head. Thus were
we butchered by those merciless heathen, standing
amazed, with the blood running down to our heels. My
eldest sister being yet in the house, and seeing those
woeful sights, the infidels [hauling] mothers one way,
and children another, and some wallowing in their
blood, and her elder son telling her that her son William
was dead, and myself was wounded, she said, "and
Lord, let me dy with them," which was no sooner said,
but she was struck with a bullet, and fell down dead
over the threshold. . . .
—From the writings of Mrs. Mary Rowlandson,
a captive taken during the attack on Lancaster

▼▲▼▲▼ Reports of the frontier warfare traveled to Boston, and finally to Deer Island, where Aiyana waited with the
community of displaced praying Indians. More than fifty
English were killed at Lancaster, and another twenty-four captured, including Mary Rowlandson, wife of the minister who
had gone to Boston on the town's behalf to plead with the Council for more protection.

The frontier villages were like a string of firecrackers, and Lancaster the first one lit. Medfield burned ten days after Lancaster.
As the plunder-laden savages withdrew from that settlement, an
English soldier found a slip of parchment attached to a ruined
bridge:

Know by this paper, that the Indians that thou has pro-
voked to wrath and anger will war this twenty-one

years if you will; there are many Indians yet, we come
three hundred at this time. You must consider the Indians lost nothing but their life; you must lose your fair
houses and cattle.

"Only their lives!" Aiyana blurted when John Eliot reported
the contents of the note. "Do they think so little of life itself?"

"They have nothing else to lose," the minister answered, staring thoughtfully at the shoreline as they walked along the beach.
"You forget, Aiyana, that an unredeemed Indian does not see
himself as created in the image of God. He believes that he is
part of nature, no more or less important than a rock, a tree, a
deer." He frowned and clasped his hands behind his back. "The
most disturbing bit of that note is the fact that the Indians have
realized how much we prize our houses and cattle. Have we
scrambled so for material possessions and wealth that the Indians infer that we hold those things above all others?"

"Is there any word of my father?" Aiyana said, carefully
changing the subject. The minister had singled her out for this
conversation, and she suspected that matters more substantial
than the spiritual progress of the war pressed upon his mind.

"Yes." Reverend Eliot's frown deepened. "Yesterday I
received a message from Daniel. Your father is well and in good
health. He bids you peace and hopes to see you soon, for he is
returning to Deer Island. But he regretted to tell me that—"

"Forest," Aiyana gasped, stopping in her place. The bitter
wind suddenly stung her eyes.

The minister's gaze softened. "Yes, my child. I hate to be the
bearer of such grievous news."

The sea roared in her ears. "He is dead?"

"No, no." Reverend Eliot shook his head. "He is missing, and
feared captured. He was with Major Savage's force, as was your
father, and they were giving chase to the Indians who are known
to be holding English captives. According to your father's report,
the natives managed to cross a swollen river, but the English
feared to follow deeper into the wilderness. Your father suspects

that your young man wanted to try an idea of his own. . . . In any case, he disappeared. The others waited for him to return—" the minister lifted his shoulder in an eloquent shrug—"but he did not."

Aiyana stared out to sea while her thoughts raced. If Forest had managed to cross the river, surely he would not have tried to follow the Indians alone! Had some sort of mad heroic energy possessed him? One man could not fight the entire Indian army!

The minister's gentle hand fell on her arm. "Mayhap we should turn back, Miss Aiyana. The wind here is cold, and you have grown thin. I cannot have your father return to a sick daughter."

"I am fine," Aiyana protested in a flat voice, but she turned automatically and followed the minister back to the camp.

One of the Indians carried my poor wounded babe upon a horse. It went moaning all along, I shall dy, I shall dy. I went on foot after it, with sorrow that cannot be expressed. At length I took it off the horse and carried it in my arms till my strength failed, and I fell down with it . . . but the Lord renewed my strength still, and carried me along, that I might see more of His power. Yea, so much that I could never have thought of it, had I not experienced it.

. . . Nine dayes I sat upon my knees, with my babe in my lap, till my flesh was raw again. My child being even ready to depart this sorrowfull world, they bade me carry it out to another wigwam (I suppose because they would not be troubled with such spectacles) whither I went with a very heavy heart, and down I sat with the picture of death in my lap. About two hours in the night my sweet babe, like a lambe, departed this life, on February 18, [1676], it being about six years and five months old.

. . . I cannot but take notice of the wonderfull mercy of God to me in those afflictions, in sending me a Bible. One of the Indians that came from [the] Medfield fight, and brought some plunder, came to me and asked me if I would have a Bible. He had got one in his basket. I was glad of it, and asked him whether he thought the Indians would let me read. He answered, yes, so I took the Bible. . . .

And here I cannot but take notice of the strange providence of God in preserving the heathen. They were many hundreds, old and young, some sick, and some lame. Many had papooses at their backs; the greatest number at this time with us were squaws, and they traveled with all they had, bag and baggage, and yet they got over this river aforesaid; and on Monday they set their wigwams on fire, and away they went. On that very day came the English army after them to this river, and saw the smoke of their wigwams, and yet this river put a stop to them. God did not give them courage or activity to go over after us. We were not ready for so great a mercy as victory and deliverance. If we had been, God would have found out a way for the English to have passed this river, as well as for the Indians with their squaws and children, and all their luggage.

—Mary Rowlandson

Aiyana paced for the better part of the afternoon, a feverish energy flushing her cheeks and driving her forward. Several of the older women, frightened by her aspect and the urgency of her steps, urged her to sit and talk with them. One old woman caught her sleeve. "If you cannot talk," she whispered in Algonquin, her voice grating against the howling of the bitterly cold wind, "come and pray with us. The heart knows another's sorrows, my child, and we can help you bear whatever you must carry."

But sharing her burden would mean that she would have to confess her loss, and she could not force the words across her tongue. Forest could not be dead—maybe he was not even captured. He had become separated from his men, he was wandering in the woods, and he could feed and warm himself until a friendly face appeared. . . .

What friendly face? Someone from one of the English villages, if anyone still lived in the smoldering frontier towns, or someone from the army. Or even Mojag himself. . . .

Mojag. She stiffened and caught her breath. If Forest had been captured, Mojag could plead for Forest's life. Forest had once saved Mojag's life, and Mojag could repay the debt of honor, but only if he could find Forest and speak on his behalf. But how could the two find each other in the wilderness? The miles of frozen forest and rimed wilderness teemed with Indians of every tribe and nation.

But she could find at least one of them. God had given her this face and form for a reason; she could be all things to all men, either Indian or English, copper-skinned or white. She could hide her dark hair beneath a cloak and speak not a word until someone spoke to her. If Mojag could live off the land and find his way through the forest, so could she. Reverend Eliot and Magistrate Gookin had kept her abreast of the progress of the war, so she knew where the Indians camped and which English villages were safe.

She had to find Forest, or she would lose him forever. The Indians cared only about important English captives. Women were valuable if they had husbands to redeem them. Political figures and ministers were esteemed. But Forest was none of these. Master Glazier, if he still lived, had almost certainly been impoverished by the war. By all accounts, little remained of Rehoboth but a smoldering pile of rubble, so Matthew Glazier would have no money with which to purchase his son's freedom. Forest would be a useless captive, fit only for slave labor. And if he proved at all troublesome, the Indians would kill him.

A hard, steely determination overrode all of Aiyana's other feelings. Leaving the shelter, she walked to the communal cook pot in the central fire and helped herself to a generous portion of corn stew, not knowing when she might eat again. After her meal, she tore small bits of bark from a nearly stripped tree and lined the inside of her moccasins, fortifying her shoes for the miles ahead. In a crate of cast-off clothing she found a tattered, loose-fitting cloak. She wrapped herself in it, pulling the hood over her head.

Without speaking a word of her intention to the others, she moved toward the shore and lingered in the shadows of sunset. When a small shallop raised its anchor to pull away from the island, Aiyana wrapped her cloak about herself and waved a cheery greeting at the man who steered the boat, telling him that she had urgent business in Roxbury.

"Reverend Eliot didn't say anything about you coming with us," the boatman protested, gaping in earnest confusion. "You'll be in awful trouble, miss, if you're found ashore without a military escort."

"Why, you're my escort, sir," she said, flashing him her warmest smile. "And you'll find that Reverend Eliot won't be at all surprised to know that I have left this evening. Ask him on the morrow, and you'll find he understands."

"All right," the boatman said, shrugging. "It's your neck at risk, not mine."

The oarsmen waited until she had settled in the bow; then they began to row away from the miserable island.

Forest clenched his teeth as one of his captors shoved him forward. His swollen ankle, wrenched as he had attempted to run from the pair of Indian scouts who had found him near the river, burned with pain, but he knew he did not dare complain. If at any time the Indians thought a prisoner too weak to manage the journey ahead, a musket shot or a tomahawk would end the captive's travail. Already he had watched them kill two women and three infants who would never have survived the arduous overland trek.

The scouts had crept up and surprised him on the eastern side of the river. They pursued him through his brief and frantic flight, and then he twisted his ankle and was forced to surrender. At gunpoint they urged him across a narrow place in the river. The cold water swirled around his knees in a current so strong that it nearly pulled him off his feet, but Forest knew that falling would mean certain death. A man could not breathe this frigid air if his lungs were frozen, too.

Within three hours after his abduction, his captors brought him to join the rest of their company. Hundreds, perhaps thousands, of Indians were passing through the wilderness, and occasionally he caught sight of pale, bewildered English faces.

Each prisoner seemed to have a particular Indian master. For a moment Forest thought he might have two, but when he looked around, he realized that one of his captors had departed. The remaining man, a tall, fierce-faced warrior whose hair was totally shaven but for a tall roach on his crown, pointed to Forest and then to himself. As Forest blinked in pretended confusion, the warrior pulled an extra pair of moccasins from a pack on his back. These he threw at Forest's feet, then motioned that he should remove his wet, squeaky boots.

Forest hesitated, then decided to obey. His new master bore an ugly, vivid scar upon his cheek, and Forest feared the man might still be out of sorts about the disfigurement of his complexion. And it would do no harm to don different shoes. He had already marched enough miles in his stiff, leaky boots to know that moccasins were bound to be more comfortable.

He had just finished tying the leathern laces of the moccasins when his other captor returned. "If the Yangeese follow us," the man said in English, his hands on his hips as he stared at Forest with the cold light of hostility in his eye, "we will kill you. This man, Sunukkuhkau—" he pointed to the other warrior—"is your master. Obey him, and all will be well with you."

"And who are you?" Forest asked, looking up at the man. This second man was not tall, but carried himself with a commanding air of self-confidence.

"I am Tihkoosue, brother to Sunukkuhkau," he said, lifting his chin as if a world of meaning could be found in that statement. "The Yangeese call me Alderman. But you shall call me nothing, slave, for the Yangeese have no manners and do not understand what a name truly means."

Tihkoosue moved away through the tide of humanity in the woods, and Forest froze in horror when the warrior stopped before an English woman with a baby in her arms. While the woman screamed in helpless anguish, the warrior pulled the baby from her, placed it on the ground, and then crushed its skull with a war club. An Indian woman pulled the hysterical mother away from the dead child while Tihkoosue moved on. Forest stood, intending to gather the child's body and bury it, but his master pointedly gripped his musket and gestured to the trail ahead.

Furious at his sudden vulnerability, Forest hobbled along the trail, seething with mounting rage. "If I only had my gun," he muttered, but another voice interrupted him.

"Do not wish to make things worse," a woman said, her clear

English diction cutting through the foreign chatter around them. "The baby would not have survived. Mine did not."

He turned, surprised that another captive would speak to him. The woman coming up behind him was a tall, thin lady of middle age. An apron about her waist defined its smallness; a brown bloodstain smeared her kirtle. Her eyes did not turn to him as she passed but rested squarely on the back of the Indian woman who led her up the trail.

"Who are you?" he called, hoping she would speak again.

In answer, his Indian master rushed forward and pointed his musket at Forest's chest. Sighing, Forest held up his hand in submission and followed the women up the trail.

They walked about five miles that afternoon. Trying to ignore the white-hot pain in his ankle, Forest trudged mindlessly ahead as his brain and body absorbed sensations, sights, and sounds he had never imagined. Though he had been in the wilderness with the militia for many days, the woods seemed different from an Indian perspective. The forest lived; amid its dark shapes, shadows moved like stalking gray cats. In a short bout of disconnected thoughts, he realized that he walked in buckskin moccasins as Aiyana's ancestors had. Surely her people had moved in this same steady rhythm, for though they knew that the English army followed in the woods, the natives walked at a consistent, controlled pace. Overexertion caused sweating, which led to chills. Too slow a stride produced the same numbing effect.

At nightfall the entire party stopped to make camp. The women, English captives included, gathered slender saplings that they bent into frames for their wigwams. Others gathered spruce branches for roofing material while the children spread evergreen branches on the frozen earth to provide a fragrant matting.

Exhausted, Forest sank to the ground beside a tree and leaned back upon it. Stretching his legs, he pulled his purpling ankle to his knee in an effort to lift it and relieve the swelling. Men, women, and children ignored him, working with an astounding

single-mindedness of purpose. Any Englishman who described
the Indians as lazy, Forest thought, had never seen them work.

Amazingly, Forest's master did not demand any effort from
him. Sunukkuhkau even lit a fire near Forest, then left him alone.
He knows I will not run away, Forest thought, leaning his head
back against the tree. *My ankle is in no condition to bear a run, and
the trees are a prison wall with no way out.*

His thoughts wandered as he drifted in and out of consciousness. Aiyana's delicate face floated before him, even appearing
in the silver orb of the moon that hurried from one dark cloud to
another. What would she say if she saw him now? She'd be
upset, she'd worry about his well-being, but maybe a part of her
would rejoice. *"Look, Forest,"* she'd say, her smooth skin glowing
with pale gold undertones. *"Observe how they live outside Rehoboth. Then you will know. You will understand. You will hear the call."*

Forest stirred and opened his eyes, feeling the weight of a
rope upon his hands, but he said nothing as his master tied his
wrists and anchored the rope to a stake in the ground. When Forest was secure, Sunukkuhkau moved into the wigwam his wife
had prepared. Others joined them, men, women, and children,
until Forest doubted there could be room for all to stretch out
and sleep.

Night drew down like a black cowl. The men smoked around
the wigwam fire and conversed in low tones, their eyes frequently darting through the open doorway toward Forest. The
women tended the children and the fire, occasionally crooning
songs of a distinctly foreign melody. As his stomach growled and
cramped with hunger, Forest realized with a pang of surprise
that the Indians had not eaten because they had no food. The
men had no time to hunt; the women had been too busy preparing this camp to forage for food in the woods.

The men lay down; the women silenced the children. Forest
did not know whether or not they slept, but his master's wigwam, like the others, became as silent as death. Tilting his head
back to study the stars, he watched a cloud grapple with the
moon for possession of the night. Who would own this land

when the struggle had ended? The burned-out English or the starving Indians?

It is a good thing that war is horrible, he thought, closing his eyes. *Else we would grow too attached to it and so destroy ourselves.*

▾▴▾▴▾ Miles away, Aiyana wrapped her damp cloak around her and crept deeper into the pile of spruce boughs she had collected for her bed. Lying flat upon her stomach under a sheltering evergreen, she pillowed her head on her arms and groaned. She had probably walked twenty-four miles in the hours since sunrise. Near the end of the day, her legs had begun to tremble and her eyes to water. She had eaten nothing and had drunk only water from an abandoned well. But tomorrow she would be near the ruins of Lancaster. If God smiled upon her and the weather held, she should be able to find the trail left by the pursuing army. Though the Indians moved in a single line, disturbing little of the underbrush, the English walked five and six men abreast over the trails, leaving a clear track.

"And," she murmured sleepily, trying not to think about her aching feet and bones, "mayhap the English left some corn in the fields or food in a house." She fell into a shallow sleep, her mind creating dreams in which the image of her father's face blended with Forest's, then Mojag's. The three most dear and important people in her life waited somewhere in this wilderness, shivering under the same dark sky, retreating from the breeze that knifed lungs and tingled bare skin. But here in the woods, hiding from both Indians and English, Aiyana felt closer to them than she had on Deer Island.

▾▴▾▴▾ A disquieting sound broke the stillness of morning, and Aiyana's eyes flew open. A painted Indian crouched before her, a tomahawk in his hand and an expression of intense interest upon his face. *The enemy.*

The native stared at her in silence until her heart raced and her fingers fluttered with fear.

He is planning to scalp me. He wants to carry my head to his village as a trophy. Can I run? No, he will be faster.

"Rise," the man ordered in Algonquin, and she stiffly pushed herself up.

He is on his feet, but if I pushed him I might escape and hide in the woods. Surely he has heard about the English atrocities. He will torture me to exact blood vengeance for his tribe.

Withdrawing from the man before her, she leaned against the tree. A branch above her bobbed, raining snow upon her head.

The warrior's eyes blazed down into hers. "To which tribe do you belong?" he barked.

Momentarily speechless in her surprise, Aiyana gaped at him. *He sees me as an Indian! Despite these clothes, this cloak, he thinks I am like him!*

She took a deep breath and forced a note of calmness into her voice. "I am from the nation Wampanoag and the tribe Pokanoket on the island Noepe," she said, naming the tribe with which she had grown up. It was a true and safe answer, for the Pokanoket were Metacomet's people.

To her great surprise and relief, the warrior stood and stepped back a half step.

"Why are you here alone?" he asked, a suspicious line at the corner of his mouth.

Holy Father, give me wisdom.

Rising to her feet, she met the warrior's eyes and told the truth. "I am escaped."

"From what place?"

"Deer Island." She heard a murmuring in the bushes and knew that other natives lurked out of sight. The warrior tilted his head as if he did not believe her, so Aiyana rushed on. "I am trying to find my brother. He is called Mojag and travels with Metacomet of the Pokanoket."

His eyes, sharp and assessing, narrowed for a moment; then

he nodded. "Come," he said, gesturing to her. "We go to meet Metacomet."

Blinking in unexpected gratitude, Aiyana stepped out from beneath the sheltering evergreen and brushed the damp snow from her cloak. She had expected God to take care of her, but she had not anticipated a personal escort to the sachem.

▼▲▼▲▼ On the morrow morning we must go over the river, i.e., Connecticut, to meet with King Philip . . . we traveled on till night, and in the morning, we must go over the river to Philip's crew. When I was in the canoo, I could not but be amazed at the numerous crew of pagans that were on the bank on the other side. When I came ashore, they gathered all about me, I sitting alone in the midst. I observed they asked one another questions, and laughed, and rejoyced over their gains and victories. Then my heart began to fail and I fell a weeping, which was the first time to my remembrance that I wept before them. Although I had met with so much affliction, and my heart was many times ready to break, yet could I not shed one tear in their sight, but rather had been all this while in amaze[ment], and like one astonished. But now I may say as Psalm 137:1, "By the rivers of Babylon, there we sat down. Yea, we wept when we remembered Zion." There one of them asked me why I wept: I could hardly tell what to say, yet I answered, they would kill me. "No," said he, "none will hurt you." Then came one of them and gave me two spoonfuls of meal to comfort me, and another gave me half a pint of pease, which was worth more than many bushels at another time. Then I went to see King Philip; he bade me come in and sit down, and asked me whether I would smoke [a pipe], . . . but this in no way suited me. . . .

During my abode in this place, Philip spake to me to

make a shirt for his boy, which I did, for which he gave
me a shilling. I offered the money to my master but he
bade me keep it, and with it I bought a piece of horse
flesh. Afterwards [Philip] asked me to make a cap for his
boy, for which he invited me to dinner. I went, and he
gave me a pancake, about as big as two fingers. It was
made of parched wheat, beaten, and fryed in bear's
grease, but I thought I had never tasted pleasanter meat
in my life. . . .

—Mary Rowlandson

▼▲▼▲▼ After three days of bone-numbing travel,
Aiyana and her warrior escorts walked into Metacomet's camp on
the west side of the Connecticut River. The joyous atmosphere of
the encampment caught her by surprise. Though the wigwams
were sparsely furnished and the cook pots nearly empty, warriors
joked around the fire, and the women went about their work with
contented faces. She looked into one pot as she passed by: A handful of peas, a slab of fat, and a spoonful of meal bubbled in clear
water. It was hardly enough to sustain one person, and yet this
meal would have to serve an entire family.

The warriors who had brought her to this place disappeared
into the crowd, leaving her to fend for herself. Aiyana walked
alone for a few moments, feeling strangely disconnected. She
spoke the language of these people, she shared their lineage, and
yet she felt like an absolute foreigner. These people were so different from those of the praying villages! Around her, in the
middle of the day, people laughed uproariously; they cried and
sang and danced; they ran throughout the camp in exuberant
pleasure. Neither the praying Indians nor the Puritans behaved
with such abandon. No wonder the English considered them
uncivilized.

Ducking her head, she shyly peered into a nearby wigwam,
then quickly withdrew, blushing furiously at what she'd seen.
Even in the face of war, they took time to love.

Embarrassed, she walked aimlessly, hoping that Mojag would have the decency to show himself and spare her the trouble of searching for him. God had answered her need to find Metacomet so efficiently that she had almost expected Mojag to be waiting for her with open arms.

"Think, Aiyana," she told herself sternly, stopping in midstride. This was Metacomet's camp, and if she was a Pokanoket, he was her sachem. Surely she had the right to speak to him, and he would of certain know where Mojag was. Squaring her shoulders, she approached one woman at a cook fire and asked for directions to Metacomet's wigwam.

The squaw turned away without answering, but a tall English woman came out of the nearest wigwam and stared at Aiyana in surprise. "Philip's hut is nearer the river," she said, obviously understanding a bit of the Indian language. Her brow furrowed as she continued to stare, and she stepped closer to whisper in Aiyana's ear, "Do you speak English?"

Holding her breath, Aiyana nodded slowly. A satisfied light came into the woman's eyes; then she jerked her head toward the trees, motioning for Aiyana to join her. After checking to be certain that the Indian woman did not care what her servant did, Aiyana followed.

"My name is Mary Rowlandson," the woman said in English, keeping her voice low as she took Aiyana's hand. "You wear English clothes, and you have not been here before. Are you one of those they call the praying Indians? Have you been sent as a—" her eyes darted left and right—"a spy?"

Aiyana shifted uneasily. "Please, do not repeat that charge. I am a Christian, and I come of my own volition to search for my brother and another Englishman who may have been taken captive."

The woman tightened her grip on Aiyana's hand. "Is the English army nearby? Will they send someone to parlay for the exchange of prisoners? I have begged my master to take me to Albany and sell me for gunpowder, but he will not—"

"I know not where the army is," Aiyana whispered, a little

frightened by the woman's frantic grasp. "I am here alone, I tell you. I want to see Metacomet and ask about my brother—"

The woman stiffened at Aiyana's use of the sachem's Indian name. *You are one of them,* her eyes seemed to say, and she dropped Aiyana's hand as if it had suddenly become diseased.

"Philip's hut is down there, near the river," she repeated, pointing toward the riverbank. "You will see his little son playing in front of the wigwam. The boy is wearing a cap I made. When Philip is among us, he does not let the boy out of his sight."

Moving slowly away, Aiyana thanked her, then turned toward the river.

▼▲▼▲ *He is an ordinary man,* Aiyana thought, a little annoyed that her first impression of the dreaded King Philip was less than spectacular. He was handsome, though his intelligent eyes were ringed with dark circles as if he had not slept in many days. He looked tough, lean, and sinewy, but so did the other warriors of the starving tribe. The great sachem was reclining upon one elbow on a grass mat near the fire before his wigwam, talking with a boy of about nine or ten years. The boy wore an English shirt over a leathern breechcloth, and the cap on his head seemed strangely out of place in the wilderness. Philip wore leather leggings and a breechcloth. Several highly decorated wampum belts hung from his shoulders and crossed his chest, the insignia of his rank and station among the Wampanoag tribes. Aiyana shuddered when she saw a vivid red scar upon his hand and other vicious marks upon his upper arms and chest. Though she could not guess how he had damaged his hand, she knew the wounds on his arms and chest were self-inflicted cuts of grief and mourning.

She advanced cautiously. The bustling Indians had paid her scant attention, but she knew the sachem was as at home in the English world as she. He would recognize her English clothing, maybe he would even be able to pinpoint her identity by her accent in Algonquin.

"Greetings, great Sachem," she said, bowing her head before him in a sign of respect.

Philip's dark eyes left the dancing form of his son and focused upon her. For a moment he seemed to weigh her presence and her intention, then he lifted his brows in an unspoken question. She was not surprised. Not even in the praying villages did Indian men often speak directly to their women.

"I am Aiyana Bailie, lately of the Pokanoket tribe upon Noepe," she said, her words coming out at double speed, as if they'd been glued together. "I have come to seek my brother, Mojag, who has traveled with you since Monthaup."

"He-Who-Talks-Much," the sachem said in a dry voice, his grin flashing briefly, "is now known by another name: He-Who-Waits. He and his wife have erected a wigwam near the water's edge."

"His wife?" she burst out, shocked. Even though Mojag had spoken of his desire to marry an Indian girl, she had never dreamed he would actually take a wife without first speaking to their father.

An inexplicable, lazy smile swept over the sachem's face as he watched her reaction. "Yes. Askuwheteau is one of the daybreak people now."

His son asked a quick question, and Metacomet turned away for a moment while Aiyana struggled to overcome her surprise. When he had answered the boy, the sachem turned back to her. "Have you come alone, Aiyana Bailie?" he asked, squinting slightly. "Have you brought those who wish to murder me?"

"No, great Sachem, I have not," she answered, grateful that she spoke the truth. "I have been in the company of your warriors for many days and have come only to find my brother." She hesitated, wanting to speak of Forest, but decided to hold her tongue. Mojag would have more influence on Forest's behalf than she would.

The sachem tilted his head slightly, then waved his hand to dismiss her. "Find your brother in peace," he said, turning to smile at his son.

Ootadabun

Though an host should encamp against me,
my heart shall not fear:
though war should rise against me, in this
will I be confident.

—Psalm 27:3

Grabbing up her kirtle, Aiyana hurried from Metacomet's wigwam and zigzagged through the cook fires and shelters of other families along the river's edge. Her hands trembled in eager anticipation, yet her heart was heavy. She wanted to find Mojag, but her imagination had obviously painted a false picture of his ministry. She had expected to find him telling Bible stories to wide-eyed, innocent children who sat at his feet and drank in the gospel. She had *not* wanted to find him with a wife and on friendly terms with that fiend Philip!

He had mentioned falling in love when he visited her in Rehoboth, but Aiyana had been certain he would soon put such thoughts out of his head. He could not have followed the example of David and Solomon; his heart was too pure to be corrupted by the beauty of a heathen woman. He had always been spiritually strong, much wiser than she, and he would never marry an unbelieving woman unless—

She covered her mouth with her hand, nearly choking on the sudden realization. Forest had tried to tell her about this! *A man is not like a woman. There are strong desires that should not be encouraged until after a man's marriage.*

Her face grew hot with humiliation. She ducked behind a tree and leaned into it, resting her head on her hand. An Indian woman squatting at a nearby fire lifted her head in a curious gaze.

"Mojag, how could you?" Aiyana whispered fiercely, ignoring the woman. Their father would be mortified when he learned that his son had abandoned his work to live with a heathen woman. Reverend Eliot would be utterly disappointed. How could Mojag have allowed manly lust to sway him from his calling?

No matter how thrilled she was to find Mojag, she couldn't escape the dull ache of foreboding. She turned and slid to the ground, folding her arms. Her brother had taken a wife from the heathen, and she could do nothing about it. One of the savages might have no qualms about walking away from a woman, but Mojag, no matter how low he had fallen, would not abandon a wife in the middle of a war. So he would not want to go home with her, and their father would go on mourning the loss of his son.

Aiyana clenched her fist. It wasn't fair. Mojag didn't belong here. He couldn't remain with this heathen enemy; she'd make him leave. After he had helped her find Forest, they would slip away and take Mojag's wife with them, though only heaven knew what would become of her. Unless, of course, the woman chose to stay with her people. The Bible gave permission for an unbelieving spouse to depart from a believer if she chose to do so. . . .

Once she was confident that she could face Mojag without revealing too much of her disappointment, Aiyana stood to her feet, brushed the dirt from her kirtle, and smoothed her hair around her face. Three wigwams stood next to the river's edge; Mojag had to be in one of them. In this hour, she would be reunited with her brother and meet his wife. If God gave her grace, she would pretend to be pleased to find him married.

She moved through a knot of talking women, skirted a pair of warriors, and spied a wigwam set a little apart from the others on the riverbank. An iron pot bubbled in the fire, and a pair of young children squatted near it, their eyes intent upon holes they were digging in the earth. Aiyana approached the fire, then peered into the dim light of the wigwam.

Mojag reclined there in a slash of sunlight. His eyes snapped with joy when he looked up and saw her. "Aiyana!" he cried, leaping to his feet. Before she could call out a proper greeting he had bounded through the doorway and caught her in a ferocious bear hug. He spun her around, rumpling her hair with one hand while he whirled her with the other.

"Mojag! Stop it, I'm too tired for this nonsense!" she fussed, but her reserve thawed as the children squealed in laughter and clapped their hands.

"Aiyana, how did you ever come to be here?" He spoke Algonquin more easily than she had ever heard him, but his dark eyebrows slanted in a frown. "Were you among the captives taken at Rehoboth?"

"No." She shook her head. "Forest Glazier took me to Deer Island, where the English have interned all the praying Indians. But after Forest and Father left to fight in the militia—"

"Father is fighting?" Lightning bolts of worry darted into Mojag's eyes. "He is too old, Aiyana."

"He is one of the best trackers in Massachusetts. When I last heard, he was on his way back to Deer Island. But Forest Glazier is missing and believed captured." She folded her arms and came directly to the point. "I thought you might be able to help me find him."

Mojag stepped back, giving her a sidelong glance of utter disbelief. "You came here *alone?* to find one of the Yangeese?"

"Forest is no ordinary Englishman. I love him, Mojag. We are to be married, *properly*, when the war is over."

Mojag looked away, his square jaw tensing visibly. "When this war is over?" he said, an edge to his voice. "Surely, Aiyana, by now you have learned that men grow tired of sleep, love, singing, and dancing sooner than they tire of war."

She opened her mouth to protest, but a young woman had come toward them, and Mojag gestured for her to come closer. When she did, his hand fell possessively upon her shoulder. "Aiyana, I'd like you to meet Ootadabun, my wife."

No explanation, no excuse, just an introduction. Aiyana nodded stiffly to the girl, who flashed her a rare, intimate smile, beautiful with brightness. "I am so glad you are here," Ootadabun said, coming to take Aiyana's hands in her own. Tall and graceful, Mojag's wife possessed a rich, fawnlike beauty. Thick braids hung softly over her thin shoulders, her long neck curved between them like a bird taking wing. She had a genial mouth and sparkling eyes that held Aiyana's in a long and interested search.

The warmth of Ootadabun's touch left Aiyana feeling uncomfortable. "Thank you," she stammered, pulling away. Part of her wished Mojag had chosen a brasher, more dislikable wife.

"You are very beautiful," Ootadabun said, shyly dropping her gaze as she turned and tended to her cook pot.

▼▲▼▲▼ Ootadabun held her tongue while Mojag's sister begged him to come away and walk with her. A strong affection obviously existed between the brother and sister, but Ootadabun had not missed the flicker of distrust in the woman's sharp blue eyes. They were like an apple and an oyster, she thought, both delicious on the tongue, but with decidedly different flavors. His sister's beautiful face bore the lines of proud humility Ootadabun had often seen in preachers who came to the Indian villages, but Mojag's countenance had never evidenced such pride. Confidence, yes, particularly on the day when he had delivered the elk to Metacomet's wigwam. But though Mojag was sure of himself and his God, he had never made her feel as inferior as his sister had with just one glance.

"Mojag, I need to talk to you," Aiyana was saying now, her eyes wide with pleading.

"Why should we walk?" Mojag said, sinking to a mat near Ootadabun. "Anything you have to say should be said here. The woods are full of eyes and ears."

Reluctantly, Aiyana knelt on another mat, then fastened her eyes upon the children. "Those two can't be yours," she said, lifting an eyebrow.

"They are Keme and Chepi. We have cared for them since they were orphaned." Leaning forward, he shooed the children away from the fire and told them to go play elsewhere. Nodding soberly, the boy gripped his sister's hand and pulled her toward the riverbank.

"Their parents?"

"Their father was killed by the English; their mother died of a fever soon after the fighting began." His faint smile held a touch of sadness. "Sometimes I think more of us die from disease than from English bullets."

Ootadabun raised her eyes from her cooking to find Mojag watching her. His mouth curved into an unconscious smile. "But my wife takes care of the children—and of me."

"I can see that she does," Aiyana answered, but her words sounded flimsy in the cool air. Passion returned to her voice as she gripped her brother's hand. "Mojag, I don't care what has happened in the past—we must think of the future! We've got to find Forest and leave this place. Look at you! You are as thin as a vine. And I've seen enough to know that things will not get better. You've spent months praying for Philip, you've told him of the gospel, and he has of certain rejected it. So why do you remain here? You can take this woman and return with me to Boston. We'll have to wait on Deer Island until the war ends, but spring is coming, and the wait will not be too long—"

"Leave my people?" Mojag looked at his sister as if she had just suggested that he commit some unspeakable crime. "Aiyana, God called me to this place. He calls all of us to the world, not to some enclave on an island to wait for sufferings to end—"

"They suffer on Deer Island, too." Aiyana's voice cracked with weariness. "There are Christian saints there, Mojag, who would appreciate the comfort you could give them. How can you ignore them? Father needs help, and John Eliot. Of certain Philip does not want you here. He only tolerates you."

"His name is Metacomet," Mojag answered, a look of intense, clear light pouring through his eyes. "And mayhap God has called *you* to minister to the saints in the praying villages, but he has called me to this place, to pray for Metacomet. We are part of the same family, Aiyana, but we are not the same part. I will not leave this place unless God or my sachem tells me to go. As long as they allow me to remain, I believe that Metacomet remains open to the truth of the gospel. He knows salvation comes at the price of his life, and he is not willing to surrender until he has tested all his other options. God is forever patient with you and with me, Aiyana. Can we deny that patience to Metacomet?"

Aiyana fell silent, her hands twisted uselessly in her lap. A flood of compassion poured through Ootadabun's heart. She had never heard him speak so harshly to a woman.

Aiyana's chin quivered. "Why is God doing this, Mojag?" she whispered in a broken voice. Her mantle of certainty had vanished. "We have given our lives to serve him. The English are praying and fasting and repenting of their sins, and yet the Indians continue to attack. And the Christian Indians, as innocent as babes, suffer for the wrongs of their brothers and are starved, hung, and tortured. Why is God allowing this war? If he wants to prove one side right and the other wrong, could he not speak through his ministers?"

"War cannot prove which side is right," Mojag said, drawing his sister to his side in a comforting embrace. "It only proves which side is stronger. There is good and evil in the heart of every man, just as there is good and evil in every nation. The stronger people will win this war, Aiyana, and yet the battle between good and evil will continue. And that is why I must remain here, for this—" he lifted his arms to the expanse above him—"is the true battlefront. If we suffer, we do so that others might live."

His gaze shifted from his sobbing sister and met Ootadabun's eyes across the fire. She warmed in his glance, knowing that he was thinking of their conversation the night before. In their private time together in the woods, he had told her the story of how God allowed Jesus, the perfect warrior of God, to surrender his life and strength in order that others might taste victory over death. Jesus endured death, Mojag had said, like a kernel of corn that falls into the ground and dies yet brings forth much fruit. And because he defeated death, all who believed in him would one day rise to live forever in his heavenly kingdom.

"Except a kernel of corn die," she whispered to her husband. Still cradling his weeping sister, he smiled at her in approval.

The bubbling kettle in front of Mojag's wigwam contained two spoonfuls of meal, a half-dozen acorns, three chestnuts, and a sliver of hairy flesh that resembled horse meat. At midday, Ootadabun divided this mixture between the two children, Mojag, and Aiyana, then drank the pitiful leavings herself.

During the wearisome journey west, Aiyana had eaten only a few pine nuts and a small cake one of the Indians had given her, so even this meager repast warmed her belly and gave her strength. She could not help but notice, however, that Ootadabun's slender face shone with the translucent look of an invalid. Though the young woman's sinewy arms and legs appeared strong, Aiyana suspected that it was but the illusion of health. It was likely that Mojag's wife fed on the love that radiated from her husband's eyes and existed by a sheer force of will.

After they had eaten, Mojag reluctantly agreed to escort Aiyana through the camp to search for Forest. "It is not as though we are one people," he explained as they set out. "We move more or less together, but occasionally the warriors go off into the woods to hunt or fish. If Forest has a master, they may be away from us for days at a time, or his master may have left us to journey farther into Nipmuck territory." He lowered his voice. "Metacomet will not admit it, but many of our number are turning aside to search for land on which they can plant crops. They have families, Aiyana, and they are thinking of the summer to come. We have no food except for that which we find in the forest or plunder from English villages."

And so you eat stolen meat? She bit back the accusation. Mojag and his family were struggling to survive; she knew she ought not judge them. Even the praying Indians on Deer Island would eat stolen meat if it miraculously appeared before them. In a time of war, only the fat and prosperous could afford scruples about food.

But physical hunger had not driven him to marry a heathen woman. When they were safely away from his wigwam, Aiyana crossed her arms and turned to her brother. "Why did you do it?" she asked, a critical tone in her voice.

His head snapped around. "What do you mean?"

"'Be ye not unequally yoked'—isn't that what the Scripture says? Why did you marry one of these savages, Mojag? You were sent to preach to them, not to become one of them, not to draw one of them to your bosom."

"Unequally yoked?" His eyes flashed sudden fury, and she stepped back, surprised at the depth of his reaction. She had expected remorse and repentance, not anger.

"Who are you to say I am unequally yoked?" He threw the words at her like stones. "When I first saw Ootadabun, I sensed in her a hunger for the truth. I have taught her these many months, and with her own eyes she has seen how God answers prayer and how he provides for his own. She is a more sincere Christian than many, no, *most* of those black-hearted scoundrels in Rehoboth who wanted to hang me. And yet you have come here, risking your life, to find one of those Puritans who talks of God and yet does not acknowledge God's movement among the Indians—"

"Forest is different!" she yelled, flushing to the roots of her hair. His words lacerated her. She would admit she had seen love shining from Ootadabun's eyes, and such unquestioning and open acceptance could only have come from God. But how could Mojag judge Forest so harshly?

"Forest saved your life!" she hissed, not caring that curious eyes had begun to look their way. "He is not like the others at Rehoboth! He is honorable and true. He is open to new ideas." A sob caught in her throat. Her voice, when she was able to speak again, was strangled by a host of advancing emotions. "Why else would he be willing to marry *me?*"

"Oh, little sister," Mojag whispered, his expression softening as he placed his hands on her shoulders, "do you still think so little of yourself?"

He opened his arms, and she stepped into them, huddling in his embrace, protecting that place in her heart that only Mojag knew existed. A lifetime ago, they had been half-breed children, neither fully Indian nor fully English, not civilized enough to be Puritans or strong enough to be Wampanoags. Though he had also been subjected to the cruel taunts of the other children, Mojag had had an easier time of it than she had, for his eyes were brown and his skin dark, but she had been the blue-eyed outcast from the children's games, forever lost and lonely, out of place even in the praying village.

"Shh, hush your weeping," he said, closing his arms around her as he whispered in her ear. "If Forest is alive, we will find him. And I will make certain that you are allowed to leave together." He stroked her hair. "Though Metacomet does not heed my words, he respects my voice. This, at least, is something I can do for you."

"Thank you, Mojag," Aiyana whispered, thumbing tears from her eyes. "Thank you."

▼▲▼▲▼ They searched for the remainder of that day, but though Mojag tried to cover the entire camp, its boundary was nebulous, always changing. Families rarely stayed in one spot for more than a day; when the ground had been picked clean of pine nuts and sticks for the fire, the family would move forward a mile or two. One day an area might be covered with Indians, but by the next sunrise only a clean-swept ground and a few charred embers would remain.

Though Mojag could tell Aiyana was frustrated and discouraged by their lack of success after many afternoons of searching, she settled into their family wigwam without complaint. How-

ever much she might resent Ootadabun, she offered her help
with the chores. Though Mojag suspected that Aiyana searched
more for English captives than for food, she often volunteered to
take Chepi and Keme exploring for ground nuts and whatever
else might be edible.

Many Yangeese were scattered through the company, probably thirty-five by Mojag's last count. Most of them moved freely
throughout the encampment, foraging food for themselves and
their masters and occasionally sewing or writing letters for one
of the sachems. But no matter where he looked, Mojag could find
no trace of Forest Glazier.

▼▲▼▲▼ The council of sachems met and deliberated;
news of their decision spread through the camp. They would
move north toward the confluence of rivers, where fishing was
good.

On the morning of the day appointed for the camp's northward migration, Aiyana crawled out of the wigwam at sunrise
and peered into shaggy corridors of white snow. Overnight the
evergreen shrubs along the riverbank had become white
mounds; puffy white powder obliterated the river trail. Gray
clouds swirled overhead like angry, warring dragons, and cold
air brushed across the back of her legs. She shivered inside the
new buckskin skirt Ootadabun had made for her. The change in
the scenery amplified the unruly feeling of disorientation she
had felt for several days. She was uneasy and nervous, and she
didn't know why.

She had thought the trail difficult when it was slippery and
damp, but how could they escape the Yangeese if they slogged
through deep snows? *Dear God, what am I thinking? I want to find
the English. I want these captives to be freed. I want to return to my
father. Help me, God, because I no longer know who my enemy is. . . .*

Sighing, she pulled the fur mantle Mojag had given her more
tightly around her shoulders and ducked back inside the wigwam to help Ootadabun ready the children.

▾▲▾▲▾ They traveled for days, stopping only when an hour of daylight remained in each day. While the women began fires and hastily erected wigwams, the men ventured into the woods to hunt. More of the hunters carried bows and arrows than muskets, Aiyana noticed, conserving their shot for warfare, not food.

On the third night, after darkness had fallen, Ootadabun tugged on Aiyana's sleeve as she sang the two children to sleep. "What?" Aiyana asked, a little annoyed at the interruption. But the children's dark lashes fringed their cheeks; they were already asleep.

"Come," Ootadabun said, leading her out of the wigwam.

Curious, Aiyana pulled a blanket about her shoulders and followed Ootadabun to another wigwam. A circle of wailing women sat inside, their attention focused on a pale and lifeless child lying on the ground. Another woman, apparently the child's mother, sat next to the corpse, cutting her arms and thighs with a dagger as she whimpered in grief.

Ootadabun turned expectant eyes upon Aiyana, who blinked in consternation. What was she supposed to do? She did not know this squaw, and she had no idea how to comfort a grief-stricken heathen. Shrugging to hide her confusion, Aiyana looked toward the other women and saw the English captive Mary Rowlandson in the circle.

One by one, women stood and drew near to comfort the grieving mother, but Aiyana slipped around the circle until she knelt by Mary Rowlandson's side. From what Ootadabun had told her earlier, she knew the weeping mother was wife to Mary Rowlandson's master, but Aiyana could find no sign of commiseration or sympathy in the Englishwoman's eyes.

"Is this your mistress?" Aiyana whispered, nodding toward the woman with the dead child.

"It is," Mary answered, wiping her nose with the back of her hand. "The babe took sick last night and died. There has been a great company come to mourn and howl with my mistress, though I must confess, I cannot much console with them. A few weeks ago, I lost a child, too, and there were none to mourn with me." Her eyes flickered to Aiyana's face, then returned to the melancholy sight of the anguished mother. "There is one benefit in it. There will be more room in the wigwam tonight."

Aiyana gasped, stunned by the harsh sound of the woman's words. Mary noticed her reaction; her mouth twisted in an uncomfortable smile. "Oh, I know I am a heartless wretch. I have been a careless creature and sinner against God—that is why the Lord has oppressed me." She swayed slightly as the wailing of the women continued. "On Sabbath days I used to go to the house of God, have my soul refreshed, and at dinner eat my fill of the good creatures of God. At night I would go to my house and lie on a comfortable bed with my family around me. But now I have only a little swill for my body and must lie like a swine upon the earth." She paused and scratched nervously at her hands. "These lice are as constant as time passing; they eat at me until I shall be no more. Still, 'tis what I deserve." She gave Aiyana a bleak, tight-lipped smile. "I have sinned against God."

"As have we all," Aiyana said, her blood running thick with guilt as she remembered her own harsh judgment of Mojag and Ootadabun. "But God is merciful to sinners and promises to refresh those whom he loves."

"Do you think he will?" Mary's eyes went wide with hope. "One day I am confident of my release, but then my master is cruel to me or we move deeper into the woods, and my heart sinks. Some days they give me my load to carry and my burden is more on my back than in my heart, and other times I feel that I possess my life alone and little spirit with it."

"I am confident," Aiyana said, reaching for the woman's hand. "God will restore us when we are near to despair. We must wait upon him."

The words took hold of Aiyana's own heart, bolstering her spirit with the encouragement she had hoped to offer the Englishwoman. She squeezed Mary Rowlandson's hand. "We will pray together, you in your place and I in mine, that we may soon be restored to our loved ones."

"Yes," Mary answered; then her smile faded. "But you, surely you are among your family? I have seen you eating with the man and his woman—are you his second wife?"

Aiyana smiled and shook her head. "Mojag—Askuwheteau—is my brother. I am searching for an Englishman among the captives. His name is Forest Glazier, from Rehoboth. If you see him, will you tell him that Aiyana Bailie seeks him?"

Mary Rowlandson nodded thoughtfully. "I will."

"Thank you, and may God renew your spirit yet another night," Aiyana said, releasing the woman's hand. The mourners had departed to bury the baby in the woods, and as Aiyana watched, Mary Rowlandson turned and followed them.

▾▲▾▲▾ Through the winter and into spring, warriors regularly rode forth to conduct assaults on the frontier towns, burning most and plundering several. Back at the camp, Indian women and children scrounged for food and shelter. Metacomet's spirit grieved to see the suffering of his people, but as the earth warmed and renewed its life, spring revitalized his heart with strength and purpose.

As a spring snow melted in the warmth of the March sun, the sachems began to negotiate in order to return their English captives. The government of Connecticut had sent a letter suggesting an exchange of prisoners, but Metacomet and many of the other sachems were unwilling to consider the terms of negotiation. Willing to release the English, they were. But willing to sue for peace, never.

"They still do not understand," Metacomet told the council, his eyes blazing as he sat in the gathering. "They still think they can say that they are sorry for the wrongs of the past and all will be well. They do not understand that they have stolen our land, our lives. Only when they are gone will all be as it should be."

His gaze flew around the circle as he sought signs of agreement. Askuwheteau, He-Who-Waits, listened behind the elders, his striking face as unreadable as stone. But several of the younger sachems nodded eagerly, the fire of battle still hot in their veins.

"Perhaps we should make peace with the Yangeese," Annawon countered, looking around the circle. He was old and wise; the circle stilled when he spoke. "If we continue, my brothers, there will be none of us left to fight. Already sickness has taken many of our women and children. Our warriors will be next to die."

"Our children are hungry," Corbitant spoke up, "but the land itself will feed us. We will eat dirt if we must, but the land will be ours again. I say we fight hard and drive the Yangeese back into the sea. Canonchet has told his old friend Roger Williams that this fight will be to the end. The Yangeese have brought this war upon themselves. *They* violated the ancient treaties, not us."

"Very well, but we cannot meet them in large numbers," Annawon said, holding up his hand. "We must strike like the rattlesnake: quickly, silently, swiftly."

"No, no," Corbitant argued, his deep voice simmering with barely controlled passion. "They come at us with large forces and many guns. They will think us cowards if we hide in the woods to shoot at them."

Leaning his head upon his hand, Metacomet closed his eyes against the buzzing around him. So many disputes, so much disagreement. The young ones resisted the wisdom of the elders, and none of them saw the truth as he did.

Once one of his brother sachems had boasted that the Indians lost nothing but their lives while the English lost their fair houses and cattle. But cattle meant nothing, and houses could be rebuilt. Women and children were the lifeblood of a people; unless they were protected, the Wampanoag could never replace their slain warriors and fathers.

Their hope and future lay in the falls of a far-off river where they would find fish enough to feed themselves and rest to grow strong for another year of battle. They could no longer fight hungry.

John Eliot shifted in his chair, easing the strain upon his back. An attack of sciatica had left him unable to sit or ride a horse without discomfort, but there was no avoiding the pain. His work demanded his attention, and the praying Indians depended upon his help. If not for Daniel Bailie, he'd be truly hampered. A word to the right ear in Boston, coupled with Daniel's brilliant service with the Massachusetts militia, had resulted in official permission for Daniel to remain in Roxbury instead of returning to Deer Island. But though he no longer lived with the interned Indians, they were never far from his thoughts.

John and Daniel were now making plans to transfer many of the starving Indians from Deer Island to Cambridge in mid-May. At Cambridge, if all went well, the natives would be allowed to settle on a neck of land adjacent to the Charles River. A nearby garrison had promised to provide shelter in case they fell under attack from either Indian or English enemies.

John picked up a letter that had arrived that morning and broke the seal. Squinting at the message for a moment, he slapped his hand upon the desk. "Daniel!" he cried, his voice ringing through the room. "Come here! You'll want to hear this!"

Daniel appeared in an instant, his face taut with worry. "In faith, have you news of my children?" he asked, his knuckles white around the edge of the door frame.

"No, but I believe this is good news," Eliot said, scanning the letter again. "'Tis a report from Captain Denison. His men surprised a party of Indians, believed to be those who recently burned both Rehoboth and Providence. They gave chase to one native who wore a fancy coat and a belt of wampum. He ran well, dashing through a small stream but slipped on a wet rock and fell into the water, wetting the pan of his gun. A young Mohegan captured the man, who was determined to be Canonchet, come into Narragansett country to obtain seed corn for his people's planting."

"Canonchet!" Daniel sank into a chair and folded his hands. "A prize! I am surprised they proved able to capture him."

"Indeed," Eliot said, smiling at his friend. "They could not have done it alone, but Denison's company was made up of forty Englishmen and eighty friendly Indians. The Indians knew how Canonchet would run." He sighed for a moment, tapping his fingers upon the desk. "Now, if God is willing, the Indians will lose the heart for war. I have often heard that Canonchet is the most respected of the warring sachems. Now that his voice is absent from their council fires, the others may listen to the cries of their starving children."

"What happened to Canonchet?" Daniel asked, leaning forward. "Will he be brought to Boston for questioning? John, he might know something of Mojag or Aiyana—"

Eliot turned to the parchment and shook his head. "I'm sorry, Daniel. The Mohegans in Connecticut demanded his death. Captain Denison reports that Canonchet was beheaded by Oneco, son of the Mohegan who had killed Canonchet's father many years before."

The tiny handwriting swirled before his tired eyes; John brought the parchment closer. "Denison writes that Canonchet was content with the swiftness of the judgment: 'I like it well; I shall die before I speak anything unworthy of myself,' he said. The Mohegans sent his head on to the Council at Hartford as evidence of their loyalty and their victory."

Daniel groaned and let his head fall against the back of the chair. "Was no attempt made to negotiate with the sachem? to reason with his people?"

"Yes," Eliot answered, continuing to read. "Captain Denison offered to spare Canonchet's life if the Narragansett would surrender. But the sachem replied that Denison's offer made no sense, for the Narragansett would go on fighting, thousands of them, with or without him. And in response," Eliot shook his head in disgust, "Denison ordered the death of Canonchet and the forty-three captives taken along with him."

Daniel closed his eyes against the constant pain of his worry and loss, and the minister felt his heart swell in sympathy for his friend. John knew intimately the grief of losing a child, but in the past two years Daniel had lost wife, son, and daughter. Oh, that God might be merciful and restore the man's children so his heart might be comforted.

But Daniel did not seem to have God's comfort in mind. "Cursed be he that first invented war," he muttered, rising from his chair.

On Tuesday morning they called their General Court (as they call it) to consult and determine whether I should go home or no, and they all as one man did seemingly consent to it, that I should go home, except Philip, who would not come among them. . . . I was with the enemy eleven weeks and five dayes, and not one week passed without the fury of the enemy, and some desolation by fire and sword upon one place or other. . . . O the wonder-full power of God that I have seen, and the experience I have had! I have been in the midst of those roaring lions and savage bears that feared neither God, nor man, nor the devil, by night and day, alone and in company, sleeping all sorts together. And yet not one of them ever offered me the least abuse of unchastity to me, in word or action. . . . God's power is as great now, and as sufficient to save, as when He preserved Daniel in the lyons den, or the three children in the firey furnace.

. . . And I hope I can say in some measure, as David did, it is good for me that I have been afflicted. The Lord hath shewed me the vanity of these outward things . . . that we must rely on God Himself, and our whole dependence must be upon Him. If trouble from smaller matters begin to arise in me, I have something at hand to check my self with, and say, "Why am I troubled?" . . . I have learned to look beyond present and smaller troubles, and to be quieted under them, as Moses said, Exodus 14:13, "Stand still and see the salvation of the Lord."

—Mary Rowlandson

▼▲▼▲▼ Aiyana thought that the atmosphere of the Indian camp changed somewhat with the departure of Mrs. Mary Rowlandson and several other high-ranking Yangeese. Though she would not have dared voice her disloyal thoughts aloud, it seemed to her that the captives' release was a conciliatory gesture, an effort to curry favor. If the sachems had felt more certain of victory, she reasoned, the captives might have been tortured, killed, or kept in slavery. Surely this was the beginning of the end.

As the English began to disappear from camp, her heart grew more desperate for news of Forest. He might have been injured or killed or ransomed already, and she would never know unless God chose to send word through a messenger. Though every evening she walked about the camp and asked questions of those she met, no one had seen a captive of Forest's description or heard his name. She always returned to Mojag's wigwam empty-handed and heavyhearted, but Ootadabun never upbraided her for wasting time and energy that could have been spent gathering food.

God always seemed to provide. Ootadabun's kettle always brimmed with something— -nuts, acorns, lily roots, beans, weeds, and various plants that Aiyana did not recognize. Once or twice Aiyana saw Ootadabun pick up an old bone, cut it at the joint, and scald it over the fire to make the worms and maggots scurry out before she tossed the bones into the kettle. During the last few months Aiyana had eaten various parts of horses, wild birds, bears, venison, beavers, tortoises, frogs, squirrels, dogs, skunks, and snakes. Her stomach, which she had always considered tender and rather particular, rejoiced even to drink the juice of boiled bark.

One afternoon the women ignored their growling bellies, for the sachems ordered the camp to pack and move on. All women and children were to journey to Peskeompscut, a native village near the northern falls of the Connecticut River. The moon of the salmon migration had finally come, a traditionally joyful time when women speared the jumping fish as they leaped upstream through the falls.

"There is food at Peskeompscut," Mojag said, helping Ootadabun and Aiyana gather their supplies. "Cattle and horses, and a smithy where the men can repair their broken muskets. We need time to rest and restore ourselves, the sachems say, and the women and children will stay there for many months."

"If we stay there, where will you go?" Ootadabun's voice trembled with a vibrancy that Aiyana had never heard before.

Mojag gave his wife a warm smile. "I will be with you, my wife. Philip knows I do not fight for him. I will remain by your side for as long as I live."

Busy packing her bedroll, Aiyana paused, shriveling a little at the intimate tone of their voices. Bitter jealousy stirred inside her; she closed her eyes, her heart aching with pain. Forest should be with her. He had promised to love and protect her, but where was he? Like a fool, he'd followed his honor off into battle and left her to wait in a cocoon of anguish. He was probably dead, rotting somewhere in the woods, his bones scattered by marauding animals as hungry as the Indians.

"There is more news," Mojag said, his eyes gleaming toward Aiyana. "Annawon told me there are several English captives at Peskeompscut. The Indians have used Yangeese to work the forge at the river."

Aiyana blinked in astonished silence. Why couldn't Forest be at the river village? He had been captured near the river!

"Mojag, let us hurry," she said, tying her bedroll with renewed energy.

Ootadabun and Mojag laughed at Aiyana's sudden change of mood.

▼▲▼▲▼ Trails lined the winding course of the river on both sides, but Metacomet's Indians avoided them. Leaving the woods around Mount Wachusett in late April, they trekked toward the northwest through the unbroken expanse of forest.

Untouched timber stretched as far as Aiyana could see, disturbed only by occasional broken branches and splintered trees, the footprints of a past storm. New golden green leaves on the maples, beeches, and giant oaks stood out against the darker green of the stately conifers.

As the company neared Paquoag, an Indian village on a tributary of the river, clean meadows marked the valley. "The *pocconocks*," Mojag remarked, pointing out the cleared fields as they walked. "If we were at peace, this would be a fertile cornfield." His smile twisted in yearning. "Mayhap in summer we will be able to plant. Then this field will truly be beautiful."

"It is beautiful as it is," Aiyana answered, adjusting the load on her back as she followed the others. "It is unburnt. The English army has not yet been here."

At Paquoag the party turned westward, following the river and the setting sun, and within two days they had reached Peskeompscut. Aiyana thought her heart would burst with gratitude at the sight of so many tendrils of smoke lifting from wigwams. The village wore a settled, prosperous look; she could almost believe the war had not touched this place. Well-groomed Indian women came running from wigwams to welcome the newcomers. Chubby children cavorted near the water's edge, their faces wreathed in happy smiles. From a pen deep within the woods, Aiyana could hear the lowing of cattle, probably taken from the burned-out English town of Hadley. The aroma of roasting beef wafted on the afternoon breeze.

"I could almost sit down and die happy," she murmured to no one in particular as she stood on a bluff over the river and surveyed the prosperous village. Mojag laughed and followed Ootadabun down to the camp. "Help my wife with the wigwam," he called, his smile more carefree than it had been in days. "Then go with her to the falls. She has promised that we shall feast on salmon tonight."

Thunder rolled through the dark clouds overhead, and Aiyana laughed as she followed her brother down the path to the village. For the first time in months, she felt safe. This place was wet and wild and dense, and English muskets could not fire in the rain. Surely God had brought them all to this place for rest and renewal. Here she would find either Forest or the strength to face life without him.

She and Ootadabun hurried to chop saplings and lash them together, and they assembled the wigwam in a pouring rain. When the sun returned, Aiyana sent Chepi and Keme to play with the other children, and she followed Ootadabun to the falls. Here banks of rough stone encased the river, and a chain of rocks broke the normally smooth flow of the water. Forced between boulders on the banks and a series of small stone islands, the flowing water churned white, then roared over a deep drop, where it tumbled and swirled before resuming its southward flow.

More than a dozen women worked beside the majestic falls, their faces wet and beautiful in their glowing happiness. With spears in hand, they stood on tall platforms that loomed out over the swirling water. As the determined salmon leaped through the falls to reach their spawning grounds, the equally resolute women held their sharpened sticks above the water and speared the fish.

They made it look easy, but Aiyana's spear harmlessly brushed the first three fish without even grazing their scales. Watching Ootadabun carefully, she learned how to twist her wrist at the last moment to position her spear above the approaching fish. The creature then impaled itself by the force of its own weight. Within ten minutes the two women had five salmon, more than enough to feed their entire family. When they returned to the camp, Aiyana heard other cries of jubilation: A pair of hunters had killed a deer with a fawn in its belly. The tender meat was divided equally among every family in the vicinity.

They behave like people of the early church, Aiyana thought as she helped Ootadabun cut the salmon. *Such generosity did not exist in Rehoboth. What Englishwoman would give a captured Indian her last sliver of meat? But the Indians ofttimes showed kindness to Mary Rowlandson and other captives. Oh, if only someone is being as kind to Forest, wherever he is!*

A quiet, comfortable air descended over their small family that evening. The rain had come and gone; the sun hovered behind a line of grayish pink clouds against the paling horizon. Restless, Aiyana tossed wet branches into the fire as Ootadabun put the children to bed inside the wigwam. Respecting Aiyana's mood, Mojag said nothing, but sat by the fire whittling a piece of wood. After a moment, Ootadabun came to join her husband. As the air of the clearing vibrated softly with the insect hum of the wood, Ootadabun wrapped her arms around Mojag's neck, then nuzzled his cheek. As Aiyana stared at the ground in silent frustration, Ootadabun took her husband's hand and led him into the wigwam.

Fire shadows danced on the walls of the lodge, and Aiyana stood up, unwilling to wait alone with her thoughts while her brother took the wife he loved in his arms. How unfair life was! Had God totally abandoned her? She had remained in her God-ordained place. She had given herself freely to God's work. She had joined the Puritan church. She had taught the children. She had served her master well. She had done nothing but try to please God while Mojag left all that was holy to go live in the wilderness, but *he* had found love among the savages. And as much as she wanted to, Aiyana couldn't resent Ootadabun, for the girl's conversion seemed genuine and her spirit was as gentle as a child's.

Why, God? she cried, turning her back on the flickering shadows in the wigwam. *I risked my life to leave Deer Island. I have surrendered all to find Forest, and yet through weeks of searching and suffering there has been no sign of him. Even here there is not the vaguest reassurance that he still lives.*

Pulling her shawl about her, she stood and moved away from the wigwam. The rain-washed evening was sweet and clean; the air vibrated to the haunting cry of a whippoorwill. She followed a northward trail, away from the falls and the women's fishing places. The river was calmer upriver, and blue-white ripples glistened in the moonlight while scattered fires dotted the darkness of the bank. A group of warriors worked the forges there, repairing their weapons. Two large pigs of lead, probably stolen from one of the English towns or purchased from the French in the north, sat by the forges, ready to be melted into musket balls.

Standing on the bluff above, Aiyana stared down at the men working the forge. Their powerful, well-muscled bodies moved with easy grace. Sounds of their laughter and jesting rose to her ear. A sudden fierce pride stirred in her breast. *They say we are ignorant, that we had no wheel or books or forges until they came,* she thought, lifting her chin. *And yet my people learn quickly. And we can live off foods the English would fain avoid. We crawl over mountains and through swamps. We thrive in conditions that would break the spirit of civilized men and women.*

Her eyes fell upon a pair of bearded men working at the forge—Yangeese, no doubt. Their slender backs glistened with sweat despite the cool air. Had they been surprised to experience so rugged a society when they were first captured? Maybe they were among the English who liked Indian culture so well that they would not return to the English settlements.

Her cheeks burned in remembrance of her own feelings. It was only last winter that she thought the unredeemed natives a savage, merciless race. Though she had lived among Indians throughout her lifetime, Mojag was right: She had never really understood their culture. The praying villages were but hybridized versions of English colonies, in many ways as regimented and stagnant as Rehoboth.

One of the Englishmen limped slightly as he moved from the fire to his iron implements. He wore only a breechcloth and buckskin leggings; dark brown hair spilled over his shoulders as he turned to say something to his companion—

Forest. Her blood rose in a jet as she stared at his profile. Though the figure below was leaner and more muscular than the man she had known, she recognized the intelligence, pride, and resolute strength etched into every feature of his face.

"Forest!"

He turned in surprise; from across the distance his eyes touched her, gripped her. Scarcely aware of her actions, she flew down the slope as lightly as a bird, her feet skimming the scree among the rocks, her heart flying to meet his. Suddenly she was trembling in his arms, crushed by his strength.

"Forest," she whispered, lifting her hand to his cheek. "Thank God, you are alive!"

"Can it be Aiyana?" His hands were tumbling through her hair, drawing her near as if he could not believe he held a flesh-and-blood being. "Can it be you?"

"Oh yes," she whispered, half laughing. She heard deep-throated chuckles arise from the men on the riverbank; tonight the tale of this reunion would be repeated around many a wig-wam fire.

"But how did you get here? Have they released the Indians on Deer Island?"

"I heard that you were missing, so I slipped away. I knew that if I could find Mojag, he could help me find you."

"Mojag is here?"

"Now he is." She locked her hands behind his neck, closing her eyes to the wonderful feeling of happiness that enveloped and overwhelmed her. "We have been traveling with Metacomet. Our band has just arrived at this place."

Pulling out of her embrace, he stepped back, his appreciative eye traveling from her moccasins to her free-flowing hair. "Aiyana, my love, I'd forgotten how beautiful you are. There were times I thought I had imagined you."

"Oh, no." She laughed in sheer joy, unable to believe that he stood within the reach of her arms. "Are you well? What is wrong with your leg?"

"'Tis nothing." He shrugged away her concern. "I sprained my ankle when I was first captured. But it is healing, though I may never be as fast as I once was." The warmth of his smile echoed in his voice, and she trembled before the fire that smoldered in his gaze. If not for the wide and curious eyes about them he might have kissed her—

But they were not in a Puritan village, and she no longer considered herself a member of civilized society. "Forest," she whispered, locking her arms about his waist. "Life is too short to worry about what people will think. If God approves, so should man."

"Aiyana," he breathed, bending his lips to her ear, "how I adore your forthrightness!" Without further hesitation he bent to kiss her, moving his mouth over hers with exquisite tenderness. A small sound of wonder came from her throat; then she heard nothing but the pounding of her heart accompanied by yips and yells from the watching natives at the forge.

Pulling away with reluctance, Forest locked his hands behind her back. "Aiyana, we must do something about this."

"Yes," she whispered, looking fully into his eyes.

"I would like my father to be present at our marriage."

Her heart sank. This was not what she had hoped to hear.

"But he is dead." She looked up quickly to see that Forest's eyes had darkened with emotion. "I have been here since winter, and other captives have come to this place, even men from Rehoboth. The Indians attacked on March 28. Father, Witty, and Constance were killed, caught unawares at sunrise."

Sharp sorrow slashed at Aiyana's heart. Though she and Constance had not been good friends, she could find no real fault in the young girl. And Master Glazier and Witty did not deserve to die in war.

"I'm sorry, Forest," she said, blinking back sudden tears.

"Aye." He nodded, a weight of sadness upon his striking face. For a moment his thoughts left her; then the pressure of his hands increased as he drew her closer. "But those things are past, and you are here. Aiyana, my father could never have foreseen what would happen. And because he has given me his blessing, will you marry me now? What say you? I won't be parted from you again."

"You know I adore you," she whispered, her fingers tracing the line of his cheekbone and jaw. "But you are not free. Don't you belong to a master here?"

"If he won't let me marry, I'll convince one of the others to buy me from him." His arms fell upon her shoulders. "Please,

Aiyana, I love you. Whether I am a slave among the Indians for one more day or for the rest of my life, I want to spend my life with you. Please say you'll marry me."

The tenderness in his expression amazed her. Gone were his reticence and his reserved control. Like her, he had seen sights that could not be forgotten. Life was for living . . . and loving.

"Yes, Forest," she answered, looking up at him. "I will marry you. And I think I know a warrior who might be willing to buy you, if you promise to be a hard and willing worker."

His brows slanted the question. "Who?"

She tilted her head and gave him a secretive smile. "You shall see."

▼▲▼▲ Forest slept easily that night, secure in the knowledge that Aiyana lived. For months he had feared that all his loved ones were dead, that he was alone in the world. But once again God had demonstrated his goodness. Though every tie to Rehoboth had been cut asunder, his love for Aiyana remained. That was all that now mattered.

The next day, shortly after sunrise, Forest lifted his eyes from his breakfast bowl as an Indian approached. He did not immediately recognize the man's clothing or the design of the paint on his shoulders and face, but then his smile widened in recognition. Mojag! Aiyana meant for her own brother to purchase him, knowing that Mojag would have no quarrel with their marriage.

"Well met, Forest Glazier," Mojag said, squatting by the fire. His smile was sincere, and Forest grinned in relief.

"Well met indeed, Mojag Bailie," Forest answered. He extended his hand and shook Mojag's, a completely English gesture that seemed out of place in this forsaken wilderness.

But Mojag shook Forest's hand warmly, then sat on the ground and crossed his legs. "My sister has worn me out with searching for you, so I am happy you are finally found. And now she tells me that you would like to marry her as soon as possible."

"I do not want to wait," Forest said, resting his arm upon his knee. "I have learned that life is too precious to pass in waiting."

Mojag did not seem either surprised or alarmed. A flicker of a smile rose at the edges of his mouth, then died out. "I have learned the same lesson," he said, staring at the fire. "And I, too, have taken a wife. Though we may not live to see another winter, we have enjoyed many days of happiness."

Forest sat still, not knowing how to answer. After a long moment, Mojag looked up. "I have two gifts for you. The first rightfully belongs to Aiyana, but I give it to you in faith that she will be your wife." As he spoke, Mojag pulled a gold ring from his smallest finger, and Forest recognized the family ring Aiyana had worn in Rehoboth.

"Boldly, faithfully, successfully," Mojag said, dropping the ring into Forest's palm. "If you love her, that is how you must pursue her. Do not let this war or these privations dissuade you. She has endured much to find you, Forest Glazier, so do not disappoint her. I pray this will soon be the wedding ring you will place on her hand."

"I thank you," Forest answered, sliding the band onto his own finger. "And I will not give up, Mojag. Though I know there are obstacles ahead—"

"That is my second gift to you," Mojag answered, his smile broadening. "Today I will purchase your freedom from your master. I have several shillings in my purse; God must have known I would need them now. And since my father is not here to give his blessing, I give it in his place. I am Aiyana's older brother; it is right that I should do this."

"And the marriage?" Forest leaned forward eagerly. "I do not know how the Indians arrange these things."

"She will be yours when the sachem agrees," Mojag answered, leaning back. "Metacomet must be consulted. But until then, you will live in my wigwam as part of our family."

"Thank you," Forest answered, his heart flooding with the wonderful sense of going home. He looked at the Indian who would soon be his brother. "Thank you, my friend."

▼▲▼▲▼ A warning cloud settled on Metacomet's features as his obstinate mouth tightened. "She will not marry the Englishman. He will be ransomed like the others. But none of my people shall be given to one of the Yangeese."

Aiyana swayed on her feet, caught up in the sickening sensation of her life plunging downward. Across the wigwam, sitting beside Mojag, Forest looked vacant and spent, all emotion wiped from his face. Had they dared ask for too much? God had brought them back together; how could Metacomet keep them apart?

"Sachem," Mojag said, speaking in the low voice he reserved for serious matters, "my sister has an English grandfather. And your elders, even your father, have always welcomed the Yangeese into their villages. Your father would not have prevented this marriage."

"There will be no peace as long as the Yangeese remain in our land," Metacomet snapped, his handsome face distorted with anger. "Your sister has been among us for many moons; I have seen that her spirit now walks with ours. She is one of us, as you are, praying man, and she will not leave. He—" the sachem's dark eyes glowered toward Forest—"is not one of us. This marriage will not be allowed."

Metacomet stood, signaling an end to the discussion, and Aiyana turned on wooden legs and followed Mojag and Forest from the sachem's wigwam. An hour ago, she had supposed that she would pass this night in the arms of her beloved husband, and now she must lie in the same hut with him and know that again they had been kept apart. Was she wrong to love Forest Glazier? Why would God allow her to find him if they were not meant to be together?

Ootadabun's lovely face fell when the three of them reentered the hut. No one spoke, but Mojag's wife must have discerned from their troubled expressions that there would be no wedding. Silently, she turned and unrolled a mat on the far side of the hut. For Forest. The children would sleep between Forest and Aiyana; there would be no sin in the Christians' wigwam.

Aiyana blinked back tears as she looked at the lonely mat; then she lay down in her own place and closed her eyes to Ootadabun's sympathetic gaze. Let them pity her; she did not care. She had seen Forest's face. He felt more defeated than she.

Perhaps Metacomet was right—she had become one of the tribe. Maybe God wanted Forest to marry a civilized, proper English girl. . . .

"Aiyana," Forest said, his words echoing in the anguish between them, "I promise you, this is not the end of the matter. I will not give up. I will make a way for us, no matter what we have to do."

Tears of relief came in a rush so strong it shook her body.

▾▴▾▴▾ "Aiyana." Forest's voice came softly through the trees the next afternoon. She paused from her berry picking and looked up.

"What?" she asked, peering through the brush. Despite her sorrow, the sight of his sunburned face brought a smile to her lips. "Why are you whispering?"

He burst out of a tangle of shrubs, then dusted broken leaves from his shirt. "I didn't want the others to hear."

"What others?" She gestured to the empty woods around her. "We are quite alone."

"Then come here." He reached out, placing his hand on her shoulder in a possessive gesture. She stepped toward him, a little alarmed at the increased beat of her heart.

"What?" she asked, her eyes searching his face.

"I wanted to see you," he said, stepping closer. He stood so close she could feel the heat from his body, and her pulse skittered alarmingly. "I need to know that you still love me despite all that has happened. Last night you seemed so quiet. . . ."

"Forest," she whispered, closing her eyes as his hands slipped over her shoulders, "I do."

His mouth moved over hers then, devouring its softness. His arms encircled her, one hand at the small of her back and the other tangling in her hair. She clung to him, returning his kiss with all the pent-up frustration, love, and hunger within her.

After a long moment, he whispered into her hair, "I'm a free man now. You can come away with me."

"I can't," she protested, though a pulse beat at the base of her throat as though her heart had risen from its place in her bosom.

"We're not far from Hatfield," he went on, ignoring her protest. "We could be there within a few days and be properly married by a magistrate. You made it through the wilderness to find Mojag. Surely we can safely reach Hatfield."

The thudding of her heart slowed abruptly, and she pulled away, confused. "You want me to leave these people? Leave Mojag?"

"Your brother is a grown man—he doesn't need you to stay with him. You said you looked for him only to find me. Well, I'm here, Aiyana, and we're together, and the only way we can *be* together is if we're married. Since Metacomet won't allow it, let's go to Hatfield."

Mixed feelings surged through her. "Forest, I am an Indian," she whispered, pushing her hair away from her face, "and we are in the midst of war. I would be *shot* if we went anywhere near Hatfield."

"I'll protect you. We'll put your hair up. If you dress in an English kirtle and blouse, they won't know."

"The man on the dock at Boston knew, remember?"

"Aiyana." His tone was hurt, reproachful. "You almost sound as if you don't want to marry me."

"Forest, of course I do," she insisted. "I love you! But you are asking me to risk my life to marry you now. I have prayed and wept over this, asking God why he would bring us together, and I can only assume that he wants us to wait."

"Wait?" His hands slipped up her arms, bringing her closer. Her skin tingled when he touched her, and she could feel his uneven breathing on her cheek as he held her tight. "Can you tell me you really want to wait?"

She closed her eyes to the brief shiver that rippled through her. "This isn't fair, Forest," she said, pressing her hands to his chest. With an effort, she pushed him away.

"Aiyana," he said, breathing hard. A vague hint of disapproval edged his words. "This is not the life for me. I am a merchant. A colonial. I am not an Indian. I don't hunt. I don't fish. I don't like sleeping on the ground and picking lice off my clothes."

"Leave your clothes on an anthill overnight," she remarked offhandedly, frowning. "The ants will eat the lice."

He thrust his hands to his head, growling in frustration. "Dear *God*, why did you make me love this woman?"

"Do you know what I think?" she said, seething with sudden humiliation. "I think you just want to go back to your old dreams, Forest Glazier. You're free of your Indian master now. You can run away, and you will because you can't be a ten-thousand-pound man here in the wilderness! Your store, your treasures, were burned up at Rehoboth, but you want to get back to your work! Well, I've got news for you, Forest. God allowed that city to be destroyed, and I know the reason why. Do you?"

He looked up, disoriented by her sudden attack.

"Mojag and I talked about it this morning. The Puritans are fond of comparing themselves to the children of Israel in the Promised Land, but they forgot God's warning to the Israelites. God predicted that they would say, '*My* power and *my* might has gotten me this wealth.' They forgot the Lord, Forest, and God allowed them to perish just like the nations they had driven out of the land."

"There is nothing wrong with hard work," he answered, his eyes glazing as he looked past her. "God commands us to labor diligently. He blesses the fruit of our hands."

"But your father, Forest, and so many others, came to esteem their goods as highly as they did their God. Don't you see? Every morning they said their prayers and gave God lip service, but all they really thought about was working to lay up their treasures. You frighten me when you talk about going back to one of those villages, because the lure of work is so strong—"

"Merchandise is my calling, can't you understand that?"

Thrusting his hands behind him, he gazed at her with a confused half smile and leaned back against a tree. "Every English boy chooses a calling when he is young. I was apprenticed when I was fourteen. I don't know how to be anything but a merchant."

"That was man's calling, not God's," Aiyana whispered, daring to move close to him again. "Forest, I don't know what God has planned for you, but if I'm a part of that plan, I don't see how we can live in a city where I'm likely to be ridiculed or even shot just for being who I am. I love you, and I'll go with you anywhere, but I'll not take foolish risks just because you want to return to your selling and shopkeeping. I won't do it, Forest." Her voice gentled as her eyes moved into his, and she ran her finger along his cheek. "I can't."

"You can't." His voice was dull, final. "So you are an Indian, and I am a merchant, and there is no place where we can be together."

She stepped back, rebuffed by the cold light in his eyes. "Perhaps there is not."

"Then I should return this to you." Aiyana was barely able to control her gasp of surprise when he slipped a gold band from his finger and pressed it into her palm.

The family ring. Mojag must have given it to Forest in anticipation of their wedding. *Boldly, faithfully, successfully . . .* The inscription silently mocked her.

The pain in her heart became a sick, unbearable gnawing, and she flung the ring away into the woods, then turned and ran from the sight of Forest's haunted face.

On the thirteenth day of May, while the Indians at the forge gossiped about the Englishman who had been forbidden to take a wife from among their people, another English captive, Thomas Reed, slipped into the woods.

Two days later Reed staggered into Hatfield, an English settlement far downriver. As the citizens of that town pressed him for information, Reed told Captain William Turner about the large numbers of Indians at the falls. "They eat and drink and refresh themselves," he said, shrugging. "Many of the warriors are away hunting, and the women fish and laugh and sing of how they will plant corn in their old villages before summer's end."

Turner fingered his goatee, thinking. He knew he ought to send word to the militia. But what if the savages fled while the message was en route to Boston? Entertaining fantasies of personal glory and heroism, Turner made other plans. Though he was yet weak from a recent illness, he summoned all able men who were willing to attack the Indians.

On May 18, one hundred and fifty volunteers, many of whom were boys, mounted their horses after supper and rode out to engage the enemy. Their nighttime journey took them across Bloody Brook, a place where seventy-one Englishmen had been killed in a grisly ambush, and past the charred ruins of the town once known as Deerfield. Turner pointed out the destruction with impassioned eyes, determined that the sights should rouse and vitalize his men.

About a half mile from the falls at Peskeompscut, Turner gave the order to dismount. The makeshift army tied its horses to trees and tramped through the darkness on foot. Though the

English had never learned to move through the woods as silently as their tawny foe, the pounding and roaring of the falls drowned out the sounds of clinking weapons and snapping branches.

The woods vibrated softly with insect life, but no sounds or signs of movement came from the wigwams in the clearing. Reed had reported that the Indians were confident and careless because they knew no divisions of the English army were in the north. Flushed by the color of war and a lingering fever, Turner sniffed the air. His stomach cramped in sudden hunger at the scent of roasting beef. The Indians had obviously eaten a full meal and were now enjoying the deep sleep of satisfied souls.

A blurred and bloodred sun peered over the horizon, purples and golds forcing away the darkness. Turner's men looked to him for a sign. He lifted his musket and stepped out of the woods, walking boldly into the midst of the wigwams. Amazing. Not a single guard stirred. Had someone warned the savages and set them to flight?

Keeping his finger on the musket's trigger, Turner walked to the first wigwam and stooped down. Four adults and two children lay asleep under blankets. Indiscriminately, he pointed his musket toward one of the figures and fired.

The silence was shattered as other musket fire answered his single shot. Wounded savages screamed, others tore through the bark-covered walls of the wigwams in panic. Turner's men fired at anything that moved. He understood a few startled cries: "Mohawks! Mohawks!" but then the Indians came out of their wigwams and recognized their enemy.

"No, we are the Yangeese!" Turner yelled, pointing his musket toward another warrior in his hut. The man jerked to grab his own weapon; Turner shot him dead.

The camp boiled to life. Whooping in glee, the Hatfield men shot the fleeing Indians like wild game. Several of the screeching natives ran to the river, leaping into canoes or into the water itself, but the Englishmen followed the Indians to the riverbank and picked them off in the water. Canoes spilled in the panic; the dead and wounded Indians bobbed helplessly in the turbulent water until the river carried them over the falls.

Like determined hunters, Turner's men swept through the camp, searching every wigwam. They flushed men, women, and children from their hiding places and shot them on the run. Some of the elderly who could not run were dispatched with the sword. Others were herded together, marched to the riverbank, and executed at the water's edge.

One lad ran up, breathless. "Captain! We found their forge by the river, and with enough lead to supply an army!"

"Throw it into the deep," Turner answered, wiping sweat from his forehead. "All of it. And fire the wigwams!"

Shivering in weakness and excitement, Turner leaned back on a tree and loosened the collar of his shirt. Such a victory! They had not only killed at least two or three hundred, but they had destroyed a number of children, so in years ahead there would be fewer Indians to walk the warpath of their fathers. The old ones had died, too, and with them the ancient memories of hostilities past.

He would be rewarded for this, possibly promoted. It was the biggest score of the war, and it had been conducted not by the army but by well-trained settlers under one determined man—

"Captain!"

Terror rang in the voice that hailed him now, and Turner stepped out from beneath the tree, both excited and aggravated that his attention was in such demand. "What is it? Can't you handle anything by yourself?"

"Captain, look! On that western bluff!"

Turner lifted his eyes to the far side of the river, then a chilly sweat formed on his skin. On the opposite bank, a host of warriors had assembled. Their weapons gleamed in the bright light of morning. Their faces were masks of hatred distilled to its essence.

I stayed too long. The thought was the only solid reality in a mad world; he had given every thought to advancing and attacking and none whatsoever to retreating in good time.

War cries rent the air as the warriors descended from their bluff. They would be across the water and upon him in no time. Desperate, Turner gave the order to retreat, then sprinted through the woods toward the place where they had tethered their horses. But someone had planned better than he. The advancing savages had sneaked through the woods and encircled the camp; they fired through the woods at the escaping English. Many of the horses were mounted now by the encircling Indians.

Turner ran toward the river, hoping to cross and find safety on the opposite shore. But a shot rang out; a blinding pain tore through his back as he splashed into the water. His legs went numb beneath him, and he fell, turning over in time to see the proud sun in the white-blue eastern sky.

▼▲▼▲▼ High on the western bluff, the people in Metacomet's camp woke to the sounds of gunfire from the opposite riverbank. The Wampanoag warriors sprang from their beds and silently gathered their weapons, their moccasins kicking up dirt as they sprinted toward the river.

The shrieking, beastly noise of the attack rose from the riverbank, and Aiyana's heart turned to stone within her chest, weighing down her legs so she could not move. Forest and Mojag, their faces set like stone in protective determination, squatted in the doorway, ready to fire upon anyone, Indian or English, who entered the wigwam.

But neither of them, Aiyana knew, would leave to fight. Mojag had sworn not to injure the English or the Indians except in self-defense, and though Forest was free now to depart any time he liked, Aiyana believed he still loved her too much to leave her in danger. But if the English came here to release him from captivity, would he love her enough to stay?

"God in heaven, help them," Mojag murmured, his eyes misting as he listened to the shouts and screams of women and children.

Chepi and Keme whimpered softly, and Ootadabun drew

them to her breast, covering their black heads with her own as she urged them to be brave.

"'Tis a massacre," Forest said, listening to the battle below with a horrified expression of disapproval. "Why are they killing the children? Is there to be no quarter for the enemy?"

"A day of battle is a day of harvest for the devil," Mojag said, pulling Keme to him as he stared out the doorway with wide, guilty eyes. "All those children, all those *people*, had not yet heard the gospel. I was going to go among that camp tomorrow or the next day. . . ."

"What will we do?" Aiyana whispered, moving closer to Forest as she looked at her brother. "What will Metacomet do?"

"Metacomet will rout this enemy and put him to flight," Mojag answered, an artery throbbing in his neck. "Then the people gathered here will flee, the Nipmuck to one place, the Narragansett to another. Those of us who are left of the Pokanoket will follow Metacomet." Tears welled within his eyes. "Today the war is ended, Sister, but our sachem does not yet know it."

From out of nowhere, like a runaway horse, came the thought that hundreds of people had suffered and died for nothing. Aiyana gave a soft cry of despair, then rested her face on Forest's shoulder and began to weep.

▼▲▼▲▼ As the English fled toward Hatfield, Metacomet returned to the scene of the slaughter and gazed at the carnage. Nothing in Algonquin warfare allowed for the butchering of women, children, and elders. And the attack had come completely without warning! The colonial army was days away. His people should have been safe here in the woods, yet the hand of death had, in the last hour, snatched three generations of life from the native peoples. The Wampanoags who had made the mistake of camping near the river were virtually destroyed. The Nipmuck and Narragansett had also suffered heavy losses.

Moving stiffly, like an old man, he sat in the mud beside the reddened river. His hopes for the future were as dead as the bodies before him. His warriors had lost the heart for war. They were more interested in extolling the victories of the past than in planning for the future. The hunger of their bellies, which would worsen now that Peskeompscut had been destroyed, would propel them toward the Yangeese bargaining table. And his fellow sachems had already threatened to send Metacomet's head to Boston as a prelude to negotiations for peace. They no longer listened to his voice.

Oh, they were blind, his people! They had been so close to victory. If they could only have put aside their tribal difficulties, if only the Mahican had joined him, if only the Mohegan and Mohawk did not hate the Wampanoag so resolutely. Together they could have pushed the Yangeese into the ocean, sent them back to the island from which they came.

The sky, serene and blue, opened above him, and he lifted his gaze to it, though the afterimage of the bloody scene still rested upon his eyes. He ought to go home. Hunger and disease now plagued the warriors who had once praised him as the source of their courage and bravery. Their women had not been able to plant corn. There would be little food this summer and none at all this winter. This northern land belonged to the Nipmuck; it housed the bones of their fathers and grandfathers. He would go home to Monthaup. He had run out of time.

Who would go with him? His wife and son. His most faithful and loyal warriors. Unkompoin, his uncle, and Annawon, his trusted counselor. And Askuwheteau, He-Who-Waits, the stubborn and stupidly persistent prophet of Jehovah God and Lord Jesus.

The corner of his mouth dipped as he thought of the young man who would neither fight nor leave. With Metacomet's people he had endured starvation and cold, sickness and health. His advice had always been sound, even if ignored, his manner patient and respectful, his message unwavering. "Turn to the

God whose son is Christ Jesus," he had almost daily urged Metacomet. "He will bring peace to you and your people."

Yes, Askuwheteau was as clear as spring water, a man with no secrets or hidden motives, save one. From the first day until this, Philip couldn't understand why the praying man had named himself He-Who-Waits. For what was he waiting?

▾▴▾▴▾ Weeks later, after Metacomet's band had left the river falls, Mojag paused outside the sachem's wigwam, arrested by the sound of a new song coming from within. The Indian women sang often, usually lullabies or grinding songs, but this song was meant to encourage a man for war. Mojag stiffened. Metacomet must be preparing to launch another raid. Ever since the massacre at Peskeompscut, it seemed that Metacomet journeyed with one eye open for food and the other for the Yangeese. *A cornered bear fights fiercely*, he thought, thrusting his hands behind his back.

The singing stopped, and Metacomet's voice called from inside the hut. "Praying man! I have wanted to speak to you."

Mojag stooped to enter, surprised to find Metacomet alone with his wife and son. The sachem reclined on a grass mat, fingering a bowl of pine nuts, but these he gave to the boy. Wootonekanuska gave Mojag a timid smile, then left, pulling Mukki by the hand.

"Your son grows tall," Mojag remarked, sinking to the ground by the sachem.

Metacomet's eyes were red and rimmed with deep gray circles, and they glistened as he watched his son's retreating form. "Yes. Even in this, he grows."

Mojag sat silently, waiting, as Metacomet composed his thoughts. When he finally spoke, the sachem's voice was troubled. "Do you believe in dreams, my brother?"

"Dreams, Sachem?" Mojag moved his hand to his chin, caught off guard by the question. "God often speaks to men in

dreams and visions. Joseph and Daniel were two who had the
gift of interpreting them."

Metacomet shook his head. "I do not care about your God,"
he said, his smile utterly without humor. "I know that gods
speak through dreams. Since my wintering I have often been visited by the spirit of a fox. But since the beginning of war, my
father has come to me in dreams. I am almost . . ." His voice fal-
tered, the line of his mouth tightened. "Sometimes I am afraid to
sleep. My father is sad. He tells me I was wrong to make war.
But the Yangeese were not so bold while he lived. They did not
rob and cheat us while he was sachem."

"Your father does not speak to you," Mojag said, taking pains
to gentle his tone. "This is the voice of your conscience, of guilt.
Part of you weeps for the people who have suffered, for those
who have died. If you will turn to my God, Sachem, his Holy
Spirit can still this voice. He can remove your guilt and give you
peace."

"There is more." The sachem's eyes burned with feverish
intensity. "The ghost of my father warns me that even my wife
and son are not safe. He says they will die if I do not sue for
peace."

"No one is safe in war," Mojag answered, tenting his hands.
"Not even the wife and son of a sachem. Even the great Canonchet has fallen, and others will die unless the fighting ends."

"You must help me." Metacomet's voice rang with command.

Mojag's smile broadened in approval. "You know, Sachem,
that I have been willing to help ever since I came to you. If you
will turn to Jesus—"

"No." The sachem's voice was hoarse with frustration. "You
will help my wife and son. You do not fight with the warriors,
but you are skilled with a weapon or you could not have
brought in the elk. You said you would defend your wife and the
children in your wigwam; defend my wife and son, too. Remain
in the camp with them when the warriors ride forth. There are
not many of us left, and there is none to guard my wife but you."

Mojag bit down hard on his lower lip. This was not what he

had hoped for, but God worked in strange ways. Perhaps if he did this job well, Metacomet's heart would stop resisting the gospel.

"I am honored to serve you," he said, recognizing the desperate gleam in the sachem's eye. "I will defend your wife and son as vigorously as I would protect Ootadabun and the children she shelters. You have my word on it."

The desperate look suddenly left Metacomet's eyes, and he nodded in what could have been relief.

In faith, God may be in this, Mojag thought as he left the hut. *If the sachem's wife and son are preserved through my hand, I will give God the glory, and Metacomet will see that the true God is all-powerful.* Encouraged by this thought, he hurried to his wigwam to share the news with Ootadabun and Aiyana.

Realizing that starvation had become their most powerful ally, in the early summer of 1676 the English moved from a defensive position to an offensive one. Breaking into small companies, the colonial militia moved through the country, burning any and all growing cornfields save those of the English. The Indians, broken now into migratory groups of a few warriors and many women and children, moved from place to place like restless shards of glass in a kaleidoscope. Hunger drove them to rivers where they could fish and to abandoned villages where fields might be gleaned for remnants of food.

No place was safe. Not only did the English prowl the woods and fields, but bands of fierce Mohawks swooped down from the north, determined to win favor and improve Mohawk-English trading policies. Whenever an enemy appeared, the Wampanoag and their allies retreated into the lowlands, but more and more often the English came with well-fed native armies that glided smoothly through the swamps like shadows.

The scorched-earth policy began to bring results. Throughout June and July, various rebel sachems approached the English and begged for terms. The colonial authorities turned a deaf ear to words of peace, telling the repentant Indians that those who had begun the war or engaged in atrocities must die. Many surrendering Indians, grateful for food and shelter, proclaimed that they had not engaged in any warlike activities and gratefully served the English as spies and scouts against their former comrades.

The formerly helpless militia became an informed army, as adept at skulking as the Indians they had once decried. Company by company they pursued the enemy through the wilderness, killing or capturing scores of men, women, and children, most of whom were sold into slavery in the West Indies despite the cries and protests of men like John Eliot.

But through the summer months, no matter how hard the English captains tried to find him, Philip slipped through their traps and schemes, always just out of sight, forever one hill or river beyond the militia's reach.

▼▲▼▲▼ On July 24, Governor Josiah Winslow of Plymouth issued Benjamin Church a new commission. The order, which had been approved by all governors of the United Colonies, granted Church broad discretionary powers. Under its terms he was authorized to appoint his own officers, pursue the enemy anywhere within the bounds of Connecticut, Massachusetts, or Plymouth, and make treaties with the Indians who wanted to abandon Philip's war effort. At his insistence, one final clause had been added: If he so desired, Church could even grant mercy to all but the most notorious enemy leaders.

On the morning of July 30, Governor Winslow himself pulled Church from worship in the Plymouth meetinghouse. With a smug expression on his round face, the governor explained that two messengers from Bridgewater had brought word that Philip had been sighted near their town. The time had come for action.

Church's body vibrated with new life and purpose; he had a company of men and supplies assembled by that afternoon. They set out immediately and stopped for the night on the shores of Monponsett Pond. The two messengers from Bridgewater went on ahead to spread the news that Church's company was en route.

The next day twenty-one men marched out of Bridgewater to rendezvous with the approaching Plymouth force. On the way they encountered a party of enemy Indians trying to cross the Taunton River on a great tree that they had felled to serve as a bridge. A skirmish ensued, and the Bridgewater men managed to inflict a number of casualties and seize several of the enemies' guns. Church, approaching from the east, heard the sound of battle, but was unable to locate the action in time to join in.

Safely arrived in Bridgewater, Benjamin Church could not sleep that night. Philip was near; Church could practically taste victory. Apparently the sachem and his people had come down from Nipmuck country into the eastern part of Plymouth Colony and now wished to cross to the western side of the Taunton River.

According to the reports Church had heard, Philip was progressing steadily southwestward toward the Mount Hope peninsula. Had he come back to his own territory because he knew it best? Or had he come home to die?

It mattered little. If he had tried to cross the river today, he would try again on the morrow. But this time, Church would be ready. This time, Philip would not escape.

▾▲▾▲▾ Mojag stirred uneasily upon his blanket, his ears filled with the rumbling sounds of thunder. He had heard the distant sounds of musket fire during the afternoon; even now Metacomet and the others could be dead. He and Forest were the only men present in a small camp of women and children hidden deep in English territory.

He knew the English would not fight in the darkness, but his fevered imagination would not let him sleep. What if the English burst in upon them? Should he shoot or surrender? Perhaps with careful bargaining he could save their lives, but what if the Yangeese stormed in and fired at women and children the way they had at Peskeompscut?

He sat up and brushed the hair from his eyes in a frustrated gesture. Metacomet's request that Mojag guard his family, at first an honor, now hung as heavy as a tombstone about Mojag's neck. They were all exhausted, sick with the struggle, weak from hunger, drowning in the ashes of dreams. Aiyana and Forest, sleeping far apart in the wigwam, had found each other but not happiness, for still Metacomet forbade their marriage. Next to

Mojag, Ootadabun slept with the children curled into the gentle curves of her body. The taut skin of her face had slackened in sleep, and she looked strangely old, like a forty-year-old woman instead of a young girl. The sleepers wore somber expressions on their faces as they clung to soft darkness and the escape it offered.

Maybe the English knew where they were. They might have watched all afternoon, realizing that Mojag and Forest had been left alone to defend a camp of women and children. If the English were coming, they'd come at daybreak, the same time they had come at Peskeompscut. Mojag would need his strength at sunrise, but if he lay down now, he'd sleep too long and they'd find him unaware, helpless, unprepared.

Thoughts of what might happen tore at his insides, and Mojag stood to walk outside into the cool dark. *He-Who-Waits*, he thought, lifting his face to the caressing night breeze. *I am still waiting.*

▼▲▼▲▼ The night died without incident. The moon nervously hid her face in the clouds as she lingered in the midst of the triumphant sun's advent. Dewdrops, like stars of water on leaves, gradually steamed away in the summer heat, and the sounds of everyday life stirred in the camp. Children's laughter threaded through the hustle and bustle of morning, and women's voices lifted in quiet song. From where he stood by the tree, Mojag lowered his head in thankfulness. Sunrise had come and gone without incident. They were safe. The English had not found them.

Forest came out of the hut, staring at Mojag with a perplexed smile. "Are you well?" he asked, rolling up the sleeves of his shirt. "You don't look like yourself."

"I am fine," Mojag answered, moving stiffly toward the wigwam. He felt like an old, tired man. "I just want to sleep for a while. Tell the children to let me rest. I just want to . . . sleep."

Relief throbbed dully in his brain as he closed his eyes; then his mind went blessedly blank. Some children ran by, their trail of laughter reaching into the wigwam, and the sound registered in his ear as normal and good. His hands relaxed; his breathing slowed. Time stopped. The moment or hour or day seemed to be lost in the gray space between dawn and day, between dusk and dark. Images of warriors long gone moved through the fog of his dreams. A dog brayed, the deep, booming note of a proud bloodhound, and a rabbit squealed in fear as the warriors cheered the hunt. Mojag knew he should rise to watch, but as the hunters bore down in slow and stately deliberation, he could make no move to stop them.

Something warm and soft nudged his belly. "Wake, Father! They are here!"

Mojag breathed in the scent of Chepi and reached for the child. "Later, little one," he murmured, forcing the words from his thickened tongue.

"The Yangeese! Please, Father, wake!"

The fog vanished as Mojag's eyes flew open. The English! It was not a dog he heard but a gun! Not a hunt but a massacre!

Even now he heard screams of fear and the rough voices of conquering men. He sat up and pulled the little girl to him. "Quick, tell me, Chepi—where is your mother? Where is Keme?"

The girl pointed wordlessly to the woods behind the wigwam.

"Good. And where are Forest and Aiyana?"

Again she pointed to the woods.

"Good." Mojag crept forward, hiding behind the wall of the wigwam as he peered out. The English, bold and sure, had fanned throughout the camp. At least two dozen Indians stood with them, and Mojag realized with puzzled fascination that these were traitorous Sakonnets who had joined the English. A circle of captives stood in the center of the camp, mothers with their arms about their crying children. Occasionally a soldier fired a shot into the air, but Mojag could see no bodies on the ground.

One man in a red uniform walked toward Metacomet's wigwam.

Without taking his eyes from the soldier, Mojag reached for his musket.

"Come out, and we won't hurt you," one of the Indians called in the Algonquin tongue. "Come out, and the English fathers will feed you. You will have clothing and food and will suffer no more."

Under the point of a musket, Metacomet's wife and son stepped out of their wigwam. Silently, with great dignity, Wootonekanuska led Mukki into the circle of captives.

They don't know who she is! Mojag thought, watching from the gloom of his own hut. *She and Mukki are just two among many. The English will not realize what they mean to Metacomet. . . .*

Chepi tugged on his leggings, her eyes wide with fright. "Shh, be still," Mojag cautioned, watching the scene beyond. The fate of Metacomet's family was now out of his hands. And Ootadabun and Aiyana waited in the woods beyond.

After gathering Chepi into his arms, he turned and used his dagger to cut an opening through the wall of the wigwam. Slipping into the darkness of the woods, he left the camp behind.

Pausing before the gate of John Eliot's house, Daniel struggled with his too-tight collar as he wrestled with the news he had to bring. It was uncomfortably hot, sticky, and humid, not a good day for bad news. John wouldn't like the report from the Council; he'd storm for an hour and then grow quiet before finally writing a pensive letter to the governor. Then Hannah would pull Daniel aside and remind him that such news wasn't good for her husband's health, that the war had been very hard on him, that the pains in his back and legs made even sitting unbearable—so how was he supposed to survive yet another trip to Boston?

And this news would certainly press him to Boston, probably to Plymouth as well.

Summoning his courage, Daniel pushed the gate open and walked up the path, greeting the housekeeper with a smile. "Good morning, Miss Liza. Is the master in?"

"Yea," the young woman replied, curtsying respectfully. "He's with Master Gookin."

Daniel breathed a sigh of relief. Mayhap Gookin had brought the same report Daniel dreaded to share. If so, the onus of bad news would be on Gookin's shoulders.

But no. The two men were sitting in the keeping room. Two cups of tea steamed on a small table between them, and open books rested on their laps. Each man glanced up and smiled at Daniel when he entered, and he waved a hand so they would not interrupt their conversation on his account. "I'm telling you, John," Gookin went on, leaning forward in his earnestness, "though it pains me to say it, I don't think either the London company or the Boston commissioners will allow another printing of the Indian Bible. They will say the idea is preposterous. Why should they give the Word of God to savages who are killing our people on the frontier?"

"Mayhap they would not be killing anyone if the gospel had been more fruitfully spread among them," John answered, acknowledging Daniel with a nod. "Forgive me if my age makes me importunate, but if I may but leave the Bible among the Indians, I shall depart this life joyfully. It is the word of life, and there may be some godly souls among even the most savage of them who will live by its words."

"They will say it is time for the Christians among them to read an English Bible," Gookin answered as Daniel took a seat. Gookin gestured to him. "Daniel, you have worked for a long time with the praying Indians—don't you think 'twill be necessary for them to speak and read English if they are ever to be civilized?"

"Teaching is certainly more effective if the natives have a Bible in their hands," Daniel answered, tugging uncomfortably on his jacket. "And only a few of the refugees managed to take their Bibles when they were harried away to Deer Island. But today only fragments of the Indian Bible remain."

"But the English version—," Gookin began.

"Is unintelligible to them," Daniel interrupted. "The great mysteries of God are deep enough in one's own tongue, how can they be understood in a foreign one?" He turned to John Eliot and softened his tone. "I think the Indian Bible should be reprinted because of what you have invested, my friend. Your time, your great personal dedication, the long patience you have spent in order that the Indians might have the Word of God—"

"The commissioners might be persuaded to reprint the Psalms and the Gospels," Gookin interrupted, slapping his knees. "But not the Old Testament."

"But the Old Testament means so much to them!" Eliot protested, wagging his gray head. "They name their children after the patriarchs. They love the stories of the Old Testament saints."

Daniel sighed. This discussion about the Algonquin Bible

could go on for hours, and neither man would change his opinion. He leaned forward and placed his hand on the old minister's knee. "My dear friend," he said, unable to keep his news to himself any longer. "I have some information that may vex you more than this debate. Shall I continue, or would you like to rest for a moment?"

"Continue, Daniel, by all means," Eliot said, stiffening in his chair. "I have seen much sorrow in the last year, and still the Lord has not allowed me to suffer more than I am able to bear."

"By your leave, then." Daniel took a quick look at Gookin, then eased back in his chair. "A report has just come from Bridgewater."

"Is there fighting there?" Gookin said, frowning. "So far south?"

"A brief skirmish between Benjamin Church and a band of Indians," Daniel went on, frowning to hide his own flustered feelings. "Philip himself was discovered sitting on the far bank of the Taunton River. Church was about to take a shot at him, but a friendly Indian yelled that the man was an ally, whereupon Philip took off into the brush."

"So close," John Eliot whispered. "If we could capture Philip and arrange terms —"

Gookin snorted from his chair; Daniel shook his head. He and Gookin knew that the colonial authorities would sooner return to England than let that notorious sachem live, but John was ever an idealist.

"This is the troubling part," Daniel went on. "The English captains have seen that the Indians are very affectionate toward their children."

"Indeed," John answered, lifting a brow. He leaned his chin upon his hand. "I have known a father to take so grievously the loss of his child that he cut and stabbed himself with anguish and rage."

"Yes," Daniel went on, choosing his words carefully. "The Sakonnet have defected from Philip's cause, and on the thirty-first of July they led Benjamin Church to a spot near Bridgewater. Philip escaped during the skirmish, but the Sakonnets killed or captured one hundred seventy-and-three of his Wampanoags. Among the dead was Philip's uncle, Unkompoin, and in a circle of nearby wigwams, Church's party found Philip's wife and son. They were identified by friendly Sakonnets and have been turned over to the ministers in Boston."

John Eliot's face paled. "To the ministers?" he asked, his breath quickening. "Why did no one consult me? This is God's provision for us. Now Philip will be willing to arrange terms."

"No, John," Gookin said, casting a hasty look at Daniel. "I believe they are hungry for blood. They may even execute the boy for the crimes of his father."

Daniel nodded. "I have already heard several ministers citing Scripture for and against such an act. 'Tis a raging debate in the courts of Boston."

"They must offer the boy to Philip in return for peace," Eliot said, his face flushing as he clasped the arm of his chair. "'Blessed are the peacemakers.' Can they have forgotten our Lord's words? If they will handle the woman and child gently, Philip might be entreated to lay down his arms."

"I believe they are more inclined to sell both the wife and son into slavery," Daniel said, wishing he had better news.

"And so we lose them to the gospel!" John said, his voice rising. The corner of his mouth twisted with exasperation. "And so the war goes on. And if death and slavery are the only alternatives to victory, Philip will fight even more desperately than he did before. And now he will hate us and will contend with us from a desire for blood vengeance."

"Daniel," Gookin asked, twisting in his chair. "Your son is with Philip, is he not?" His voice dropped into an infinitely compassionate tone. "Was he among those captured?"

Daniel shook his head, relieved that the burden of his own heart had been uncovered. "No, thank God," he whispered, looking at the floor. "Though I do not know what I will do when— if—I hear that Mojag waits in Plymouth for sentencing. And my Aiyana—"

His voice broke. He had witnessed too many painful scenes to imagine that his family would escape death and sorrow. As tears blinded his eyes and choked his voice, the other men fell into an uncomfortable silence.

"God has his hand upon your children," John Eliot said after a moment. He leaned back in his chair and studied Daniel intently. "I speak what the Spirit of God tells me, Daniel, and I rest in this knowledge: Your children, wherever they are, are safe."

Quinnapin, one of the greatest of the Narragansett sachems, fell to the English days later. Colonial forces captured One-eyed John, Sagamore Sam, and Muttawmp. Weetamoo drowned in a river as she tried to escape the pursuing army. And Benjamin Church dogged Metacomet's footsteps, once coming so close that the sachem saw the white gleam of the hunter's eyes.

Metacomet learned of the Sakonnets' treachery through his spies. Two of his men brought him word that Awashonks of the Sakonnets had made a peace treaty with Benjamin Church. In celebration of her betrayal, the squaw sachem staged a joyous dance on the shores of Buzzards Bay at Mattapoisett. All the Indians of her tribe, great and small, gathered around a huge bonfire. Awashonks and her elders made a ring around the fire; her robust warriors encircled the elders, the rest of the tribe mingling outside these two rings.

"Then the one they call Captain Church stepped in between the rings and the fire, with a spear in one hand and a hatchet in the other," Tihkoosue told Metacomet, a muscle flicking angrily at his jaw. "He danced with the sachem around the flames. He fought with the fire and made mention of all the nations and companies of Indians that were his enemies. This I saw with my own eyes; this I swear to you."

Metacomet bent his head and studied his scarred hand, understanding the significance of the dance. One by one, Benjamin Church had symbolically disposed of the enemies of the English, including Metacomet himself. One by one, Awashonks's warriors would have joined him, swearing their allegiance in the traditional Algonquin way.

Had his name been the first spoken? Or had they reserved his name for last, when their fury was at its peak?

Metacomet shrugged in mock resignation, though a raw and primitive grief overwhelmed him. Benjamin Church now had a very fine Wampanoag army, composed of men who had previously vowed to fight to the death in Metacomet's cause. He grimaced in misery so acute that it was a physical pain. His own people had turned against him.

Yet all these things he could have borne if not for the loss of Wootonekanuska and Mukki. Metacomet felt as if whole sections of his body were missing, torn away. His father's dream ghost wore a mournful expression now; the line of sachems had come to an end because of what the English called King Philip's War. "My heart breaks! I am ready to die," he had cried when he learned the news, and the passage of days had not lightened the misery that sat like an iron weight inside him.

He was exhausted, drained of will and of any thought but going home. Dashed dreams and disillusionment raked at his heart—the fight was lost, the lights fading. He and the pitiful remnant of his people traveled with shoulders drooped, their gait slow and unsteady. The horses were gone. They had eaten the last one, Metacomet's prized black stallion, on the banks of the Taunton River because the forest yielded no other meat. They lived and breathed and moved in the twilight world of the half alive; darkness pressed down on them.

And yet they continued toward the tidal basins of Monthaup, home, their fathers' burial grounds. Metacomet walked in the dark with pain and loneliness, a handful of warriors and counselors, and the praying man and his family.

Lord Jesus had preserved the praying man's family but not Metacomet's. Askuwheteau's Lord Jesus had power, but he would not save the Pokanoket from the harsh hand of English justice. The Yangeese would have no mercy; they had shown none to his wife and son. Wootonekanuska and Mukki should have died in the camp with honor, but he'd heard that the greedy Yangeese planned to sell them like cattle. They would be lost to the land they loved, torn from the existence they had known.

Alone in his wigwam later that night, Metacomet faced hopelessness. His experiment with the praying man had failed. One day, he thought with a wry smile, he might have called upon the Jesus God just to see why men clung to him so resolutely. But not now. The Yangeese called themselves God's people, and they would not give him a chance. They would strike him, chop his body into pieces, hang his head upon a pike, and laugh at his broken brow and wasted visage. They had done it to others who offended them far less than he. He had heard already that Weetamoo's head was on display in one of their towns, and they had stolen Sunconewhew's head, leaving a headless corpse for Metacomet to bury.

He would not submit! Let them come; let them find him! They would earn their bright badges of honor!

Lifting his head in a proud imitation of his earlier strength, Metacomet summoned his counselors. Only five remained, a mere handful. Annawon, his faithful war captain; Segenman; Pannoowau; and the two brothers, Tihkoosue and Sunukkuhkau. They sat at the fire outside the hut and looked at their sachem with a kind of sardonic weariness, their eyes narrowed by pain and doubt. Only Annawon looked at him with a clear countenance. Only Annawon believed the Fox was still elusive and clever.

Metacomet sat beside them in silence for a moment, measuring each man's mood by his expression and gestures. Finally Sunukkuhkau spoke. "My Sachem, my brother and I spied for you. We saw Benjamin Church make peace with Awashonks. And now we are starving."

"So we are hungry. Have any of us died from an empty belly?" Metacomet asked, lifting a brow. He crossed his arms. "I will not talk of peace. I will not sit back and let the Yangeese fill the land until we have no place of our own. It is far better for a leader to dare great things than to do nothing. A warrior will have honor if he wins glorious victories even though he endures defeat. I will not rank with pathetic creatures who neither savor nor suffer much because they live in the gray twilight that knows neither success nor failure."

"The Yangeese are numerous here. They have built forts and will set a trap for us. If we value our lives, we should treat for peace," Sunukkuhkau insisted, rebellion in his eyes.

"Our lives?" Metacomet snapped. Fury almost choked him. "Why should we value *our* lives? The lives of our wives, our children, our fathers, are gone. My brother lies in the earth, his head resting upon a pole at Rehoboth. While his soul searches for his head, the Yangeese jest and spit in his face. My wife will never greet me again, and my son—"

His anguish peaked to shatter the last shreds of his control. He would weep if he could not channel this unbearable emotion. Wrapping his palm around the handle of his tomahawk, he stood in the tense silence and walked forward with stiff dignity, then whirled toward Sunukkuhkau, burying the blade deep in the man's skull.

The others flinched but said nothing. The dead man slumped sideways toward his brother, Tihkoosue, who gaped at Metacomet, his long nose pinched and white with silent, resentful rage.

"We will not speak of peace, for there will be none until the Yangeese are dead or gone," Metacomet said, his anger hovering in the air like an invisible dagger. "I have spoken."

Annawon tilted his head slightly and offered a trembling, diplomatic smile. "Sachem," he said, his voice fragile, "Askuwheteau lives with an Englishman in his wigwam. If there can be peace in this camp with one of the Yangeese—"

"There is no peace here." Metacomet stepped forward and grabbed the handle of the tomahawk, jerking it from the dead man's head. Even Annawon stiffened as Metacomet straightened and turned again to face the circle. "Call Askuwheteau. Call his wife, his sister, the Englishman, and the children who live with them. Bring them before me. I will no longer suffer their presence."

▼▲▼▲▼ Aiyana caught Mojag's eye when the summons came; then she looked at Forest. She had expected this, and her dread had grown ever since the raid upon their camp. More than sixty of them had managed to escape when the English came, but Wootonekanuska and Mukki had not. And for that, she feared, Forest and Mojag might now suffer.

"What is happening?" Forest asked, his expression wary in the fire-tinted darkness. "Why does Philip send for us at this hour of the night?"

"He is Metacomet," Mojag reminded him. He extended a hand to Ootadabun, who had been asleep by the fire. "And do not make the mistake of speaking his name to his face. He will think you have no manners whatsoever."

"You have often assured me that I do not," Forest answered, but he smiled as he stood and waited for Aiyana to follow Mojag and Ootadabun.

"All of you must come," Annawon said, peering inside the wigwam. "Even the little ones."

Ootadabun's face paled, but she crawled back inside the wigwam and woke the two sleepy children.

Aiyana walked beside Ootadabun as the men led the way to the sachem's fire. Whatever this was, it was not good. Metacomet's mood had been black and heavy ever since he had returned from the Taunton River. He might hold Mojag responsible for his wife and son's capture, she thought, but Mojag had also helped to gather the survivors in the woods and move the camp to a more distant location. And when Metacomet had returned and cut himself with grief at the news about his family, Mojag had offered no excuses. He-Who-Waits had simply . . . waited. For this?

She shivered with a cold that was not from the air, then lifted her chin, determined not to expose her fear. Metacomet was not a devil; he was a frightened, lonely man. God had brought her and Mojag to this place. God would protect them, even here, and show them what they must do.

Metacomet was sitting on his ceremonial mat outside his

empty wigwam. He wore his heaviest wampum belts around his shoulders, his arms folded, his eyes large and fierce. In front of him, a ceremonial bonfire had been laid but not lit. Aiyana felt sweat bead on her forehead and under her arms when she saw that a man's body had been tied to an upright pole in the center of the mounded rushes.

"I have something to say to you," Metacomet said, his voice cold. His dark, gun-barrel eyes strafed their group, then trained in on Mojag. "You are no longer one of the Wampanoag."

"If I have failed, I beg your forgiveness," Mojag said, bowing his head.

Metacomet pressed his lips together. "I left my wife and son in your care, and you promised to protect them. And yet they are gone, stolen from me, while your wife and children and sister live. Your God helped the Yangeese, and you did not keep your word. I have no use for either you or your God." His eyes were like black holes in his somber face. A tear rose, but he dashed it away, smearing the war paint on his cheek. "I allowed you to come among us," he said, his compelling eyes riveting Mojag to the ground, "not because I wanted to hear about your God but because I wanted to see if your heart could be turned from him. And when it could not, I thought you were a man strong enough to protect my family. But you were not."

Suddenly Metacomet turned to Aiyana and Ootadabun. "Take these children from your wigwam when you go. They do not—" He paused, unwilling or unable to speak more, and Aiyana thought she understood what the sachem meant to say. The war had left him with a nation of widows, orphans, starving scarecrows. Nothing but ill remained for those who stayed with him, and he desperately wanted the children of his tribe to survive. Doubtless he also thought of his own son, now in the vengeful hands of the English.

So he was sending them away! Mojag had said he would never leave unless God or Metacomet demanded it, and now that time had come. The wait was finished; she and Forest would soon be parting. He would find an English village, and she would return to her father.

"We will take them, my Sachem," Aiyana whispered, nodding in respect.

"And you, Englishman." A creeping uneasiness rose from the bottom of Aiyana's heart as Metacomet looked at Forest. "You have no parents to ransom you, no wife to miss you. You are a captive of war. Tonight your life will pay for the evil of the Yangeese. You will burn in the fire with the dead traitor."

Speechless with horror, Aiyana felt the woods swirl around her.

"No, Sachem!" Mojag said, kneeling. He spread his hands in a gesture of entreaty. "You do not want to do this! You think you can erase the bitterness in your heart by killing one of the Yangeese, but this man has done you no wrong! If you must take a life to feed your anger, take mine."

"Mojag," Aiyana pleaded, her heart thumping madly.

"Let me do it," Forest called as two of Metacomet's men seized his arms. "The sachem is right; no one waits for me."

Waves of grayness passed over Aiyana. What did he mean? She had been waiting since they first met!

Scowling at Mojag, Metacomet lifted his hand as if he would slap him away. "Stand up or sit," he muttered, the words a low growl in his throat. "The blood of the people flows in you. Do not grovel like a worm!"

Mojag ignored him and remained on his knees. "Sachem, you have cast me off from the tribe I have vowed to serve. Your anger and grief are great, I understand! But do not blame God for my failures. I slept while the English came. Your wife and son are with the Yangeese because I did not stand guard. Take my life and free this Englishman. He has lived with us in peace. He will protect the women and children so the Wampanoag will not altogether vanish from the earth."

"Mojag, no!" Aiyana ran forward and clutched his arm.

Metacomet placed his hands on his hips in a defiant gesture. A strange, unpredictable light glittered in his eyes. "The fire of my fury will be fed," he answered, his eyes moving toward Forest. "One of you must die. Make your choice."

Aiyana glanced quickly left and right, but the sachem's warriors and counselors had surrounded them, muskets in hand. There was no escaping Metacomet's justice.

"Quickly," Metacomet commanded.

"Mojag!" she entreated. Her brother lifted his face, and Aiyana's heart broke at the sight of sorrow and defeat in his eyes. "Mojag, this is not why God brought you here! 'Twas not your fault!"

"Would you rather see your Englishman burn?"

"No!" She lowered her voice to a desperate whisper. "Talk to the sachem. You were always skillful with words. Surely you can say something to change his mind."

"His mind is made up, Aiyana, and he will not back down before his warriors. This is the only way."

Turning to face Metacomet, Mojag folded his hands. "It is decided—I will die. You meant to test my God when you asked me to protect your wife and son, but 'twas only me you tested, Sachem. I am only a man, and I did not hear the Yangeese approaching."

"So be it." Metacomet inclined his sleek head toward a warrior at the bonfire. The man stepped forward with a torch; the heaped rushes flickered and then burst into flame.

Forest strained against the men who held him. "No, Mojag, the women need you. I will volunteer so you may live. Rehoboth is dead—" his eyes caught Aiyana's and held; an easy smile played at the corners of his mouth—"and I suppose I was never meant to be a merchant. Aiyana, if we are not to be married, let me give myself for your brother."

Aiyana groaned as blood roared in her ears. This was a living, flesh-and-blood nightmare; surely she would wake soon. . . .

"You choose, Sachem!" Mojag's voice rang through the crackle of the flames. "You have two men willing to die, so choose which one would best satisfy your rage."

Metacomet's eyes flickered at Mojag, then focused on Forest.

Grief and despair tore at Aiyana's heart as her love turned toward the bonfire, ready to offer himself to the flames.

Metacomet folded his arms and nodded at Forest.

Leaving Mojag, Aiyana ran forward and caught Forest's hand. "Forest," she whispered, sobbing, "I love you! Don't do this. I was wrong. We can find a place to be together. I'll go anywhere with you, only don't do this."

Tenderly, resolutely, he pried her fingers from his arm. The warriors who had held him stepped back, grudging respect on their faces. Aiyana fell to her hands and knees in the dirt, tasting the blackness of sorrow as Forest gave her a last look.

A sudden scream clawed through the darkness, a terrible, soul-rending cry. Aiyana shifted her tear-blurred gaze. Struggling between two warriors, Mojag fought to reach the flames, his hands extended, his face distorted into a paroxysm of terror. A new kind of fear shook Aiyana's body from toe to hair, twisting her face as she turned toward the towering fire. Two figures stood in the leaping flames, the dead man and . . . Ootadabun.

Dear God, no!

The girl's long hair blazed in the heat. Her arms clung to the pole as if it were a life preserver. The fire moved around Mojag's lovely wife, a dancing nimbus of light with caressing fingers of smoke and flame. As Aiyana stared in horror and Mojag's plaintive wails rent the air, the fire woofed and puffed and sent streams of sparks whirling off into the night, throwing the darkness back.

The shock of terror and despair held her immobile. *Let it end now. Let the English come. Let us all die. Defeat cannot be worse than this.*

▼▲▼▲▼ Aiyana woke at sunrise. Lifting her head, she was surprised to find herself lying by a stream in the woods. Chepi and Keme slept beside her, the dirt on their faces streaked by tears. Mojag lay not far away, curled into a tight ball, his face layered with soot, his hair and eyebrows singed. He murmured distractedly in his sleep, his reddened, blistered hands reaching for something he would never hold again.

Careful not to wake the children, Aiyana stood up and walked to her brother's side. Forest must have brought them to this place. Though she could not see him, she knew he was nearby.

She lay down behind Mojag and wrapped her arms about him, drawing him close.

▼▲▼▲▼ It was nearly sunset when Forest returned with two fish on a string and a pouch filled with gooseberries. Aiyana divided the berries among the children, then set about gathering kindling to roast the fish. It felt good to find work for her hands, but she could not think of cooking without remembering Ootadabun at her kettle.

Like an old man, Mojag crouched upon his haunches by the stream, his hands in the water, his eyes glued to the ground. He had not spoken a word all day, internalizing his grief and his questions. When Aiyana approached with the roasted fish, he waved her away, preferring to watch the river. She and Forest left him alone.

Peggy Church rested her chin on her hand, a bemused smile on her lips as she watched her husband from across the dinner table. Benjamin found it difficult to tear his eyes from her delicate face even though Major Peleg Sanford insisted upon engaging him in conversation.

"Yes, we believe King Philip may be somewhere in the area," he remarked offhandedly, transfixed by a glimpse of his wife's apricot skin. The lace at her throat parted, and he glimpsed the softly shadowed hollow of her neck. "But you needn't worry, Major Sanford, when my men are about."

His wife cast him a smile of gentle rebuke, and he grinned at her, delighted by the effectiveness of his surprise visit. She hadn't expected to see him this afternoon when he had appeared at the major's house; she had swooned most dramatically and had heartily embarrassed him. "Indeed, I had scarcely hoped to see you alive again," she had said, clutching his hand when she awoke in the major's keeping room. "For I had heard that you were close to that devil Philip. . . ."

Church had played a hunch, traveling from Plymouth to Aquidneck Island, for he believed with every sinew of his being that if Philip was near the Taunton, he journeyed homeward. The Indian ran from death itself, but the quarry was nearly spent. Even the most daring and sly fox eventually fell into the trap laid by a wise, risk-taking hunter.

"Excuse me, Major Sanford," a maid said, coming to the doorway of the dining room. "There's a soldier out here who says he has an urgent message for Captain Church."

Peggy's eyes widened with concern, but Church threw her a

bold smile and noisily pushed back his chair. "Excuse me, Major and Mistress Sanford," he said, forcing a remote dignity into his voice. "I must see what trouble is afoot."

Pleased by the rippling whispers that followed him from the room, Church picked up his hat from the table near the door and hurried to the front room. "You have a message for me?" he asked the soldier standing there.

The young man, sunburned and windblown, doffed his cap. "Yes, sir, Captain Church. One of Philip's own men has just arrived on the Portsmouth shore. He slipped away from the fiend's camp because Philip killed the man's brother."

"Why would Philip kill one of his own?"

"According to the Indian, the dead man dared to suggest that peace might be made with our authorities."

Church turned away, unable to contain the expression of smug delight that spread across his face. "Is he recently escaped? What is his name?"

"Within two days. The Indians called him Tihkoosuc. He says he will now use only his English name, Alderman. He knows where Philip is, and he is willing to take us there forthwith."

"Then we should not waste time," Church answered, rejoicing in the power of knowledge. He turned toward the door, then hesitated on the threshold. He would have to tell his wife that she must content herself with a short visit. The fox was in the field; the bugle had sounded.

"Have my horse saddled. We will put spurs to flanks momentarily," Church said, casting the words over his shoulder as he turned again to the dining room "Let me say a quick good-bye to Mistress Church."

"Aye, sir," the soldier answered, hurrying to the barn.

▼▲▼▲▼ Alderman, the deserting Indian, was frank and free with his information. Church listened carefully, his hands steepled before him; then he closed his eyes to consider this latest twist of fate. Some thought that the savage intended to lead the English into a trap, but Alderman's eyes glowed with such resentful hatred that Church could not help but believe the man.

Nodding abruptly, he looked at Alderman and smiled his thanks. "We will leave immediately. Prepare yourselves," he called to his men. "We are traveling to a small piece of upland in a miry swamp on the southwestern side of Mount Hope. If this man speaks true and the Fox has not stirred from his lair, God may make all of us heroes on the morrow."

The moon was but a sliver of silver in the sky as shallops ferried Church and his men across the half mile of water from Portsmouth to Mount Hope. With the darkness as a cloak and Alderman as a guide, Church led his men through the woods and into the swamp in search of their dangerous quarry. An indefinable feeling of rightness filled his being; he had no intention of permitting himself to lose Philip again. This time he would fight *his* way with his hand-selected woodsmen, not the prison castoffs and old men of the militia. He would skulk like the Indians, approach like a shadow, and ring Philip's den so the sleeping fox would have absolutely no chance of escape.

His men had cast off the bright uniforms and heavy matchlocks of the colonial militia. They carried lighter, shorter muskets with brown barrels that would not glint in the sun. Instead of armor, they wore moccasins and heavily padded coats dyed dark green. Instead of shining swords, they traveled with hatchets and knives in their belts.

In his months of warring with the Indians, Church had discovered three tactics that the other English captains routinely ignored: First, a war party must never return from an area via the same route it took going in; second, an army must "march thin and scatter," avoiding travel in a congested heap; and finally, a captain must trust the native allies, even men like Alderman who had but recently reversed their allegiances. If a captain wanted to be loved and trusted, Church had learned, he must first love and trust his men.

The moon, sailing through a sky of deepest ebony, cast a bar of silver across the swamp floor but left the trees in shadow. A confusing rush of anticipation and dread whirled inside Church as the darkness pressed down on him. Suppose it were to end on the morrow? His pursuit of Philip had become an all-encompassing quest. How could he go back to farming and trapping after this?

Alderman tugged on his sleeve, then indicated a spot in the distance. Church squinted into the gloom. A strangely horizontal line appeared among the trees—a shelter. Silently, he held his hand aloft, then drew a circle in the air and motioned toward the structure.

Moving with the sure grace of forest creatures, his Indian-and-English company ringed the open shelter where Philip and his remaining warriors slept. Everything, Church noticed with satisfaction, was exactly as Alderman had said it would be. Once the alarm had been given, Philip and his men would rise and run in the opposite direction of the first shot, but Church would be waiting.

The circle was formed; the night still full dark. Church and his men settled down onto the moist earth and waited for the first beams of sunrise. Captain Roger Goulding, commander of the ship that had rescued Church from the Pocasset swamp in the early months of the war, had been chosen to fire the first shot and drive the enemy forward. All was in readiness; they waited only for the definitive moment when dawn would jimmy the horizon.

Church eased his back against a tree and rested the barrel of his musket against his shoulder. *What are you thinking, my foxy friend?* he wondered, staring through the gloom toward the open-fronted shelter in which the Wampanoags slept. *Are you dreaming of me? Surely you know that Alderman is missing from your band. You must also know that he hungers for vengeance . . . and yet you have not moved your camp. You are trapped on this peninsula, but you know that, too. Are you even in there, or am I staring at a sleeping bundle of straw? Do you count yourself as a man already dead? You first raised your tomahawk against the English here; do you mean to die here as well?*

Fear kept him at the peak of intense feeling; his nerves hummed at a full stretch as the forest chirped, sighed, and echoed with night noises. His men waited in the woods, their bodies rigid, their fists clenched around the stocks of their muskets.

The sliver of moon disappeared behind a cloud; the darkness of the swamp deepened until Church felt as though he swam in a black lake, filled with monsters that might rise at any moment. Was that crack behind him a footfall? Then, without warning, a breeze blew the cloud away, and a hint of thinner darkness appeared in the east.

A savage had stirred from the hut. Church now saw him shuffling toward the brush. Did he know they watched him?

No, he did not, Church decided, watching the hunched figure. The Indian was only sleepy and urgently needed to answer the call of nature. *Let him go. Do not begin shooting yet. 'Tis too dark to know friend from foe. . . .*

A musket fired. Too soon! Church winced as if his flesh had been nipped, then raised his musket and held his breath. The solitary savage fled into the woods, but figures stirred in the hut beyond, men struggling in shades of black and gray. *"Iootash! Iootash!"* someone shouted, "Stand and fight!"

The next instant, a volley from the forward line of soldiers tore holes in the Indians' shelter, and a wave of men raced wildly toward the safety of the woods. The men who had fired the first shots shouted so their hidden comrades would not mistake them for the enemy, and the sound of their cries swept the Indians toward the hidden ambush.

Church caught his breath as a solitary Indian threw his pouch and powder horn over his head, caught up his gun, and ran as fast as he could without any more clothes than his breechcloth and stockings. The corner of Church's mouth dipped in a wry smile when he realized that the man ran directly toward Alderman and his English companion, Caleb Cook. *Ah, if I am not to snare this fox, at least Alderman will be satisfied. "Vengeance is mine; I will repay, saith the Lord."*

The Englishman pulled the trigger of his musket, but the damp powder in his gun failed to ignite. The Indian then opened fire, and the fleeing savage spun around and fell forward, falling facedown into the muck.

From his position, Benjamin Church watched . . . and knew that the much-feared King Philip was dead.

While his men pursued others of Philip's band, Church joined Alderman and Cook by the body in the mire. Turning the man over, he beheld that one musket ball had penetrated the man's heart, another a spot not two inches from it. "A great, naked, dirty beast he looks like," Church muttered, staring at the mud-spattered face and form.

What was it about this man that had drawn thousands to his cause? What charisma or power had he possessed? Church had heard many stories, but each portrayed a different and often unbelievable aspect of the sachem's nature. Philip had summarily murdered Alderman's brother, but he had reportedly given aid and friendship to Mary Rowlandson during her captivity. He had hung dismembered English bodies upon poles at Swansea, and yet he had tenderly returned two English boys to their parents before the war broke out. And though he had fought fiercely, his people, the Pokanoket, not the sachem himself, had fired the first shots of the war.

Whatever qualities he may have had were gone.

"Take him," Church told Alderman, "up there, to higher ground, and announce to our company that the monster is dead."

The English broke into loud hoorays when Alderman proclaimed the news. Church ordered Philip's head to be chopped off and his body quartered, the usual procedure for a vanquished enemy whose remains should not be honored by a proper burial. As the Indian executioner lifted his hatchet, he remarked, "He was a very great man and made many a man afraid of him."

The executioner wrapped the head in leaves and carried it back to Aquidneck. Soon Church would have the pleasure of presenting it to the Plymouth authorities, where it would be mounted on a spike for public viewing. The four quarters of Philip's body were hung on trees, here and there in the Pokanoket swamps, so his flesh and bones would be scattered and never remembered or honored by his people.

As an afterthought, Benjamin Church allowed Alderman to cut off and keep Philip's scarred hand. The informant had done the English a great service; he deserved a reward. The devil's very hand would be worth many rounds of free drinks in future tavern visits.

▼▲▼▲▼ The war in southern New England drew down to a steady and anticlimactic close. Less than a month after Philip's death, Annawon, Philip's war captain, surrendered to Benjamin Church with great dignity and resolve. On the night of his surrender, Annawon absented himself from Church for a moment, then reappeared with something in his hands. Falling on his knees before the English captain, he presented the regalia of the sachem Metacomet, known to the English as King Philip. In his hands he carried two enormous belts of wampum, one of which was edged with red hair from the Mohawk country, two horns of "glazed powder," and the red cloth blanket upon which Philip would sit when appearing before his people.

"Great Captain," Annawon said, nodding in stately dignity, "you have killed Philip and conquered his country, for I believe that I and my company are the last that war against the English. The war is ended by your means; therefore, these things belong to you."

▼▲▼▲▼ But Forest, Aiyana, Mojag, and the children did not know of Philip's death and the war's end. Hiding from Indians and English alike, they slipped along the forest trails, eating whatever they could find and sleeping in the woods with only moss and leaves to shelter them. Aiyana was afraid to build a wigwam for fear the English would spy it and fire upon them.

Mojag was reluctant to approach any English settlements lest they be shot on sight.

They were walking to Roxbury, to John Eliot and Daniel Bailie. As they ventured north, they passed through the blackened ruins of Swansea. Abandoned dogs and cats skittered away from their approach, bewildered by the war that had stolen their masters and decimated the places they had called home.

Aiyana thought that Forest might want to examine the ruins of Rehoboth in hopes of finding the graves of his loved ones, but he resolutely shook his head when she suggested it.

They camped for the night after a long day of walking, the children snoring already. Aiyana sat next to Forest by the small fire, hugging her knees. "We do not need to go to Rehoboth. I will not mourn for what lies behind," Forest said, his fingers warm and strong as he slipped his hand over hers. "You are an Indian, and I a merchant, and we will find a place to be together. We will make our own place, if we must."

Too moved for words, she clung to his hand, pressing it between her own. When her fingers encountered an object on his smallest finger, she looked up, startled. "My ring!" she said, gaping at the gold band that glimmered in the firelight. "But I threw it away!"

"And it took me the rest of the day to find it," Forest answered in mock severity. His tone gentled as he smiled. "I knew the ring was precious to you, just as you are undeniably precious to me. I couldn't let you lose it, Aiyana, any more than I could bear to lose you."

His fingers curved under her chin and lifted her face so that she looked into eyes that brimmed with tenderness and passion. "My battle is over, Aiyana. When the Almighty brought me to the flames of Metacomet's fire, suddenly I realized how empty and useless were my ambitions, my *calling* as a merchant. Though my body escaped the fire, my pride and vainglory did not. Forgive me for being blind."

Leaning back, she nestled against him in response, and for a long moment neither of them spoke. "I thought Mojag was crazy when he talked about God's call," he whispered, laughter in his voice, "and lately I've realized that I'm the odd one. I never thought to ask God what he intended for me. I just assumed I was to be what my father was."

"God will reveal his plan for you—for us—in his time," Aiyana whispered, wrapping her arms about his waist. She let her head fall on his chest, content to wait. They had overcome obstacles presented by their families, the war, Metacomet, and even themselves. Their love was strong enough to withstand time. She would never question it again.

"For now, I can promise you this," Forest answered, his fingers threading through her hair. "I will remain by your side. We will trust God to show us where we can be happy . . . together. But we must go forward. All of us."

She heard the warning undercurrent in his voice and turned her face to look at Mojag. He sat by the fire, a blank expression on his face, Chepi's and Keme's heads pillowed on his lap. He had little to say these days, preferring to spend his time caring for the children. It was as if he had been shipwrecked by grief, marooned on an island of doubts. His unflagging certainty, his faith, and his confidence had vanished in the flames that had consumed Ootadabun.

As they made their way over the trails leading from the Wampanoag ancestral home, Aiyana thought the woods themselves seemed to mourn, exchanging the living green of summer for the fading colors of fall. A year ago they could not have covered twenty miles without encountering at least a dozen Indian villages, but the Wampanoag people had vanished from the land that had birthed, fed, sheltered, and buried them for countless generations. Occasionally she spied the rag-clad skeletons of Indians or colonists in the woods, and she marveled that she and her loved ones had survived at all.

The sun was sinking toward a livid purple cloud bank piled low on the western horizon when she and her companions finally reached the gate outside John Eliot's home. Aiyana held her breath as Forest looked at her, his hand on the bell rope. They had been away so long, anything could have happened.

"Your father might not be here," Forest said matter-of-factly, his eyes meeting hers. "And Reverend Eliot is not a young man and was much pressured by the work."

"Ring it," Mojag called, his voice heavy.

Aiyana drew the children to her side as Forest pulled on the bell rope. After a moment woven of eternity, a serving woman came to the porch and shaded her eyes from the setting sun. Aiyana frowned when the servant gasped and rushed back into the house.

"Either she thinks the savages have come to call," Forest said, his voice dry and mocking, "or I am not as handsome as I once was."

"Reverend Eliot has never feared an Indian," Aiyana answered, peering into the yard through the fence. "Look, there! She is fetching her master now."

She let out a long exhalation of relief when the aged minister stepped carefully onto the porch. Another man walked with him—her father!

"Aiyana?" Joy and relief rang in Daniel's voice. "Thank God! Is that Mojag with you?"

"Yes, Father!" Forgetting her manners, Aiyana pushed open the gate and flew down the path and into her father's arms. Mojag followed, joining her in their father's embrace. Forest followed also, bringing the children.

Daniel embraced each of them warmly, exultant tears flowing freely down the fine creases in his face. "We have not ceased to pray for you," he whispered, slipping an arm around Aiyana's shoulders. His eyes focused on Mojag's face. "We feared you were forever lost to us. When we heard that Philip was killed and many of those with him—"

"I am not lost, Father," Mojag answered, his voice shattered. "Never lost. Though my heart has been broken and my mind confused—"

"Come inside. It grows cold out here," Reverend Eliot interrupted, taking the children's hands as he led the way into the house. "We shall talk, and you will unburden your hearts. The world has changed, children, and we shall see how we must change with it."

"And so, Master Bailie, I do most humbly beg for your daughter's hand in marriage," Forest proclaimed, standing before Aiyana's father. "I don't know where God would have us serve him, but we are open to do his will wherever he calls us."

Aiyana looked at Forest, marveling that a man could change so much in so short a time. Cleaned up, shaven, and dressed once again in a proper English suit, Forest was the picture of success and prosperity, but gone were the indomitable pride and the aloofness that had been chiseled into his handsome face. Yet confidence remained in his features, and a sober strength born of experience beyond his years.

"I am surprised that you waited to ask my blessing," her father answered, smiling with warm spontaneity. "And yet I am glad that you did. I would be very disappointed if I were not personally able to give my daughter to the man she loved."

"And now, Aiyana," Forest whispered, turning to her and lightly taking her hand. "I loved you in Rehoboth. I loved you on Deer Island. I loved you in the wilderness. No matter where we are, I shall always love you. Will you be my wife now and till death parts us?"

"That all depends," she whispered, running her finger over the fabric of his new jacket. "Will you love me carefully, like a good Puritan, or passionately, as a woman wants to be loved?"

He laughed in answer and swung her into the circle of his arms before the entire audience in Reverend Eliot's keeping room. "I will love you," he whispered into her ear, his voice suddenly almost unbearable in its tenderness, "with every act and thought and breath from this day until my last. We have seen the worst life has to offer. The time has come for us to seek out the best."

Standing on tiptoe, she pressed her lips to his, sealing their bargain.

▼▲▼▲▼ They were married within two weeks. After taking their marriage vows before a magistrate of Roxbury, Forest returned the simple gold band to Aiyana's finger, promising that they would boldly, faithfully, and successfully seek God and love throughout their days. As they knelt in prayer, the Reverend John Eliot placed his hands on their heads and blessed them.

In October 1676, soon after Aiyana and Forest were married, the Massachusetts legislature proclaimed that "of those several tribes and parties that have hitherto risen up against us, which were not a few, there now scarce remains a name or family of them in their former habitations but are either slain, captivated, or fled into remote parts of this wilderness, or lie hid, despairing of their first intentions against us, at least in these parts."

Fire, theft, or destruction had laid waste to the fourteen praying villages, John Eliot's life's work. The recently founded settlements in Nipmuck country would never be reestablished. And volunteers to continue the work among the remaining Indians were rare indeed.

After much prayer and counsel, Forest and Aiyana Glazier moved to Natick, one of the first praying villages to be rebuilt. Unwilling to grant the praying Indians complete freedom, the colonial authorities designated four villages as places where they could live under close supervision. Fifty Christian Indians returned to Natick in November 1676, sixty-two were released to Newton, twenty-five to Nonantum Hill, and twenty-five to Medford. A total of one hundred sixty-two praying Indians left Deer Island and returned to rebuild their homes, thirty-eight fewer than had been forced into exile on that first march one year before. Some of the thirty-eight had died of hardship on Deer

Island; others had been killed in combat as they fought with the English against the Wampanoag. A few did not return to the praying villages because they had been corrupted by alcohol—drinks offered by Englishmen eager to thank the friendly Indians for their undeniable role in a great victory.

Despite his declining health, John Eliot continued his work with the Indian converts. "I can do little, yet I am resolved through the grace of Christ that I will never give over the work so long as I have legs to go," he wrote to a friend. As proof of his devotion and steadfast labor, many of the Christian Indians, despite their cruel treatment and internment during the war, remained firm in their faith.

After building a home in Natick, Forest and Aiyana adopted Chepi and Keme. Aiyana spent her days teaching other orphaned Indian children while Forest helped the converted Indians who struggled to adapt to life as farmers. The schools and farms of Natick had no supplies, so Forest ordered hoes, spades, rakes, and iron plows, joking to Aiyana that God had called him again to the merchant business. Daniel Bailie continued to assist John Eliot, who divided his time between his Roxbury pulpit and the four Indian towns.

Mojag remained at Natick for nearly a year, but Aiyana knew he would never be happy in a praying village. Whether his heart was burdened by memories of Ootadabun or Metacomet, she could not tell, but he had little patience with either the agricultural or spiritual problems of the praying Indians, and his countenance was often downcast.

One night she approached him as he stood at the gate of her house, his eyes on the wooded horizon beyond. The cool evening air was as stringent as alcohol, and she shivered at the wounded look in Mojag's eyes.

"Speak your thoughts, Brother. 'Tis not for nothing you were named He-Who-Talks-Much," she whispered, placing her hand upon his.

The quick smile he cast her did nothing to soften the pain

carved in merciless lines on his face. "There is a time for talking
and a time for being still."

"Ootadabun would not want you to mourn her forever." She
waited, hoping he would speak, but he did not. "You can be
happy again, if you will let God heal the hurts of the past."

"God has healed my heart, as much as he will," Mojag
answered, after clearing his throat. "After the war, I believed I
was wrong to go to Metacomet's people. The sachem did not
turn to Christ, and my coming brought Ootadabun's death. I
denied God's calling and his message. I thought Ootadabun
might yet be alive if she had not met me."

"No. She would be among the dead of Metacomet's people,"
Aiyana answered, her fingers tightening around his hand. "Like
Metacomet, she heard about the Lord's salvation. But while he
chose to reject it, she accepted it. If you had not gone to the
Wampanoag, Ootadabun would be as lost as Philip for all eternity. You brought her light and salvation, Mojag; you did not
cause her death. You introduced her to life; you opened a world
she loved better than this earthly one, and she chose to enter it for
our sakes."

"She should not have had to die." Unspeakable pain glowed
in his eyes.

"God ordains our length of days. 'Tis he who holds us in his
hand and not we ourselves. And can you be forgetting that the
blood of Christians is seed? Ootadabun gave her life so that we
might live, so that we might continue the work among her
people. Don't take your grief so much to heart, Mojag. Don't let
it become an idol between you and God."

He smiled slightly at her words. "You speak like a good Puritan," he said, taking hold of her hand. "You have found your
place here."

"This is your home, too," she said, taking a step toward him
as though being closer would make him understand what she
wanted to say. "I was wrong to doubt you, Mojag. You *were*
called to go to Philip's people, and you were wise to pray for
him. He was a great sachem. He needed to hear a witness to the

truth. In opposing you, Father and I were too bound to tradition
to see what God wanted. He wanted a voice to go among the
Indians, so he chose *you*, He-Who-Talks-Much. Keme and Chepi
will tell future generations how Ootadabun defied Philip and
gave her life for the man who dared to live with Metacomet and
pray for his soul."

"They knew me as Askuwheteau," Mojag answered, his eyes
dark and remote. "He-Who-Waits."

"God is waiting for you, Askuwheteau," she answered,
squeezing his hand. "You can be at home here if you will put the
past from your mind."

"Is God waiting?" Mojag laughed hoarsely. "Sometimes I wonder if he still cares."

"He does," Aiyana answered. "He cares about the world, and
he has called each of us to do our part in it. The Puritans, bless
them, will remain cloistered in their churches and teach their children. Forest and I will work with Father among the praying Indians. And you can work with us. . . ."

His eyes narrowed slightly in resistance. "Aiyana," he said,
his eyes still fastened on the distant horizon, "Jesus prayed that
we would remain in the world and that we would be protected
from the evil in it. God has sheltered us through the worst bloodshed this land has yet seen. You and Father and Forest have
found your place, but my heart is still restless. He preserved me
for a reason but not for a praying village. The church here is like
a boat in the harbor. You are doing a safe work; your sea is calm;
you are steering Christian souls across the bay to dry land. My
heart yearns to ride rough waves by faith, to venture into
uncharted waters where souls are perishing."

"What souls?" Aiyana cried, the old anguish searing her
heart. "Philip and his people are *gone*, Mojag. The few that
remain are forced to live in our villages. The land is *empty*. The
souls you speak of are dead or in slavery." In a rush of bitter
remembrance she recalled the thriving Wampanoag villages, the
people's stoic perseverance in the face of defeat and starvation,

their pride and fierce resistance. Philip had gambled his nation's existence in an all-or-nothing venture, and lost.

"They are not all gone," Mojag answered, his voice firm, final.

She felt the chasm between them like an open wound. The hunger to leave obviously gnawed in Mojag's heart, but where would he go? There were no other praying villages, nothing but miles of charred country, fledgling colonial villages, and the wild, untested frontier beyond.

She looked away to the horizon, where he stared so intently. Darkness was gliding across the eastern sky with the silken slowness of an infinitely languid tide. The heavens seemed to pull her heart up and over into the west beyond. Suddenly, a stab of feeling pierced her heart, and she sensed a message across the darkness. Not for her, but for Mojag.

Blinking, she peered out at the empty field in front of her house. At the edge of the forest a man sat upon a white horse, waiting. The setting sun illuminated his flesh, his waist-length silver hair, his countenance. Even from this distance, she could feel the pressure of his bright eyes.

"Is that—," she gasped, the hairs on her arms lifting.

"Yes." Mojag's mouth curved into a surprised smile. "Excuse me, Aiyana, but I must speak with an old friend."

She clung to his arm, suddenly as anxious as a child who has stumbled onto something she doesn't understand.

"It is time, Aiyana," he said, slowly peeling her fingers from his flesh. "I'm ready to go where God sends me." He nodded toward the man in the field. "I think my orders have just arrived."

Choked by the sudden certainty that she would not see him again, Aiyana twisted her wedding ring from her finger. "Here," she whispered, pressing the gold band into her brother's palm. "Take this and boldly, faithfully, successfully do what you must. I love you, Mojag. And . . . I trust you."

"But this is your wedding ring!" His eyes widened in surprise.

"No." She smiled, grateful that she had been allowed to share this moment with him. "This is but a symbol of Forest's love, and I have no need of symbols when the man himself waits yon-

der by the fire. But to you, Mojag, it is our charge, our family.
Take it with you." She bit her lip, fighting back the sudden tears
that swelled heavily in her chest. "And know that I love you
always."

There was a depth to his smile that had been missing far too
long. He stepped close, kissed her on the forehead, then moved
through the gate toward the field. Aiyana watched him go until
the coming night cloaked his form; then she slipped into the
house to join Forest and the children.

In the morning, Mojag and his things were gone. A simple
note lay on the board in the keeping room:

> For God so loved the *world*. . . .
> You will remain in my love and prayers.
> He-Who-Talks-Much

Philip's desire to take action in the face of English aggression, bigotry, greed, and racism only succeeded in fanning the flames of those vices. In less than two years, the Indians killed twenty-five hundred colonists and erased an entire generation of settlement. But the cost to the Indians was high: six thousand dead, wounded, or enslaved.

Captain Samuel Mosely, the fierce sea-captain-turned-Indian-hunter, captured two hundred and twenty-three Indians, who were shipped from Boston and sold into slavery. For a time they served as galley slaves in English oared ships. History does not record what happened to Metacomet's wife and son.

Nearly 40 percent of the Massachusetts Indian converts survived the war with their faith intact, but seventeenth-century missions in New England never again enjoyed the fervency of John Eliot's early work. Twenty years after the war, Eliot's colleagues reported only seven Indian churches with twenty preaching stations and schools. Natick remained strong for more years than did other mission towns, but its population declined to 166 by 1749 and to about 20 by 1797. In 1855, only one Christian Indian remained in the village.

The Puritans came to New England to establish a visible kingdom of God, a society where outward conduct would be managed according to God's laws. Why didn't the zeal that led them to establish prosperous towns and colonial governments lend itself to evangelism? Because their churches and their towns became refuges from the world, exclusive societies for saints and their children. "Instead of an agency for bringing Christ to fallen man," Edmund Morgan wrote, "[the church] became the means of perpetuating the gospel among a hereditary religious aristocracy" (Edmund Morgan, *The Puritan Family* [New York: Harper and Row, 1944, 1966], 174). And before the end of the seventeenth century, the Puritan system teetered on the verge of collapse. Not until the Great Awakening of the next century would New England come back to her knees and her reliance upon God.

REFERENCE LIST

Historical information for this book came from the following sources:

Banks, Charles Edward, M.D. *The History of Martha's Vineyard, Massachusetts*, vol. 1. Edgartown, Mass.: The Dukes County Historical Society, 1966.

Bourne, Russell. *The Red King's Rebellion: Racial Politics in New England 1675–1678*. New York: Oxford University Press, 1990.

Bowden, Henry W., and James P. Ronda, eds. *John Eliot's Indian Dialogues: A Study in Cultural Interaction*. Westport, Conn.: Greenwood Press, 1980.

Chartier, Roger, ed. *A History of Private Life*, vol. 3, *Passions of the Renaissance*. Cambridge, Mass.: Belknap Press, 1989.

Demos, John. *The Unredeemed Captive: A Family Story from Early America*. New York: Random House, 1995.

Hawke, David Freeman. *Everyday Life in Early America*. New York: Harper and Row, 1989.

Josephy, Alvin M. Jr. *The Patriot Chiefs: A Chronicle of American Indian Resistance*, rev. ed. New York: Penguin Books, 1993.

Kotker, Zane. *White Rising*. New York: Alfred A. Knopf, 1981.

Leach, Douglas Edward. *Flintlock and Tomahawk: New England in King Philip's War*. New York: W. W. Norton & Company, Inc., 1958.

Marcus, Robert D., and David Burner, eds. *America Firsthand*, vol. 1, *Settlement to Reconstruction*. New York: St. Martin's Press, 1989.

Morgan, Edmund S. *The Puritan Family: Religion and Domestic Relations in Seventeenth-Century New England*. New York: Harper and Row, 1944, 1966.

Rowlandson, Mary. *The Captive*. Originally published as *The Sovereignty and Goodness of God, Together with the Faithfulness of His Promises Displayed, Being a Narrative of the Captivity and Restoration of Mrs. Mary Rowlandson*, Tucson, Ariz.: American Eagle Publications, 1682, 1990.

Webb, Stephen Saunders. *1676: The End of American Independence*. New York: Alfred A. Knopf, 1984.

White, Jon Manchip. *Everyday Life of the North American Indian.* New York: Indian Head Books, 1993.

Winslow, Ola Elizabeth. *John Eliot, Apostle to the Indians.* Boston: Houghton Mifflin Company, 1968.